Also by Cathryn Grant

Cathryn Grant

An Affair With God

A Novel

D2C
Published by D2C Perspectives

Contact Cathryn through her website at CathrynGrant.com

Cover design by Lydia Mullins Copyright © 2015

ISBN: 978-1-943142-09-5

All Saints' Day

THE KITCHEN WAS nearly silent, thick with the absence of sound that takes over the suburbs in the hours after midnight. The only disturbance in the perfect stillness was the hum of the pewter clock hanging on the wall behind Gabrielle. Across the table, a pair of blue eyes stared past her. It was impossible to read the thoughts lurking behind those eyes.

The clock hummed like an overfed horsefly, perched on the back of her head. She tried lifting her hand to brush a hair off her face, but her arm was too heavy, weighted to the table. A cup of cinnamon tea sat in front of her, growing cold. She wanted another sip, but the silence and those unblinking eyes immobilized her. The cup across the table was still full. Steam had risen from it steadily for some time, winding its way to the window, leaving a foggy spot on the glass. The spot was gone now. The darkness outside turned the window into a mirror, reflecting the single light and the framed poster of water lilies that hung next to the clock.

"All I ever wanted was a little sex," Gabrielle said. She felt compelled to talk, moving her mouth, saying words, even though they sounded hollow. At least it was activity — the shifting of her jaw, working the joints, her tongue tapping the back of her teeth. "I didn't think it was perverted to want my husband to make love to me."

The sound of her voice was sucked into the silence. The blue eyes were swallowed by pink, swollen flesh. They refused to look at her. She could be talking to anyone. Or no one. It didn't really matter, because for months, years, maybe her whole life, she had talked only for her own ears. "You're not going to say anything, are you? A woman wanting sex is normal, you know. Like needing to eat and sleep."

No sound came from the other side of the table, not even a small cough. Was it her imagination that the eyes hadn't blinked for at least five minutes? A chill threaded its way down her spine. Moving her lips, her jaw, keeping the words flowing out of her mouth, was the only thing that kept her warm. If she talked long enough, would her words be acknowledged?

"It's not fair. Everyone in the whole world has sex. Except me. Every day I see women who don't look half as good as me, and their husbands can't keep their hands off them. I want that. I deserve that. I shouldn't have had to beg for it." She leaned on the table, pressing the knobs of her elbows and the tiny bones of her wrists against the oak surface. She spoke in a whisper — "I shouldn't have to beg."

When she stopped talking, when the tea turned icy cold, the dead body at the other end of the house would have to be dealt with. Time was slipping away. But those hard blue eyes kept her seated, kept her talking. The solid force of the stare, the glittering spots of blue shining out of the shadows that hung in every corner of the room, had the power to keep her seated. Action was called for, removing the body, working fast before the watery sun seeped over the horizon like runny egg yolk.

"Vengeance belongs to God, right? That's what you're thinking."

It might be that vengeance was not in her hands. It was also true that sometimes human beings were required to act on God's behalf. And she was nothing if not a woman of action. She wanted to lift the cup of tea. She wanted to stand up, stretch her legs, get a sweatshirt. Action was called for. She wanted to gulp down the lukewarm tea, and get out of the chair, move the body to another place. She needed to get it out of the house, but she needed help. She needed another pair of hands, another set of shoulders, and all she was getting was that blank stare. It irritated her that so many people allowed life to flow past them without doing anything to change it. They might as well be dead, like the body lying on her bed — no blood pumping through the veins, muscles slack, lungs collapsed. Death had looked more frightening than she'd imagined. Although there was no exposure of internal organs, there had been the convulsions, the vomit mixed with blood…she shuddered.

The hum of the clock swelled, seeming to gain speed. She wished they had a normal clock that ticked, but this clock was more upscale. It probably had some important brand name she was supposed to remember. She tried to ignore the humming. It was getting on her nerves. It was funny when she concentrated on other things like cooking or feeding her son, she didn't notice the humming. It was strange that something could be right next to you all the time, and you never noticed because you were busy paying attention to something else. Then suddenly, it loomed out of proportion, took over your thoughts. The clock wanted to take control of the remaining hours of the night. It was doing its job, reminding them that morning was coming quickly. There was no more time to sit at the table, doing nothing. In a few hours, the blackness pushing against the window would start to slip back, lifting out of the side yard, sliding over the fence. Then it would be too late. Peter would rattle the rails of his crib. The sky would grow light, and it would be too late.

Those eyes kept staring — wanting her to admit she had done something horrible.

"You can call it murder, but it's not. I only did what God told me to do," she said.

One

LOOKING BACK, GABRIELLE could see exactly when everything started to go wrong. The rough patches in her marriage, visible but unacknowledged since the beginning, began to get rubbed raw on Pentecost Sunday — fifty days after Easter. On Pentecost, the Spirit of God had descended upon the eleven remaining disciples. According to the Biblical record, the eleven men were in a room, mourning the crucifixion of their Savior. A fierce wind that had no source in the natural world had blown through the room. The men spontaneously began speaking in languages they'd never studied.

Gabrielle sat in the front row every Sunday. That Sunday had been no different.

She was a small woman. At twenty-four, she still looked like a girl. This was partially caused by the clothes she wore. She clung to clothes left over from her teen years, proud of not squandering her husband's limited income. She was pleased with her slim figure and knew the other women at church noticed. Even after giving birth, her jeans and skirts fit as smoothly as they always had. Her round, full breasts were the only fleshy part of her body. Although her pride wasn't pleasing to God, she couldn't help noticing what she saw in the mirror every day. Fortunately, the mirror didn't capture her feet, and she tried not to think about their potential for marring her appearance.

This morning she wore a faded pink denim skirt, a sea-green t-shirt, and a narrow black belt edged with silver beads. The belt was one of her dollar finds at the Salvation Army store. Because the belt was too long, she had the excess length looped at the side, with the end dangling over her left hip. Her thick, brown hair was pulled high into a ponytail that reached the center of her spine.

Peter snuggled against her shoulder, saturating her chest and throat with his body heat. They were alone in the first row of folding chairs. With no other voices singing beside her, Gabrielle's voice sounded extraordinarily loud in her own ears. The tempo of the hymn was lethargic, straining from note to note as if it were climbing a steep hill. The organ sounded like a lost soul, moaning for its life. She missed the music of the fundamentalist summer camps she'd attended in high school, piano tunes that made her feel like dancing. As the hymn neared its end, her husband stood up, a silent signal that the sermon was about to begin. Behind her, people rustled, trying to settle themselves more comfortably on the metal folding chairs, re-crossing their legs and tugging at clothing that twisted in the wrong places. Mark looked out across the rows of faces, not allowing his gaze to linger on Gabrielle any longer than it did on any other member of the church. He closed his hymnal and stepped to the pulpit.

While Mark's glance skipped lightly over her face, Gabrielle stared intently at his. Did any of the women seated in the rows behind her pay attention to how good looking he was? He wasn't very tall, two inches short of six feet, but everything was compacted into a neat, well-formed package. His reddish-blond hair was cut very short at the sides and back, thinning slightly on top like dry grass at the end of August. His gaze was steady, taking in everything around him, but holding his thoughts tightly inside where they couldn't be touched. Hidden beneath his liturgical robes, he had sculpted shoulders, his muscles defined enough to swell when he worked hard, but not over-developed. His waist and hips were narrow, and he walked with determination.

Gabrielle sat up straighter. She was supposed to be listening to his words, not admiring his body.

Peter squirmed on her lap. He raised himself to a standing position, digging his heels into her thighs. He was getting stronger and more difficult to control every week. It was a quirk of Grace Lutheran Church that they didn't believe in childcare, convinced that children should attend church services every week of their lives, starting at infancy. When a child cried, the parents left the hall until the storm passed.

Gabrielle was in and out of her seat multiple times every week. She hated that Mark wanted her to sit in the front row, where the entire congregation could see his little family. It took all her strength to keep Peter from slipping off her lap, crawling between the chair legs, dragging his knees across the faded linoleum floor. She leaned down and dug a plastic cup of crumbled rice cake out of her purse. When Peter saw the cup, he yelped. As he began nibbling, he stopped murmuring and sat still.

Mark opened the Bible lying on the pulpit and began to read from the Old Testament book of Ezekiel. Wrapping his words in an ominous tone, he read: "…there was a noise, a rattling sound, and the bones came together, bone to bone. I looked, and tendons and flesh appeared on them, and skin covered them, but there was no breath in them."

This was the same passage Mark read every year on Pentecost Sunday — a prophecy that God's Spirit would arrive on earth like a gust of wind.

Gabrielle closed her eyes. The dead bodies rose behind her eyelids, stiff and lifeless. Bones, dry and brittle as dead branches, tendons tying themselves to the joints. Flesh, before the skin appeared to cover up the nauseating mess. Liver and other organs — did they pulse with life, or hang limply, exposed and naked, anxious for the tight wrapping of skin to protect their ugly, slippery surfaces? A shiver of disgust ran across her skin. Sometimes, she felt like that — raw and unbearably vulnerable. When she married Mark, she'd thought the exposed feeling would go away. Finally, someone adored her. She had one person in the world devoted completely to her, a man who had stood in front of God and everyone else, promising he would cherish and hold her close. That day was still vivid in her mind.

THEIR WEDDING HAD been on May first, dry and sunny most years in California. But that year, the spring rain dragged into early June. May first had been cold and gray. Not the milky gray that promised light or occasional showers, but heavy charcoal clouds bloated with water. The church members, who couldn't be more thrilled that their pastor had found a sweet wife to take care of him, clucked that it was a shame the weather was so unfriendly.

Gabrielle loved the rain. She didn't care if they had a hurricane. All that mattered was Mark. Their love. Although she didn't say it, she wouldn't care if the weather was so horrible the entire church stayed empty. She wasn't like other girls, dreaming of some silly queen-for-a-day wedding. In fact, it was kind of funny that Mark wanted a more elaborate ceremony and reception than she did. *The parishioners expect it*, he'd said. She wasn't interested in what they expected. The important part was their promises to each other. And to God, of course.

She had a narrow wedding band that Mark would slip on her finger and a thin engagement ring with a diamond the size of a dried pea. Nothing too showy that might offend parishioners who didn't want to see a minister's wife with a lavish display of money. Her dress was slim, ivory satin, a tight bodice with a wide, round neckline, not too low cut. There was no train dragging behind her, and she didn't wear a veil. Her hair was straight, trimmed to the tops of her shoulders. She carried one white rose. But none of that mattered. She was in love. Better yet, she was loved.

She stood in front of the minister. The sleeve of Mark's suit brushed against her arm. Through two songs and the sermon, her mind drifted pleasantly, soothed by the pattering rain and the warmth of Mark's hand holding hers. His grip was snug, his hand dry and smooth, warming the cold tips of her fingers. A hand that would keep her safe. A hand that would hold her, touch her face, sweep through her hair, and stroke her skin, holding her close while she slept, every night for the rest of her life.

On their wedding day, none of that had happened quite yet. Mark had been very careful, insisting they keep their distance so they didn't get too heated up before they were married. *We might both have things in our past that aren't completely pleasing to God*, he'd said, *but we can start our marriage off with the right promises.* It was so romantic, he was so strong. He knew about Gabrielle's one disastrous love affair, if you called it a love affair when you were eighteen. He was somewhat vague about his life before her. There had been lots of girls, nothing important.

MARK'S SERMON VOICE interrupted her thoughts. His words buzzed in her ears, rhythmic but unformed. The chair was unbearably hard, and Peter's weight intensified the pressure on her back. Their wedding was so long ago. All the promising, exciting words had withered. When had she ever been the center of his soul? From the beginning, it had been a silent battle between her and Grace Lutheran Church for Mark's attention. How demanding they were. Meetings at night, people getting sick and going into the hospital, dying, delivering babies. And there was never any break. Just because Mark had three evening meetings in one week didn't mean someone wouldn't have a heart attack on a Friday, keeping him away for several hours on the weekend. And then there was Sunday — arriving each week like the drip of a leaky faucet. Feeling him crawl out of bed before the sun rose so he could make sure his mind and the building were prepared for two church services and an hour of Sunday school.

Not only did Grace demand him six long days a week, but they had wormed their way into the center of his heart, where she belonged.

Just a few months ago, Elaine Brackner, an opinionated woman with a large mole above her upper lip, sprouting a single dark hair that Gabrielle longed to pluck, had murmured — *He's a workaholic as much any CEO.* Gabrielle had shrugged, wishing Elaine would pay attention to that wayward hair instead of plastering her inflammatory observations onto Mark. Besides, he wasn't a workaholic, it was nothing common like that. It was more insidious. Something Elaine didn't notice. Mark loved to be in demand. He created need where it didn't even exist. He spent hours each day visiting elderly people, shut up in rank smelling convalescent homes. They rewarded him with tearful faces and gnarled, grasping fingers that soothed him more than his wife's tender hands. He invited the borderline mentally ill members to call his home landline whenever they needed him. And they needed him frequently, begging Mark to listen to the details of the conspiracies against them, or injustices of twenty years ago. Injustices that were murky, perhaps real events, perhaps imagined. And he listened until their frenzied thoughts unraveled and relaxed. He played electronic games while they droned on, but they didn't know that. And they loved him for his listening ear. What made a man more satisfied by the love of the insane than the love of his wife?

Her thoughts were punctured again, this time by the honking of the organ. Ushers glided down the center aisle and began to pass the gold-coated offering plates up and down the rows. While they collected crumpled bills and envelopes primly covering checks, Bob Schneider walked up the side aisle. He was a tall man with white hair, his skull prominent through his skin, wearing a tenderly pleading expression on his face. He was scheduled to spend a few minutes talking about the start of the fundraising program. After decades spent worshipping God in a nondescript hall, most of the members of Grace had decided He needed a real sanctuary. They wanted Him to have the stone floors and stained glass windows He deserved. They wanted marble and polished wood — a building that inspired awe and respect.

For more than forty-five years, Grace Lutheran Church had stood like a forgotten woman on the corner of Hamilton Road and Fremont Avenue. The property was large — two acres of prime real estate in the center of Silicon Valley. Fremont Avenue curved to the right where the property line began, and at the center of the curve was a large lawn, landscaped with shrubs and fruitless Mulberry trees. Set at the back of the parking lot was the education wing with four classrooms. On the opposite side of the parking lot, at the edge of the lawn, was the main building. It housed the large multi-purpose room with a kitchen at one end, and offices for the minister and church secretary at the other end. The hall was used for Sunday morning services, potluck dinners, children's craft fairs, and the Christmas boutique. It had green linoleum floors and a stage at the front. A row of large windows lined the side that faced a small garden at the edge of the lawn. The garden was graciously laced with a curved, pebble-encrusted concrete path that led to both buildings and the parking lot. Along the path were prize-worthy rosebushes and a few concrete benches used, not for meditation, but for gossip during the Sunday morning coffee hour.

New construction had been discussed for over a year. Plans to build had been debated about three years earlier, just before Gabrielle and Mark were married, and another time, ten or twelve years before that, but the project was always abandoned. This time, it looked like it was finally going to happen.

Gabrielle couldn't get caught up in Mark's excitement over the building plans. *Shouldn't people come to church for a spiritual life, not an exotic building?* He dismissed her question, though she asked it often. *People need tangible objects to help them focus*, he said. *Physical beauty will deepen their worship experience. Just wait and see.* He saw it as the start of a bright future. In his mind, a real sanctuary meant higher church attendance.

But today, all she could think about was the end of her son's babyhood. That morning, she had just put a slice of homemade bread on a plate. She turned to the refrigerator to get the pitcher of orange juice. Using the handle of a drawer beside the refrigerator, Peter tugged himself into a standing position. Before she could open the refrigerator door, he released his grip on the drawer and took two lurching steps toward the center of the kitchen. He looked like a drunk trying to stay upright, and at the same time as if walking was the most natural thing in the world. Gabrielle scooped him into her arms, pressing kisses onto his firm cheek. "What a big boy! Daddy will be so proud of you." The praise gushed out of some instinctual part of her, but as she mouthed the words, a rush of sadness filled her throat. She clutched him to her chest. Her little baby — ready to walk away from her.

The organ music began again, indicating the offering collection was complete. She stood up, settling Peter onto her hip, so he straddled her waist. As if to prove he was growing up and she couldn't stop it, Peter threw his upper body forward. She clutched him tighter, singing from memory the words of the four-line offering hymn. Mark moved to the side of the stage and walked down the steps to take the wide gold plates from the ushers. He stacked them into a nested pile, then turned his back to the ushers. They stood with their hands clasped behind their backs, their heads bowed. Mark lifted the plates high, straining toward the wooden altar that was now several feet above him. He spoke the words of a prayer printed in the hymnal.

Already in position behind the pulpit, Bob Schneider cleared his throat. The congregation sat down. Mark climbed the stairs and set the offering plates on the altar. Then he walked back down and stepped toward the front row. He sat next to Gabrielle. Peter giggled and reached out his arms. Mark kept his body straight, watching Bob. Peter strained against Gabrielle's arms. He whimpered and twisted, pulling at the stiff fabric of her skirt.

"Mark!" She nudged him with her elbow.

Mark kept his eyes focused on Bob, who was making an awkward attempt to tie the subject of Pentecost to the beginning of the fundraising drive.

"Mark, he wants you," she said.

"Not now." Mark leaned closer. "He won't go back to you if I take him now."

"Then why did you sit here?"

"Shhh."

Peter started to chatter. "Da! Da. Da." He said it louder, "Da!" Not caring if she distracted the entire congregation from Bob's instructions on the importance of stretching their giving, she grabbed the backpack, stepped around Mark's feet, and walked toward the back of the room. With each step, Peter became more frantic until his chattering turned to crying. By the time she walked down the hallway, past the kitchen, and out the back door, Peter was screaming. She went around the side of the building and stood a few feet from the sliding glass door that opened from the hall onto the garden. The rose bushes were in full bloom, smelling even sweeter after the cool, damp odor that never seemed to evaporate from the multi-purpose room. She could see the back of Mark's head, his straight shoulders. She closed her eyes, imagining what it would be like to sit close to him every Sunday, taking turns holding their child.

The only sound in the garden came from the doves, cooing in the fruitless Mulberry tree behind her. She swayed from side to side so Peter would be happy to remain on her hip. His body felt strong and solid against her ribs. The fresh air calmed him. Already, he'd forgotten how desperately he wanted his father.

She and Peter had that in common — both of them wanted Mark. Everyone wanted Mark. She longed to bury her face against Mark's throat, feel his arms holding her tightly, his biceps pressing against the sides of her arms. She ached for him to pull her close until every part of their bodies touched — their mouths, hips, thighs. But the only touch she was likely to feel any time soon was either Peter's thrusting legs or an old lady's brittle hug, smothering her with a cloud of perfume. It had been so long since she'd felt Mark with her entire body. There was always something in the way.

She moved under the leafy tent of the Mulberry tree, humming to Peter, content to be out of the stuffy building, her thoughts wandering without interruption.

Why did every event in their lives conspire to keep her and Mark from making love? First, her pregnancy had been a problem in more ways than one. There was that whole business with Mark insisting she should have consulted him before abandoning her diaphragm. She hadn't understood why he'd been so upset. No one would have consulted him if they'd been a part of the six percent failure rate. If she and Mark had allowed complete control to be in God's hands, rather than interfering with an artificial barrier, Mark wouldn't have had a choice in the matter either. The timing had been right for a child. Besides, she wanted someone who adored her the way Mark's parishioners adored him. She regretted it now, but her decision hadn't seemed like a betrayal at the time. She'd been too caught up in the exciting possibility of becoming a mother.

For a while, he hadn't touched her. She'd known he would come around. And finally, he did.

But when he finally got over his fit about that, he was

overcome with a fear of hurting the baby. For a man who was supposed to be so smart, so educated, he stupidly believed that making love would risk a miscarriage or early delivery. No matter how many blogs and articles she emailed to him, assuring him sex was perfectly healthy and had absolutely no effect on the baby, he refused to change his views. Before they walked into the waiting room for her first ultrasound, he'd grabbed her arm. *If you talk to her about sex, I'm leaving. It's none of her business.*

She wasn't going to beg him to make love to her. She told herself she should be thankful her husband was so sweetly concerned for the safety of their child. And he made up for it, sort of, with long, soothing foot massages. He took her foot in his hands, pressing his hard fingers into her swollen arches, making her forget, for a few pleasurable moments, about his idiotic belief.

After Peter was born, it was one thing after another. Gabrielle was sleep-deprived, terrified they would wake Peter. Then, Mark was tired from pacing the length of the house, jiggling a fussy baby. When Peter started sleeping through the night, Mark had heartburn, a late meeting, a hospital visit to make. Gabrielle had her period. Peter got the stomach flu. Then Gabrielle and Mark had serial bouts of a feverish, coughing flu. Mark hadn't finished preparing his sermon. When she mentioned their withered sex life, he dismissed her — *Don't put so much emphasis on sex. It's only one part of a marriage. We just had a baby for crying out loud.* When she pointed out that their baby was five months old, he'd said, *I've never heard of a wife hounding her husband for sex.*

They don't have to, Gabrielle said.

It wasn't that they never made love. There was that one time when Peter was seven or eight months old, right after Mark told her once again that she thought too much about sex. And another time, just three or four weeks ago. It was a fuzzy wad of tissue in her memory, but she was almost sure Mark had touched her first. She hadn't asked or prodded him with sarcastic words. His hands had been hesitant. He tickled her ribs, teasing. His fingers brushed across her breasts. Before his feeble move died, Gabrielle turned toward him, stroking his chest. She kissed his lips, so smooth she wanted to lick them.

SQUINTING TO SEE beyond the reflection on the windows, she studied the congregation. It was like watching television on mute. People were uncrossing their legs, folding their bulletins, glancing casually at the door, and not so casually at their phones. For a man who had been a Lutheran all his life, Bob Schneider seemed to have forgotten that a church service was only supposed to last one hour. It was five minutes to twelve, and they hadn't listened to the general prayers or sung the final hymn.

Gabrielle smiled and breathed in the sweet-smelling air. She put Peter on the grass. He spread his fingers among the blades and stuck his butt up as he straightened his arms and legs. The skin of his face stiffened as if he needed every cell in his body to complete the task of standing upright. The set of his lips looked like Mark's when he was practicing his golf putt on the living room carpet. Seeing the mirror image of Mark's face on her son, she felt her irritation subside. She let the backpack fall off her shoulders and pressed her toes against the straps of her sandals, prying them off her feet. Down at the roots, the grass was still damp. It was cold but soothing on her bare feet. She performed a few demi-pliés, all that the tight hem of her skirt would allow, loving the burn that ran through her muscles. Pressing her feet against the unyielding earth made her think again of Mark's foot massages. He really was a very sweet husband, and they had been so busy the past year. Now their baby was a toddler. Things would change.

The voiceless figures behind the windows flattened in her vision, turning into shadows. They looked like the breathless bodies from the book of Ezekiel. Every week was the same. The service followed its orderly course, the minister spoke his words at the proper time. It didn't cross their minds that they were acting out the scene of the dry, rattling bones. She was the only one who saw the similarity. She closed her eyes. It could only mean one thing. God had slipped out of the building. She alone was paying attention, and in return, He was paying attention to her.

A shiver started at the roots of her hair, streaking down her spine. Her whole body trembled. Overhead, the leaves in the

Mulberry tree tapped against each other, rattling like they did at the start of a storm, but there was no breeze. The same tremor that was shooting through her muscles must also be filling the tree. The single-note cooing of the doves and the sound of traffic on Fremont Avenue were swallowed by a rushing sound that filled her head. She knew what was causing all these strange sensations — this was her own personal Pentecost. The chill evaporated, and a sweet warmth melted over her body like heated oil, filling her parched, hungry pores.

Limp, lifeless bodies were of no value. God demanded passion. Making love was the force of life. Flesh. Breath. He admired and rewarded unpredictable action, not stiff, robotic rituals. Another tremor raced through her heart, filling her with overwhelming love for her husband. God wanted love. Warm, blood-filled, breathing flesh. As if she was floating above their bed, she saw herself and Mark, their naked limbs wrapped around each other. The message was clear. Speaking out loud, she said, "Yes. Yes. I'm listening. You want to breathe life into my marriage." She hummed to herself, ecstatic with unbearable desire for the day to fade into night. She opened her eyes, stunned by the vivid sensations. A vision! She'd been given a vision! Tears ran down her face. Her heart pounded heavily against her ribs.

Inside the building, Mark stood and moved toward the steps leading to the stage. Bob bent his head over the pulpit as if he was ashamed of speaking past his allotted seven minutes. He stepped to the side, keeping his head bowed while Mark walked up the steps and took his place in front of the altar. In a solid wave, the congregation rose to their feet. As heads nodded forward, she knew Mark had started the litany of prayers. A few bodies swayed as they lost their equilibrium from standing with locked knees and closed eyes.

The sound of the organ began to leak out around the edges of the windows. The congregation began to sing. After a few minutes, the glass doors slid open. People filed past Mark, shaking his hand and complimenting his sermon, before they scurried to their cars eager to get home to lunch. When the building was empty, Mark went back inside. Gabrielle followed. He began picking up fallen bulletins and pulling others out of hymnals.

"Hi." She put her hand on her collarbone and tried to breathe, shocked by the reality of his presence after her vision.

"Where are your shoes?"

"Huh?"

"Where are your shoes? You're barefoot."

"Oh. I took them off. Are you ready to go home?"

"I have a few things to take care of in my office, first."

"You always have things to take care of." Her voice was brittle. "Always!" She felt yanked back to the earth, rotting like all the other drooping bodies trudging to their cars. She refused to let it be like that. The warm creamy feeling, edged with adrenaline, couldn't be gone already. Words rose in her mind and flung themselves out of her mouth before she could stop them. "Why is it always the church? What about me?"

"Why can't you think about anything but yourself?"

"Your son started walking this morning, and you don't even know it."

That got his attention.

He left the stack of bulletins on a chair and straightened his back, glancing out the window at Peter. "Really? That's terrific. It'll just be ten minutes, I promise."

"See you in a while, then." She smiled, stepping closer, wanting to kiss the pale skin on the back of his neck. Before she reached his side, he turned and began pulling chairs back into alignment.

She walked outside. Peter sat plucking at the grass, watching his fingers slip off the blades. She picked up the backpack, grabbed the straps of her sandals, and lifted Peter onto her hip for the two-block walk home. He felt heavier than usual. She feared the moment when God had turned His attention onto her would slip away as quickly as Peter's infancy.

The sidewalk was hot when she turned off the church lawn, but she was glad for the burning on the soles of her feet. It made her feel alive. She sighed, lifting Peter a few inches to settle him more securely at her waist. She couldn't stop him turning into a little boy. She swallowed around the lump in her throat, lifting her thoughts back to Mark. Her husband. Peter had taken up too much space in their lives. She quickened her pace. She would make herself so soft and desirable, Mark would be overcome with his need for her. Making love tonight would be beautiful and perfect. The only thing she needed to do was stay calm. She couldn't start screaming, ripping with bared teeth at his quiet control. It was always a mistake to let rage take over. Always a mistake when she slammed a plate against the tile counter, or clawed at his skin, hating him for making her beg, for not longing to touch her aching body. There was no reason to hate him for rejecting her. Their dead sex life needed a fresh, peaceful breath. Love, not fury. Tonight would be different.

Two

GABRIELLE AND PETER were finished with lunch, and Peter was asleep in his crib when she heard Mark's motorcycle rumble into the garage. She went into the kitchen where bowls and plates dotted the counter like stepping stones. She opened the refrigerator and took out a plate of sliced cantaloupe. She put it on the table and peeled off the plastic wrap. She collected a loaf of bread, mustard, mayonnaise, and a package of turkey. She lathered one slice of bread with mustard, the other with mayo, and placed five pieces of turkey on the mayo side. She slapped the other piece of bread on top and sliced it diagonally. She looked out the window, trying to rid her mind of a sandwich that contained nothing but gooey spreads and animal flesh. It baffled her that most of the people she knew were immune to their daily consumption of death. She couldn't walk through the grocery store without thinking about the creatures who had been brutally slaughtered, their bodies ripped apart. She picked up a plate and opened the dishwasher door. Loading up dirty dishes and wiping the counter while Mark ate would prevent the nauseating images from taking over.

Mark stood by the table and ate two pieces of cantaloupe. He took the sandwich into the living room. He sprawled on the futon, a thin pad draped over a wood frame that had started life as their bed when they were first married, and now functioned as a sofa. His stretched out on his back, knees bent, with his tablet propped on his thighs and his head supported by a fat pillow. His finger was in constant motion, scrolling through headlines while he chewed. It made her stomach tighten, thinking of the food trying to make its way past hardened muscles and along the intestines that were folded over each other, but he didn't seem uncomfortable.

After she finished the dishes, she curled on her side in a patch of sunlight on the living room carpet and fell asleep. When she woke, Mark was flat on his back. The pillow was on the floor, and his eyes were closed. The tablet on his stomach moved in time with his breathing, like a small boat near the shore of a lake.

For dinner, she served fettuccine with marina sauce and fresh mushrooms that she'd made herself. Mark ate two helpings. She cleared the table and put away the leftovers. On the back patio, they pulled their plastic chairs close to the low wooden table. While Mark lit his pipe, Gabrielle pleaded with Peter to demonstrate his walking skills, but he sat stubbornly, rooted to the ground like a pumpkin. He tugged pieces of grass out of the ground and dropped them into the bed of his yellow dump truck.

When Mark's pipe had gone out, leaving only the stale smell of tobacco, and it was almost too dark to see, Peter pushed himself up to his feet, using his truck as leverage. He teetered in the direction of the patio. As he lurched closer to the concrete slab, the toe of his sandal caught on the edge, and he crashed forward. There was no blood, but he started to cry.

Gabrielle jumped up. Her chair skittered away behind her.

"Don't rush over there," Mark said. "Let him decide how much it hurts. When you get upset, he copies your mood."

Peter howled, refusing to lift himself off the ground. Gabrielle sat down on the edge of the patio and pulled him onto her lap. His howls grew louder. She lifted her t-shirt and moved Peter's slippery face to her breast. Mark stood up and walked to the kitchen door. The screen scraped on the metal track. After a minute, light burst through the sliding glass door that opened from their bedroom onto the patio.

Peter sucked frantically. Gradually, his gasping, phlegmy breathing subsided. His eyelids closed until only a thin line of blue was visible. Not wanting to disturb his milk-drugged serenity, she carried him into the house and dressed him for bed without a bath. She thought about her own bath, filled with crunchy scented crystals nipping at her skin, wiping away perspiration and milk and saliva.

In the hall bathroom, she scooped the plastic boats out of the bathtub and ran the hot water until steam crept up to the open window and slipped out through the screen. She slid the window partially closed and watched in the mirror as the steam turned the wisps of hair around her face into tiny curls. She unwrapped a fresh bar of almond soap and lathered her hands. She spread the suds on her left leg. While the water ran into the open drain, she shaved slowly, rinsing the blade under the faucet after each stroke. It wasn't good for their water bill, but this was important. They followed all the drought regulations. Surely one splurge was allowed. Each pass of the razor left a strip of silken skin. After shaving the other leg, she plugged the drain, dumped in two handfuls of apple-scented bath crystals, and lowered herself into the water. She leaned back, letting the warmth loosen her muscles and dissolve the knots in her joints.

When the water started to cool, she shaved under her arms. She climbed out and brushed her hair. She smeared lotion on her arms and legs, rubbing the excess into her belly. She squirted another puddle into her hand and spread it slowly across her breasts. They weren't as swollen with milk now that Peter received most of his nourishment from solid food, but they were still larger than normal. She pulled on a pair of lime green lace underpants and a matching satin top that clung to her breasts and left a ribbon of skin exposed below the hem.

A sigh of pleasure escaped from her lips as she stepped

into the bedroom. A lot of creativity had gone into creating a perfect sanctuary, a place that whispered love from every corner. The room was modeled after an image she'd gazed at with longing when she was eight years old. Watching marathons of the sixty's sitcom, *I Dream of Jeannie,* she'd formed her own dream. Someday, she would have a bedroom that looked like the inside of Jeannie's bottle — a circular, completely enclosed universe. Originally, she'd imagined a haze of purple and gold, exactly like Jeannie's bottle. But when she bought purple chiffon to drape over the bar above the vertical blinds that covered the sliding glass door, Mark had said, *Absolutely not.*

She compromised and bought navy blue chiffon and fifteen pillows in various shades of blue and gold to match the navy satin spread. She'd stripped and sanded their second-hand dressers and painted them with cream-colored enamel. The wooden knobs were painted gold. The frame of the mirror that hung over her dresser was painted with dark blue enamel to match the bedspread. It was a stroke of luck that the bedroom had already been carpeted in dark blue when they moved into the house. It was an unusual color for a carpet, making it seem as if the room had been waiting for her touch. When the house was quiet, and the blinds were closed, bathing the room in pearly light, she felt she was secure inside a magical blue and gold bottle. Their bedroom was a place guests never saw, safe from invasion by the ever-present specter of Grace Lutheran Church.

Mark was on his back with his eyes closed. Light from the house next door glowed through the semi-sheer gold curtains covering the window on his side of the bed. His breathing was shallow, his face tight with consciousness. She closed the door and walked to the bed. For a moment, she watched him breathe, wanting him to open his eyes and see how luscious she looked in her thin, silky top. Any moment, he would feel her presence, smell the aroma of almond and apples. His eyes would open and soften with longing. They remained shut.

She peeled off her top and slid into bed. She moved her hand slowly under the sheet, across his firm belly, then up, slowing to feel the soft, sparse cluster of hair on his chest. She rubbed her hand through the hair, fluffing it into a cloud that tickled her fingers. His eyes opened, but he didn't turn toward her. Moving closer, she stroked the soft skin below his armpit, then ran her hand down the opposite side of his body. She lowered her face to his chest, letting the cloud of hair caress her lips and nose. She rested her head on his chest and pulled him closer. His skin against her breasts made her feel weak. Waves of tenderness filled her throat and eyes. She gasped. She kissed his chest and neck and slipped her fingers under the waistband of his boxers, feeling the stiff hair on his groin and the hard muscle below his navel. Her throat ached with love for him, but deep in the pit of her belly was a worm of despair. He didn't move his hands to touch her.

She stroked the silky tip of his penis, petting it gently as if it were a timid animal. She wrapped her hand around it, lifting it. She slid deeper beneath the sheet, letting her breast brush against him, and then moved lower. She kissed the satiny skin. "I love you," she said. Any moment now, he would be overcome by the enticing touch of her hands and lips, the feel of her body against his.

"I love you too. Is Peter asleep?"

"I'm sure he is."

"Maybe you should check."

"He's fine." She kissed his penis again, pulling gently to bring him closer to her lips.

"Then, I'll check."

"He's fine. If he's not asleep, he's almost there." With supernatural effort, she bit off the words — *pay attention to me.* She cupped his testicles in her hand, drinking in his scent. She propped herself up on her forearm, letting the sheet slide off her shoulder so he could admire her body. A prickle of irritation ran through her. Any man would be thrilled to have a wife who looked like her. Her breasts were round, and the skin was smooth, not rippled or stretched. She let go of him and scooped her hair off the nape of her neck. She slid her hand back under the covers and wrapped her fingers around him. "What's the matter?"

He flinched as if she'd snapped him with a wet towel. "I think you should stop nursing Peter," he said.

"What?" she sat up.

"You heard me. It's annoying when you say *what* or *huh* just to say something. You heard what I said."

She shivered at the cool air on her skin. "He's only a baby." She softened her voice, "I don't want to talk about that right now."

"I do want to talk about it. In two weeks we start the every-member visits. I don't want you whipping up your shirt when we're talking to someone we hardly know. At least half the visits will be to delinquent members. What kind of introduction to their pastor and his family would that be?"

"How do you know they'll let us visit to ask for money if they don't even come to church? Besides, Peter's staying with Susan and Jack when we make our visits." This was not what she'd wanted at all. Why did he have to force her into an argument when she was trying to seduce him?

"I don't want to argue," he said.

Gabrielle hugged him, burrowing her face in his belly. "Neither do I."

"I just think you need to stop feeding him like that. He doesn't need it."

The panic she'd felt when Peter took his first steps that morning returned. "It's too soon."

"It's not." He shifted as if he wanted to turn on his side. When she didn't move, he lifted her arm off his waist, forcing her to raise her head. He rolled away from her.

"What are you doing?" she said.

"Going to sleep. It's been a brutal day. You know Sundays take a lot out of me."

"You had a nap."

"I'm exhausted."

Her touch was supposed to entice him. She didn't want to ask him to make love to her. She shouldn't have to! God had come to her in the garden, told her their marriage would be transformed, that He wanted Gabrielle and Mark to be alive with passion. God despised the dead, lifeless bones! She'd waited patiently all day. She'd remained calm. Now, he was forcing her to beg him to touch her, just like every other time. A spark of hatred sizzled in her chest. Whispering so that it wouldn't sound harsh or complaining, worst of all pleading, she said, "I thought we could make love."

"Is that why you're not wearing anything?"

She sat up, leaned over the side of the bed, and grabbed her top off the floor. "You are so *dense*." She sat up and yanked the top over her head. It twisted, and the strap cut into her shoulder. She whimpered and straightened the fabric. "I don't know if you pretend to be thick-headed or you really are. I can't even remember the last time we made love. All you care about is church and having the perfect child, the perfect family. Oh, and golf."

"Come on, Gabby. Not now. I'm really tired."

"I hate it when you call me that."

He sighed and turned onto his back. "I said I'm tired. I don't feel like having sex right now."

"You never feel like it." She threw back the blankets and climbed out of bed.

"Where are you going?"

"What do you care?"

Maybe he would get up and follow her. They would make love in the living room, the risk of someone seeing in the window adding excitement to their reconciliation. She walked to the door slowly.

He yawned. "Aren't you going to turn out your light?"

She gripped the doorframe, wanting to hurl herself onto the bed and pound her fists against his chest, rip off the covers and his boxers, making him feel as exposed as she did.

A soft snore drifted out of his mouth. She grabbed a long t-shirt from the chair in the corner, pulling it on as she walked. She hoped the thumping of her feet on the hardwood floor in the hallway would wake him. She stepped down into the living room and flopped on the futon. She stared out the glass door at nothing. Her mind felt rinsed with icy water. Cool air rippled across her skin, and goosebumps rose on her legs. She rubbed them furiously. He wasn't going to wake and come looking for her.

The blackness outside pressed against the glass. She couldn't see more than a few feet into the backyard. Someone could be out there, watching. She scooted off the futon, yanked the cord to close the drapes, and pulled the crocheted afghan off the back of the rocking chair. That chair and the blanket made of chartreuse, orange, and purple yarn, were the only things in the room that had belonged to her before she married Mark. She pulled the afghan over her legs. She couldn't stop shivering. He treated her as if she was just another church member demanding his time. She did everything for him. She created a warm sanctuary inside their home. She was a wonderful mother. She cooked delicious, healthy meals. She was friendly with everyone at Grace, even the people she didn't like. There was nothing in her life that wasn't for him and the church. He should be grateful and thrilled that he had such an attractive wife. Her hair was long and thick, her skin was smooth, and she didn't have any flab except the slight pouch in her belly. Her only flaw, taunting her from under the afghan, was her over-sized feet. Size eight. Much too large for her five-foot, five-inch body. But he shouldn't notice her feet. He should notice the rest of her.

If he wasn't a minister, she might think he was having an affair. She couldn't quite picture that. Couldn't see Mark approaching a woman or being outgoing enough for a strange woman to come on to him. Besides, where did he ever go that he might meet someone? He spent all his time at church, old folks' homes, and hospitals. Maybe at a hospital. A parishioner's daughter that wasn't a member of Grace? She shook her head, trying to dislodge the thought. He wouldn't risk his career for something like that. There must be some repulsive thing in her. Something she was blind to, something hideous that had been there since she was a child. Some ugly, unlovable thing.

Her thoughts drifted closer to the darkest crevice of her mind. No one wanted her. People told her she was beautiful. They commented on her gem-like green eyes, her thick, milk chocolate hair with golden highlights, her creamy skin. Why, then, didn't they want to touch her? Hold her? A sob rose from a place deep inside. She gagged on the nasty taste of bile.

When she was little, her mother had adored her, whispering into her ear every night. "You're my sweetness. Never forget that your name means the strength of God. You brought me strength to raise a child by myself. A name as beautiful as your little face, as precious as your little lips and toes."

FOR SIX MONTHS of the year, Gabrielle's father was floating on the ocean with the US Navy. When her father was home, Gabrielle had her own tiny bedroom, a bed with a white headboard, a bright pink spread, and a pink and white ruffled sham for her pillow. She loved her bed. But even more, she loved it when her father went to sea, and she was invited to sleep in her mother's bed. The first night he was gone was the most exciting. Gabrielle climbed into her pink and white bed and burrowed under the covers, waiting for her mother. Soon, her mother's finger, tipped with glossy pink polish, touched the light switch, lingering, drawing out the anticipation until shivers ran down Gabrielle's slender legs.

"I could use some company," her mother said. "Want to sleep in my bed tonight?" She always said *tonight*, but Gabrielle would sleep on her father's side of the bed for the next one hundred and eighty-two nights.

Her mother swept up to the side of Gabrielle's bed, her

silky white robe with the shimmering purple flowers billowing behind her. She grabbed the blankets and yanked them down to the foot of the mattress. Gabrielle squealed. They ran down the hall and jumped into the big double bed, not bothering to turn off the light in Gabrielle's bedroom.

Even when her father was in town, Gabrielle and her mother spent their days doing everything together. They walked to the park. Sophie sat on the swing next to Gabrielle's, and they had a contest to see whose toes could go higher into the sky, frantically pumping their legs until the swings flew up so high the chains went slack. In the summer, they sometimes packed cream cheese and jelly sandwiches and peanuts in their rough shells and stayed at the park until dinner time. They ate tomatoes and cucumbers and breadsticks, sitting on a blanket in the backyard. Her mother read stories and rubbed Gabrielle's back until she drifted to sleep at nap time. They colored pictures, painted with watercolors, and cooked.

Cooking was the best. Sophie loved to experiment. After they read *Stone Soup*, they plopped a small, smooth rock into a pot and added all the vegetables left in the refrigerator. The soup was delicious — just as the story had promised. Another time, giggling as she danced around the kitchen, Sophie combined anise, basil, cinnamon, and sage into a boiling pot of potatoes. She mashed them with a whole cube of butter. They pinched their noses and ate nothing but mashed potatoes for dinner. If one of their cooking experiments failed completely, Sophie tossed it in the garbage, and they drove to the *Dairy Belle* for hamburgers, fries, and shakes.

When she was five, Gabrielle didn't go to school. Sophie taught her the alphabet and numbers. The next year, she taught Gabrielle how to read and how to add and subtract.

Nights were the best. They cuddled close so that Gabrielle felt the warm nylon of her mother's nightgown. The gowns were lined up in Sophie's second dresser drawer like colorful clouds — pink, coral, yellow, pale green, pale blue, lavender, and white. While they slept, the silky stuff floated across Gabrielle's arms and legs, caressing her throughout the night. When her father was away, her mother's room became Gabrielle's room. Once a week, they sat at the vanity, and Sophie painted their fingernails. Every morning, Gabrielle lay on the bed, watching her mother apply make-up. Gabrielle stared with an open mouth that mirrored her mother's as she outlined her eyes in black, and her lips in red, before filling in the shadow and the rest of the lipstick.

Then, everything changed. One night, when her father had been home for a few months, Sophie pushed away her dinner plate and announced that a new baby was joining their family. Frank shoved his chair back, stood up, squared his shoulders, and walked around the table. He pulled Sophie up and kissed her hard on the lips. Gabrielle stared, wondering what it meant. Maybe she would have a sister, and the three girls would have fun. That might be okay.

"It'll be a boy!" Frank said.

Gabrielle scowled. A boy wouldn't be any fun. She knew already, boys didn't like their fingernails painted. And where would the boy sleep when her father was gone? Or did this mean her father was staying home now? No more ships. Maybe he wanted to stay home, for his son.

Daniel was born when Frank was at sea. *God knows where*, her mother said.

Gabrielle spent three days with Mr. and Mrs. Eckhart next door. The night Mr. Eckhart brought Sophie and Daniel home from the hospital, Daniel slept on the double bed.

"He's our new baby," Sophie said. "If you're very, very careful, and sleep on your back without moving, he can sleep between us."

Daniel made her mother grouchy. She complained of being tired. She complained the bed wasn't big enough for all three of them. She complained that Frank wasn't around, and how in the *hell* was she supposed to take care of two kids by herself? She was too tired to color or paint. Now, Gabrielle went to school. Sometimes her mother was late picking up Gabrielle from second grade because she'd been napping. *With you two in my bed, I never get any sleep.*

"It's not my fault," Gabrielle said.

"I didn't say it was. But even when I fall asleep, I don't sleep well. I'm perched on the edge of the bed as if I'm ready to fall over a cliff. You have no idea how many nights I dream about sliding down a cliff into the ocean. I wake up, and half my body is hanging off the mattress."

A few months later, Frank came home, and Sophie's mood improved. Gabrielle went back to her princess bed, but Daniel got to stay in his parents' room in a wood cradle.

The next time her father went to sea, Gabrielle lay in bed, waiting. She fell asleep with the light on. When she woke, the house was silent. She crept out of bed and down the hall toward her mother's room. The bedside lamp spread a milky glow into the hallway. Gabrielle peeked around the corner. Her mother was feeding Daniel, her breast poking out of the top of her nightgown like the fat white bratwurst they'd had for dinner a few weeks before.

"You didn't come into my room," Gabrielle said.

"You're a big girl. I think you can manage to turn off your own light."

Gabrielle waited for her mother to remember Frank was gone, to remember Gabrielle would be sleeping in her mother's bed for the next six months. All she heard was Daniel's sucking noises.

"Aren't I sleeping here?"

Her mother sighed. "You're a big kid. You take up a lot of room."

Tears spilled out of Gabrielle's eyes.

Her mother sighed again. "If you're going to be a crybaby about it, come on in. It's just so crowded."

Gabrielle didn't like being called a crybaby. If anyone in the house cried too much, it sure wasn't her. She felt silly and strangely ashamed. She walked slowly to the bed and climbed up, inching herself closer to the middle. "Can't Daniel go in the cradle?"

"No. Then I just have to get up when he fusses." Sophie plucked the suction cup of Daniel's mouth off her breast, pulled the strap of her nightgown back over her shoulder, and laid Daniel on the bed next to her.

"Can't he sleep on the other side?" Gabrielle whispered.

"He'll fall out. Now lay down and go to sleep." Sophie turned off the light.

Gabrielle slid under the covers, pressing up against Daniel.

"Careful," Sophie said.

Gabrielle wanted to poke Daniel in the belly, make him cry, show her mother who the real crybaby was. But what if her mother sent Gabrielle back to her room?

When Daniel woke to eat again, he didn't wake slowly. He opened his mouth and let out a howl that made Gabrielle and her mother jolt up in bed. While Daniel nursed, Gabrielle drifted into a half-sleep. She inched closer to her mother, feeling the edge of her mother's gown tickle her bare leg. She turned on her side, pressing her face against her mother's hip. The flesh and the thin nylon felt so warm and soft.

Speaking in a low voice so Daniel wouldn't be startled, Sophie said, "You can't stay there."

Gabrielle burrowed her face deeper. Just a few more minutes, he wasn't asleep yet, she could hear him sucking and gulping.

Suddenly, her mother's elbow was poking in her eye. "You have to move. When he falls asleep, I don't want to jostle him. Now move back. What's the matter with you? You're too big for this kind of thing."

It wasn't fair. Daniel should go. He wouldn't even know the difference. She clenched her eyes and fists and pointed her toes, trying to hold the tears inside. After a while, her muscles relaxed, and she fell asleep. When she woke again, everyone was sleeping. She smelled Daniel's milky breath and sweaty head. She turned on her other side. Soft, snoring noises came from her mother. She would never know if Gabrielle moved Daniel, just for a minute. She'd put him right back.

She wriggled toward the foot of the bed until Daniel's pajama'd feet were at the top of her head. Carefully holding his head, like her mother had shown her, so he didn't wake, she rolled him onto his stomach, then his side and onto his back. Now there was a narrow space, just perfect for her. She slithered back up and pressed herself into her mother. She turned on her side and pressed her back against her mother's arm, pretending she was having her back patted and rubbed. Daniel hadn't woken, and her mother hadn't moved at all. Gabrielle was pinched between the two of them. She rolled Daniel again. That was better.

There was a thud punctuated by a scream.

Sophie leaped out of bed and switched on the light. "What happened? Oh, my God! My baby!" She rushed to the other side of the bed and picked up red-faced, howling Daniel.

"You pushed him out of bed! How could you? What kind of monster have I raised?!"

"What?" Gabrielle shook her head. "No. No. I didn't."

"You're evil, Gabrielle. I don't know what's the matter with you. This is our tiny baby, you should love him."

"I didn't push him." Gabrielle's lips trembled. "I just…"

"You didn't *just* anything. There's no excuse."

"I didn't push him," Gabrielle cried. "I just moved him a tiny bit."

"You pushed your baby brother on the floor. I'm so ashamed of you. Go back to your room. You can't sleep here anymore."

"I didn't push him." Gabrielle could hardly breathe. "I didn't. I want to be here with you."

"No. You're too big. You move around and take up the blankets. You snore, and your breath is sour. Your big, bony feet are always poking me in the shins."

For a long time after, Gabrielle hated her princess bed. The blanket came untucked, and her big feet poked out the bottom. She woke cold and shivering. Most nights, she cried herself to sleep with the light on, afraid of being alone, but even more afraid because her mother didn't want her anymore.

By the time her father came home, Gabrielle was able to sleep without crying. She never allowed her mother see her cry again. Let Daniel be the crybaby. She hated him. There were no more cooking parties or back rubs. When Daniel got older, he was sulky and quiet. Useless. When Gabrielle complained that he never did anything but sit in the living room with the drapes closed, staring at the TV, her mother gave her withering looks. Sometimes, when her mother was at the store, and Daniel was staring at the TV, Gabrielle tiptoed into her parents' room and lifted one of the pastel nightgowns out of the drawer. She rubbed it against her cheek. It wasn't the same.

THAT HAD BEEN A LONG TIME AGO. She never thought about it. Now her mother was gone. Dead from cancer one year after Gabrielle and Mark were married. Had her mother ever altered her false belief? Gabrielle didn't know, didn't care. She felt ashamed, begging her mother to believe her, to adore Gabrielle like she had before Daniel poked his dumb face into their lives. Why did she always have to beg someone to love her?

She needed Mark's body, his touch, but was ashamed of her need. Hadn't God promised her a living, breathing marriage?

Three

ON THE FIRST Sunday after Pentecost, Mark got up at five, as he did every Sunday. He ate a piece of buttered toast, drank a cup of coffee, and was ready to leave by five-forty-five. He opened the front door, forcing his eyes to look past the Bird of Paradise plants crowding closer to the front porch as if they wanted to come inside the house. The porch looked like something in the middle of a jungle, filled with man-eating plants. The Birds of Paradise mocked him as he stepped onto the path. The thick leaves brushed against his arms, making his skin crawl. He couldn't understand why Gabrielle was so fascinated by them. She said she didn't want their house looking like every other house on the street. Sometimes, it seemed that her whole purpose in life was to draw attention to herself. He hadn't noticed before Peter was born. Now, it was embarrassing to watch her vie for attention, competing not only with the church but with their son.

Instead of firing up his motorcycle for the short ride to

church, he decided to walk. The exercise would drive his thoughts back to the morning worship services where they belonged. It worried him when he couldn't keep his mind under control. If he wasn't strictly focused, his thoughts ran wild. Lately, they'd become more difficult to control, and he wasn't sure why. Like the uncontrolled Birds of Paradise — why did he have to fixate on those damn plants every time he stepped out the door?

The air had a satiny stillness, foretelling another hot day. The horizon was fuzzy with light, colored pink by the smog. Finches chirped frantically, determined to have their say before it was too hot to move. The long week of hot weather hadn't helped anyone's mood. Gabrielle hadn't said a word to him about weaning Peter since they'd argued about it. Mark had been patient enough, saying nothing when Peter started crawling. He'd been waiting for her to realize it was time, but the months crept past until he wondered if she planned to breastfeed until Peter went to Kindergarten. Some women did. It was hard to tell with Gabrielle. She had intense, unconventional opinions, and she would fight to the death to defend them. She was fanatical in her insistence that she stay home to raise their child, even if it meant buying clothes at thrift stores. If a piece of beef or a preservative touched her tongue, she behaved as if she'd been poisoned, curling her lips, making soft gagging sounds. He turned the corner onto Fremont and once again forced his thoughts back to the morning worship services.

The church parking lot was empty. He liked it when no one else was around. A chance to be alone with his thoughts. Sometimes he felt like he was paid just to listen to other people talk. The women who volunteered in the office knocked on his door regularly, eager to describe in detail the phone calls from the mentally unbalanced who called the church looking for an available ear to ease the pressure of their delusions. Once a week, he listened to the widows' sewing circle members, all hungry for a man to talk to. On a daily basis, he listened to people who called him in various stages of crisis — the death of a loved one, financial pressure, marriage problems, child-rearing traumas, poor health — everyone wanted to talk. And to think he went into the ministry believing people would treat his opinions with reverence. They claimed they came to him for counsel and advice, but they didn't seem that interested in what he had to say at all. They wanted to talk. The world was starving for someone to listen.

He cut across the lawn toward the offices. It was thrilling to think that he was cutting through the spot where the new sanctuary would sit if everything went according to plan. Images of stone floors and stained glass windows, polished wood and dim lighting, filled his mind as he made his way toward his office. He unlocked the flimsy door and went inside. He settled into his chair and pulled his sermon notes out of the center desk drawer. The drawer was reserved solely for his sermon notes. It had become a ritual, as if being alone in a drawer, his sketched thoughts would remain unblemished and take on a life of their own.

Most of the ministers he knew either followed an outline or typed out their sermon several times over, letting the words seep into their subconscious. Mark liked to use small sketches to illustrate his ideas. He was certain it worked better than any other method for remembering the stories and examples needed to embellish the Biblical words. He often thought he should write a book about his technique. Using a conventional outline made it easy to stumble too abruptly to the next thought, forgetting a key point, and getting so far ahead of yourself, it was impossible to artfully return to a missed concept. His detailed drawings kept the stories clear in his mind. The sketches were effective because they engaged his creative right brain, making the messages more cohesive, less memorized, and more conversational.

He chose his sermon topics ahead of time, announcing the titles in the church newsletter months in advance. This morning's topic was marriage, not an easy subject under normal circumstances. Today, it was fraught with land mines for a follow-up argument with Gabby. For the introduction, he planned to tell a humorous story about miscommunication. A few months after they were married, Gabby had spent an entire week weeding and raking the yard for her enormous vegetable garden. Because of her hard work, he'd wanted to surprise her with a nice dinner. He'd even planned a vegetarian offering, convinced it would make her feel extra loved.

The meal would be comprised of sautéed green beans, mushrooms, finely shredded carrots, and garlic served over brown rice. He was making a salad filled with her beloved avocados. He crept into the house and spread his supplies on the counter. Through the screen door, he could hear the tines of her rake hitting the hard clay as she diligently removed each and every rock. Pulling up a jazz playlist, he started the rice cooking. He settled into slicing the ends off the green beans. He chopped the mushrooms and garlic into precise slivers. He sautéed everything quickly with the gas set high, slightly browning the beans, then reduced it to simmer. After he set the table, he stepped out the back door and called to Gabrielle. She jumped, nearly falling backward in the loose dirt. He walked over and took the rake out of her hands and leaned it against the lemon tree. "Come wash up. I made a spectacular dinner for you. I even chilled a bottle of Chardonnay."

"What?"

"You have sautéed veggies and salad waiting for you. I know how hard you've been working on all this." He swept his arm above the swath of fresh, dark earth that consumed almost a third of the backyard.

She took a step forward, put both her small hands on his chest, and shoved him. He stumbled back into the branches of the lemon tree. They scratched at his neck and head.

"What's the matter with you?" He regained his balance and

glared at her, not sure whether to feel hurt or angry.

"I already made dinner. Didn't you smell it cooking? There's a bean casserole in the oven."

He hadn't noticed. Fumes of fresh garlic had filled his nostrils. He'd noticed the kitchen was warm but hadn't realized the source was the oven. They argued over which dinner would prevail. He won, insisting the casserole would keep for a day. Gabrielle sulked through dinner.

Her sullen face and the description of her shoving him into the tree would be eliminated from his sermonized version of the story. The story was funny if you left her temper out of the picture. To illustrate it, he'd drawn a stick figure of a man and a woman with their backs to each other, each preparing a meal. Over their heads was a sketch of a garden growing nothing but garlic. Although the garlic looked like mutant onions, it was enough to create a vivid image in his mind. In the retelling, he hoped to elicit a few laughs by putting himself at fault, emphasizing how oblivious he'd been to the fantastic aroma coming from the oven. The congregation would be engaged by his story-telling skills and continue to listen eagerly when he reached the less entertaining portion — instructing them to follow the command to put their spouses' well-being ahead of their own. People were addicted to stories, and they loved his, especially stories of his charming, newborn marriage.

When he finished reviewing his sketches, he walked into the church hall. The folding chairs were constantly shifting their positions as if a poltergeist wandered through at night, creating disarray. Just a half an inch here and there turned the rows into waves of beige metal. He couldn't wait to be rid of them. Soon he would stand in a real pulpit instead of behind a wobbly podium. He'd look out at wooden pews, bolted to the floor, unable to taunt his need for order. He'd probably save an hour a week once he was rid of the task of repositioning chairs.

His heels echoed as he walked to the back of the building and into the kitchen. He made a pot of coffee and rummaged in the refrigerator for something to eat. A plastic container with a few slices of cheddar cheese was left from the Wednesday night Working Moms' fellowship group. He nibbled on cheese while he waited for the coffee to drip into the pot. What he really wanted was a few puffs on his pipe, but he couldn't risk one of the members who categorized smoking as a sin observing their pastor puffing on tobacco. After gulping one cup of coffee, he poured a second cup and went outside. He crossed the parking lot to the covered corridor that ran the length of the education wing. He unlocked the classroom doors and opened the drapes in each room. From the far end of the building, he marveled over the size of the property for the hundredth time. It was incredible that the members had let it sit semi-developed for all these years.

It was the ongoing disagreement over money that continuously derailed the discussion and kept them from building. The financially conservative members refused to begin a building project until all the cash was on hand, while another group thought it was more realistic and not ungodly to take out a loan. Since Mark had become the minister, there'd been a gradual shift in power. Younger people with more disposable income wanted a real sanctuary. They were also used to carrying large mortgages on their homes and didn't see why the church couldn't do the same. This faction was also open to other non-traditional ideas, such as hiring a fundraising consultant. The investment in a consultant ultimately saved money, because churches which had an outsider to deliver all the controversial statements about money didn't splinter as easily over the divisive topic. Money and God. They all wanted to please God, but there was nothing like a disagreement over money to rip a church in half and destroy all efforts at Godly behavior, depleting the membership, and the church income.

Their professional fundraising consultant, Grant Miller, had met with a group of ten leaders in the early Spring. He'd assured them that with a little targeted effort, they would have no problem raising funds for a sanctuary and a new office wing, including a welcoming room filled with comfortable furniture, featuring a gas fireplace. Grant's salesmanship had convinced nearly everyone who was actively involved that a massive fundraising drive would *strengthen the community feeling at Grace*. He fired them up to trust that the program would increase their faith once they saw the results of a unified team effort, blessed by God. Usually, Mark was distrustful of salespeople, but this guy hadn't pressured them. He quietly and reasonably persuaded them, even the frugal Brackners, that his twenty-five-thousand dollar fee was worth every dime. *Like the mustard seed that falls into the earth*, Grant said, *this tiny investment, only a little over eighty dollars per name on the church roster, will grow into a massive blessing.* The remainder would come from a loan.

The only roadblock was Susan Geller Ormiston — Gabrielle's best friend, a life-long member of Grace, and the daughter of the former minister. Before he'd died and Mark was called in as an unseasoned, sub-par replacement, Susan's father had been the minister of Grace for over thirty-five years. Susan had been baptized as an infant, passed through the rite of confirmation as a teenager, and walked down the aisle toward her soon-to-be-husband at Grace. Her children were baptized at Grace. Three local ministers and a regional official, all wearing elaborately embroidered chasubles, officiated over Reverend Geller's funeral at Grace. The building was littered with her childhood memories. The walls of the nondescript building pulsated with the tangible emotions of every significant event in Susan's life. If the aging multi-purpose room was good enough for her wedding and her father's funeral, it was good enough to last the remainder of her lifetime. She saw no use or reason for an expensive new sanctuary. Enlisting Gabrielle as the messenger, she'd informed Mark — *If people only come to church to sit in a nice looking building, then they're here for all the wrong reasons, and we don't want them.*

His thoughts were halted by a car pulling into the parking lot. He hurried back to the kitchen, washed and dried his cup, and went to the tiny room behind the stage where his robes and vestments were stored. He slipped his arms into the ankle-length black robe and buttoned the front. Over that, he put the seamless white cape that hung to mid-calf. He draped the narrow red brocade stole around his neck, checking to make sure the embroidered cross was centered over his spine, so the fringed ends hung at equal lengths. On top of this, he added a four-inch 18-carat gold cross on a thick chain that reached almost to his waist. Ministers in other denominations conducted services dressed in dark suits, but he was pleased that he was in a tradition that demanded elaborate garments. They set him apart from the rest of the congregation. If a visitor wandered into the building on a Sunday morning, there was no doubt about which man was the spiritual leader. Putting on his robes was a ritual that silenced every stray thought. The robes transformed him into a spokesman for God.

As if the robes truly had given him a supernatural power, the eight-thirty worship service passed flawlessly. When everyone scattered to their age-appropriate Sunday school classes, he escaped to his office. He looked over his calendar for the coming week. Then he read, for the third time, the packet of materials explaining why it was critical to the fundraising program that the leaders visit every person listed on the membership role, even those who hadn't walked through the church doors in ten or twenty years. It was a blend of business theory, stating that leaders had to communicate clearly with all stakeholders, and a belief that God's supernatural power was unleashed through a meticulous effort to touch every single life attached to the church. According to the organization that developed the program, these factors would bring a *startling* number of delinquent members back into active participation, if all the visitation guidelines were adhered to. Of those returning members, a certain percentage would donate *miraculous* sums of money to demonstrate their overwhelming joy at returning to the arms of their church family. He was tormented with doubts each time he read the over-hyped words. Still, the back page of the brochure was filled with quotes from ministers recounting how the program had not only allowed them to successfully complete their building plans, it strengthened their churches beyond anything they could have imagined.

With an admirable sanctuary and office complex, the church would also attract new members. This could be a turning point in his career. At thirty-one years old, the next twenty years would be his most powerful. A larger church membership would raise his status among other churches and in the secular community. It was his chance to lead the most significant Lutheran church in Silicon Valley, possibly in the state of California. Ministers from large churches were often welcomed and listened to when they spoke at city council meetings. They were invited to participate in other community activities, working diplomatically to insert Godly practices into public affairs.

The new sanctuary would change everything. He didn't just want it for himself. Sure, it would be great for his career, but part of his career was about dreaming of big things for God. Mark was simply the vessel. His stomach knotted when he worried the plan wouldn't work, that it was more effective in other denominations, that the branch of the Lutheran church to which he belonged was too immersed in tradition, too conservative, too practical. While their denomination interpreted the Bible literally, unlike other literalists, they dismissed modern-day miracles and some of the more stringent practices such as the expectation that members tithe ten percent of their incomes. They weren't inclined toward enthusiasm for anything outside the church documents that spelled out what the correct literal interpretations ought to be.

The second worship service began as smoothly as the first. While the congregation sang the final verse of the pre-sermon hymn, he closed his hymnal and moved toward the pulpit. He looked down and smiled at his family. Peter was climbing up and down, from his pile of plastic blocks on the floor to Gabrielle's lap. Mark looked out over the pool of faces, re-focusing his mind onto his sermon.

The music stopped, and Peter yelped. Mark shut out the

sound, read the passage that formed the basis of his sermon, and launched immediately into the story of the redundant dinners he and Gabrielle had prepared. At the end of the story, he foolishly allowed his glance to dart in Gabrielle's direction. She was scowling. He looked away quickly, and continued speaking, the words seeming to flow on their own, while Gabrielle and Peter claimed his thoughts. The chair next to Gabrielle rattled as Peter pulled himself up into her lap. One of the plastic blocks clattered onto the floor. Peter cried out. Mark forced the noise to the back of his mind.

After a few minutes, he heard a snorting sound. It couldn't possibly be what he thought it was. Months ago, they had agreed — it was better to take Peter into another room if he wanted to nurse. But that was when he was an infant. By this age, there was no reason for Peter to eat right in the middle of the service. Mark allowed his gaze to travel back to the front row. Sure enough, Gabrielle had her shirt bunched up around her left armpit. Peter happily slurped his human pacifier. Mark glared at her. Then he softened his expression, worried that someone else would pick up on his contorted features. Gabrielle refused to meet his eyes. She was smiling with that half wicked, half sleepy Madonna demeanor she adopted when she was feeding Peter. She seemed to think breastfeeding her son was some sort of spiritual accomplishment that transported her to another dimension. It wasn't as bad when Peter was tiny, wrapped snugly in a blanket. But now, his legs dangled onto the chair next to

Gabrielle. He looked like a little boy with his thick leather sandals, his miniature blue jeans, and a blue and black striped shirt. Mark wanted to jump off the edge of the stage and pull her shirt over the exposed skin. His hands trembled. He wanted to grab her shoulders and shake her, demanding to know why she was doing this to him. His face felt flushed. Half the congregation must be staring at the suggestion of his wife's breast, not hearing a word he was saying. It felt like the retina was tearing away from his eyes as he forced his attention away from Gabrielle and out over the others. Sounds of Peter's satisfied grunts filled his ears. The snuffling noises echoed off the linoleum floor up into the rafters.

He cut the sermon short, another excellent feature of his pictorial method for arranging his thoughts. There was no need to search through layers of paper or find a new place in an outline, he simply identified a picture and mentally obliterated it. The offering and prayers drowned out the noises coming from Peter. By the final hymn, Peter was asleep on Gabrielle's lap.

Gabrielle didn't join him at the side door to shake parishioners' hands as they left the building. This morning, he didn't care. He could put his attention on the faces in front of him, push his anger into a narrow space, and direct his concern toward the people filing past him, smiling and complimenting his sermon. He grinned ridiculously and handed out vigorous handshakes with personalized comments to each person who waited in line to shake his hand. When the last one had stepped out of the cool building and into the blinding sunshine, he hurried to the vestment storage room. He removed the stole and his robes, placing each item on its proper hanger. He washed his hands to remove the odors of perfume and cologne that had been passed to him through handshakes and hugs. He closed the door, locked it, and went to his office, skipping his usual habit of picking up discarded bulletins off the chairs and floor.

Gabrielle was there, staring out the window. Peter toddled from the couch to the desk to the filing cabinet, pausing at each piece of furniture to re-establish his balance.

"Hey, Buddy." Mark held out his arms.

"Da!" Peter cried. He wobbled toward Mark.

Mark scooped him up and tossed him in the air. Peter giggled.

"Please don't do that," Gabrielle said.

It was like pulling a lever. When he tossed Peter in the air, he could count on laughter from his son and a directive from his wife. All fathers, since time began, Mark told her, threw their children in the air. It was what fathers did. He suspected it had sociological significance — helping children develop confidence. Gabrielle thought that was ridiculous. She persisted with alarmed intakes of air and stern comments.

She stared out the window as if she were peering into a world that was invisible to him. The sharp line of her shoulders assured him she was waiting for his complaint, preparing to start an argument. Seeing his son's grin, the small collection of tiny white teeth, made Mark smile. His anger started to dissolve. Why make an issue out of one defiant act? Maybe if he didn't press her, she'd come around more quickly to his way of thinking. The more Peter moved around on his own, the less interested he'd be in sitting on his mother's lap. Time might resolve the whole problem.

Gabrielle turned from the window, and in one sweeping motion, lifted her tee-shirt and the spandex tank top she sometimes wore instead of a bra. Her breasts wobbled just below the folds of the yellow shirt she was holding in her fists. "Why are you afraid of these?"

"What are you doing?" His voice was rough. He looked out the window at the empty garden, then jerked his shoulders around in an awkward motion that made him lose his balance for a moment. The office door was closed. His heart thudded against his ribs. When he turned back, she'd dropped her shirt, but his heart continued its rapid beating. If it weren't for the wrinkled spots along the bottom edge of the shirt, he'd think he'd imagined those seven seconds of horror.

Gabrielle laughed. "Afraid one of your parishioners is going to find out your wife has breasts?"

"What's the matter with you?" His heart wouldn't settle down. He felt weak and slightly out of breath. He backed up toward the couch and flopped down.

"You're such a prude," Gabrielle said. "I saw your snarly looks when I was feeding Peter. I have nice breasts. Why are you so afraid someone will see one? But more important, why don't you like them?"

"Do we have to fight about this right now?"

Peter picked up on Mark's emphasis on the word *fight*. "Ite," he said. "Ite."

Mark patted Peter's head and got up from the couch. "Let's go. I'm finished here."

"I want to know why you're so ashamed that I breastfeed your son. No one is going to leave the church because I'm feeding our baby. You act like you're terrified of my body."

"He's not a baby." It was the wrong thing to say.

"He is a baby."

There was a hesitant tap on the door. Great. Who had been standing outside, listening? He felt an uncomfortable combination of relief over postponing the argument and anxiety over the possibility of exposure. "Come in."

Gabrielle grabbed the strap of the backpack she used as a diaper bag. She scooped up Peter and settled him on her hip. He didn't care if she stormed out. It was better than fighting about breasts in the church office, worrying she'd uncover herself again, and this time, someone would pass by the garden window.

Tentatively, the door opened. Susan Ormiston stepped into the office. She wore her standard leggings, showing off muscular legs. A large knit top covered her barrel-shaped torso that had evolved out of two pregnancies and the resulting loss of freedom to play softball and soccer as often and vigorously as she once had. Her hair was stiff, a pale yellow color that looked dyed but had changed texture because of some weird hormonal change after the birth of her daughter. Long bangs covered her eyebrows, giving her indigo eyes a slightly surprised expression.

"Hey, Susan." Mark was aware of his voice slipping into the deeper, smoother tone that emerged when he spoke to a member of the church. He hated the phony sound, certain that Gabrielle noted it. He shook the hyper self-awareness from his mind and smiled, "How are you?"

"I'm fine. I was looking for Gabrielle." Susan's voice was low and seductively hoarse. She looked at Gabrielle, "Hi."

Mark stepped toward Susan and folded his arms around her. "It's good to see you," he said. Susan liked hugs. Her father had been a hugger, and he'd passed it on to his children, as Susan regularly reminded him. She pressed her hands firmly against the center of his back. When they moved away from each other, he kept his gaze locked on her face, looking for a sign that would tell him whether she'd listened for a moment outside the door. His heart still thumped so heavily he wondered if she'd felt it when she hugged him.

Susan smiled at Gabrielle. "Sorry I haven't called. Things have been *completely* crazy. I was in charge of Cara's end-of-school picnic. Then teacher appreciation day. Plus, regular life. Two kids keep you going twenty-four-seven." She laughed. "Or at least eighteen-seven. You have no idea." She laughed again. "Be thankful you only have one. So…why'd you disappear after church? I've been looking all over for you."

"I wasn't feeling sociable," Gabrielle said.

Susan smiled sympathetically. Mark was certain she hadn't overheard anything. Susan wasn't the kind of person to listen outside a closed door. There were more than enough of those in the church, but Susan wasn't one of them. She accepted people and situations at face value. She let others' quirks roll off her back. He wished Gabby could be less complicated, easy-going, like Susan. But then, the entire reason he'd been captivated by Gabrielle was because she was a challenge. He needed to accept the bad with the good. It was just that lately, there had been more bad than good.

"I wanted to know if you can come for lunch and a swim Tuesday," Susan said.

Gabrielle set Peter on the floor, slipped her other arm through the strap of the backpack, and picked him up again. "Sure."

Mark sighed. She made it sound like she was doing Susan a favor. Once her anger flared, she forced everyone to work like mad, pleasing and teasing her out of it. He stepped behind Susan and turned off the lights. Following his cue, Susan backed toward the door. "Eleven-thirty. Okay? We'll eat early, and I'll put Sam down for a nap. Hopefully. Does that sound good?"

"Sure. Okay." Gabrielle moved toward the door.

He waited, letting both of them walk ahead into the hallway while he pushed the lock on the doorknob and made sure the door closed snugly. He couldn't remember if he'd locked the door that led to the garden on the opposite side of his office. He shoved his key in the lock, went back inside, and locked the interior door behind him. He crossed the room. He had locked it, but he went out that way and cut across the lawn. Jack Ormiston was jiggling Sam on his hip, watching Cara attempt forward rolls on the thick, soft grass. Sam was squalling, but Jack looked placid. Nothing phased Jack or Susan. Life must be tranquil at their house.

He shook Jack's free hand. "Susan's on her way out."

"Catch the Giant's game yesterday?" Jack said.

The question was a testimony to Mark's ability to act as if there was common ground where none existed. He'd known Jack for a little over five years, they'd spent countless evenings at each other's homes, talked frequently about golf, fatherhood, and church matters. Despite the years of friendship, Jack still believed Mark was interested in baseball.

"I missed it."

Jack covered the highlights as they watched their wives walk toward them.

After they said their good-byes, Mark waited while Gabrielle strapped Peter into his seat and climbed into her side of the minivan.

"I need to stop at the market to get something for dinner," she said.

He nodded — five and a half miles in hot, lazy Sunday traffic. He turned right out of the parking lot instead of left, giving a final wave to the Ormistons in the rearview mirror.

Gabrielle leaned her head against the back of the seat, closed her eyes, and let her hands fall face up in her lap. She never fiddled with her hands or clasped them like most people did. She didn't secure them in her pockets or tuck them under her arms. He felt uncomfortable when his hands weren't occupied. Was it a subconscious fear of attack that kept his hands in one protective stance or another? He felt vulnerable if he left his hands limp. It had taken a while to zero in on Gabrielle's unusual relationship with her hands as the reason she always looked a bit different from other people. When she wasn't holding Peter, she stood with her arms at her sides. They didn't dangle awkwardly. Her arms were graceful, elbows straight, her hands brushing lightly against her thighs, her fingers extended but not rigid. He'd observed the reactions of others, wondering if they knew why they backed away from her, clutching their arms tightly around their waists, or shoving their hands deeper into their pockets.

Sometimes, when he looked over at her idle hands, her skyward palms, she seemed like a stranger. Instinct drove human beings to search for mates. When they discovered a man or woman who tweaked their hormones or fit easily into their own lifestyle and plans, they hooked together for life. It was a cold view, but one he couldn't avoid when he looked at her, trying to imagine what was going through her mind. No one really knew who they were marrying. How could they?

Even after living together for years, you couldn't know for certain what another person was like, what they thought about. People revealed only what they wanted you to know.

He thought about these things frequently, more so since Peter had been born. They said women's hormones changed, but no one ever specified how much or for how long. Or if the change was permanent. Maybe it had nothing to do with hormones — just a slow revelation of more facets of the woman he'd married. He hadn't noticed the changes immediately after she got pregnant because he'd been so upset about the pregnancy to begin with. He should have noticed when she stopped bugging him about having a child. She became sweet and compliant, wanting to make love nearly every day. Late in the summer, she asked him to sit beside her on the futon one evening and announced she was pregnant.

He'd stood up, backing slowly away from her as if she were diseased. "How did that happen?" Before he finished saying the words, he knew his question would elicit a sarcastic response.

"How do you think?" She smirked, but her eyes were hard.

"I thought the diaphragm was almost a hundred percent safe."

"It's not. And I quit using it."

"You quit? Why?"

"I told you I wanted a child."

"You don't make that kind of decision on your own."

"It was God's decision."

"No, it wasn't."

"If we had an accident, you wouldn't have had a say in it either."

Although it had been a pointless disagreement once a child was growing inside of her, the argument had lasted for weeks, punctuated by Gabrielle's accusation that he was destroying the happiest time of her life. "The baby senses our lack of harmony. This is the most important phase of her development. The emotions she's absorbing are full of toxins."

Gradually, he let it go. Arguing wasn't going to change anything, and he did want their child to come into a tranquil home. That's when he noticed the next bit of aberrant behavior. Gabrielle referred to the baby inside of her growing belly as *she*.

"If you want the child to feel welcome," he said, "call it he or she."

"It's a girl."

He'd been cleaning leaves out of the gutters when she made this startling prediction. "You don't know that." She'd insisted the doctor not reveal the child's gender. She couldn't possibly know.

Gabrielle stood next to a black plastic garbage bin where she'd been collecting the leaves for mulch. "Yes, I do. I want a girl. If we're only having one child, I want a daughter."

He was so startled by her attitude, that he didn't ask

whether it occurred to her that he might want a son as much as she wanted a daughter. He didn't have a preference, but it irked him that the thought never crossed her mind. He didn't care what sex the child was, why was Gabrielle so emphatic about it? Her desire should be for a healthy child.

His thoughts scattered as the minivan bumped over the apron of the driveway into the Whole Foods market. He drove up and down several rows of cars before finding a spot with a lacy canopy of shade. Peter was asleep in his car seat, his head flopped over against the side. Gabrielle got out of the van, closing the door softly.

Mark leaned his head back. His thoughts returned to that fall day when she'd announced she was carrying a girl. He'd never finished cleaning the leaves out of the gutters. He'd climbed down the ladder to look her in the eye. "It doesn't work like that. We get what we get."

"You said we're only having one child. God knows I want a daughter. The Bible says He gives you the desires of your heart."

He couldn't think of a response to this simplistic view of God's thought process. He supposed some would call her attitude *faith*. There were people that approached God that way, he just didn't know many of them. When he encountered them, he did his best to keep the conversation light. There was no intelligent discussion with people like that. If you disagreed with them, you were accused of lacking faith. They didn't want to hear that the Hebrew meaning of the original text suggested desires that God planted in your heart, not whatever whim you grabbed onto. Not selfish desires. Not longings that were contrary to the revealed will of God. "The verse doesn't mean that you get everything you want."

"Yes, it does. That's what it says."

"Well, that's not how you're supposed to interpret it."

He tried to explain that it was meant to be taken spiritually. She wouldn't be reasoned with. The verse said she would receive the desires of her heart, and the desire of her heart was a daughter. He wondered what she would do if she gave birth to a son, but he stopped trying to change her opinion. Maybe she had some sort of woman's intuition that told her she was having a daughter. He just hoped she wouldn't be disappointed.

Disappointment was an understatement for her behavior when Peter emerged. The doctor informed them it was a boy, and Gabrielle said — *You're lying.* The doctor looked up and said, — *A healthy baby boy.*

Gabrielle had screamed, "Noooooo!" It was the most pitiful sound Mark had ever heard, a wailing he'd expect if their child were stillborn. Shame reddened his face and neck, spread down his chest, making his t-shirt feel heavy against his skin. He avoided eye contact with both the nurse and the doctor, forcing himself to look at his son rather than speculating about what they thought of a woman who howled at the introduction of her child.

Over the next few days, no one was spared from her ranting that God had let her down. She wanted a girl, she'd expected a girl, she actually said she deserved a girl, whatever that meant. *What good were the promises in the Bible if you couldn't rely on them one hundred percent?*

And then, as if God had miraculously changed her desire, she became Peter's devoted slave. She marveled and cooed over him as if she were the first woman on earth to produce a child. The smallest whimper sent her running to lift him out of his crib and offer him her breast. She changed his clothes multiple times every day. Although she never cared much about buying expensive clothes for herself, she came home with something new for Peter every few weeks. The kid had a bigger wardrobe than both his parents. She held him constantly, never allowing anyone at church to take him in their arms until he was over six months old. By then, he'd developed separation anxiety and refused to leave his mother's arms.

A sharp cry from Peter broke his thoughts. He was straining to break free of the straps on his safety seat. His face had an angry red gash where it had pressed against the plastic edge, and the hair on the left side of his head was damp. Mark pulled off one of Peter's sandals. "This little piggy went to market," he said, squeezing the first toe. Peter stopped crying and stared at his toe. By the time Gabrielle returned, Peter had a weak smile on his face.

Peter's short nap in the minivan sabotaged any hope of

sleep that afternoon. Mark wanted nothing more than a nap of his own, or at least a chance to watch a little golf on TV. Instead, he sat beside the wooden sandbox he'd built for Peter's first birthday, constructing sand towers by filling a bucket with damp sand and turning it upside down. There was no end to Peter's enthusiasm for smashing the towers as fast as Mark could build them.

Gabrielle sat in the vegetable garden, plucking weeds from between the rows of green beans, tomatoes, onions, and whatever else she had sprouting there. It fascinated Mark that she could look at the shoots spread across fifteen square feet of soil, and know which ones didn't belong. She pulled them out by the roots and dropped them into a white bucket.

Throughout the afternoon, he waited for Gabrielle to resume her complaint that he wasn't sufficiently fascinated by her breasts. Was she waiting for him to pick up where they'd left off? If he didn't, that failure would be woven into their next argument. But he didn't have the energy. Better to put it off and deal with the whole tangled mess of dissatisfactions at once. His desire to avoid talking to her fed his willingness to keep building sand towers. As long as Peter was having fun, so was he.

While Gabrielle made dinner, Mark buckled Peter into the child's seat on the back of his bicycle. He pedaled down the street, gaining speed. They flew past houses that sat silently in the heat, families dozing inside, or out of sight in their backyards, warming their grills for barbecued meat. Defying the drought, underground sprinklers sprayed water onto the sidewalk in front of a few houses, and Peter screamed with excitement when Mark rode through the mist.

All evening he continued to wait for Gabrielle to launch into her unfinished thoughts. It was like waiting for the aftershock of an earthquake. You knew it was coming, but no matter how alert you were, you could never be prepared, and the jolt always threw you off balance. This time, the jolt never came. Even after Peter was in bed, she maintained her superficial friendliness. She was like the fruit smoothies sold at the health food store, sweet, refreshing, but bitter sediment from the vitamins waited at the bottom.

Four

GABRIELLE TOOK A jar of canned apricots off one of the metal shelves along the side wall of the garage. In the gray light, the slightly blanched fruit looked like unidentified internal organs suspended in syrup. It was hard to believe that when she boiled, peeled, and shoveled the apricots into these jars, Peter was a tiny baby. The shelves that had been lined with rows of jars were almost empty now. The apricots on the trees in the backyard were turning orange, and Peter was walking all over the place.

She loved the feeling of accomplishment that came over her after she'd preserved two trees' worth of fruit. At the start of the day when the sky was navy blue, and the air felt slightly wet, the bags of apricots covering the kitchen table looked overwhelming. But a few hours later, she could step back, wipe the perspiration off her face and see an army of jars stuffed tight with fruit, accompanied by smaller jars of bright orange jam. She felt safe. No matter what happened, there would be something to eat. In California, the mild weather insulated her from the anticipation of disaster. They would never be buried by a fierce snowstorm or their house flattened by a tornado. And in the Santa Clara Valley, there were no floods. Earthquakes happened so rarely, it was easy to forget about them. Still, she felt calmer knowing that in summer, the trees and vines were filled with food, and in the winter, her garage was stocked with preserved fruit and vegetables. Nothing terrible could touch them.

A thin layer of dust coated the jar. She went into the kitchen and wiped it clean with a damp towel. The apricots were for Susan, a casual hostess gift. She put the apricots and two beach towels in a small box so the jar wouldn't roll around in the back of the minivan. It was only nine-thirty. There was plenty of time to stop by Nordstrom's for a new pair of sandals. She'd bought a pair of black sandals at the discount store on Memorial Day weekend, but they'd been a mistake. They made her feet look much larger than they had looked in the store. The mirrors were distorted. There was no other explanation for the fact that no matter how many times she'd walked past the mirror, studying her feet from every angle, they now made her feet look enormous. Her feet made her look like a hick. Big, flapping things that drew attention away from her smooth, muscular legs. Wide and flat, with very little arch to give them even the suggestion of elegance. Toes that were too long, with large spaces between each one, like the tentacles of an octopus. She was on a constant mission to find shoes that minimized their size.

Mark hated it when she bought extravagant shoes, but what was she supposed to do? Inexpensive shoes were designed so that sizes six and down looked adorable. When shoes were removed from a box marked size eight, they looked like they'd been slapped together for a freak fashion show. The black sandals had a small heel. The right shoe was a bit loose on her foot, and the combination of the loose strap and the heel forced her foot to slide forward. Her toes hung over the edge so that her right foot appeared to be a half-inch longer than the left. Cheap shoes. When would she learn? Burying them at the back of the closet was the only solution, trying to forget her shameful waste of money. The next time she went to the thrift store, she would slip the offensive sandals in her backpack and leave them at the drop-off site behind the store.

The minute she stepped onto the carpeted floor of the shoe department, she saw what she was looking for — wide, camel-colored buttery leather straps crisscrossing the foot, partially hiding the toes, crafted to give the illusion of smaller feet. Solid stitching that would prevent the sandals from slipping around when she walked. They had thin flat soles and a large buckle. Eighty-five dollars was outrageous, but there was no other choice. She'd be even more careful with household expenses over the next few weeks.

With a sturdy box containing her new sandals on the back seat, she drove fast in the nearly deserted left lane of

Highway 280. The highway wound through the foothills to the little town of Los Altos, whose borders flowed almost seamlessly into Sunnyvale, but was recognizable by streets without sidewalks, large lots, homes hidden by brick walls, and ancient trees. It was a small, exclusive community with highly rated schools, minimal crime, and property values triple those of Sunnyvale.

Susan and Jack lived closer to the foothills where the homes were newer and more lavish, looking up to the sparkling estates spread across the hills behind them. The Ormiston house was two stories, with five bedrooms, four and a half bathrooms, and a three-car garage.

Gabrielle pulled into the wide, curving driveway. She got out of the minivan and opened the side door. She lifted the lid off the shoebox, took out her new sandals, pulled off the ugly, synthetic material on her feet, and stuffed them into the tissue paper. She slipped her feet into the leather sandals and inspected them. So much better. She walked down the driveway to the sidewalk and back to the minivan. It was a good sign that she could walk easily and gracefully without even thinking about her feet.

She smiled and unfastened the buckles that held Peter in his car seat. As she picked him up, he struggled to escape from her arms. She squeezed him, kissing his warm cheek, breathing in the scent of him. He smelled sweeter than freshly baked bread. She pressed her nose into his skin. He screeched. She put him on the ground, and he started making his way to the front door. With the apricot jar in one hand, Peter's things and her swimsuit in the backpack, and their towels draped over her arm, she left Peter to his own pace and walked past him. The doorbell sounded like a church carillon. Before the series of notes were complete, five-year-old Cara opened the door. Peter was still making his way to the front porch. When he saw Cara, he shrieked and quickened his pace, but he arrived at the edge of the porch without stumbling.

Cara stepped outside. She held out her hand so he could balance himself as he stepped up. "Mommy told me he can walk. He's really getting good."

"He didn't take long. Thanks for helping him." Gabrielle stepped around Cara, and into the house. Cara and Peter followed and turned down the hall to the right, headed toward the family room, which contained enough toys to function as a child care center.

Gabrielle called after them. "Make sure he doesn't get his hands on anything tiny."

"I will." Cara's voice was firm, with a suggestion of irritation.

As Gabrielle walked toward the back of the house, savoring the soft tension of leather straps binding her feet, she heard Susan's voice. It was hoarse and low, softer than usual. "I know. Uh, huh."

Gabrielle stopped outside the doorway, clutching the apricots and towels to her chest.

"It's disgusting, all these people thinking our church isn't good enough for them. Just like their cars, they have to have the newest, the biggest and best." Gabrielle smiled at the thought of Susan in the upscale kitchen of her 4000-square-foot home complaining about people who wanted the biggest and the best.

"I know," Susan said. "He's letting his ego get caught up in it, instead of thinking about what's right. He's doing a decent job overall, but he absolutely needs to pay more attention to the long-time members on this subject."

There was a pause.

"I need to go. I heard the doorbell."

Gabrielle waited a decent interval after Susan said good-bye. Mark was doing a *decent job*. He devoted everything he had to that church, to Susan and the others. Susan was acting like a self-righteous gossip. She walked into the kitchen and plunked the jar on the white tile counter. "Hi. I brought you some apricots."

"Thanks." Susan was stirring the contents of a deep pot. Hotdogs chopped into tiny triangles covered the bamboo cutting board.

Susan's standby — macaroni and cheese with bits of hot dog.

Susan laid the spoon on the counter and scooped the hot dogs into a bowl then dumped them into the boiling water. "I wanted to fix something more interesting, but the time got away from me. Anyway, Cara loves this. I know Peter will make a mess, but he seemed to like it last time. You can pick out the hotdogs for him."

Susan chattered about Cara's summer enrichment activities while she drained the macaroni, stirred in the powdered cheese with a cube of margarine, and added low-fat milk. She emptied the colander of macaroni and chopped hotdog into the orange mixture. She paused to put the jar of apricots in the cabinet.

They sat at the round oak table in front of a large window that looked over the swimming pool. Susan held Sam on her lap, and Peter sat in Cara's old oak high chair. Cara scooted close to the table. She gobbled up half of her macaroni and hot dogs before anyone else had even lifted their spoons. Gabrielle choked down her own clotted mass of pasta and cheese-flavored sauce while watching Peter smear Day-Glo orange goop in his hair, on his face, and across the front of his shirt. As the layer of sauce grew thicker, she could almost see the poisonous glue filling his arteries. She tried so hard to keep his body pure from junk like this, but she didn't want to be rude. "You know this isn't really that good for you," she said.

"I told you to pick out the hot dogs. It's just that Cara loves them, so I like to add them in."

"I don't just mean the hot dogs."

"Sorry." Susan popped the last hot dog chunk into her mouth. Spooning more macaroni onto her plate, she shifted Sam to the other leg and plugged a bottle into his mouth.

"I don't mean to hurt your feelings," Gabrielle said. "But you know how it drives me nuts when people put all this effort into keeping their bodies free of cigarettes and pollution, but they don't even think about the garbage they consume at the dinner table."

"I'm not offended. I know how you are. I think of this as healthy because of the cheese and milk. The hot dogs don't have nitrates."

Gabrielle went to the sink and ran water over the corner of a clean towel. She returned to the table and began wiping Peter's cheeks. When she knelt to clean the liquid cheese that had somehow found its way between his toes, she noticed Susan's feet for the first time. It was surprising they hadn't caught her attention the minute she'd walked into the kitchen. Checking her friend's toes had been a habit ever since Susan made her big announcement to the Young Mothers' Bible study group.

The women had been sitting in a circle of folding chairs in the center of one of the Sunday school classrooms. There were only four women that day. They'd been working through a booklet that provided discussion questions around the topic of maintaining a Godly marriage. Susan had slipped off her flip-flops and kicked them under her chair. Suddenly, she stretched her legs toward the center of the circle, wiggling the toes of her bare feet. Elaine Brackner, starting a second round of children now that her first two were teenagers, interrupted her own comments on creative meal planning and complimented Susan on her flashy red toenails. Susan blushed. *Jack did them.* She smiled. *Before we make love, he likes to paint my toenails.* Thankfully, she hadn't said anything more. She didn't have to. The eyes of the other two women grew vacant as they imagined their husbands holding their feet, caressing them, softening their tired skin with lotion, then painting the nails bright, glossy, frivolous red. Gabrielle had felt a sharp pain that ran from her navel to the base of her throat. The other two women sighed. No wonder Susan was barefoot in the middle of February.

For a moment, Gabrielle squeezed her eyes closed, trying to blot out the significance of Susan's freshly painted toenails. She checked Peter's feet again, they were pale and clean. He still had cheese in his fingernails, but it could rinse out in the Ormiston's swimming pool for all she cared.

"Let me change Sam's diaper and put him down for his nap," Susan said. "I'll be right back."

Gabrielle took Peter into the family room and sat on the floor. She built a tower of red and blue blocks. Peter knocked it over. He laughed and let out a shriek. She built a second, larger tower. He shrieked again as he knocked it down.

"He's going to wake the baby," Cara said.

"Oh, he can't hear us way upstairs."

Cara looked at Gabrielle, holding her gaze. Cara narrowed her eyes.

Where had Cara learned to flash disapproving expressions like that? Now that she was in school, she probably picked up all kinds of unwanted mannerisms from teachers and other kids. It terrified Gabrielle to think of Peter going out into the world without her, learning things she didn't want him to know, picking up habits she didn't like.

It felt as if everyone was drifting away from her. Peter was gently prying himself loose, and her husband was locked inside his own world where she couldn't break into his thoughts. She wasn't sure she liked her best friend anymore, flaunting her freshly painted toenails. Susan appeared to be boasting — *My husband can't keep his hands off me.*

Peter knocked over the tower of blocks. Gabrielle grabbed him onto her lap and rolled sideways to the floor, holding him close, kissing his plump cheeks. He laughed, then squirmed out of her arms, scrambling over to where Cara was coloring an outline of a horse, using every shade of brown in her crayon box.

When Susan walked into the room, bitterness rose in Gabrielle's stomach. Susan's face was smooth with contentment, free of want. Susan ran her fingers through her hair, pushing it back into stiff waves. She planted her hands on her hips. "Ready for a swim?"

"Sim!" Peter shouted.

Cara eased her crayons into their slots and closed the cardboard lid. She stood up and pushed her miniature chair under the table. "I'll need my swimsuit."

Gabrielle dressed herself and Peter in the downstairs bathroom.

When they were settled by the side of the pool, Gabrielle studied Susan's barrel-shaped torso, stuffed into a brown spandex suit with a white triangle slicing across her breasts and down to her navel. Why didn't she choose a less ridiculous design to minimize the swell of her body? Next to Gabrielle's slim figure in a turquoise bikini, Susan looked like a brown baked potato with sour cream bursting from the swollen center. And yet, Jack adored her, kneeling at her feet with a bottle of nail polish to demonstrate his rapture. Gabrielle lowered her sunglasses from the top of her head and stared at the darkened water. She stepped into the shallow end of the pool.

They paddled around for over an hour. When she finally pulled Peter out and sat him on the edge of the pool, he pouted and whimpered. Cara climbed out, spread her towel on the cement, and lay on her back. Her tiny body sparkled with drops of water, her skin golden next to her white swimsuit. Susan spread out her towel beside her daughter's. After a few minutes, her face was slack, her breathing deep. While the Ormiston women sunned themselves, Gabrielle trotted around the pool, teasing Peter away from the edge. After a while, she lured him to the swing set at the opposite side of the backyard.

The afternoon drifted by, pushed by shadows creeping across the pool. Just when Gabrielle was thinking of packing up and heading home, Cara announced it was time for her favorite television program. She took Peter's hand and led him toward the family room. Susan went into the house to get Sam out of his crib and settled him in the family room with his sister.

She returned to the backyard. "Do you think it's too early for a glass of wine? Now that the kids are occupied, we can have a real conversation."

Gabrielle shrugged. "I guess wine sounds good."

Susan went into the house. Her voice drifted out through the open window. "Make sure you're keeping an eye on Sam and Peter, okay Cara?" A few minutes later, she reappeared at the screen door, pressed the handle with her hip, and stepped out carrying two glasses of white wine. She let the screen clatter shut behind her.

They sat with their feet dangling in the water. Gabrielle stared at the offensive red toenails bobbing below the surface. They looked like clots of blood. The silence between them danced over the dimpled water around their legs. She took a large swallow of wine. The toenails swam in front of her eyes, taunting, announcing that bland, pudgy Susan was worshipped by her husband. Gabrielle wanted to grab those undulating feet and chop off the perky little toes, one by one.

"Nice nail polish." She tossed her head back and swallowed the rest of her wine. It made her brain hum, but it took away the sharp thorn pressing against her windpipe.

Susan looked up. Tightening the muscles of her thighs, she straightened her legs, so her feet lifted out of the water. She wiggled her toes. "Jack likes to put polish on them when…"

"I know what he likes to do. You announced it to the mothers' Bible study, remember?"

"Oh, that's right." Susan's laugh bounced off the water as she lowered her feet below the surface.

Gabrielle bit down hard on her tongue, tasting salt and sour wine. Sex was a funny thing. Women talked about it constantly when they were single, but once the march down the aisle had taken place, it became a forbidden subject. "It sounds like Jack was anxious to get back to sex after Sam was born," she said.

"Are you kidding?" Susan pulled her feet out of the water and levered herself to her feet. "Another glass of wine?"

Gabrielle put her glass in Susan's outstretched hand. Susan walked back to the house. Her wet toes left damp spots on the concrete.

When Susan returned, Gabrielle reached for the glass and took a careful sip. As if the conversation had continued unbroken, she heard herself say, "Mark's not that interested. In sex." She was shocked by her words. But it was too much. She had to talk to someone, and who else was there? She couldn't keep it inside anymore. But there it was — she'd betrayed her husband. That was what the taboo was really all about. Once you were married, if you talked about sex, you weren't just talking about yourself. Sex was transformed into something that belonged equally to another person. If you laughed about it or discussed it, you laughed or gossiped about the man you were supposed to love and respect. The man who was supposed to be the other half of yourself. But what about her feelings? Either way, there was no going back now that she'd exposed him. In her case, the betrayal was a thousand times worse, talking about Mark to one of his parishioners — one of his hundreds of employers. She knew already it was a terrible mistake, almost like being unfaithful. But right now, she needed reassurance as desperately as she needed his hands on her skin. Still, it wasn't just Mark. She had a right to talk to her best friend about her suffering.

Now, it was easy to let her thoughts keep spilling out, words careening downhill. "When we found out I was pregnant, everything stopped. It just stopped, Mark was... we've only done it two or three times since Peter was born. He keeps saying he's busy. He's so tired, and I know he feels a lot of pressure about the building program, but I always have to ask. It's like he never even thinks about it." She wanted to tell Susan how it made her feel. Ugly. Disgusting. Unlovable. But she stopped. "All I think about is sex."

"That's odd," Susan said. Her down-turned mouth screamed — *three times! What a freak!* She sipped her wine.

Gabrielle waited for her to say more. "I know it's odd. I..."

"You should talk to him. Not me."

"I tried." The words bellowed out of Gabrielle's lungs and bounced off the water.

"Don't yell."

"Don't tell me to talk to him. Why do you think I'm talking to you? He won't talk. He changes the subject. He manages to bring seven other things into the conversation until it's all muddy, and we get sidetracked onto something else and end up in an argument."

"Maybe you haven't tried hard enough."

Gabrielle hated her. She wanted to shove Susan into the swimming pool. Watch her big tee shirt turn into a wet pillow while her wine disappeared into the water, and her glass sank, invisible, to the bottom of the pool. Instead, she took another sip of wine. It had been a terrible mistake. She could never take it back. Susan would know, forever. She would tell Jack.

The sun had moved below the tops of the fir trees behind the fence, giving the water a grayish cast. Crows sat in the trees, cawing so loud Gabrielle couldn't hear her thoughts. The almost black trees and gray water looked cool and soothing. Still, she felt overheated and bloated. Her head spun from drinking too fast. Only her feet were comfortable. Even though the wine increased the pressure in her head and neck, she continued to take quick sips. The alcohol made her lethargic. It prevented her from pushing Susan into the pool, holding her head under the water. She would force Susan to understand. She had a physical need for someone else to feel the thick, heavy ache of Mark's rejection that pressed on her continuously. She longed to make Susan squirm with shame, admitting her husband was more interested in toenail polish than actual sex, admitting he was repulsed by her thick body. Gabrielle couldn't be the only one. "I try to seduce him, and he makes up excuses that he's tired or has other things on his mind."

Susan peered into the water as if she expected to find fish swimming along the bottom. A rubber raft floated toward them, moved by the thin breeze. Susan kicked it away, but it was partially deflated and only moved wearily toward the center of the pool.

"I want him to touch me, and he won't. I put my arms around him, and he lays there like that raft, all limp and spineless."

"Should you be telling me all this? I don't know what to say. He's your husband. You really, really need to talk to him."

"I told you, I *have* talked to him!" She knew she should stop. She was making it worse, but the wine, her muddled brain, the heat. "I've cried and yelled and talked. I've begged him to touch me. Do you know what that feels like?" She grabbed Susan's arm and squeezed as if she meant to produce juice from Susan's flesh. "Do you have any idea what it's like to beg your husband to touch you because you need his body like you're an alcoholic?"

"You're hurting me," Susan whispered. "Let go."

Gabrielle released her grasp. "I'm sure you've felt that way."

"No." Susan looked miserable. "I haven't."

"The other night, I wanted to make love to him, and before I knew it, he was preaching to me about breastfeeding. He wants me to stop. It embarrasses him. Can you believe that?"

"Lots of men are embarrassed by it."

"That's not true. Men love a chance to see a woman's breasts."

"That's why it embarrasses them."

The discomfort disappeared from Susan's face. Gabrielle could see she was thrilled to be back on comfortable ground. She loved to play the wise, spiritually mature woman offering advice. "Men think of women's breasts as something sexy. They get confused when they're supposed to see them as functional."

"How do you know that?"

"Maybe the reason Mark seems uninterested in you is that he's confused. One minute you're nursing your child. And the next minute, you want to be his lover. He doesn't know how to put those two images together."

"That's ridiculous."

"Are you sure?"

Gabrielle wasn't, but she refused to say so. She still had a tickling desire to see Susan plunge into the pool. A deeper, overwhelming urge to break the wine glass and use a chunk of glass to scrape the mocking red paint off Susan's toes made it difficult to focus on what she should do next. Susan's words prodded like a baby's fat finger at some logical spot in her mind, urging her to think about giving Mark another chance. Still, she hated that she had to think about it at all. "It doesn't make sense."

"Maybe you're thinking about it too much. Ask God to satisfy your desire."

Ask God. How did *that* work? Why shouldn't she have a man who wanted her? The kind of man who appreciated her beauty and wasn't distracted by stupid ideas about motherhood and sex. Susan might be right about Mark, but it didn't cool the burning. Everything felt hot. Her skin, her heart sick with boiling shame, knowing Mark didn't need her body like she needed his. Tipping her head back, she took a final drink from her glass. "I need to get going."

"Don't be upset. It's normal for marriages to have ups and downs."

Gabrielle wanted to lie. She wanted to say she wasn't upset. But she would rather inflict pain on Susan. "You may have a point about Mark. Sometimes it's hard to see things right under your own nose. It would be terrible if Jack wanted someone thinner and started noticing other little toes he wanted to paint. Maybe he gets tired of red polish."

Susan looked smug instead of shocked. "I'm sorry you're hurting. I want to help, I really do, but please don't take it out on me." She stood up and put her arm around Gabrielle. "I'm glad you came over."

Gabrielle pulled away. The thin lines across Susan's forehead made her look hurt. Thick chunks of hair fell over her face, and she raked them back with the hand that wasn't laced around the stems of the empty glasses.

"Thanks for lunch and the swim." Gabrielle tossed her ponytail over her shoulder and did a few, shallow pliés to get the kinks out of her legs, feeling Susan's eyes on the taut muscles. She went inside and gathered Peter and their supplies. As she closed the minivan door, Susan waved from the porch. "I'll pray for you. It'll work out, just be patient. Let the Lord satisfy you."

Gabrielle got into the minivan, tossed the wet towels across to the passenger seat, slammed the door, and started the engine with too much pressure on the gas pedal. Shame burned just beneath the surface of her skin.

Five

THE NEXT MORNING, Gabrielle woke feeling anxious. She'd dreamt that Mark was squalling like a one-year-old. "I'm too old," he'd cried. He wanted to drink milk from her breasts. Big, clear tears rolled down his cheeks, and he clutched his stomach, complaining he was so hungry he couldn't stand up straight. Through gasps for air, he complained that she was depriving him, that she gave all her love and attention to Peter. She was disturbed, unsure what the dream meant. She tried to push it out of her thoughts, but while she nursed Peter after breakfast, the vivid sounds and images increased. Usually, dreams faded quickly until she couldn't recall the details or the way she'd felt, stumbling through a murky, senseless world. This time, she couldn't shake the feeling it had really happened. The reality frightened her. Was it a message of some kind? The dream might be telling her she was supposed to wean Peter.

After lunch, she nursed Peter, letting him fall asleep at her breast as he usually did. She didn't carry him to his crib for a nap. She watched him sleep, feeling the warmth of his breath on her exposed skin. Tomorrow, she'd skip the after lunch feeding. She'd wean him gradually, cut down to twice a day, first. The hardest part would be when he woke whimpering in the middle of the night. She'd never denied him. She was in the habit of drifting toward his room, feeling her way in the dark hall by running her fingers across the molding around the bathroom door, grazing them over the framed pictures that covered half the wall outside of his room. Just a few minutes of sucking, and he slipped back to sleep.

FOR THREE NIGHTS, Gabrielle and Mark listened to Peter howl. His pitiful sobs tightened around her heart like wire. She curled into a ball, hugging her knees while Mark got up and tried to comfort his son, carrying him around the house, pointing out the moon, talking to him. But Peter wanted Gabrielle. It was crazy. She was doing this, hoping her husband would desire her, while the one male who did ache for her was deprived. She squeezed her eyes shut and whispered to herself, "You have to do this sooner or later. Now that you've started, it's not worth turning back." Peter screamed, and she wrapped the pillow around her head. They craved sleep like a drug, their veins twitching.

That evening they had to face a meeting concerning the new sanctuary. The purpose of the meeting was vague — *community building*. Everyone was supposed to express whatever they felt about the building plans. There were no boundaries. They were expected to talk about their fears, their pride, their doubts, what they wanted the building to look like, and anything else on their minds. Speaking freely was a crucial first step, according to Grant Miller. *Everyone gets their feelings out in the open right up front*, Grant had explained to the leadership committee. *That way, negativity doesn't fester and disrupt the program midway through.*

Mark worried that nothing would be accomplished except the further entrenchment of people in their various opinions. Meetings without a prescribed agenda made him nervous. Gabrielle thought it sounded entertaining. She was curious whether the members would be able to shake themselves loose from their Lutheran restraint to talk about fears and dreams. As a child in her mother's fundamentalist church, people regularly spilled their guts in personal testimonials and long, intricately woven prayers. Lutherans were private people, submitting their requests for divine intervention on tiny lined cards via the offering plate. They didn't stand in public and state their feelings, those were whispered to the pastor or intimate friends behind closed doors. Sometimes, not even then.

At seven-thirty that evening, Gabrielle, Mark, and the most faithful members of Grace sat in the church hall, waiting. The temperature was still in the high seventies. Inside, cool air seeped up from the earth through the thin linoleum floor. Peter toddled around after Cara, who was drawing the small children into a cluster of baby ducklings, waddling behind her. Technically, the small children were in the care of two teenagers hired for the event, but they were happy to let Cara keep the children entertained while they checked their phones and shared pictures.

Grant Miller stood at the edge of the stage. He wore a perfectly tailored charcoal gray suit and a white shirt, open at the neck. His blonde hair was combed straight back, and his face looked almost hairless. Seated beside Mark at the front of the hall were the president of the congregation and the head elder, each waiting his turn to speak, looking nervous without their usual scripted set of readings.

Susan sat in the second row, encircled in Jack's arm. Often Gabrielle sat next to them at congregational meetings, but she wasn't in the mood to spend the next two hours looking at cherry red toenails while her husband sat far away on the stage and carefully avoided meeting her gaze. She chose a seat in the back row, a new experience for her. She liked it. There was only one other person in her row, a woman she'd seen sitting in the same row during the morning service, but had never met. Musk perfume drifted off the woman's turquoise gauze blouse. She wore a matching turquoise and orange skirt that fell in uneven folds to the floor. Her bare feet poked out from under the skirt. The thin gold sandals she'd slipped off while Gabrielle was getting settled lay hidden somewhere underneath the skirt. Just looking at her, Gabrielle liked her — a woman practical enough to cool her feet on the floor.

She had dark, thick curls, with loose strands billowing into a frizzy cloud, and the rest spiraling down her back. Her fingers were covered to her knuckles with silver rings.

Gabrielle turned her face toward the stage. Grant Miller switched on the hand-held microphone. He introduced himself and talked about his theories and successes. He strolled around as if he were following a pattern of dance steps painted on the floor — one step forward, two to the side, back to the center, and repeat. "One church where I consulted saw their weekly attendance grow by twenty-five percent when they followed this program. They moved into a new building with renewed life."

He rattled off three examples of old antagonisms that were buried for good because of the increased attention to prayer that was an integral part of the program. He told stories about people who had shut themselves off from church for years because of hurt feelings. Through the power of every member visits, they'd been restored to the fold. Gabrielle sensed cautious excitement pulsing through the hall as people imagined how Grace would change — all for the good. Mark sat straighter in his chair. The doubt that had flickered in his eyes all week danced to the background along with the choreographed steps of Grant Miller.

"Now, I'm going to open up this mic to you good folks." Grant walked down the steps at the side of the stage and stood at the head of the center aisle. "Now look what I've done. I came down here to get close to you, and left our first three speakers stranded up above."

Everyone laughed a bit too eagerly. The woman seated next to Gabrielle didn't smile.

Led by Mark, the men who had been seated on the stage marched down the steps in a line and arranged themselves slightly behind Grant. As if he was reluctant to let the microphone leave his hands, Grant hesitated before slowly handing it to Mark. Grant sat down in the front row.

Mark's warm voice filled Gabrielle's head. She closed her eyes and breathed in the heavy musk.

"I'm always preaching that God doesn't live in buildings of concrete and stone," Mark said. "But doesn't it give you a sense of awe when you walk into a church that's been around for fifty or sixty years? A hundred years?" He lowered his voice to a sexy stage whisper. "The vaulted ceilings and the dim light remind me I'm in a place that's been set apart for worship — dedicated to the most important thing in life."

Why didn't he talk to her in that voice? Gabrielle couldn't see the connection between a sanctuary that wasn't even built yet and a church that had been around for decades, but no one coughed or shuffled in their chairs. The congregation stared at him, most nodded gently at his description. A few heads remained stiff on their shoulders, as if their muscles and bones were repelling his words.

"New offices and meeting rooms will show the world we care about what goes on here. Gathering in a room with comfortable furniture and a fireplace will make us feel even *more* like the family we are."

The microphone was passed back and forth from one man to the next —

Linoleum floors are slippery and give off a terrible echo. We need a worshipful atmosphere.

This building was never designed to be permanent.

Working toward a common goal will draw us closer together.

The office roof leaks.

There isn't enough space to even consider increasing church membership.

Our teenagers need a room that they can call their own.

It was time for the members to speak. Mark and the other men sat beside Grant. A few older people quietly, hesitantly, worried aloud about the ability to pay for the construction.

Grant Miller leaped out of his seat and broke in with a silky apology for talking when he *wasn't really a part of this fine family, but I feel like I might become one,* which was a lie because he'd help them raise cash and then move on. Like the Bible salesmen of the early twentieth century, he had no home base.

For several minutes, he talked about faith and the power of unity.

It wasn't really fair to tell people they could express all their fears and then talk vaguely about faith, implying they didn't have any. Gabrielle felt the woman next to her shift in her chair, rearranging her skirt. Susan lifted Jack's arm off her bare shoulders, stood up, and stepped toward Grant. She held out her hand for the microphone.

Arching her back, trying to sit up taller in her chair so she could get a better look, Gabrielle felt a hum of anticipation vibrate through her muscles. Susan's opposition to the construction plans was well-known. She hated, more than anything, to stand up in front of people and talk. She would rather build the sanctuary herself than have to speak in front of a large group — this must be important. She plucked at the front of her tank top and straightened the twisted waist of her skirt. She cleared her throat and whispered into the microphone, "Can you hear me?"

Heads bobbed.

Susan had been baptized in her father's arms in this very room. When he died of a heart attack at the age of fifty-seven, the church was without a pastor for almost three years. When Susan's mother moved to the east coast to look after her own aging mother, Susan became the caretaker of her dead father's ghost. Although it wasn't explicitly mentioned, Susan's blessing was desired for every decision. Susan enjoyed the attention, liked being the center of everyone's concern, liked feeling she was still that beloved child with a hundred parents to watch over her.

Gabrielle felt the swell of Susan's memories hovering in the rafters, ready to descend in a deluge of emotional words. Susan cleared her throat a second time. A quiet, echoing cough came from the woman next to Gabrielle. Turning to look, Gabrielle saw the woman lower her head until her chin rested on her collarbone. Thick hair hung like curtains on either side of her face. Gabrielle turned her attention back to Susan.

"I'd like to say something." Susan coughed into the mic. "As most of you know, this church is the foundation of my whole, entire life. There isn't a single part of my history that wasn't connected to Grace, and to this building. I know I'm not the only person with strong feelings about what's best for Grace, and some of the feelings people have expressed are valid. But please listen to my point of view."

Susan's chest swelled visibly as she took a deep breath. "I don't need a fireside room to make me feel like this is my home. I've eaten hundreds of meals in this hall. I've sung hymns and prayed and been preached to every Sunday of my life in this plain building. I played here as a child and cooked in the kitchen as a woman. I cried through my father's funeral and cried almost as much through my wedding."

This brought a nervous, sympathetic laugh, like gurgling water.

"I lived my life inside these walls that are now being condemned as inadequate and temporary. I've worshiped God without a marble altar and stone floors and stained glass."

The woman beside Gabrielle still sat with her head bent forward, hair swept over her arms. Gabrielle hoped she wasn't sick.

Susan went on. "Feelings associated with the church don't

have anything to do with what kind of building we have. Let's not get caught up in society's obsession with a flashy exterior. The focus of our church shouldn't be physical, it should be spiritual. People shouldn't want to join because of glamorous buildings. What matters is how they're accepted and cared for. This project feels a bit like an ego trip."

Gabrielle closed her eyes. Susan was the last person to talk about ego trips, wiggling her red toenails to the women's study group.

"I think my experience should give us something to think about. I love this place, and I feel worshipful in this old building because I've felt *loved* here. It doesn't matter that the floor echoes — it's echoing our voices, even the voices that aren't here anymore. When I come into church feeling tired because I've been up with my baby all night, and Mrs. Olefson asks to hold him, I feel God's presence, allowing me to see my precious baby through new eyes." She paused and raked her fingers through her hair. She lifted her chin. She pulled the microphone close to her lips like she wanted to kiss it. "I love Grace because of the people and the simplicity. I love it because the people that visit and decide to join do so because they feel the same things I do. In the Old Testament, people worshipped in tents. When they built an elaborate temple, they ended up turning away from God." She paused. Someone coughed. She handed the microphone back to Grant and scooted back to her seat, slipping onto the chair and under Jack's protective arm in one fluid movement.

Gabrielle couldn't wait to see Grant twist Susan's speech into something that confirmed the need for a building program. Susan had just told them they were turning away from God if they proceeded with their plans. Gabrielle leaned forward and unbuckled her sandals. She slipped them off her feet. The floor felt cold and firm, pulling her attention back to the barefooted woman at her side. At some point during Susan's plea, the woman had lifted her head. Her eyes were wet with tears. A tiny smile flickered over her wide mouth.

Susan's walk down memory lane didn't puncture Grant's persuasive ability. His voice was low, copying the quiet intensity and gravelly sound of Susan's as if he'd sucked her voice into his own throat. "That was a beautiful testimony to your father and your faith, Susan."

How did he know her name? This guy was good.

"You are absolutely right. God doesn't only make His presence felt through the strength of stone and stained glass, or behind marble altars." His voice rose, letting the remnant of Susan's whisper fall to the floor as he carefully walked over her words, burying them with the formula designated to overcome that particular objection. Gabrielle could see the printed guidelines in her mind — *Overcoming the Sentimental Memories of a Well-respected Member.*

"Susan has an incredible love for the people and history of this place called Grace," Grant said. "What a beautiful name — Grace. I sensed the moment I walked in that God's grace surrounds this community. As Susan said, this place called Grace is blessed because of the people. And the *people*, all with their hearts tuned to heavenly concerns, these same *people* who showed love to Susan throughout her life, these *people* feel God has put a desire in their hearts to expand the ministry of Grace. They aren't selfish and stubborn, plowing forward like a steamroller. No. The *people* of Grace, the leaders of Grace, are gently asking whether more use could be made of this magnificent piece of land. These good-hearted *people*, full of grace, want to *build* on what Susan's father did. They want to extend His grace into the middle of the twenty-first century." Grant bowed his head.

No one stood up to speak. Who would dare to express objections, now? Mark and the other two men sat meekly in their chairs in the front row. If this were a movie, music would burst out of the walls. After several minutes of uncomfortable silence, there was nothing to do but end the meeting.

Grant handed the microphone to Mark. Gabrielle was certain that all the thoughts and opinions that Grant applauded at the start of the meeting had not been expressed. In fact, most of the feelings that had been expressed were Grant Miller's.

Mark began praying, filling the room with words that were more dramatic than his usual style, cluttered with pauses and exclamation points. "We know…oh God!…our future here is…magnificent!"

Gabrielle sighed. A whiff of musk rose next to her. She willed Mark to finish his weak imitation of Grant so she could introduce herself to the musky woman. As soon as Mark said *amen* and lifted his head, Gabrielle turned. "I don't think we've ever met. I'm Gabrielle Atwater."

"Pastor Mark's wife." The woman didn't smile. "I'm Allysan Krohl." She held out her silver shrouded fingers.

Gabrielle didn't let the rings prevent her from taking a firm grip.

"I like a woman who isn't afraid to shake hands," Allysan said.

"You're new," Gabrielle said. "How long have you been coming here?"

"Five or six months."

People moved around them, but no one interrupted, as if the musk formed a bubble that made them invisible to the bewildered congregation heading toward the side doors. They moved swiftly and silently out to the patio where plates of cookies, tiny paper cups of juice, and a pot of coffee waited.

"Why did you flop your head down in the middle of the meeting?" Gabrielle said.

A large, toothy grin spread across Allysan's face. She laughed from deep in her chest. "You're so refreshing. I like you. Anyone else in this room would have chosen a safe and very boring topic like the weather, or where I went to church before I came here." She leaned closer to Gabrielle, thin silver necklaces gliding out from beneath her shirt and tinkling against each other. "I felt a weight pressing on my heart for that poor woman. She's so confused. She hasn't recovered from the loss of her father and the disintegration of her family of origin. All her unresolved emotions are tangled up with this building. I was directed to pray for her." Allysan closed her eyes and let out a heavy sigh that seemed to rise from the floor under her bare feet. "Of course, in a way, she's symbolic of everyone here. Whether or not a sanctuary should be built, I can't say. But they're unable to discern the correct path because they're trapped by their desires."

No one Gabrielle knew talked like this. She could linger all night and listen to this low, commanding voice. With her gypsy clothes, the perfume, and all that fantastic hair, Allysan gave the impression she'd just stepped out of an Old Testament story. At any moment, the woman might deliver a message from God.

"Gabrielle, you have a very sensitive spirit. You have the beauty of a child, an angel, a creature who hasn't been tarnished by the world."

The words spread through Gabrielle's chest like melted butter.

"And your name is so beautiful. Do you know what it means?" Before Gabrielle could answer, Allysan continued, "It means *strength of God*. And you look to me for the answer to your questions?"

Gabrielle stared at the dark chocolate eyes, ringed with thick black lashes that curled up long and lush, free from mascara. Allysan seemed to know what Gabrielle had been thinking because she hadn't asked any questions. But that was silly. It was just her imagination, captured by the exotic clothes and hair.

"They want a new building because they think it will remove their doubt. If they have new buildings, more people will come, and more people will make them feel secure in their beliefs. Safety in numbers. Some think the aura of the building will make them feel closer to God. Others think bringing back old members will make them feel like God really *is* doing something in their lives. All different manifestations, but the same seed of doubt."

"What about Susan?" Gabrielle felt as if she was making inquiries of a fortune teller.

"Susan doubts that she's loved. Her father is gone — she needs things to stay the same so she can feel secure. Everything that defines her life will be torn away. But Susan was right about one thing."

"What's that?"

"Selfishness. Wanting to improve your public image. Trying to raise large quantities of money, asking people to give more than they can afford, will open the door for Satan to creep into your community."

"Did Susan say that? I didn't hear her say anything about Satan." Gabrielle shivered.

People at Grace didn't talk about Satan. They stuck to safe topics. They didn't spend an excessive amount of time talking about God either. They mentioned His name in passing, but they didn't dwell on the subject. They might talk about the instructions from the Bible, saying God wants us to do this or that. But anything beyond the visible was mildly frightening territory. When the subject came up, the corners of their lips twitched with discomfort. Their voices trembled as if someone was delving into the most intimate part of their lives. You might as well ask when they last had sex. No wonder they were so intent on looking to Mark when they ran into rough spots in their lives. Only the pastor was credited with understanding God's will. Words from his lips carried weight close to, if not the same as words from the Bible. The pastor was educated. The pastor knew what all the confusing passages meant and how they applied to individual lives and circumstances. After all, he could read Greek, the language of the New Testament, and he was even able to translate a few words of Old Testament Hebrew. The pastor had an inside track with God.

Gabrielle needed to hear God speak to her. The experience on Pentecost Sunday had whet her appetite, creating an addiction. She needed to hear a distinct voice, clearly telling her, she would get what she was promised. All the rest of the members of Grace thought that kind of thing — personal messages, visions — was finished, left behind in ancient times.

The building was almost empty. Everyone was outside in the darkening garden, munching cookies and drinking coffee that would keep them awake half the night. Allysan looked into her eyes, waiting for Gabrielle to speak.

"You don't talk like a Lutheran," Gabrielle said.

Allysan smiled. "Neither do you. You're bold, and you believe God has a personal plan for your life."

"I do," Gabrielle said. "But I get frustrated. I don't always get the things I'm promised." She stopped. She definitely didn't want to tell Allysan that her most pressing desire, sex with the man she loved, was being withheld.

"You should come to Gethsemane Temple with me sometime."

"What's Gethsemane Temple?"

"That's where I go to church. It's my real home."

Gabrielle frowned. "I thought you were a member here."

"Yes and No. I grew up Lutheran, and I have a heart for seeing Lutherans escape from their rituals so they can get in touch with the Spirit. I pray for them. I try to bring the Spirit into the services when I'm here. But I can't possibly worship here. At Gethsemane, people believe in prayer. They believe God is active, not just a remote being that has to be invoked through correct words and structured worship services. You'll have to come with me to a prayer meeting and see for yourself."

"I should do that."

Allysan took hold of Gabrielle's left hand, squeezing it between the rings and her dry, smooth fingers. "It was a true pleasure talking with you. I'll give you a call, and we can arrange a time to go to a prayer meeting." Allysan swept her thick hair behind her shoulders.

Gabrielle was excited. The pressure of Allysan's hand and the movement of her jewelry and hair as she turned to go, all promised something different, something supernatural.

Six

WHEN SHE'D TOLD Mark she planned to attend a prayer meeting at Gethsemane Temple, he was not happy. He viewed it as a rejection of Grace. He didn't say, but possibly he viewed it as a rejection of him. But she wasn't rejecting anyone. She simply wanted to experience the shivering ecstasy she'd known in the church garden on Pentecost Sunday. Her motives were spiritual desire and friendship. Even though Allysan was easily ten years older than her, Gabrielle felt a connection with her. Having a friend that wasn't one of her husband's parishioners was a good thing.

She kissed Peter's nose and handed him to Mark. She walked up the living room steps to the entryway and turned. Mark was holding Peter under his armpits as if he didn't quite know what to do with him. They both stared at her, bewildered and uncertain.

"What if he wants to nurse?" Mark said.

"We're done with that."

"Are you sure?"

"That's what you wanted."

"I still can't comfort him sometimes. He cries, and he won't stop."

"Yes, he does." She dug her keys out of her purse.

"Be careful."

"Of what?"

"Getting caught up in false doctrine."

She laughed. "If I speak in tongues, I'm going to hell?"

"Those gifts were unique to the Apostles."

"How do you know?"

"I understand that you feel smothered at Grace. I really do."

She clenched the doorknob. If she hadn't been walking out the door, she would have hugged him, squeezing Peter between them. They hadn't done that in a while. He was acknowledging her feelings. He hadn't done that in a while either. But his timing was all wrong, and maybe he was just trying to keep her from humiliating him, as he put it, by going to a church where he wasn't in charge. "I'm going to be late." She opened the door and stepped onto the front porch. "Bye." She didn't look back into the room, didn't see his face, or Peter's. Mark said something, but she couldn't make out the words. She closed the door.

GETHSEMANE TEMPLE WASN'T actually a temple. The name referred to the temple inside each worshipper. The building used to be home to a grocery chain that had been swallowed by a more profitable chain, which then proceeded to close the smaller stores. The church had also taken over the units on either side — one, a former Italian restaurant. The part of the building that had been divided into meeting rooms smelled like garlic. The odor wasn't overpowering, but it was disconcerting.

Allysan met Gabrielle at the entrance to one of the meeting rooms. As the woman hugged her, Gabrielle breathed in strands of tangled hair and musk. The garlic odor was pushed to the side for a moment.

The room embodied the characteristics of the fireside room envisioned by the members of Grace — without the fireplace. Pale blue Berber carpet covered the floor. Sofas and chairs were arranged to form intimate circles, each their own tiny living room with a coffee table at the center. Each coffee table held a fat white candle, the flames steady despite the gentle movement of air from perfectly tuned air conditioning. Most of the seats were occupied. People bent their heads close to each other, talking softly. Some had retreated into their own worlds, reading the Bibles lying open in their laps. A woman near the left side of the room sat alone on a love seat, strumming a guitar. The words of her song blended with the voices rather than fighting for attention.

Allysan led Gabrielle to the group closest to where they stood. She introduced Gabrielle to John, Byron, Peter, Claire, and Paula. They smiled as if they'd been waiting all evening for Gabrielle and Allysan to arrive. Maybe they had. Paula, an undernourished, mildly frightened-looking woman in her twenties, said Gabrielle's name was beautiful and remarked that she felt she'd known her all her life.

They sat down. Allysan pulled her Bible out of her purse. It fell open of its own will, revealing a page filled with blue ink and pale yellow highlighter, tiny printing in the margins, and several arrows pointing to other passages. Gabrielle hadn't brought her Bible. She worried that her empty lap labeled her as someone who wasn't as attached to the Word of God as she should be. No one seemed bothered by the lack, but she felt bare and vulnerable without a heavy leather-bound book spread across her thighs like the others.

The woman playing the guitar began to strum more loudly, picking up the tempo. Without any obvious direction from her, the others began singing the words to the song she played. Gabrielle had heard it before, but she only knew the chorus. She joined in confidently when the chorus came around, and let her voice fade to a self-conscious humming when they reached the verses. The next song was softer, and only a handful of people continued singing. The others closed their eyes, some lifting their arms toward the ceiling. Gabrielle closed her eyes. It was easier that way. The woman continued strumming and then stopped as the voices filled the room, some speaking discernible words of praise, others murmuring sounds that were comprehended only by themselves and God, maybe only God. It sounded beautiful but frightening. Gabrielle couldn't shut off Mark's voice, reminding her that the gift of tongues described in the Bible referred to known languages, not a mystical prayer language, as some churches believed. His voice echoed inside, explaining that chasing after emotional experiences meant a loss of focus on obeying the words of the Bible — God was an object of faith, not a physical experience. He'd reminded her of the correct views daily, ever since she'd informed him she was attending a prayer meeting with Allysan. He'd even touched on the subject in the previous week's sermon.

She was here to pray! To get caught up in the energy of her new friend, and all these other believers, so passionate in their faith. She was here to find out what God wanted her to do about her marriage. She was not here to listen to one of Mark's sermons. She had plenty of opportunities to do that. This was for her. This was a place to meet God face to face without the interference of rituals and pre-printed words and dull, plodding music. This was a place where her body could worship as fervently as her soul. This place was alive — the dry bones invigorated with breath.

Now, they were praying, pleading with God, pouring out more words of praise. One of the women laughed when she spoke, as if she and God were best friends — little children hiding under a tent made of blankets and sheets, whispering and giggling. Gabrielle wasn't sure when she should pray because they didn't go around the circle in an orderly fashion. She hoped Allysan would nudge her, but even more, she hoped a supernatural sensation would take hold of her tongue, and she'd start speaking without having to plan her words. She couldn't say what she really wanted, not in front of all these people. She'd already betrayed Mark to Susan, she couldn't reveal his failure to a bunch of strangers. She loved him. He was her husband, and he deserved her respect. Maybe that was God's voice inside, telling her to give Mark more respect.

The group fell silent. It might be the nudge she'd been waiting for, but she wasn't sure how to begin. Allysan spoke, her voice like a hum in Gabrielle's ear. "Release our fears. Make Yourself known. Unbind our tongues and let our words flow like the Jordan River. Reveal Your will, make Your Voice known to us, make us the creatures You want us to be. Open our ears, so we listen to *Your* voice, speak *Your* words. Make our hands do what *You* desire, and take our feet where *You* want us to go." She went on like this for several minutes. The odor of musk coming off her body grew stronger as if speaking had opened her sweat glands. Her rings clicked against each other, and the chains around her neck shivered with an echoing whisper.

Gabrielle knew she needed to take her turn, but she had no idea what to say. The others had been very specific, asking for healing for headaches and back pain, pleading with God to release a friend from addiction, asking for jobs, money to pay bills, and supernatural intervention for their car engines. Allysan had been more vague. Was that because Gabrielle was here? Did she make detailed requests for the members of Grace Lutheran Church during other prayer meetings? She'd said the members of Grace were her mission. It wasn't clear what that meant. Allysan seemed to think she was a conduit to bring God into the church as if He'd been missing in action. Maybe He was. Except for that single Sunday morning in June.

The woman with the guitar began to pluck the strings. The people in the other groups continued praying, their words indistinct. Gabrielle felt movement in the cushions, Allysan shifting position. Then, Allysan's hands were on her shoulders. She'd stood and moved behind the small sofa. Her hands were surprisingly cool through the fabric of Gabrielle's shirt. The pressure of her hands increased, easing the tightness along Gabrielle's spine. She felt she was going to cry. Allysan's hands moved across Gabrielle's shoulders and down her upper arms. The pressure of her fingers broke something loose inside Gabrielle's chest. Her breath grew tight, and the tears increased their pressure, spreading beneath her eyelids, trickling out from the corners. The tears ran across her cheekbones. She continued to feel the weight of Allysan's hands, warmth spreading through her entire body. Her awareness of the rest of the room faded. The others seemed to drift away, leaving an ever-expanding space between her and them. Their voices were faint, and the vibrating strings of the guitar were no longer audible. She heard something else, maybe her breath. No, it was the tears. She could hear the sound of her tears dribbling against her skin, falling onto the backs of her hands. Her breathing was clear and steady, not labored like it normally was when she cried.

Allysan's hands were back on the stops of her shoulders, pressing gently as if she were trying to keep Gabrielle from floating off the sofa.

"Please love me." Gabrielle hadn't known she was going to speak, hadn't planned the words. They'd come out of a place deep inside, or maybe not inside at all, maybe God speaking through her. "Please." Her voice was louder. "Love me. Love me. Love."

"Yes!" Allysan cried out. "God is love. The church is love. Everything is love."

Gabrielle's skin was on fire, her brain melting inside her skull. The tears were gone, and she knew everything there was to be known. Everything was love. Everyone needed love. Mark needed it, and Allysan needed it. Susan. Peter. Even *God* needed love! She wasn't the only one. She wasn't alone at all. Her heart pulsed as if all her tears had run down the inside of her and filled it with liquid.

Allysan lifted her hands off Gabrielle. Rings and chains rattled softly. Without looking, Gabrielle knew Allysan was raising her hands toward the ceiling. She began speaking words that Gabrielle couldn't understand, but she was sure she heard her name, and the word *agape*.

Then, Allysan was no longer behind her.

Gabrielle wanted to peek to see where Allysan had gone, to

notice what the others were doing. How unspiritual. She was disgusted with herself. But she hadn't felt the cushions move, hadn't smelled the musk. If she didn't peek, she might start believing Allysan had been sucked up through the ceiling, floating up to the heavens. No one spoke. They seemed to be humming softly, but she couldn't be sure if that were inside her head, or she was truly hearing the sound of their voices.

The woman with the guitar began strumming faster, louder. All at once, the entire group was singing a song Gabrielle had never heard before. The tension of worrying about Allysan faded, replaced by the solid comfort of people doing something predictable. There was nothing more expected of her. She opened her eyes.

Everyone was looking at her, gazing with knowing smiles, as if they hadn't just heard her prayer, but heard every silent word she'd said to God and the words He'd spoken to her. Blood rushed to her face. They knew what she knew. She was afraid they knew even more. That they knew about Mark's rote spiritual life, that he might not be a very good minister, not really leading people to God after all. They knew he didn't want to touch her, knew that even the casual touch of a woman's hands on her shoulders had made her weep with pleasure. She swallowed and turned slightly. Allysan was still behind her after all. She gave Gabrielle the same knowing smile.

They sang several more songs, then a few people stood and spoke about what God had told them to do. Then, everyone stood, picked up purses and Bibles, and began moving toward the doors.

Allysan suggested they go for coffee.

"I'm not sure. I should…"

"It would be good for you to talk about your experience," Allysan said.

"I don't think I want to. Is that okay?"

Allysan smiled. "Of course it's okay. I just thought you might want to. Sometimes that's important. To solidify it, make it real."

"It wasn't real?"

"Of course it was. But later, it might seem that it wasn't. Doubt can creep in."

Gabrielle knew all about that. Her experience in the garden felt like a dream. She had to remind herself it had happened, remind herself how she'd felt, even though she could never get the feeling itself to return. "Not yet," she said.

Allysan patted her upper arm. "Of course. You don't want to dilute it."

They walked out to the parking lot. Allysan put her arms around Gabrielle and held her for several minutes. She put her face close to Gabrielle's ear. "Be strong."

Gabrielle wasn't sure what that meant, but she didn't want to ask. She'd rather not know. She needed to cling to the idea that Mark needed her love. God needed her love. She didn't feel quite so alone.

Seven

MARK OPENED THE top center drawer of his desk and grabbed his keys. He closed the drawer and walked around the desk, tossing the keys in the air. They missed his outstretched hand and fell on the floor. He instinctively glanced around the office, as if his animal brain worried he was being observed. He rarely caught the keys but was still compelled to toss them, newly surprised each time that such a simple maneuver eluded him. He locked his office door and the door to the main office and stepped outside. It was ten past five, and the hot white sun had penetrated the west side of the building. In spite of the heat rising off the asphalt, he looked forward to the short walk home. He cut across the lawn, dried tips of grass crunching under his shoes. Fremont Avenue was even hotter, the sidewalk exposed to the unclouded sky for ten hours a day. Two lanes of cars in both directions blew fumes at his face, but once he reached Cherry Street, the magnolia trees covered the sidewalk with shade.

Dried magnolia leaves clattered around his feet.

Tonight he and Gabrielle were scheduled to visit Miriam and Tom Heddelson. The Heddelsons would be their third visit of ten. It had been five weeks since the congregational meeting with Grant Miller. Each member of the leadership committee had plowed ahead, diligently making appointments to visit their designated list of members. When Susan Ormiston saw she wasn't going to prevent the project from moving forward, she'd taken her assigned list like the good sport she was, but Mark worried that the feelings she'd expressed would re-surface at the worst possible time.

The Atwaters, Ormistons and four other couples each had ten families to visit. Each couple was also responsible for supervising a subgroup of six couples with visitation assignments of their own. The members of Grace hadn't known how to respond to Grant Miller's salesmanship, and many of them surely felt pricks of guilt over Susan's passion for preserving the status quo, but they knew what to do with a list.

Overall, the every-member visits were going well. There had been one or two not-so-pleasant experiences. Larry and Elaine Brackner's visit with Boris Dunning had been painful in every way. Boris had made sure they were uncomfortably seated on narrow wooden chairs in his living room. The furnace spewed out heat on a seventy-two-degree summer evening. According to Larry, Boris had kept them captive for three hours, alternately yelling and whispering about the failures of Grace. Everything from the church's lack of attention after his wife's death eight years earlier, to the unruly behavior of children during the coffee hour. The man's primary complaint, which surfaced every fifteen minutes during the diatribe, had been that the only time he saw anyone from the church was when they came looking for money. Larry and Elaine had tried to excuse themselves, sweating from the motionless air and their discomfort in the face of Boris' rage. Boris had slammed his fist on the heavy oak table beside his armchair and shouted — *You asked to visit me. You'll sit there until I'm finished.*

After that, the Brackners had fallen behind on their visits for a week or so. When they got back to it, subsequent visits had been pleasant and uneventful. Knowing the Brackners, it was likely they'd exaggerated their terror, pinned to torturous chairs, perspiring while Boris heaped eight years of grief onto their ample laps.

So far, Mark and Gabrielle's visits had proceeded smoothly. If one of his visits did become uncomfortable, the disruption was more likely to come from his wife than from a church member. When he and Gabrielle were dating, he'd adored her spontaneity. Now, he'd realized a more appropriate term was instability. He couldn't put his finger on when the change had taken place. It seemed to be more than the normal progression of marriage — an endearing trait transformed over time into something else. Like the initial charm of watching her kick off her shoes and point her toes as if she were a ballet dancer warming up for a performance. She rested her fingertips on the edge of a counter or a table and performed shallow pliés. The moves showcased her muscular legs and extraordinary posture. Now it annoyed him.

Why couldn't she stand still like a normal person? Why did she always have to be pointing and flexing and wafting her arms over her head? It made her look like an overgrown child. In the winter, she compounded the impression by wearing bright, thick colored tights to match her tops and twirly short black skirts. Her movements and clothes screamed — *Look at me!* Inevitably, the question arose — *Are you a dancer?* Gabrielle would smile as if humbly admitting she'd been found out. Her smile lingered, implying she lived to dance and couldn't restrain her well-trained body. As the questioner leaned forward into the tension of an answer that was too slow in coming, Gabrielle would suddenly shake her head — *No.* The questioner would step back, confused by an exchange that didn't conform to an expected pattern.

He saw how unnerving it was. Like comedic timing, she'd perfected the pauses in her responses, improved her knack for throwing people off balance, making them retreat anxiously to a safer group of people — a group that wasn't leaping about, but decorously moving their arms, lifting cups of coffee to their lips.

He shouldn't waste so much mental energy on her quirks, but that's all he could think about lately. The unconventional aspects of her personality seemed to have grown disproportionately. People mouthed the cliché that marriage was hard. He'd repeated the same phrase himself. It was doubly hard to keep loving someone who seemed to go out of her way to create trouble. It was impossible to keep fights from breaking out over the smallest things. It was hard to find subjects to talk about when the number of conversational land mines increased every year. What must it be like after ten or twenty or forty years? He stepped out from beneath the last magnolia tree, and the thought flamed through his skull, burning with more intensity than the unrelenting sun.

He'd never thought of himself as someone who needed to be in control, but Gabrielle kept pulling and prodding, intent on stretching to the breaking point beliefs he didn't even know he had. Such as his belief that she should support his ministry by attending worship services and social events. They were supposed to be a team. After the fundraising kick-off meeting, she was eerily calm for almost two weeks. Then she'd announced she was attending a prayer meeting at Gethsemane Temple, invited by Allysan Krohl, the only member of Grace who gave him the creeps. When he told Gabrielle that visiting another church implied Grace wasn't meeting her spiritual needs, she giggled. Then, she threw back her head and cackled. She gasped and snorted, but refused to explain what was so funny.

He turned onto the walkway connecting the driveway with the front porch. His stomach clenched like a fist as he neared the Bird of Paradise plants surrounding the porch. The name was fitting — the orange wing-like shape of the blossoms had the appearance of mutated birds. The purple at the base looked like blood pumping through the abstract bodies. They scraped his arms as he stepped onto the porch.

The house felt like the inside of an oven. In the dining area, Peter was already seated in his high chair. Mark kissed the top of his head, then kissed Gabrielle's cheek. Her skin was cool and firm, like kissing an apple. She smelled equally sweet. There was only one place setting on the table. Gabrielle carried bowls of corn and mashed potatoes to the table, dancing between the counter and Peter's high chair, where she lifted a spoonful of potatoes to his mouth.

"Aren't you eating?" he said.

"I'm not hungry."

"You should eat something."

"I don't feel like it." She put a plate with four slices of meatloaf near the bowl of corn, pirouetted to the refrigerator, and took out the bottle of ketchup.

"Well, sit down. You're making me nervous." He looked down, ignoring the sneer that passed over her mouth. He spooned potatoes and corn onto his plate. "You haven't forgotten we're visiting the Heddelsons, have you?"

She returned to the fridge and removed a bottle of spring water. She snapped off the cap and took a long swallow.

"Did you forget?"

"Why would I forget?"

Mark ate his dinner quickly, praying she wasn't warming up to pick a fight.

They'd arranged for Susan and Jack to take care of Peter. Mark waited in the minivan while Gabrielle helped Peter walk to the Ormiston's front door. Rather than simply relinquishing his hand from her own to Susan's, Gabrielle stepped inside the house. The door closed. He rested his head against the seat back and closed his eyes, forcing himself not to check the time. He didn't want to feel compelled to calculate whether they would arrive late if Gabrielle spent ten minutes inside, giving instructions on Peter's current mood, digestive status, and beverage requirements.

THE TIGHTNESS IN his neck dissolved when they pulled up in front of the Heddelson's only five minutes past seven-thirty. The house was on a wide, curving street that managed to retain a peaceful quality despite the steady flow of traffic. The front yard was lush with flowering shrubs, large rocks, and only a small oval of grass showing they were doing their part to consider the drought. The house, like all the others on the street, was an Eichler design. It had a flat roof, and the windowless wall facing the street hid a courtyard accessed by a gate, the front door buried inside.

Stepping from the Heddelsons' courtyard into the foyer was like entering a greenhouse — the open kitchen, dining area, and living room were filled with large tropical plants. The entire back wall of the house was made of floor to ceiling windows and sliding glass doors, revealing an equally lush backyard.

Mark and Gabrielle sat on the living room couch. To his left, the graying light was blurring the outlines of fruit trees along the back fence. The Heddelsons sat facing them in identical green leather armchairs.

"Hot day," Mark said.

Miriam agreed and talked about the forecast for the rest of the week.

On the table in front of him was a glass of lemonade. Pulp floated in the liquid and clung to the ice cubes. A film of moisture coated the outside of the glass, and a damp ring had already formed on the Lucite coaster. Thirsty as he was, he was afraid to pick up the glass, knowing the coaster would hang on for dear life, crashing without warning onto the glass-topped table. He was equally afraid that the sweaty glass would slide through his fingers, leaving a sticky, pulpy mess on the area rug covering the tile floor, situated between the couch and the armchairs.

From the corner of his eye, he saw Gabrielle reach out and grab her glass with her right hand, releasing the seal of the coaster with her left, and cupping her hand under the bottom of the glass. Just when he thought she was completely impossible, she turned around and performed some graceful act that left him in awe of her lack of self-consciousness and innate practicality. He copied her movements, relieved as the cold liquid poured down his throat.

He set the glass on the coaster. "Of course, you know we're here to talk about demonstrating our faith by committing to building a new sanctuary and office complex." He gave a wry smile. Visiting people in his own age bracket was difficult. He was suddenly conscious of how out of touch he was with the rest of his generation as if a thick velvet curtain separated the landscapes of their adult lives. Talking to older people was easy, all he had to do was draw on their shared experience of church involvement. But younger professional couples like Miriam and Tom didn't view the church as the backdrop for their entire existence. It was only a small slice of full lives that included careers and sports and travel. They were smart and wary. Older people respected and welcomed him simply because he was called Reverend Atwater — Pastor Mark — as if he had a stamp of approval from God Himself. With people in his generation, there was no such aura. He was just like them, the same age with similar cultural memories, yet not like them at all.

He forced himself to concentrate on shoving the conversation forward. "Even though it might seem like this is just about raising money for the sanctuary, it's a great opportunity to get to know you on a different level. Sunday mornings aren't very suitable for talk about anything but the superficial."

Gabrielle nodded eagerly. This was one of her favorite topics. He felt his neck and back relax. She really was an asset to him. He'd been fixated on her faults lately. He took another sip of lemonade. Ice cubes knocked against his lips.

"Oh Mark, don't give a speech," Gabrielle said. She gulped her lemonade and grinned.

Miriam smiled for the first time. The slow sweep of her long, pale eyelashes and her obvious pleasure at Gabrielle's brashness, flicked away the prick of irritation he felt.

Gabrielle put her glass on the coaster with a thud. "I love your house. It's so open, and it's so cool, even in this heat."

Tom and Miriam were visibly flattered by her words.

"That's one of the great things about Eichlers," Miriam said. "There's terrific airflow because of all the doors along the back. And we're on a concrete slab, you know, so the floors stay nice and cool."

Tom and Miriam tripped over each other, applauding the features of their house as if they were persuading Gabrielle to buy it. As she nodded and sipped her lemonade, it looked like all she cared about in the world were the architectural perfections of their home. But Mark could see her eyes narrowing into a squint — she was angry about something. He heard the accompanying rise in her tone that told him her mind had wandered off on another track, chewing over some unidentifiable fragment in the conversation. He took a long drink of lemonade, glad to see the level was down by three quarters. He could turn his attention to the business at hand and stop concerning himself with leaving a half-full glass, implying he didn't like their homemade lemonade, with its thick strings of pulp that provoked his gag reflex.

Talking about the house was taking too much time. He needed to shift the conversation. He ticked through the three steps he'd memorized as thoroughly as he'd memorized the Lord's Prayer: establish a friendly atmosphere, make them feel more connected to the leaders of Grace, and guide them to admit some facet of the church was more important to them than they'd previously recognized.

Gabrielle had artfully accomplished the first, leading them delicately, although somewhat robotically, from talking about their house to their jobs. She was nodding with an increasingly vacant expression. Miriam chattered on about her job as a Marketing Programs Manager and her thoughts that she was almost ready to think about having a child. "I mean," she corrected herself, "We're almost ready." She turned and smiled at Tom. He squeezed her hand that he'd taken hold of at some point during the sales pitch for the house.

Even though Mark had lived in the Santa Clara Valley all his life, he didn't remember so many people working in marketing when he was growing up. Was that something new? He took another sip of lemonade. He had to get control over his thoughts. The heat didn't help — the house wasn't that cool after all. His mind was tired from the increasing pressure to motivate two hundred and seventy-five people, ranging from the ambivalent to the resistant, to agree to part with their hard-earned money.

His glass was empty. Tom unwrapped his fingers from Miriam's and stood up. "Can I refill your glass, Pastor?"

Mark handed the glass to Tom. In spite of whatever irritation was simmering inside of Gabrielle, she'd managed to move the Heddelsons through the second step in the visitation formula. An invisible but monumental shift had caused Tom to identify with Mark as a spiritual leader — calling him by his title. When they'd walked in the front door, Tom had studiously avoided any form of address, as he did every Sunday. But Gabrielle's simple questions and Mark's inattentive murmurs had melted the atmosphere, as gently as the warm air had molded the cubes in his glass into thin, lacy pieces of ice. Miriam hopped out of her chair and followed Tom into the kitchen. After a few minutes, she returned with a bowl of potato chips. "Salt and vinegar," she said. "I hope they're not too tart for you."

Tom brought back the glasses of lemonade with fresh ice cubes clinking dully against the sides. Mark plucked several chips out of the bowl. The vinegar stung his lips and mouth, but it was strangely soothing after the too-sweet lemonade. He reached for more. Gabrielle shook her head at the offered bowl. Thankfully she refrained from commenting on the dangerous properties of processed foods.

Mark let out his breath. The knots between his shoulder blades unwound further. What was he so afraid of? He couldn't think of an instance where she'd truly humiliated him. It was her behavior at home that rattled his nerves. There was no reason to think she'd haul one of her favorite topics out, like she pulled toys and snacks out of her bag for

Peter, and plop it on the iron and glass coffee table. Still, he was nervous. All the time. And it exhausted him. He longed for her to return to the pleasant, quirky companion she'd been before...before what? It didn't matter. He just wanted her to stop controlling what he ate. And stop hounding him about sex. And stop acting like a ballet dancer and giving him the silent treatment. He didn't want to know why she went to Gethsemane Temple, but he wanted it to stop. He wanted her to stop smothering Peter. And he didn't want her looking at him with those narrowed eyes.

While his thoughts wandered over Gabrielle's sins, she'd elicited an admission from the Heddelson's that their weekly attendance at church was a bigger part of their lives than they'd realized. Church helped set their priorities for the week before they were plunged back into the pressures of work. They would definitely be more involved in other activities when they had children. They would discuss how much they could contribute, but it would absolutely be more than their current weekly offering.

The Heddelson's were standing up. Mark rose as if pulled by strings from above. Gabrielle was nodding, and Tom and Miriam's attention was directed toward her. He couldn't see whether her eyes were the thin slits they'd been earlier. He was mesmerized by her long ponytail flowing and dancing across her back as she moved out from behind the coffee table, picked up their empty lemonade glasses, and carried them to the kitchen.

Tom extended his hand to shake Mark's. "Hey, great evening. Thanks for dropping by. To be honest, I thought you'd hit us up with some hard sell." He laughed, shoving his hands in the pockets of his jeans. "It wasn't like that at all. You fooled me. I guess I'm too cynical."

Mark smiled. It was best not to say anything.

As Gabrielle and Mark walked through the courtyard, Miriam called out, "Hope we can get together again some time."

Before the minivan door slammed shut, Gabrielle said, "Did you see that?"

"What?" He started the engine and opened his window.

"They kept touching each other. That's how couples are. They want to touch each other. It's not something you have to plan for." She had twisted her hair in one hand and was holding it on top of her head, staring at the windshield.

"So? They don't have a child. They don't work sixty or seventy hours a week like I do."

"Miriam does. Weren't you listening?"

He hadn't been, so he couldn't argue. They drove in silence. After a while, she let go of her hair and let it fall. The ponytail whipped back and forth as the breeze came at her from the open windows on either side.

He slowed to a stop. Turning onto El Camino Real was like jumping onto an overloaded conveyor belt. Cars moved past in a thick flow with just a few feet between bumpers. When they paused, the lines of vehicles stacked up as far as he could see. There was nothing to do but try to sense a hesitant driver who looked vulnerable to an intrusion. Waiting for a break, or an offer to join the flow sometimes took three or four minutes. The cars lining up behind him, also ready to turn, were willing to wait only seconds. He bolted in front of a black Porsche, always a good bet because an expensive car was more apt to be heavily invested in avoiding a rear-end collision. He drove with his eyes fastened on the tail lights of the SUV in front of him. The street was brightly lit by storefront signs and a bobbing line of headlights and tail lights. It gave a blinding glow to everything as if they were traveling through an over-lit tunnel. A tunnel that went on forever.

El Camino Real stretched beyond the horizon, an endless stream of shimmering metal banked by strip malls and gas stations. It was so unattractive, there were times he couldn't bear to drive on it. Thinking about what it used to be made his heart ache — a rural highway that meandered from southern to northern California, past adobe missions, with soft red tile roofs. It had turned into a dystopian setting. It was congested with every unattractive human endeavor possible. When did suburban cities stop caring what buildings looked like? Maybe it was just an illusion that they used to care, and now the remaining structures from other centuries appeared well-crafted only because they were different.

The new sanctuary would be aesthetically pleasing — a gem in the midst of suburban apathy. He wished Gabrielle cared about that. He wished she cared about anything that mattered to him. If he could just get home without a fight. If he could sink into their soft, rumpled bed without a marathon conversation about their relationship, he would be a happy man. He wanted to tell her how charming she'd been with the Heddelsons, he wanted to praise her contribution to the fundraising effort. The rumble of the traffic a few feet from his left ear was almost soothing. He didn't want to disturb the mindless hum. If he said nothing, she would continue to sulk, giving him a few moments of peace. He'd pay for it tomorrow or the next day, but right now, the chance for his mind to collapse into aimless thoughts was worth any future price.

They picked up Peter and drove home in deepening silence.

INSIDE, THE HOUSE was airless. Mark shut off the porch light and listened to the deadbolt thunk into its slot. He went into the kitchen. The sticky sweetness of the lemonade had quenched his thirst while he was drinking it, but now his mouth was parched. He pulled a small bottle of water out of the refrigerator and twisted the cap. The pressure of breaking the seal compressed the sides of the bottle, and water spurted onto his hand. He took a gulp, not caring that the water on the back of his hand dripped onto his face. He stood in front of the open refrigerator door. Cold air, scented with slightly overripe cantaloupe, wrapped itself around him. He drank the entire bottle of water, and put the empty bottle on the counter, too tired to walk fifteen steps to the recycling bin in the garage. He shut the refrigerator door, went to the dining area, and pulled a chair out from the table. He sat down, untied his shoelaces, and pulled off his shoes and socks. He stood and moved toward the window over the sink. There was nothing to look at but the shadow of the side fence. He couldn't stand here all night, afraid of his wife. It wasn't exactly fear but a feeling of exhaustion turning his limbs into rolls of wet newspaper. He would give anything to walk slowly down the hall, take off his clothes, and lie down on his bed undisturbed.

He turned off the kitchen light. The refrigerator hummed loudly. With only a faint light from their bedroom to guide him along the hallway, he trudged toward the opposite side of the house. He stopped at Peter's room. He bent over the crib and kissed Peter's forehead. He stood holding Peter's foot for several minutes.

Gabrielle was lying on her side, her head supported by her left arm, her hair draped across her collar bone and over the sheet that covered the rest of her. It was hard to tell what she was wearing. He unbuckled his pants, the soft clack of the metal the only sound in the room. He realized he was holding his breath. Letting it out softly, he pulled the belt out of the loops, rolled it into a coil, and put it in the top drawer of his dresser.

"I bet Tom and Miriam are making love right now. Even though it's hot," Gabrielle said.

He felt sick. He tugged off his pants and laid them flat across the bench at the foot of their bed. He took off his shirt and let it fall on the floor. He turned toward the bathroom door.

"Don't you think? You could tell he couldn't keep his hands off her. And she kept winking at him. I wish I could wink, it's such a useful skill."

What was he supposed to say? Agree that winking was a nice skill to have? Offer an opinion on the sexual habits of his parishioners? He backed into the bathroom.

"I'm trying to talk to you." Gabrielle pushed out her lower lip and forced down the corners of her mouth. "See, I'd wink right now, if I could."

He offered her a weak smile. "Can I just finish in here?"

"Ew kaaay." She almost sang the words.

In the car, she'd been ready to bite off his head. Now she acted like she wanted to host a television talk show, with him performing double duty as guest and audience, speculating on what other people did in bed. She was a voyeur, obsessed with sexual habits — theirs and those of everyone who crossed her path. He spit toothpaste and saliva into the sink. He spit several more times. He couldn't seem to stop.

He returned to the bedroom. She was still propped on one side, perky as ever, batting her eyes. She must have been trying wink while he was in the bathroom. He crawled into bed. "I'm really tired. Let's try to get some sleep."

"It's too hot. And you didn't answer my question. I'm

curious, aren't you?"

"Not really."

"Not really? That means you are a little bit. Do you think he's climbing on top of her right this minute? Or are they finished?"

He sat up. "Gabby! That's enough."

"That's not my name, and you know it."

"Well, stop it with your prurient questions. It's gross."

"I don't know what *purient* means, but I guess that means you don't want to spice up our life with a little sexy conversation."

"It's prurient."

"What?"

"It's *prurient* — there's another R — it means an unhealthy interest in sex."

"Thank you for educating me, Mr. Know-It-*All*. Or I should say *Reverend* Know-It-*All*."

He groaned. "I'm not trying to put you down. I just want to sleep. And I definitely do not want to spice up our marriage by talking about my parishioners' sex lives."

Gabrielle shook her hair, so it fell behind her shoulders. The movement made the sheet slide down her arm. She was naked. He closed his eyes, knowing he wouldn't be getting much sleep. The sleepless nights had become more frequent since she went to that weird church with Allysan Krohl. Now, she fasted once a week like she had today. Then she couldn't sleep. She wandered up and down their short hallways, drifted from room to room as if she was looking for something.

Surprisingly, Gabrielle hadn't wanted to give him a detailed description of the events at Gethsemane. He knew they elevated prayer to the status of a sacrament. He knew they spoke in tongues and believed in modern-day miracles, but he had no idea what they'd told her, or what she'd told them.

THE FIRST AND ONLY time Allysan Krohl had come to see him in his office, asking to transfer membership, she couldn't get to the point of her request to join Grace because all she wanted to talk about was Gethsemane. She'd sat in the plaid armchair several feet in front of his desk, reeking of some kind of woodsy smelling perfume. It had taken all his strength to keep his gaze on her large-jawed face, buried beneath mounds of dark, tangled hair. He clasped and unclasped his hands on the blotter in front of him, fighting the desire to get up and open the window so the scent could escape.

"What made you choose Grace?" he'd said, trying to get the words out of his mouth without succumbing to a cough.

"I grew up Lutheran, and the Spirit wants me in a Lutheran church as a ministry of light."

"A ministry of light?"

She shifted in the chair. Everything about her billowed. Her hair splashed over her shoulders, and her skirt, seemingly made of an entire bolt of fabric, draped over the seat and legs of the chair. When she reached for the glass of water on the table next to her, the sleeves of her blouse and collection of bracelets came dangerously close to knocking the glass on the floor.

"My real home is Gethsemane."

"I'm not familiar with it."

"Gethsemane Temple, in San Jose. You've never heard of it? I guess you wouldn't have."

What was that supposed to mean? He plucked the glossy black pen out of the wood stand bearing a tiny brass plate engraved with *Reverend Mark Atwater*. He turned the pen upside down, then right side up, twirling it through his fingers like a miniature baton. He felt Allysan staring at the pen, saw her lips curve slightly as if she was proud of her ability to make him fidget. He put the pen back in the thin gold cup.

Allysan remained silent.

"So, you're returning to the Lutheran church?"

"Not really."

"You want to join Grace, but you still belong to Gethsemane?"

Allysan flashed a wide, toothy smile. "My mission is to be a prayer warrior for Grace Lutheran Church, and I can't do that unless I'm fully involved."

He hadn't said much else, just led her through the minimal process of re-establishing her membership. She'd grown up Lutheran, she didn't need to take instruction classes. It was a simple record-keeping exercise.

Since then, he'd seen her sitting near the back of the hall

every Sunday. As far as her claim to be fully involved, she'd stayed on the fringe. She drifted past the other members like an apparition, never pausing to talk, just smiling and moving on. Until she sank her talons into Gabrielle.

ONE VISIT TO Gethsemane Temple and Gabrielle had picked up this new obsession — the fasting. When he was home, she had a glass of water or a cup of tea in her hand all day long. She cooked dinner and sat watching him eat, feeding Peter, her eyes glazed without a hint of desire for food. He felt guilty eating, and he hated her for that. He'd thought feeling guilty for eating meat was difficult, this was worse, and there didn't seem to be a pattern to when she chose to avoid food. The only predictable pattern was that on the days she fasted, he could count on her keeping him awake half the night. If she wasn't wandering the halls, she talked in mind-numbing detail, as if her body's need for food had transformed itself into an insatiable hunger for her own words.

She poked the tip of her index finger in his armpit. "Open your eyes and look at me. Everyone needs love. God revealed that to me. You need my love, but I think you're afraid of sex. I think you're afraid of me."

He kept his eyes closed. Who wouldn't be afraid of her?

She crept across the warm sheets. Her pale skin glistened in the light that came through the sheer curtains. He didn't know which was worse, her always simmering desire for sex or her demand for conversation when he wanted to sleep.

"Don't be afraid of me, Mark." The words slithered into his ear, sending a chill down his spine. The tips of her fingers glided across his ribs. Against his will, he shuddered.

"I don't imagine Tom Heddelson is afraid of his wife. I think at the end when they went into the kitchen together, they were kissing. Didn't it seem like they were in there a long time? When they came out, her shirt was bunched up at the waist. I know he was putting his hands up inside her shirt, feeling her breasts. Imagine, he can't resist touching Miriam even with the minister and his wife sitting ten feet away in the living room, and…"

"Twenty."

"What?"

"The distance from the living room to the kitchen is closer to twenty feet, not ten."

She pinched the flesh at his waist — hard.

"Ow!"

She kissed his neck. Her hair fell across his chest. At any moment, it would tighten around him, immobilizing his body like a dolphin caught in a tightly woven fishing net.

"When she came in with the chips, she had that little smile on her face. Her nipples were hard. What does that make you think of?"

"It makes me think you're crazy."

"That's not very nice."

"It's how I feel. Come on. Can't we go to sleep? Why do

you want to stay up all night? You're not getting enough rest. You're not eating, and it's all making you just a little crazy. I'm tired. It's hot, and I want to relax and try to fall asleep."

Her fingers moved like drops of water, touching his arms, his chest. They ran across his belly, up to his neck, across the stubble on his face. The air in their room hadn't moved all evening, and the sheets were knotted under him like stiff ropes. Moths clung to the screen, longing to get inside. When he closed his eyes, Gabrielle's fingers transformed themselves into the satiny wings of moths, flicking at his body. He wanted to scream, slap at them, scratch himself, curl into the shape of an egg.

She whispered, "Don't be afraid of me."

He rolled on his side. She tightened her grip, pressing her fingers against his neck. He *was* afraid. Terrified. But not for the reason she thought. Never, in all his plans, had he imagined Gabrielle would develop this insatiable need for sex. It hadn't been there before they were married. Or he hadn't noticed it. She'd been extremely affectionate, but he'd assumed that was because their relationship was new. His father had informed him, in one choreographed conversation, when Mark was thirteen, that girls didn't have much interest in sex. Desire was the territory of men.

He remembered that talk with his father more profoundly than any other moment with his father. Indistinct pictures of his life tickled the back of his mind, mingling with hopes and uncertainties until he had trouble separating actual memories from imagination. But he remembered every detail, nearly every word, of the talk about sex. Probably because he was forced to lie right to his father's face.

"GIRLS LOOK AT SEXUAL matters differently than boys. They have different needs." Mark's father laced his fingers together and wrapped them around his knee. "They're wired with instincts to nurture and hold together the social fabric. They like affection, but most women are not interested in the act of sex."

Mark wished his father would go away. Why couldn't he give Mark a book to read, like other fathers? Probably because he couldn't find one that had a stamp of approval from the church. Mark did not want to hear his father utter words that hadn't passed his lips for thirteen years, words that now erupted into the space between them like swarms of exotic insects. His father's face was stiff, his eyes jittered in their sockets. His gaze darted to the piano, the coffee table, the brass candle holder on the mantle as if he needed to reassure himself those objects were still where they belonged. The sky outside the wide living room window was flat. A veil of white hung behind the Mimosa tree in the center of the front lawn. The tree never stopped dropping pink fuzzy stuff on the grass. His mother loved that tree with its delicate leaves, so his father was out there twice a week, scraping up the pink fluff off the lawn, plucking it out of the shallow bowls of dirt under the roses that lined the front walk.

Turning to see what had Mark's attention, his father said, "It's like that damn tree." It was another piece of evidence that this conversation was not ordinary. His father never cursed. He frowned when either of his sons used words his wife deemed *gutter language*. His father's frowns were deep and powerful, halting unacceptable words before they fell off the tongue.

"Your mother loves that tree. And I spend my life cleaning up after it because it matters to her. The tree makes her favorably disposed toward me, and it makes her feel unloved when I criticize it. As if it's an extension of herself."

Mark couldn't follow the logic or decipher the meaning of that statement, but he wasn't about to ask a question that would prolong the amount of time he had to sit and watch his father's pained expressions. His father's thin, pale lips blended perfectly with the lightly tanned skin that was the same shade from his jaw all the way up his face and across the top of his head. The only startling interruption to that flow was the narrow fringe of white hair that ringed his scalp. Each change in his father's face, from a smile with crinkled eyes, to pressed lips and a wide-eyed stare, created a different set of creases running across that long expanse of skin.

The smile disappeared. "You're a young man now, and I'm sure you've had urges." He cleared his throat. "We don't need to talk about that. While you're young, before you're married, that is…" He coughed again. "Sometimes, after you're married, you need to find ways to distract yourself from all that. Reading the Bible every day will keep your thoughts in check. And that's why I've always encouraged sports. Your body needs that outlet, driving yourself to exhaustion."

At the mention of sports, fear creased his father's face in a different direction. He knew Mark's dismal record of throwing and catching balls. He scrambled to his next thought as if he was scratching his way up an embankment of loose dirt and rocks. "All I want to say is that girls don't have those same urges. You need to treat girls carefully. With kindness and respect. When you are married someday, you'll find those skills come in handy for, uh, helping, uhm, raising your future wife's level of interest."

From there, whatever else his father had to say became a buzzing sound in Mark's head. Words vibrated inside his skull like music vibrated against cheap speakers. He wanted to be far away from that thick white sky pressing against the window. He was tired from the effort of keeping an empty expression on his own face.

Girls and their fleeting interest in sex didn't concern him. Marriage was something he didn't want to think about now, or ever. His hands trembled. In spite of feeling relieved that his father quickly skirted the issue of his son's *urges*, Mark couldn't stop the tremor. What if his father talked his way past his own nervous thoughts and turned his attention to Mark? What if he asked about those *urges*? Could Mark provide an answer solid enough to plug his father's mouth, and end the agonizing talk? It was possible if he expressed his thoughts carefully. Altered the gender.

Would John Atwater, for whom normality was a strict adherence to church doctrine, sports, and immersion in engineering problems, be fooled? Mark thought he would be. His father's discomfort was written across his mouth, through his eyes, and burrowed deep in the ridges of his scalp. Discomfort announced itself from the way he leaned the points of his elbows on his knees. His father didn't want to be sitting here any more than Mark did. His father wanted to instruct his son to align himself with John's perception of the American norm and be finished with the subject once and for all. Disappointment that his youngest son lacked the ability to run and catch and throw with fluid movement — at one with the field, the ball, and the rest of the team — tightened around his father's words. His father didn't know how to talk to Mark about any subject. Sex was no different. Doubt over why a boy would decide to be a minister when he was still a child dulled his father's enthusiasm over Mark's report cards, which were littered with As.

John Atwater had all the ingredients of normality — two sons, a kind-hearted wife, a three-bedroom, two-and-a-half-bathroom house on a shady street, two-car garage, a comfortable church, and a two-week camping vacation every summer. He didn't want anything more than to keep plodding toward retirement, accumulating and protecting his investments, maintaining his health, and shoving his offspring onto the same, well-worn path. A boy who aimed to speak for

God was bad enough. A boy who wanted to touch and cuddle with other boys was not in John's game plan. Maybe, the possibility of his son being attracted to boys was so far beyond the boundaries, it had never crossed his father's field of vision. So Mark listened. He lied by saying nothing. Nodding as if he were sucking the marrow out of each savory bite of information on how decent men approached women.

It had worked. His father didn't suspect. The only missing piece in their talk in front of that whitewashed sky was a woman who *did* want sex, who begged for sex — a woman like Gabrielle.

When he was six years old, Mark had decided he wanted to be a minister. He gazed at the man who wore elaborate robes, who was treated with such respect, who got to stand on a platform and tell people what to do every single week. And he was paid for it! As Mark got older, his desire was less crass — less about the rituals and strange clothing and telling people what to do — but he still craved the respect, the sense that the man in the pulpit was separated somewhat from the others.

Knowing he was different from other boys didn't seem like a conflict. Once he fully realized the implications of that difference, he figured he'd simply not get married. By the time he was finished with seminary and experiencing the pressure to provide a family as part of his ministry, he'd worked out a form of Biblical approval that satisfied his conscience. Most of the time.

THE FEAR THAT PRICKLED under the roots of his hair and down his neck when he faced his father had been nothing compared with the terror he felt when he imagined Gabrielle discovering there was nothing she could ever do to awaken his desire. Breasts, hips, soft thighs and smooth legs, the scent of her hair and the sound of her voice aroused him to the same extent as one of the apricot trees in the back yard. When Gabrielle had allowed herself to become pregnant without consulting him, he was angry at what she'd done. At the same time, he was relieved. It meant the end of sex, at least for the most part. It was the end of closing his eyes and straining to summon up appealing images of men he'd known and loved. No more scenes like the one a few months after their honeymoon.

THEY'D LAIN IN BED, Gabrielle fluttering over him like she was doing now, touching him, trying to draw him into her world. Back then, her voice lacked the slightly sinister quality it had now. Knowing his life depended on it, he'd stroked her belly and legs. He'd touched the soft damp place that made him think of a soapy sponge. Then, he carefully diverted his mind to another place until he was able to transform the sensation of her hands into strong, muscular hands, shut out the feminine sound of her voice, and perform his duty.

When they were finished, she'd exploded with angry words.

He didn't care for her lips or the way she kissed. He didn't enjoy her hair. He ignored her breasts. He panicked. If she recognized that his lack of experience was actually a lack of interest in women, his career, his life, would be over. He lay with his eyes closed, trembling. Had he made a mistake thinking he could be married to a woman? But what other choice did he have?

"I'm not some video game where you can just poke at some buttons, and you're finished," Gabrielle said.

"What do you want from me?" He took a long, slow breath, trying to pull from somewhere inside a certainty he didn't feel. He wanted to bring back the assurance he'd had as he began his ministry — the assurance that God preferred him to be married to a woman. Breathing slowly to keep his voice steady, he said, "You're making too big of a deal out of this. It's just sex."

"It is not just sex. It's the foundation of marriage, the beginning of life, the force that drives the world." She flung off the blankets, shoved her legs over the side of the bed, and stood up. She planted her hands on her hips and kicked the bed with her bare foot.

Mark pulled the discarded blankets up to his neck. He'd thought performing the act would satisfy her. She'd grow bored with it like women were supposed to. Never had he heard of a woman who demanded her husband worship her body, who thought making love was the center of her life. Unable to keep looking at her glittering eyes, he ducked under the blankets, comforted by the weight of the quilt and the cooling sensation of untouched sheets near the foot of the bed.

"Don't crawl under the covers like a rabbit. Act like a man. You said you wanted to cherish me for the rest of your life. You act like I'm boring, and my body is uninteresting. It's not the way things are supposed to be. You're not even here when we make love. You go someplace else, and I don't know where that is." She started to shriek. "No one loves me. Everyone starts out loving me, and then they shove me out of their bed!"

He took a deep breath of musty air threaded through the fibers of the sheets. He pulled himself up, so he was leaning against the curved oak slats of the headboard. The wood pressed against his back so that his flesh bulged between the boards, making him feel like a ham, bound with string.

"Come here." He patted the mattress.

She remained standing, glaring at him, her shoulders trembling as she took deep gulps of air. Her skin was covered with tiny goosebumps. They spread across her arms and down her sides, but she didn't shiver.

"Come here, where it's warm," he said.

When she still didn't move, he bowed his head, so his chin was almost touching his chest. He lowered his voice to a whisper, "I'm sorry I don't make you happy."

From the corner of his eye, he saw her shoulders move away from her neck, where she'd had them pinched in to support her jutting elbows. The hard surface of her eyes began to melt. They looked soft and liquid, slipping back toward reason. After all, wasn't reason admitting that there were other human beings with thoughts and feelings different from your own?

Her hands were still firmly embedded in the soft part of her waist, right above the sharp bones of her pelvis. She looked uncertain. She let her hands fall to her sides.

"Get into bed with me," he said.

That was all she'd needed to save her pride. A third invitation, and pity for him. "I'm not as experienced as you," he said. It was a lie, but not completely. He wasn't experienced with women. "You're the only woman I've ever loved, with my heart as well as my body. I'm sorry I don't know how to please you."

"Don't say that." Gabrielle slipped under the covers and pressed herself against him. Her warm breath flowed across his skin. He lowered himself, so her head rested on his shoulder. With his other arm, he reached to the lamp on the nightstand and turned it off. In the safety of the darkness, he smiled, pleased with his ability to influence her mood.

As they lay in each other's arms, she told him about her first and only boyfriend before him.

SHE WAS NINETEEN. Paul was twenty, and the only thing he'd wanted was to make love to her. For hours at a time, he'd gazed at her, admiring every part of her body. He couldn't keep his hands off her. He told her she was perfection. He wrote poems about her lips. He wrote longer poems in overwrought language about his love for her breasts. For the first time since she was a small child, Gabrielle felt adored. Wanted. The entire time she and Paul were together, she'd listened to him dream about a trip to Europe that would come after he finished his two years at junior college. It never crossed her mind that the trip wouldn't include her.

One day, at the end of summer, they were at the beach, as they had been nearly every day since final exams. The sand was warm and soft without the dank presence of summer fog. The air remained balmy enough to sit on the beach past sunset. As the sand turned gray and the water black, Paul stood up. "I have a surprise." He jogged to the parking lot and returned with a box of supplies to make sand candles — wax, wicks, and a small camp stove and a beat-up old pot for melting the wax. "We can make candles from impressions of our feet. So we'll always remember this day."

Gabrielle was thrilled. She was so lucky. Her lover was like a Renaissance poet. They poured the hot liquid into the pits formed by their feet. As the wax cooled, Paul pointed out that she should have done her right foot, not her left foot. "We can't tell them apart."

When the wax was hard, he picked up a candle in each hand. "I was wrong, we can tell them apart, yours is bigger." He laughed.

As they carried the candles back to Paul's car, she'd asked

him why they needed something to remember the day.

"Because I'm leaving for Europe in two weeks and I have a lot to do. This is the last time I can see you."

He wanted to be free to experience life, to write his poems, to explore other women. Gabrielle had been a wonderful first lover, but there was a world of women out there. His poems to her? Writing exercises. Nothing but the heat of a boy and girl breaking away from a religious childhood, desiring sex on an hourly basis. Of course she'd fascinated him — it was all so new.

On September eighth, he left. She stopped going to her classes. An obsession with jogging took hold of her, and she ran ten, twelve, sometimes fourteen miles a day. Weight fell off until she looked like one of the stalks of pampas grass at the beach, thin, brittle, with a head of thick hair. One day she went to the beach with a huge pair of scissors. She hacked off her hair to her earlobes and threw the silky strands onto the waves.

After that, her mother dragged her to the minister for counseling, and that's when the part of her life that Mark knew about had begun.

THE STORY HAD pinched at Mark's heart. He'd whispered apologies. He clutched her hair in his fist, keeping her head firmly against his shoulder. He told her he was clumsy and didn't know how to love her. Words tumbled out of him until her gasping breaths grew softer. As they drifted to sleep, confidence bloomed in his mind. None of this had anything to do with sex. She needed verbal admiration, craved it like a junkie. Married life would be peaceful as long as he maintained a steady flow of attention in her direction. But he was wrong. So wrong.

When she was upset with him about their infrequent lovemaking, words of admiration irritated her. *That means nothing. Don't flatter me with fake words.*

She wanted sex. She wanted it all the time. He held himself to a strict schedule with long periods of abstinence and was disgusted by her lack of self-discipline. He looked in the mirror, gazing deeply into his own eyes. "I haven't had sex in two months," he said to his reflection. "What's wrong with her?"

Their lives fell into a pattern of easy companionship, interrupted only by the predictable head of steam that built up inside of Gabrielle. Sometimes, when she was close to exploding, she approached him with tickling fingers. Other times, with sarcastic words that sharpened themselves as they flew out of her mouth. After the yelling or his eventual succumbing to her tickling, the atmosphere grew calm for a few days, sometimes several weeks. When she was pregnant, it was easy. As much as she plied him with informative websites, he'd silenced her with the reminder that medical experts didn't know everything — medicine was an art. She finally backed off, in awe of his tenderness toward their child. For a short time, newborn Peter replaced her obsession with sex.

Now, her voice broke through his thoughts, even lower and more ominous. "Don't be afraid of me, Mark. Why are you so afraid?"

"I'm not."

"I stopped breastfeeding Peter just for you."

The hum of crickets invaded the room, rattling his brain. The moths still clung to the screen. He was going to be nibbled alive by Gabrielle and the insects straining to devour his skin, his mind. He didn't want to know what she meant — giving up breastfeeding for him. He moved his legs slightly. "What do you mean, *just for me?*"

"Susan told me you might not be attracted to me because of the breastfeeding. The milk. Sharing me with Peter."

He thrust himself up on his elbows and turned to look at her, straining the tendons in his neck. "You told Susan?"

"Uh-huh."

"Why? Why would you do that? What business is it of Susan's what we do in bed?"

"I didn't tell her what we do. I just told her I felt unwanted." Gabrielle's hand came to a stop on the lower edge of his rib cage. The crawling sensation continued. Her arm slid off, and her fingers brushed against the side of his thigh. Her voice was sharp. "You should be happy I didn't tell her I've felt that way since we got married. It's hard to keep it all inside. All these years of feeling unwanted. I'm all alone. I have no one to talk to about how I feel."

"It's no business of Susan's. I can't believe you'd talk to her about something so personal."

"You sure won't talk about it."

"I'm talking now."

"Only because I forced you into it. I try to touch you and love you, and you turn it into a fight so we can't make love."

"You shouldn't make sweeping statements. It's rarely accurate and…"

"I'm not someone coming to you for a damn marriage counseling session."

He decided to let the cursing pass. He wasn't the one starting fights. Overall, he was a pretty calm guy. She was the one who kept working herself into a froth. "I don't like it that you talked to Susan about our sex life. I'm her Pastor."

"You're my husband, first. Not the *Pastor.*" She flung the blankets back, yanking them off his body. He shivered. There was a gap between one side of the screen and the metal frame, and he was certain that any minute one of the moths would figure out how to work its way through the opening. And now his body was exposed to its feathery wings. He sat up to reach for the blankets. Gabrielle put her hand on his shoulder and shoved him back toward the mattress. She made a small fist and punched his shoulder.

"Ow! What are you doing? What's the matter with you?"

"Nothing is the matter with me. I want a normal husband who loves me and needs me."

"You don't want a normal husband. You want someone to worship the ground you walk on. Someone who spends twenty-four hours a day thinking about you, and what you're thinking and what you want and how magnificent you look."

She switched on the lamp and climbed out of bed. The moths tapped their wings against the screen, excited by the wave of light that splashed across the room. "It's no big deal. I had a few glasses of wine, and I needed someone to talk to. I thought she'd understand. I think about sex all the time."

"You've got that right."

"That's because I don't have it. And what's the first thing you think of? Grace, and your precious reputation as a minister. What about me?" Her voice was raw. A handful of moths, more frightened than Mark, fluttered away from the screen, giving up their craving for light in favor of silence. He wanted to slip into the darkness with them.

"Susan is my friend. I'm upset, so I talked to her about my feelings. That's what friends are for. Not that her advice did any good. I've prayed, I've fasted. I've done everything I possibly can. I keep myself looking nice for you. My whole life is about you, and all that matters to you is being the Pastor. It's like you're not even a human being. You're some eunuch, and I'm just here as a prop for your ministry."

"You're not a prop."

"You don't need me."

"Yes, I do." Mark rubbed his eyes, longing for darkness and a room without the sound of her voice, challenging him, testing him, demanding he rip open his skull and let her probe his brain. How long would it take her to pounce on the thought that he wouldn't be interested in any woman? She would catch him off guard. She would look at his face, the film of deceit over his eyes, and she would know. Thinking about it, imagining how it would happen, made his brain feel slippery. He couldn't hold a thought in place.

"How? How do you need me? To shake hands after church? To sit in the front row? To be a fundraiser? To cook? You don't even like the food I cook."

"Do we have to do this now?" he said. "I'm tired. Aren't you tired, honey?"

"Of course I'm tired. I'm exhausted from trying to attract your attention. I'm worn out from praying. I want…"

There would be no escape. He needed to try another tack. It had worked before. As tired as he was, he had to find some small piece of him that could fantasize himself into doing what she wanted. "Come here. I want to hold you."

"Yeah, right. You aren't going to distract me from what I'm trying to say."

"I don't want to distract you. You're right. We haven't had sex in ages. Come lay next to me."

"I hate it when you call it having sex. It sounds so technical. Why don't you think of making love?"

"Just come here. Please."

She turned off the light. Slowly she climbed onto the bed, lying perched at the lip of the mattress. "I want you to want me," she whispered.

"I do want you."

A simple lie, and his hands on her skin. That was all it took to silence her.

Eight

IT WAS SO EASY to get up early at this time of year when the sky was filled with watery light at five-thirty in the morning. Gabrielle's stomach groaned and bubbled, aching for food. The fasting had finally paid off, as Allysan had promised it would. Twice a week, Gabrielle had gone without food, and every morning she'd prayed for an hour, sometimes more. When her cramped stomach woke her at night, she knew it was another call to prayer. She'd come to realize that in the past, her prayers lacked the fervent devotion that was required. For three weeks now, she'd been faithful. And God had answered.

She planted the ball of her foot on the floor and spun in a circle, the other foot dragging on the carpet as she turned. Her short nightgown flared out around her hips. She wanted to run into the back yard and dance on the wet grass, let the birds see her tears of happiness. God had seen her hunger, heard her prayers, and responded. The Ruler of the Universe was paying attention to her. To *her*! She went into the kitchen, pulled a basket of strawberries out of the refrigerator, and began digging out the stems. A quick slice cut each berry in half. She dropped the pieces into a white bowl with a chip on the side.

As the pile of berries grew, she pushed away the gravelly voice inside, reminding her that this scene had taken place before. *It's not prayer! Fasting means nothing. She'd manipulated him into it. His desire was reluctant at best.*

She silenced the voice. This time was truly different. Her jealousy of the Heddleson's had evaporated. The burning pain in her stomach when she saw them touch each other had become a puff of smoke that felt like an old dream. The feel of Mark's hands on her skin, no matter how quick and evasive, sent warm waves through her mind until every painful image was obliterated, and that mocking voice was silenced.

She pulled a plastic container of granola out of the cabinet and poured a healthy pile on top of the strawberries. The hard clusters of nut and oat tumbled off the berries around the sides of the bowl like pebbles falling onto soft clods of dirt. She opened the refrigerator and poked her head inside. Behind a container of peach yogurt and a withered looking cantaloupe was a tub with a few spoonfuls of plain yogurt left in the bottom. She stirred it furiously, transforming it back into a creamy texture, and spooned it over the berries.

The screen door squeaked on the track when she opened it.

She set her bowl on the concrete while she carefully pulled the screen shut. She didn't want to wake either one of her boys. A smile spread across her face. They needed her. Mark needed her as much as Peter did. She stood in the middle of the patio, gobbling strawberries, hardly stopping to chew the granola, swallowing with huge, needy gulps. Two consecutive days without eating had been a bit much. She'd been so weak from hunger the night before, she'd had to hold the lemonade glass with two hands, afraid her limp fingers would let it slide onto the floor. Lemonade had not been the best choice for breaking her fast. The sugar went right to her blood. Her hands trembled all the way home, sending tiny vibrations across her brain.

She popped the last strawberry into her mouth and brought the bowl up to her face, licking up the last of the yogurt and stray nuts. She was still famished. But that was good. It was motivation to plan all sorts of goodies for dinner the following night.

Four couples were coming over to eat dinner and pump each other up by reporting the results of the fundraising visits. What a bore — an evening spent talking about numbers and facts. They should spend the evening in prayer. She'd visited Gethsemane Template twice more, and she wanted those experiences all the time. She felt ecstatic in that circle of people, drinking in their devotion and the expectation of miracles. When she closed her eyes, she felt God was in the room with them. Last week, when they'd all stood and moved toward her, a single organism, resting their hands on her head and shoulders and forearms, she'd felt something that couldn't be reported in a business meeting. The varying pressure of fingers and palms, some firm, some barely touching her, were channels of power into the core of her being. Her skin grew heavy on her bones, so that she felt a weight pressing around her. The constant aching for the touch of her husband dissolved, and she felt desirable, almost worshipped.

When she'd asked Allysan about the feeling of heaviness, Allysan said, *That's the presence of the Spirit. Isn't it glorious? Wouldn't you give up all you have to feel it constantly? People have no idea what they're missing. They're so bound to the earth and all its petty distractions. They're little groundhogs, burrowing down where they think they'll find safety.*

She was desperate to feel that presence now. Should she kneel on the damp grass to pray or go inside for more food? The hunger was incredible. A sharp pain shot through her temple. "No," she whispered out loud. "I'm not listening to you. My husband needs me. He *wants* me." She wouldn't allow the enemy to sneak in with those silvery needles of doubt, telling her Mark had only touched her because she'd begged. She wouldn't listen to the suggestion, lingering just beyond her consciousness, a voice that said — *Mark doesn't want you at all.*

Allysan had warned that doubts would arrive to torment her. The closer she moved toward God, the more intense the doubts would become. Gabrielle fell on her knees in the wet grass. The bowl clinked as she set it on the concrete beside her. She closed her eyes and lifted her arms toward the fence, past the power lines, up to the heavens. The demonic thoughts would disappear if she prayed out loud, if she wasn't ashamed to have a neighbor overhear her singing praises in her slightly toneless voice. Her arms ached, but people who were passionate about God lifted their arms, they danced with the music. They used their bodies.

After a few minutes, her arms became heavier. She relaxed her neck and let her head fall back. She opened her mouth. Oddly enough, the tune that came to mind was Lutheran, not one of the light rock tunes she'd learned at Gethsemane. Her voice sounded small and thin, as she sang a few words to get herself going. "Praise God from whom all blessings flow..." The doves stopped cooing, and the songbirds ceased their flute-like notes. She wished they would join her. "Praise Him all creatures here below..." She felt better. The words pushed aside her negative interpretation of the night before.

Her stomach clamored for more food. She let her thoughts run to Mark's warm hands and his sweet, almost childlike face that never failed to entice her — his gentle eyes and soft, pale lips. Her stomach growled. Her arms felt like they were going to snap off and fall to the ground. As if to confirm the possibility, she heard the soft thud of an apricot hitting the earth. The fruit that had dropped over the past few weeks lay nestled in the lawn, rotting a little more with each day's hot sun, slick fruit bursting through the skin, and clinging to the blades of grass. She needed to pick the rest before it all fell off and decayed.

It wasn't working. She couldn't remain still. Adrenaline raced through her. The empty, bubbly feeling in her stomach made her eager to start planning tomorrow's dinner. She stood and wiped the dew off her legs. The skin on her kneecaps was crisscrossed with ridges formed by grass pressing against her bones, turning her knees into small, woven mats of skin. She opened the screen door, suddenly afraid that Mark had gotten up for his coffee and newspaper and seen her on her knees, waving her hands as if she were trying to catch the hem of an angel's gown. He wouldn't like seeing her on her knees in the back yard. Prayer should be private, not showy.

The house was silent. She let out her breath. The empty bowl and spoon were still sitting on the patio. She opened the door and went back out. A fly was stepping gingerly around the edge of the bowl, interested in the skin of yogurt that covered the spoon. She blew on the fly, and it darted across the yard. She carried the bowl into the kitchen and placed it in the sink. She got a loaf of dark, moist homemade wheat bread out of the refrigerator and cut a thick slice. She spooned honey onto the slice of bread. She leaned against the front edge of the sink and took a large bite, chewing as fast as she could. When she was finished, she sliced and gobbled down another piece of bread with honey. She screwed the lid on the honey jar, wrapped up the bread, and put everything into the refrigerator. She placed the knives on top of the bowl in the sink. Crumbs lay like insects across the white tile counter. She brushed them toward the sink. Some of the crumbs refused to cooperate, clinging to the grout. She brushed harder, irritated that they were so resistant to her efforts. She wanted the counter clean but was too keyed up to take the time to dampen a cloth and wipe it thoroughly.

The wall clock read six-fifteen. She wanted Mark and Peter awake, she wanted the house to bristle with energy. She walked down the hall and into the bedroom, opening and closing drawers, hoping the sounds would wake Mark. Snores rumbled out of his mouth. The sheet was pushed down to his waist. He looked sweet in spite of the ferocious snoring. She placed her underwear, jeans, and a tight pink t-shirt on the bathroom counter. She turned on the hot water and unwrapped a new bar of soap, dumping the old one into the wicker basket on top of tissues and stiff clumps of dried soapy hair that she'd pulled out of the drain. Cleaning the bathrooms should be added to her list for the day, but she wanted to cook, not waste time scrubbing floors and showers. If she didn't get it done today, spent all her time in the kitchen, maybe Mark could stay home on Saturday, like a normal husband. He could wash the bathrooms while she vacuumed and dusted. She stepped into the steaming shower, wincing as the hot water hit her skin. She turned the second knob, adding more cold to the mixture.

After her shower, she twisted her hair into a soggy bun at the top of her head and spread moisturizer on her face. She brushed brown and beige shadow onto her eyelids and outlined them with a darker brown pencil. She coated her top and bottom lashes with mascara and stepped back to admire her face. She loved putting on makeup and didn't feel dressed until her eyes were shadowed and lined, stark against her pale skin.

A little after seven, she heard Peter jumping in his crib. His shouts carried down the hall. "Tuck! Tuck!" As she started toward his bedroom, Mark's feet thumped on the floor. She heard him yank open a dresser drawer and shove it closed. Peter shouted. "Up! Up!" He paused, "Ma! Ma!"

She quickened her pace. Once Peter started yelling, he was only a few short breaths from a piercing scream. When she entered the room, he reached his arms toward her. She picked him up and squeezed him close, breathing in the smell of his hair. She nuzzled her nose against his cheek and kissed it four times. While she stripped off his t-shirt and diaper, he ran through his litany of words, from truck to bath. She dressed him in a red t-shirt and blue overall shorts. She tried forcing his feet into his sandals, but he kept his toes curled, making it impossible. She gave up.

She was spooning oatmeal into Peter's mouth, pausing while he plucked bits of strawberry off the tray of his high chair when Mark came into the kitchen. She turned to look at him. She smiled. "Hi, sleepy."

He yawned. "Hi."

Peter gave an echoing yawn.

"I need to go to the store," she said.

"Sure. Okay."

She looked back at Peter. His tray and face looked as if they were smeared with blood. She patted his lips with the napkin and held out another spoonful of oatmeal. He turned his head. He grabbed a strawberry and stuffed it in his mouth, grinning.

IN LESS THAN two hours, she was back home with ten grocery bags of food. Peter was in the backyard, pushing his truck around his sandbox. Mark was sitting on the chaise lounge, reading on his tablet.

She sat at the kitchen table with a piece of ivory stationery and a purple pen. On one side of the paper, she listed each dish she was planning. On the opposite side, she jotted down the stages and timing required to make sure everything, or at least most of it, got done today. She was always excited by the chance to influence the poor eating habits of others. She didn't want to count how many potlucks she'd been to, wandering past tables of food, carried by waves of nausea as she contemplated casseroles featuring canned vegetables, meat, and preservative-laden sauces. For now, Peter ate the food she brought with her. But it wouldn't be long before he'd have to run the gauntlet like she did.

Women would come up close to him. With a single voice,

they'd chant — *Oh dear, you hardly eat anything. Have some cake.*
Have a piece of torte. Did you eat my casserole? You must try some, it
will put a little meat on those bones. With that, they'd push him
toward the table, surrounding him, so he had no chance of
escape. Just like Gabrielle, he would be prodded to try a little
of everything. It would be terrible to hurt someone's feelings.
Ladles full of ground beef or chicken drowning in cans of
soup and packaged seasonings would be offered. Without
realizing what they were doing, they aimed to destroy his
sweet little body from the inside. How could she make Peter
strong enough to resist their attempts to poison him? He was
so open to whatever anyone suggested. He loved the people
at church. They were always eager to admire his favorite toy
or hold his hand while he practiced walking.

Finished with her list, she scooted the chair away from the
table. She pulled a large dishwashing tub out of the cabinet
under the sink and went outside. Mark glanced over at the
sound of the screen sliding along the metal track. He stood
up quickly. "I'm heading over to the church."

She kissed him, keeping her lips on his for several
moments longer than usual. He touched her ear and stepped
back. He kissed her nose.

When he was gone, she went back outside and crept up
and down the rows of vegetables. Peter held the tub and
toddled after her. She plucked green beans off the vines and
dropped them into the tub. After a few minutes, Peter got
bored simply holding the tub, so she showed him how to

snap off beans. He broke some of them, leaving the tips of the beans dangling from the vine, but he still made the job go faster. When the tub was half full, she continued through the garden, pulling out green onions and carrots. Zucchini filled it to the top. She would pick cherry tomatoes on Saturday morning so they'd be fresh. Her dinner guests were always stunned by the taste of a tomato that hadn't been picked when it was a hard green knob and stored for weeks in a refrigerated truck. She rinsed the vegetables while Peter sat on the floor, banging a wooden spoon on the bottoms of three plastic bowls.

She was peeling the thin, wet skin off the tips of the green onions when her phone began spilling out the rhythmic strumming of a harp. Her fingertips were oily with onion juice. She rinsed them, dried them on her jeans, and dug the phone out of her back pocket.

"Hello?"

"It's Susan."

"Oh, hi. I was cooking so I didn't look at the screen. How are things?" They'd barely spoken since the afternoon when Gabrielle had foolishly bared her soul. A few times after church, Susan had asked how the weaning was going, but Gabrielle cut her off, ignoring the hurt look. Mark was so right. She never, *ever* should have said a word to Susan about their sex life. It gave Susan a weird kind of power over them. She knew now that it had been terrible betrayal, a lack of trust in God's timing. Even worse, Susan pitied her — a realization that made Gabrielle sick to her stomach.

"How are *you*?"

She ignored Susan's prying tone. If she were fishing for a report on breastfeeding, or Gabrielle's sex life, she would have to come right out and ask. Gabrielle was determined to paint over her mistake as if it had never happened.

"You've been a little cold," Susan said.

"Have I?"

"You know what I mean."

"No, I don't." Gabrielle pinched and peeled the layers of fine skin off the next onion.

"How are things going? You know, with the weaning. With Mark?"

"Oh, the weaning." Gabrielle put a note of surprise in her voice, as if it was the last thing she was thinking about. "Peter's all weaned. I think it makes him feel independent. He's doing really well with a cup. Of course, he has such good coordination." A piece of onion skin clung to her fingertip. She wiped it onto the edge of the drain and turned on the water to wash it down the garbage disposal. Susan said something, but the rush of the water filled Gabrielle's ears. She turned it off. "What did you say? I had the water on."

"What did Mark think?"

"What did Mark think about what?"

"Are you being clueless on purpose?"

"What do you mean?"

"If you don't want to talk about it, just say so."

Gabrielle rinsed her fingers and dried them on a towel. She moved the phone to her other ear. "Talk about what?"

Susan heaved an exaggerated sigh.

Gabrielle smiled. Susan would be forced to either give up the conversation or spell out her — what did Mark call it? — *prurient* curiosity.

"You...we...thought Mark might be...confused because you were still breastfeeding. Remember? You were so upset that he wasn't...you know...upset about not making love in a long time?"

We? Who did Susan think she was, sticking her nose into their sex life after one rash confidence on Gabrielle's part? The image of Susan's toenails filled her mind. Susan was sneering beneath her sympathetic tone. Gloating with the knowledge that she was desirable, and Gabrielle was not. "Things are terrific with me and Mark," she said. "All that wine you poured into me made me obsess over one small misunderstanding." She laughed.

"I didn't pour anything into you."

"Remember? We were drinking wine. I had two glasses. I hardly ever drink that much wine, especially in the afternoon. And it was hot, which makes the alcohol affect your brain even more. I was bloated from that lunch, remember? The macaroni and hot dogs? And wine? No wonder my brain wasn't working right." She laughed again. Whatever Susan remembered was not at all an accurate impression of Gabrielle's marriage.

Susan was silent for a moment. "I don't think we had that much wine."

"Maybe not for you." She knew Susan felt slimy. Susan wouldn't think any more about Gabrielle's marriage, she would be too busy trying to prove she didn't drink too much. And now, she doubted what she'd actually heard Gabrielle say. "Anyway, enough about that. What did you call for?"

"I wanted to touch base about the plans for dinner tomorrow."

"What about it?"

Susan's voice was low, defeated. "You're making a vegetable dish, bread, and salad, right? And I'm bringing beverages and a meat and cheese tray. The church is reimbursing me, right?"

"That's what Mark said." Gabrielle smirked. Susan acted as if she couldn't afford a meat tray. Gabrielle was glad she didn't feel the need to pluck money out of the church treasury. It was a pleasure to purchase and prepare fresh food.

"I guess it's all settled then."

"Sounds like it."

"Do you want me to come over early? To help you set things up? I'll do whatever you want, to help you and Mark. You know I love you two."

What had she been thinking, blurting out her painful feelings to Susan? Why had she been so stupid? She might as well have flung open their bedroom door and invited spectators inside. It felt as if Susan had crawled into their bed and was lying at the foot, watching them, giggling at how frightened Mark was of her. Susan could see that Gabrielle's body meant nothing to Mark, that she couldn't capture his attention. There was no room to move — Susan in their bed, taking up space, looking at things she wasn't supposed to see. Judging and making suggestions. Shoving herself between them, wanting to fix things.

She chased the image out of her mind. There had to be a way to make Susan forget. It was unbearable, knowing Susan pitied her. It wasn't right — thick, lumpy Susan, acting so superior. But that wasn't really the point. If Mark weren't such a...if Mark would give her the adoration she deserved, be overcome with desire for her...all she needed was a change in him. The night before had been a start, but she needed more — a permanent change. She needed God to completely transform him.

She arched her back and felt thick, silky hair brush across her spine. She was desirable, practically a goddess. She needed to recapture the feeling from early that morning when her whole body tingled with the knowledge that heaven had acted on her behalf. She'd captured God's attention with her willingness to give up food. Controlled by something beyond himself, Mark had relaxed. The chains that tied him to his work had broken apart. As she'd straddled his hips, all the strain had melted off his face. His expression was sweet, his real self, desiring his beautiful wife. The power to grab the attention of God Himself was now part of her experience. She had been lifted to a higher plane, to a place Susan couldn't begin to imagine. "I'm glad you're willing to help." She softened her voice. "Most everything is under control, but if you feel led to come over early, the tables could be set up."

"Are you sure? I don't want to intrude."

"Mark and I never consider it an intrusion when our parishioners want to be in our home." She could feel the smile spread across her face. Her skin glowed.

Like everyone else, Susan wanted to be best friends with the minister and his wife. Susan had seen herself in that role from the very beginning. She'd taken charge of Mark's future, introducing him to Gabrielle, encouraging them to date. From the start, she'd wanted to arrange their marriage, play cupid for them, and be viewed as a confidante for both of them. She felt as if she'd chosen her father's replacement, set herself up as an essential part of their lives.

Susan might possess the temporary lust of her husband, but she didn't have what Gabrielle had. Susan wasn't singled out by God to experience His power. The power to claim God's attention felt almost as good as sex. Gabrielle shivered.

Nine

ON SATURDAY, THE sun remained behind a screen of fog. An afternoon breeze kept the house cool as Mark and Gabrielle made arrangements for the dinner. The Ormistons arrived at four. After Mark and Jack set up a ten-foot table in the living room, they took the children to the park, happy to get out of the shrinking space consumed by the table and folding chairs.

In the kitchen, Gabrielle and Susan steered a wide path around each other. Susan put a tower of clear plastic cups at one end of the counter. She lifted off three cups and filled them with plastic knives, forks, and spoons. Next to the coffee pot, she formed a similar tower of Styrofoam cups.

Gabrielle tried not to watch, tried not to see the pollutants floating in rivers, bits of Styrofoam broken into bite-sized pieces, caught in the foam at the edge of the ocean, turning the white, frothy water into a pasty yellow that looked like industrial waste. Using real plates and washing dishes and silverware would have been fine with her, but Mark felt it was *inhospitable* to use real dishes. Because it wasn't a dinner party, all the pseudo guests would feel compelled to help wash plates and flatware. Paper and plastic let them off the hook and made them feel more welcome.

Susan had brought a tray from the supermarket, piled with tight rolls of turkey, ham, and roast beef. They looked like edible bullets of fat. The layers of white and yellow cheese appeared glued together. Next to the tray of death, Gabrielle's food looked colorful and life-giving. She'd made a salad of cold wild rice, cranberries, and almonds with an apricot-mustard dressing. Next to that was a platter of cut vegetables — sliced green peppers, carrot sticks, and piles of creamy white mushrooms, their undersides soft as silk. A bowl in the center of the tray was filled with ranch dip made of Greek yogurt.

Susan stood to one side while Gabrielle continued to cover the table with bowls of green salad, potato salad, and a casserole featuring thinly sliced tofu.

"You went to a lot of effort," Susan said.

"Not really, it was fun."

"I guess if you like to cook."

Gabrielle nudged bowls this way and that, trying to discover the perfect arrangement that would make everything easily accessible. "It's fun to figure out different combinations, and it's so…I don't know…it makes me feel like I'm giving life to people, you know? Nourishing their bodies, filling them up. Mark fills their souls, I fill their bodies."

"Interesting. I never thought about it like that." The dull edge to Susan's words suggested she still didn't look at it that way.

"You know what we need? Flowers!" Gabrielle dragged a chair to the refrigerator and stood on it to reach the cabinet above. She pulled out a glass vase, slightly browned on the bottom where she hadn't scrubbed it enough the last time she used it. "I'll clean out this vase. Grab the scissors in that drawer and cut some jasmine from the side fence."

"Won't the scent be sort of unappetizing when people are getting their food?"

Gabrielle sighed. Why did Susan have to be so negative? She was bent out of shape because she didn't get to hear any more about Mark and Gabrielle's sex life. Her energy came from feeding on other people's problems. That's why she didn't like to cook. Instead, Susan liked to eat, and her source of nourishment was the misery of others. Why hadn't she ever realized that? It must be her newly heightened awareness of the spiritual realm. Now that she thought about it, she could track the shape of their friendship around each difficult point in her life. When Gabrielle was miserable, Susan was kind and attentive. When things were going well, Susan withdrew, sulking. It seemed as if she lurked on the edge of Gabrielle's life, waiting for something to go wrong. Waiting for Gabrielle to cry on her broad shoulders. Gabrielle climbed down from the chair. Susan was a vampire, craving trouble, sucking the blood of disappointment.

Susan escaped to the side yard with the kitchen shears.

The sharp snap of the scissors was audible through the open window. Gabrielle held the vase under the faucet and let the warm water run for a moment. She added a few drops of dish detergent. The rough side of the sponge lifted off the stain at the bottom of the vase. She rinsed and dried the vase, then filled it halfway with cold water. She continued nudging the bowls of food around, pushing Susan's meat tray toward the back. Susan returned with a fistful of jasmine.

With the strands of jasmine draped over the edge of the vase, everything looked perfect. Gabrielle pulled two bottles of water off the top shelf of the refrigerator. She held one out to Susan.

Susan took the bottle and twisted the cap. "Thanks."

INSTEAD OF RINGING THE BELL, Larry and Elaine Brackner knocked on the screen door. Mark greeted them with a loud *hello* and a pat on Larry's shoulder. Larry was a tall man with a large, solid belly. He had round, dark brown puppy eyes, and black wavy hair. His cheeks swelled when he smiled. In contrast to the kind, gentle look of her husband, Elaine's eyes were wary. Even when she smiled, she pursed her lips. The pea-sized mole above her lip with its single strand of hair quivered excitedly when she had an opportunity to gossip. For Elaine, the smallest hypocrisy was worth talking about and considering at great length. The Brackners' stationery store provided a fluctuating income over which she worried constantly to anyone who would listen. Elaine stayed home with their three children, the eldest of which stood behind them in the entryway, ready to babysit Peter and the other children.

Jan and Rick Davenport and the Schneiders arrived at the same time. Rick was quiet with a warmth that flowed out of his eyes, unaided by a smile, because most of his mouth was covered by a fluffy beard. Watching him talk was an endless fascination for Gabrielle. His brown beard, spattered with gray, bobbed up and down. White teeth flashed only occasionally from behind the hair. Although the Davenports had been married for over twenty years and had two teenaged daughters, they gave the impression of newlyweds. Gabrielle wanted her marriage to be like theirs. They held hands and gave each other secret smiles. Every few months, they went away alone for the weekend. Other couples acted bored with each other, their eyes looking for someone of their own sex at every social gathering. Even though the Davenports were years older than Gabrielle and Mark, they seemed young. Artistically applied makeup made Jane look vibrant, and her clothes appeared to be custom cut for her body.

The Schneiders brought an air of dignity into the room. They were retired and had been married so long they looked like brother and sister — both tall and slim, white hair and a dried look that made them seem eternal.

The group made their way to the kitchen, where they formed a semi-circle around the food table. Mark said a short prayer. He thanked them for coming and swept his arm toward the food, telling them to help themselves, and that soda and water were available in the cooler at the foot of the table. "There's also white wine in the fridge," he said.

Everyone but Elaine opted for wine. Her father, she reminded them, had been an alcoholic. It was shameful to serve alcohol at church gatherings. People, they might not even suspect of having a drinking problem, would be forced into the path of temptation. Her expression, satisfied and strict at the same time, hinted that she knew all the closet drinkers at Grace Lutheran Church. Larry put his cup of wine on the counter and took a soda out of the cooler. Gabrielle let Mark pour a healthy dose of wine into her cup. She could never make up her mind whether wine contradicted her devotion to healthy eating. Alcohol was obviously on any list of unhealthy foods, but wine seemed so natural — made from grapes, aged in wood barrels. It tasted delicious, and it calmed her mood. She usually concluded that it was all about moderation. She took a sip.

After dinner, the table and chairs were stowed in the garage, and the others settled in the living room with cups of coffee. Gabrielle and Susan moved silently around the kitchen, wrapping the leftovers and inserting the dishes into whatever slots they could find in the refrigerator.

Mark stood in front of the small fireplace, piled with ashes from the previous winter. He cleared his throat. He leaned over and set his cup of coffee on the hearth. He informed them that seventy-four percent of the families listed on the church roster had been visited so far. He gave a summary of the visits he and Gabrielle had made and ran through updates on the lists of people contacted by each of the three couples beneath them in the hierarchy.

Bob Schneider started the report for his and Marlene's visits with a description of George Farnham's living room. It was consumed with towers of folded newspapers. Bob hadn't been able to follow the script because his thoughts kept drifting to the newspapers, wondering how many there were and whether every daily paper was accounted for, curious as to whether George ever re-read them. Marlene interrupted to add that Bob hadn't given the complete picture. From where she'd been sitting, the hallway was visible, lined with newspapers and magazines in unstable columns, five or six feet tall, from the living room to the back of the house. If she craned her neck, she could see into the kitchen where newspapers and magazines were stacked on the floor, the table, and all but one of the kitchen chairs, as well as the top of the refrigerator.

Mark said that when he'd first came to Grace, he'd visited George Farnham. After seeing the condition of the house, Mark had contacted George's son to see about cleaning up the place. Mark had been advised to *butt out*. George continued to welcome the occasional visit but refused to budge when it was suggested he might part with some of his papers.

In the pause after Bob's report, Gabrielle and Susan went into the living room. Susan squeezed herself onto the futon between Jack and the narrow wooden arm. Gabrielle settled on the floor, her legs sprawled out at a forty-five-degree angle, her arms behind her for support.

Most of the stories were bland — reports about people who attended church regularly. There were quite a few stories of people who had left their names and addresses listed with the church office but hadn't made an appearance in years. Some of those had aborted the proposed visit with a sharp rejection over the phone. There were heartbreaking stories of people who grudgingly allowed the visit only to vent their bitterness over the way Grace, or life, or God had treated them.

Jack began his final story. Earlier that week, he and Susan had visited Charlie Latimer, a man in his early forties who attended church every Sunday, accompanied by his intelligent, blonde daughter, and her wary younger brother. Charlie's wife, Victoria, joined them on Easter and Christmas. She wore a pleasant expression but was chilly to anyone who tried to give her more than a casual greeting. During the first half of the Ormiston's visit, Victoria had stayed in the kitchen fussing over the strawberry torte she was serving, letting Charlie do all the talking. After they ate the torte and were sipping coffee, Jack pointed out that God had blessed both of their families with financial success. Before he'd finished his thought, Victoria had flown out of her seat, nearly tipping a china cup full of black coffee onto the armchair. Her eyes blazed, and her face was contorted.

Susan wiggled forward and interrupted him. "We don't need to get into that. I thought the purpose was to report on whether or not people responded favorably to our visits and whether they were receptive to coming to a pledge dinner."

"This isn't just about money," Mark said. "The reason we're..."

"I know it's not just about money," Susan said. "But I think we're betraying their confidence. No one knew the things they said would be part of a public report. It's invasive."

Gabrielle shifted into a cross-legged position. Why did people resort to dictionary words when they were upset? Were they afraid to say what they really thought, preferring to wrap their negative emotions in some complicated word so they could avoid the plain truth? "You mean we're being nosey," she said.

"Okay," Mark said. "I don't think any of the folks we visited revealed their darkest secrets. They knew the purpose of the visit. I don't think there's any harm in sharing the stories. We have a positive intention — to make our community more connected, to pull in some of the people on the fringes. We can't pray for issues if we don't know what they are."

"It's just that Victoria's problem is ancient history. She's a bitter woman, and she took it out on Jack. She needs prayer for a forgiving heart. No need to get sucked into her unresolved issues."

Susan turned and gave Jack a look that Gabrielle couldn't see.

"That's my point," Mark said.

"We can pray for her without knowing all the details," Susan said.

"Susan's right," Jack said. "No need to go into all that. It isn't relevant. As we expected, Charlie will make a substantial contribution. So that's it for our visits."

"Your call," Mark said. "If you think it's too private, we'll move on."

"Wait!" Gabrielle said. This wasn't right. Jack wasn't going to entice them with part of a story, breaking off right before the dramatic moment. "Either we're going to report on the visits, or we're not," she said. "You don't start telling a story so we can know how to pray for these people and then not say anything about what's really bothering them. What's the point of that?"

Mark's eyes created little spots of heat on the side of her head. She resisted the urge to turn and stare him down. He hated it when she contradicted him in front of anyone from church.

Susan shot forward again. "We're not here to gossip, Gabrielle." She put the emphasis on the last syllable of Gabrielle's name.

"I'm not gossiping. Either we talk about the visits, or we don't."

The Schneiders and Davenports shifted in their chairs. Someone coughed softly. Elaine Brackner leaned forward, eager to gather all the data she could and not just information about whatever was eating away at Victoria Latimer. She was gobbling up the friction between Gabrielle and Susan.

"We have a bit of a philosophical difference," Mark said. "Let's leave the Latimers and move on to something more positive." His tone was pleading.

Gabrielle was torn. She desperately wanted to hear what Victoria Latimer had said to Jack. She was sure it was a criticism of Susan's father. Nothing else would make Susan react so quickly. Saying anything negative about her father, or anything he'd done when he was the pastor of Grace, never failed to puncture Susan's placid bubble. But if she pushed the subject, Mark would be upset. He'd accuse her again of not supporting his ministry. That wouldn't be good for their newly resurrected love affair.

The room was quiet. The voices of the children and the Brackner's daughter, unnoticeable a few minutes earlier, came through the open windows, shrill and piercing. The Brackners wouldn't rescue Mark from the uncomfortable silence, they trembled with anticipation as if they had box seats at the World Series. Gabrielle closed her eyes. Only a few hours earlier, she'd felt so spiritual. Where had it gone? The morning seemed like a faded dream. The presence of all these people sucked the spiritual life out of her. If she could close her eyes for a few moments, if the room would stay silent a little longer, that peaceful, heavy feeling would return and fill the empty cavities inside of her.

Annoyed at God for abandoning her, she decided, instead, to sink to Elaine's level. "The only ones we haven't heard from are Larry and Elaine. Any wild stories from your visits?" She laughed, but no one else joined her. Not even a snicker. Mark looked at her. His eyes were tired. She knew what he was thinking. *Why do you have to say every random thought that pops into your head?*

"Larry, how many visits did you complete?" Mark said.

Before Larry answered, the landline rang. Mark looked utterly defeated. He was trying so hard to follow the outline suggested in the fat blue binder provided by Grant Miller, but it wasn't working the way Grant had promised. Real people kept getting in the way. If he would just relax. No one would ever guess he'd just had sex the night before.

"Excuse me," Mark said. "Go ahead, Larry. I'll be back in a minute."

Gabrielle should have offered to answer the phone, but the caller would ask for Mark, and she'd have to take a message. The phone rang a third time, and he trotted down the hall to their bedroom.

Larry began describing his and Elaine's visit to a widow. He interrupted himself with his own thoughts. He voiced doubt about whether it was right to ask older people who had worshipped happily in a utilitarian building for years to contribute large sums of money at the end of their lives. The objective was stretch giving, faith giving. Meaning, giving more than was affordable. He emphasized their fixed incomes. It was harmful to pressure them to give even a dollar beyond what they already contributed on a weekly basis. Susan nodded enthusiastically.

Gabrielle wondered why these people, full of doubts about the construction, were on the leadership committee. Only because they'd always been in power. Mark wouldn't be having so many problems propping up enthusiasm if he'd spent a bit more time asking Grant to provide insight into how to select the right leaders. Instead, he went with the obvious, the expected, and now he had a group that he had to drag behind him like a sack of wet cement. If he didn't hurry up with his phone call, the reporting session, which was supposed to be inspirational, would spiral off course. Their wavering support for the building program would dry up and blow away like the Styrofoam cup the wind had swept off the table outside.

Larry ended his litany by recalling the Bible story of the widow with no spare change. He started in on the next report — a middle-aged couple who were recently told their fifteen-year-old daughter had leukemia. Elaine interrupted. She went into a long explanation of the prognosis for leukemia in all cases, and in this girl's case in particular. Larry nodded while she outlined the symptoms, the medical challenges, and all the associated problems of having a seriously ill child. As if they had orchestrated the story, Larry chimed back in to emphasize the medical costs. It was beginning to sound as if every person they were assigned to visit lived under a financial strain similar to that of the Brackners. There was a compelling reason why every single one of them couldn't give *more than a pittance.*

Perhaps God had a hand in this after all. Could it be He really didn't want a new sanctuary and office complex? It had to be more than coincidence that the Brackners were given a list of people who had the same sensitivity concerning money. Instead of pushing ahead with the fundraising agenda, Larry and Elaine had been side-tracked into the human drama.

Where was Mark? Gabrielle felt sorry for the changed mood he was going to face when he returned. Larry launched into the story of another financially challenged member. Gabrielle bent her knees and pushed herself up. She rubbed her thighs to get the circulation going. She walked quietly up the steps and crept down the hall. If she were careful, she'd hear Mark's conversation before the floorboards gave her away. The edge of the bedroom door rested against the frame, but it wasn't latched. His voice was muffled. He was talking in a normal tone, but obviously trying to keep the sound from leaving the bedroom. She moved closer, careful to avoid a sudden move that would cause the door to glide open. She stood at the hinged side, swallowing the itching sensation in her throat, trying to label his tone of voice. It wasn't the easy-going style that brimmed close to a laugh when he talked to his brother. And it wasn't the cautious tone he adopted with his parents. It definitely wasn't the voice he used with parishioners. There was a sarcastic edge, sharper. She inched closer to the opening, trying to get a peek at his face.

Mark laughed. A loud, uncontrolled sound that exploded from his chest. Although she still couldn't see him, she pictured him bending over, clutching his stomach. It wasn't bad enough that he loved Grace more than her, and it wasn't bad enough that she had to go without food and hammer her fists against the unseen walls of heaven in order to get him to make love to her. Now, he had someone capable of making him laugh with every cell of his body, in spite of the fundraising visitation team sitting in his living room, straining to reveal secrets without sounding like they were gossiping.

She touched the door gently, willing it to open just a few inches, maybe a foot, so she could slip into the open space without her laughing husband looking up. She had to see his face. He sounded like a man, not a minister. A man who finally let the shell of minister, spokesman for God, caretaker of old people and needy people, the sick and the demanding and the mildly psychotic, fall away. He was laughing like a little boy who had stolen cherries off a cranky neighbor's tree and escaped without being caught. Laughing with his best friend as cherry juice stained their lips until they looked like little devils.

His eyes were damp, and his face had a red glow. He looked up at her. The redness faded, leaving only the damp corners of his eyes to assure her she hadn't imagined his laughter. She chastised herself for not standing longer in the hallway, waiting to hear more of the conversation. She wanted a hint of why he willingly stayed away from his floundering meeting. Once he hung up, he'd revert to the man in charge. Never in a hundred years would he be willing to tell her about it now.

"I need to get back to my meeting." He turned so that only his profile was visible. He was silent for a moment. "That's really great. I can't tell you what that means to me, what it'll mean to everyone. It's a fantastic step forward." He paused again. "I know," he said. "But like I said…okay. Sure. Talk to you soon. And have a good flight." He pressed the button to end the call.

"Who was that?" Gabrielle said.

"An old friend."

"Who?"

"Joe Malik." He stood and put his hand gently on Gabrielle's back, trying to guide her toward the bedroom door. "I better get back in there."

She planted her feet firmly. The effect was as if he'd pushed her. "Why are you pushing me? What's the big hurry?"

"The big hurry is that we have a room full of people. They're wondering where I went. They're probably done reporting and don't know what to do next."

"You weren't worried about them when you were in here laughing it up with Joe Malik, whoever that is."

"You remember, I told you about him. From college. We were on the golf team together. He's a marketing big shot for a high tech company in Seattle. He wants to give fifty thousand dollars to the building program. Can you believe it?" He nudged her again, eager to report to the group the biggest news of all.

"Fifty thousand dollars! You haven't talked to this guy since college, and suddenly he calls up and says he wants to give fifty thousand dollars to a church he's never heard of?"

"Shhh. Don't scream it down the hallway. We can't talk about it now. We need to get back in there. I want to tell everyone the great news."

"You weren't very concerned about them five minutes ago. I want to find out what's going on, and you're suddenly interested in your guests."

"*Our* guests."

"Whatever."

"Come on, Gabby, not now. Please."

He nudged her again, and she took a step toward the door. Everything inside her wanted to stay rooted to the spot, but the touch of his hand on her lower back was like a flood of honey into her hips, bringing back his caresses from the night before. She let her head fall back against his chest. Her hair draped over his arm. She turned her head and breathed in the scent of his skin. It smelled like dry wheat. Kissing his neck made her pulse throb faster. She longed for everyone to get up and walk out of their house so she and Mark could escape into each other's arms. But they wouldn't. The only way to be rid of them was to go back into the living room, smile sleepily, yawn, keep her thoughts bound tightly, and wait for Mark to wrap things up. Mark shook her off his arm and stepped in front of her, hurrying down the hall. Gabrielle sauntered behind, hoping to walk in and see their guests standing up.

No such luck. They were firmly nestled in their seats, waiting like birds on a telephone wire for something to happen. Gabrielle felt an impulse to flap her arms and frighten them away

"Guess what?" Mark said. "You won't believe the phone call I just had."

They looked at him sullenly. Larry looked especially upset. He surely took it as an insult that the pastor didn't consider him as important as the others since he hadn't bothered to stay and listen to Larry's visitation reports.

No one spoke.

Mark crossed the room and turned to face them. "An old friend from college called. He's with a high tech company in Seattle. He's the Chief Marketing Officer, and he's moving back to California."

That was news to Gabrielle. Leave it to Mark to forget the most important piece, to announce something like that to the whole world rather than telling her first.

She meant nothing to him. She shoved the thought out of her mind. It was a whisper from the enemy. But it wouldn't go away. She didn't hear what else Mark said, just a chanting in her skull — *He doesn't care about you. Doesn't care. Doesn't care.*

Ten

THE NEXT MORNING the living room smelled of other people. Everything was slightly rumpled, a little bit strange, not quite her own. She straightened the rocking chair, so the runners pointed at the center of the room. She sat down and started to rock. She couldn't focus on praying, and she wasn't in the mood to read her Bible. It was only four-thirty — even the birds were sleeping — but there was no way she was letting Mark slip down the hall and out the front door without talking about Joe Malik. It couldn't wait until after church. She had to understand why that guy made Mark laugh so freely. Why on earth did he want to give fifty thousand dollars to the building fund when he'd never seen the church, never met a single person from Grace? If he was such a good friend, why hadn't he come to their wedding?

She closed her eyes and tried to picture his name on one of the one-hundred-seventy-five thick, white envelopes she'd addressed. At the time, she'd thought she'd never forget a single name. She couldn't remember any Joe Malik, but neither could she bring to mind the image of any other names from Mark's past, except his family, and people who she now knew at Grace.

At the sound of water running, she opened her eyes. Quarter to five, and Mark was out of bed. Good. That would give them time to talk. She hurried into the kitchen and ran water into the coffee pot. She filled the basket with grounds.

When Mark came into the kitchen, he was dressed in his formal black clerical shirt, featuring a white plastic collar that circled his neck and fastened in the back with a brass tab. His hair was still damp. He looked so handsome — an actor playing the part of a very proper minister.

"Hi," she said.

"Hi." He lifted his chin and sniffed. "Thanks for making coffee."

"You're welcome."

He took a thick blue mug out of the cabinet and filled it with coffee. "Why are you up so early?"

"I'm dying of curiosity. For one thing, I don't get why your college friend wants to give all that money away."

"You got up before dawn to ask me about an old friend?" He set his cup down too fast, and coffee splashed onto the counter. He grabbed a paper napkin off the remaining stack and wiped up the spill.

"You never talk about him. I can't remember if we invited him to the wedding, but we've never sent him a Christmas card. It doesn't seem right."

"What doesn't seem right?"

"Who is he?"

"A friend from college. I told you that last night. We were on the golf team together."

"Why does he want to give all that money? Do you have something on him?" She laughed.

Mark's expression remained unchanged.

"Why were you laughing so hard? You never laugh that way with me." Her voice was unsteady.

"It's five o'clock in the morning. I have to leave in a few minutes."

"I want to know."

"I'm not even sure what you want to know. He's made a lot of money, millions, from what it sounded like. He's moving back to California, and he wants to…"

"Why did you tell everyone else about him moving back to California before you told me?"

He pressed his lips together. He turned to face the window. He yanked the cord, opening the blinds, and slid the window along the track. The nearby complaining of crows filled the room. He turned back toward her and took a large swallow of coffee. "Will you let me finish?"

She put her hand on the table and performed two demi-pliés to calm her muscles. She sat down, breathing deliberately.

He sipped his coffee. "I told him about the building

program, and he thought it was great that we want to update the place, make it more appealing to a new generation. It just spilled out. He's like that. Wait until you meet him. He's a very enthusiastic guy."

"So if he's so much fun, why don't you ever see him?"

"I've told you before. I lost touch with almost everyone when I went to seminary. People outside the church don't really understand ministers, you know that. I don't think Joe's ever been in a church in his life. Unless it was for a wedding or a funeral. Maybe. Most people don't even get married in churches any more, and how many funerals could he have been to?" He drank the rest of his coffee. "I really need to get going."

"You always have to get going. Everyone in the whole world has a bigger part of you than I do."

He turned on the faucet and let it run, warming the water. He washed and rinsed the mug. He dried it and put it back in the cabinet. He walked over to the table and took her hands. He tugged gently to get her to stand up. She resisted. He let go and put his hands on her shoulders, bent forward, and pressed his face against the top of her head. He kissed her hair. She stood and slipped into his arms. Her spine softened. She clung to his waist, pulling him close until their bodies seemed to melt into a single being. He turned his head to the side and rested his chin on her shoulder. "Don't want so much," he said. He pulled back and let her go.

If only, just once, he needed her more than she needed

him. It wasn't true that she wanted too much. She wrapped her arms around her waist, the tips of her fingers feeling her ribs through her thin shirt. "Have a nice worship service." She spit the words at him. "I'm glad you're so holy you don't want anything. Too bad you couldn't have the Virgin Mary for your wife." He stood close as if he might reach to hold her again. She put her hands on his black, stiff shirt and pushed.

He stumbled back, knocking a chair against the table. He opened his mouth, then closed it. Another thing that infuriated her. He never yelled, rarely fought back. She could cry and beat him with her fists. She could yell. Scream. She could throw things, smack the table. Push him. He stood like a pillar, neat and fit, never allowing himself to lose control. That must be why he didn't care for sex. It was the ultimate loss of control. As he turned and walked out of the kitchen, unlocked the deadbolt, and went out the front door, she followed, wondering why she'd never noticed the connection before.

An unfamiliar thought planted itself in the center of her mind — something evil had entered their home. It crept up her spine, scaly and hard, then reversed direction, slithering down her throat. A man should need his wife, but this thing was choking Mark's desire. Allysan and the Gethsemane people talked a lot about demonic invasions. They daubed oil on each other's foreheads to prevent demons from gaining entry. Oil was a symbol of the Spirit that repelled demons. A demonic presence was the only explanation for Mark's coldness. Ministers' families were especially vulnerable to attack. According to Allysan, a demonic force that got its talons into a minister could gain access to an entire church. Allysan had mentioned it would be a good idea for a few of the strongest prayer warriors to anoint the Atwater house. Gabrielle could imagine Mark walking in on that scene. She pressed her forehead against the front door as if the sheer force of her skull could prevent anything from slipping inside.

Shrieks from Peter's room pierced her thoughts. She ran down the hall as his screams ripped at her brain like claws. Peter was standing in his crib. His little hands gripped the railing. Although his scream had only started a few seconds ago, his face looked like a bruised plum, swollen with tears that had flowed across his cheeks and soaked into the skin, bloating his eyes and nose. His cries didn't subside when he saw her. She lifted him out of the crib and pressed him close to her body, holding his head against her shoulder. He trembled. His terrified shrieks continued. His body convulsed, and the tears soaked the side of her face and her nightshirt. She swayed, holding him close as if she could draw him inside of her, just as she'd tried to hold Mark, tried to pull his body inside hers only a few minutes earlier, or was it hours ago?

After a long while, his sobs abated. He gasped and relaxed into her. She walked slowly to the changing table. He lay willingly on his back while she changed his diaper, which wasn't overly wet. She slipped his arms into a red, blue, and green striped t-shirt and thrust his warm, firm legs into a pair of red shorts. Even though he was calm now, he gave her a funny, sideways look. A sharp, hard stare that reminded her of Mark.

She fed him yogurt and red seedless grapes. She could hardly peel and slice the grapes fast enough to keep up with his cries for more. It could be he was over-tired from all the activity the night before, that he was hungrier than usual, the pains in his belly causing him to scream. Maybe he'd been whimpering for a while, and she hadn't heard him because her heart was eaten up with longing for Mark. Or, the evil spirit had a grip on her entire family. Mark's ignorance about the dark side of the battle between God and Satan had allowed it to gain entrance. He ignored the existence of demons. So had she, until she attended Gethsemane and her eyes were opened. All Satan and his army needed were tiny chinks in the armor. They gained a toehold, swarming into a believer's life like the clusters of flies that swarmed over the sticky apricots lying under the tree, filling the air with a sweet, rotten stench. Evil beings were intent on devouring any group of believers they could find. What better place to start than the home of Pastor Atwater?

She needn't have dressed Peter in his best shorts and shirt. They weren't going to church this morning. There were more important things to do. A cleansing was needed. She settled Peter on the living room floor with blocks and his wood trains. She linked the tabs of the track pieces together, forming a complex circuit. Running his train around the configuration would keep him happy for some time.

She started with the kitchen, sorting unused paper plates and cups, putting them in the cabinet, filling a large black trash bag with the leftovers from Susan's meat tray, coffee grounds, and soggy paper towels that she'd used to wipe spills from under the kitchen table. She swept the floor. Starting in the corner behind Mark's desk in the family room area, she mopped every inch with steaming water. She returned to the same corner and squirted a one-step clean and shine liquid on the floor, mopping furiously across the entire surface.

In the living room, her dust cloth slid gracefully over the blonde wood of the cabinet that held their music docking station. She ran the cloth along the bookshelves built into the wall on either side of the fireplace. She was sweeping the house of unseen creatures, grabbing them all in an increasing layer of dark gray fur on the white cloth. When she finished, the cloth was black. She went into the garage and tossed it into the washing machine. She got another cloth out of the kitchen drawer. Working her way down the hallway, she wiped the edges of picture frames showing every phase of Peter's life. Near the entrance to their bedroom door was a ten-by-fourteen print of her and Mark on their wedding day. She flipped the rag over to use a clean section to wipe the frame and the surface of the glass. Then she crept along the floor, dusting the top of the baseboards.

Peter's room was easy because the crib never got dusty, he had his hands over every inch of it on a daily basis, and she washed it regularly with disinfectant. She wiped the edges of the changing table and the top of his dresser. She polished the ceramic figurines of Winnie the Pooh and his companions.

In the hall bathroom, she depressed the childproof latch on the cabinet under the sink and pulled out the tub of sponges, sprays, liquids, and powdered cleanser. She scrubbed furiously until the tub gleamed white and pure, the floor was glossy, and the counter slick under a sparkling mirror. She opened the window and took a deep breath of morning air that was still damp with fog. No disease, germs, or any other unclean thing would survive now. No wonder the Old Testament made such a big deal about serving clean food and keeping clean houses. It was one thing to be free from the Old Testament laws, but another thing to forget how the physical world mirrored the spiritual. A clean house was evidence that their lives were clean, free from stains, protected against the invasion of evil. Just like pure food was symbolic.

She put away the cleaning supplies and went back to the living room.

"Peter, come in the kitchen, and we'll have a little snack. I need to vacuum the living room."

"Vackim," he said.

She put him in his high chair, holding his hands together in front of his chest so his fingers wouldn't be pinched while she lowered the wooden tray. She poured apple juice into his new Winnie the Pooh cup and broke a rice cake into pieces. She stood in front of him and nibbled on her own rice cake. While Peter inspected the puffed bits of rice, she took an apricot out of the refrigerator and cut it into bite-sized chunks. She put the pieces on the tray. "Here's some apricot too. Apricot."

"Ap-cot," Peter said.

She pulled out the vacuum cleaner from the hall closet and sucked dust bunnies from the corners of the hardwood floor in the front hall. She glided through the living room, sucking up crumbs and sloughed off strands of hair. She vacuumed around the train track, not wanting to take it apart and put it away for such a short time. Then, she changed her mind. What if there were something lingering in the carpet, waiting to invade her baby's skin? Who knew what lurked in those tight fibers. She gently pulled the track to one side so it wouldn't break apart. She ran the vacuum over the spot and then unplugged it and lifted it up the steps into the entryway. She'd saved their bedroom for last. It was the most important and the most likely candidate for whatever terrible thing was destroying Mark's passion, tearing apart their marriage.

When she came back into the kitchen, Peter had sucked all the apricot pieces and let them fall out of his mouth onto the tray.

"Why didn't you eat the apricot?"

"Ap-cot," Peter said.

She picked up a gooey piece and put it into his mouth. He spit it out. She picked up another, less soggy piece, but as her hand came close to his mouth, he jerked his head to the side.

"No!"

"It's yummy. See?" She found a piece he hadn't mangled and popped it into her mouth. It was firm and cool. Just last week, he'd gobbled up apricots. Was it possible he'd observed and absorbed Mark's dislike for the innocuous little fruit? She held another piece of apricot up to Peter's lips. Tears filled his eyes. "No, No!"

Whatever was causing disruption in their house hadn't been eradicated yet. She scooped up the mangled pieces of fruit with a paper towel and dropped them into the garbage. She wiped up the crumbs from the rice cake, wiped his hands and cheeks, and pulled him out of the high chair. She pressed her lips against his cheek. Peter made a kissing sound, and she put him on the floor. Hating herself, but knowing it was the only way to cleanse the house, she slid a DVD featuring an animated singing mouse into the player. Peter settled himself in front of the TV.

She went into their bedroom and opened the window on Mark's side of the bed. The fog was burning off, and the sky was a fuzzy blue, streaked with wisps of cloud. She stepped into the bathroom and began to scrub it like she'd done with the hall bathroom. She washed the shower wall, whispering with each upward stroke, "Be gone." And with each downward swipe, "Be Clean." The words gave a steady rhythm to her movements.

She unwrapped a clean sponge and dampened it under steaming water. She went into the bedroom and wiped the window sill. She still had to clean the rest of the bathroom, but she couldn't wait to attack their room. She left the sponge on the windowsill and yanked the blankets off the bed. She separated the sheets and pulled the pillows out of their cases. She carried the linens and mattress pad to the garage. Swallowing a sour lump in her throat, she poured detergent into the machine. It should be a pleasure to make a clean bed where she and her husband would fold themselves up, naked, between crisp, sweet-smelling sheets, wrapping themselves into a cocoon of soft touches and long kisses. Such a simple task and a common desire should not make her want to cry.

She let the lid fall closed and leaned against the machine. While she was moving and scrubbing, her muscles and bones felt strong and alive. Now, her body ached, all the way to her soul. She wasn't fooling anyone. Their lovemaking a few nights ago was no different from any other time. It may have been preceded by starvation and sleepless nights filled with long, eloquent prayers, but it was just like every other time. The only change had been her hunger and exhaustion. She'd been deluded, thinking Mark's desire had grown. Half crazed by her weakened physical condition, she'd thought he'd approached her with eager longing. It hadn't been that way at all. Nothing was different. Nothing. Every few weeks, she cried and begged. When he couldn't take it anymore, Mark yielded. Making love was more agreeable than listening to her.

The washer groaned beneath her, filling with water, squeezing the sheets, beating the sweat and dead skin out of them — cleaned for nothing. Already Mark had forgotten about the other night. He was more excited about holding a fifty-thousand dollar check from Joe Malik than touching her skin. He'd been happier laughing it up on the phone with Joe than he'd been burrowing under the blankets with her.

She didn't deserve this. She was nothing but a maid and a nanny. She chastised herself for the thought. Peter was her soul. In fact, he was the only good thing in her life. What a horrible person she was for letting that thought take shape. It was Mark. When you took away the passion, the shutting off from the world in a private castle of love and complete knowledge of each other's thoughts, all that was left was work. Cleaning and cooking and caring for her baby. Without love, all of it was meaningless. Mark didn't even like most of the food she prepared. He'd rather eat thick, fibrous meats, and gluey potatoes soaked with butter and cheese and sour cream.

The machine switched cycles, spinning and vibrating out the first infusion of water. She straightened and stretched her arms over her head. Moping in the garage wasn't going to solve anything. Putting one hand lightly on the edge of the washing machine, she used it as a ballet bar. She performed seventy-five pliés followed by seventy-five forward kicks with each leg. For a few minutes, she'd lost faith. Satan was taking advantage of that. Even if the other night appeared to be the same, it wasn't. It couldn't be. God had heard. He was answering her prayers. That was what Allysan said, that's what the minister and music leaders at Gethsemane said. Most important of all, that was what the Bible said. What were they all doing if those pages and pages of promises weren't true?

The tightness in her knees from crawling over the hard bathroom floor was gone. She would clean their bedroom like it had never been cleaned before. She'd wipe out the drawers and cabinets in the bathroom. She would vacuum the closet, not just cleaning the outside of things, but the inside also. That was what God was telling her! The *inside* needed to be cleansed. It wasn't Mark's fault at all. Look at his sweet, innocent face, his clear eyes, his nicely formed muscles, and flat inviting belly. He had a healthy appetite for sex, for his beautiful wife. Obviously, some demon had consumed him. It was up to her to follow where the Spirit led — ridding the house of the unwanted presence. She grabbed three new sponges and a can of disinfectant off the shelf over the washing machine. She went back in the house, walking to the family room area to see how Peter was doing. He was staring wide-eyed at the colorful creatures on the screen, bouncing his head and shoulders with the beat of the music.

In the bathroom, she took a towel, folded it in thirds, and knelt on the soft cushion, as if she was kneeling on a prayer pillow. She pulled everything out of the cabinet and began spraying and wiping the bottom. She threw away tiny screws that had found their way to the back corner. She tossed a nearly empty can of cleanser and a dried-up bottle of black shoe polish into the trash. She wiped the grit off the pipes. Next, she emptied the drawers. The two on the left side were filled with Mark's things. The top drawer contained his deodorant, insect repellent, and medication. The second drawer held the shaving kit he used when they traveled and his hairbrush. There wasn't much, but she took everything out and wiped out the drawers, scrubbing away the rusty ring left by the can of shaving cream.

All that remained on the floor was the brown leather case, filled with disposable razors, a miniature container of aspirin, and a decaying half-empty roll of chalky tablets for relieving indigestion. She tossed the antacid tablets in the trash. She looked at the container of aspirin. Taking chemicals went against everything she believed in, but her joints were unbearably stiff and swollen. Her head ached. The base of her skull was tight as if a big knot of fear had lodged itself there. She pulled apart the opening of the case to grab the aspirin. What did it matter? Two tiny white tablets weren't going to kill her. Underneath a blue disposable razor were three foil packets. She pulled them out and turned them over. She rocked back on her heels, dropping the case on the floor. Condoms? Why were there three foil-wrapped condoms in his shaving bag?

She stood. The blood rushed out of her head. The corners

of her vision filled with a black cloud and her head buzzed as if whatever had made Peter scream like the devil that morning had now entered her body. Her jaw trembled, causing her teeth to vibrate against each other. She grabbed the edge of the counter and let the condoms fall into the sink.

He didn't love her at all. She read all the time about men finding someone more interesting outside their marriage, especially after they had children. But never in her wildest bouts of despair had she truly believed he might be making love, expending all his physical needs with another woman. She slammed her fist on the edge of the counter. A sharp pain shot up her arm. She kicked the shaving case out of her way. It crashed into the corner, and a plastic razor fell out.

She stumbled out of the bathroom, tripping on her own foot. She threw herself on the bed. The clock glared at her. Twelve-twenty. The second worship service was over. She grabbed the cordless phone off his nightstand and punched in the number of the church. The recorded greeting came on. She disconnected and dialed again. Mark's recording spoke again — *Thank you for calling Grace Lutheran Church.* Before his voice could tell her that everyone was welcome to worship with them, she disconnected.

She rolled onto her back and closed her eyes, letting the blackness that lingered around the edges of her vision recede. No thoughts formed in her mind. Nothing but the buzzing sound and the knot at the base of her skull. She wanted a cold shower, she wanted Peter to not be in the other room, the DVD coming to an end. She wanted Mark home right this instant, lying next to her on the bed where she could pound his hard, flat stomach with her fists until he told her the truth.

The phone rang.

"Hi, it's me," Mark said. "You didn't answer your cell. I have a..."

She screamed into the phone. "How dare you! You liar! I've spent my life trying to love you. You're a rotten excuse for a human being. Liar!"

"I have a counseling appointment that was unexpected. The person will be here in five minutes. I just wanted to give you a quick call to tell you I won't have time to come home before the youth group event and..."

"Counseling." She spit out the word. "You think I believe that? I'll never believe one of your creepy lies again."

"Gabrielle, I don't have time for this. Someone will be here in a minute. I don't know what has you upset, but it'll have to wait until I get home."

"Who is it?"

"What?"

"Who are you *counseling?*"

"You know I can't tell you that."

"Yeah, right."

"Gabby. Please."

"Go ahead and counsel. Maybe I'll be here when you come

sashaying home, or maybe we won't." She ended the call and threw the phone against the wall. The ringer chimed as the phone hit and crashed to the floor. She rolled onto her side, waiting for him to call back. She wouldn't answer it, of course. The phone remained silent.

Eleven

IT HAD BEEN a marathon Sunday. Gabrielle hadn't shown up for the worship service, which had been only slightly worrying. Until the phone call. After the services, Elaine Brackner had spent nearly two hours in his office, sobbing because her teenaged daughter was *promiscuous*, asking what she should do as if he had any idea how to stem that behavior as if Elaine or her daughter would listen to him if he did make a suggestion. He'd been late to the youth group Open Space Preserve cleanup event. After that, he'd returned to the church to pick up his tablet and the Sunday morning clothes he'd changed out of for the cleanup event. Elaine had been waiting outside his office, wanting to unload more emotions. She was holding a bag from a fast-food restaurant containing a juicy hamburger, a giant container of French fries, and a chocolate milkshake. He hadn't had a dense, satisfying meal like that in a long time. The price had been listening to Elaine for another hour and a half, trying, and failing, to help her sort out her feelings.

When he walked into the house, everything smelled clean. Peter was asleep, and Gabrielle was burrowed under the covers, also asleep. He dropped his clothes on the floor near the nightstand and crawled into bed. She'd washed the sheets, and the clean fabric against his skin was reassuring. Things couldn't be that bad if she'd scrubbed the house.

He slept until the sun was halfway to the center of the seamless blue sky. He got up, pulled on a pair of jeans, and trudged down the hallway, anxious for a cup of coffee. Gabrielle was sitting on the living room floor. Next to her was a stack of Peter's books. Peter sat on her lap, leaning his head against her shoulder so he could look at the pictures while she read a story.

"Good morning," Mark said.

She didn't look up.

"Dada!" Peter climbed off her lap and ran to the steps leading up to the entryway. Mark scooped Peter into his arms, kissed his nose, and tossed him a few inches over his head. Peter squealed, and Mark put him back on the ground. "Ghen," Peter said.

"No, once is enough."

He thought about kissing the top of Gabrielle's head, but she'd turned and was looking out at the backyard. So that was the sort of day he could expect. The details of her tirade on the phone came flooding back. He didn't want to know what was bothering her. The general theme was probably the same:

his lack of attention and sex. He was tired already.

It was difficult to enjoy his coffee, almost impossible to keep his attention on the news articles sliding across his tablet like schools of fish racing nowhere. The news offered all kinds of tantalizing stories — other people's problems in which he could lose himself, problems that he wasn't expected to solve. But each article blurred in front of his eyes after three or four paragraphs. It was too much trouble to push his slightly damp finger across the screen. He took a sip of lukewarm coffee. It was disappointing that Peter wasn't spinning around his legs like he usually did when he hadn't seen Mark for a day or two. Instead, he was in the living room, crawling over Gabrielle, chattering about one of his books. She sat like a stone, ignoring his pleas for another story.

Mark tapped the logo to return to the CNN home page. None of the headlines or video links looked even moderately interesting. Peter began slapping one of his books against his mother's leg. Mark pushed back his chair and went to the entrance to the living room. Gabrielle was sitting with her legs crossed in a lotus position, her back perfectly straight. She stared at the corner of the room where a matted, charcoal-colored piece of spider web hung from the ceiling, floating slightly on an indiscernible movement of air. Peter chattered and squirmed across her legs. Now he was tugging at her hair, grabbing her face in his small hands, trying to turn her head toward him.

"For crying out loud, Gabrielle. Read the book to him."

Her back remained straight, her chin lifted. The sound of his voice hadn't caused even the smallest twitch. Peter's rough, squirmy movements had no effect as if she was in a trance.

Why was he required to deal with this? For the hundredth, maybe the thousandth time, he wondered why he'd thought he wanted a woman who was a bit whacky, different from all the other women he knew. More interesting, entertaining. She was different all right. She was a full-time job on top of his other incredibly demanding job. It was starting to seem as if God was punishing him — handing him a life filled to overflowing with moody, hysterical, needy people. They all wanted something from him. Most of the time, he wasn't even sure what that *something* was. But they wanted it, and they expected him to figure it out.

"Gabrielle! You're tormenting him!" He turned and set his coffee cup on the counter and stepped down into the living room. He sat on the futon and patted the cushion. "Come here, Peter. I'll read the story."

It would be hell trying to read the sing-song words of Dr. Seuss while Gabrielle sat in front of him, drifting off to an unknowable place, but he couldn't bear to sit in the kitchen and listen to Peter's frustrated babbling. What a way to start his day off. His only day off. Supposedly a chance to relax and replenish his energy. It looked as though he'd be spending the day distracting Peter from his catatonic mother, cut by the blades of her wordless stares.

As he finished the final page, Gabrielle leaped to her feet and snatched Peter into her arms. She carried him up the steps and disappeared down the hall. Mark leaned back and closed his eyes. If only he could disappear. Maybe he would. He went into the kitchen, warmed his coffee in the microwave, and grabbed his tablet. If his mind wasn't capable of absorbing the news, at least he could smooth out the kinks with a virtual game of golf. The coffee tasted sour, but he gulped it down anyway, tapping the screen, assured of each move, the only piece of his life with clear answers.

When he'd finished the bitter, too-hot coffee and taken his shower, Gabrielle was still in Peter's bedroom, watching Peter run his train around the track. Peter ran the train over her toes and laughed. Mark could see only a portion of her face. The shadow of a smile flitted across her lips.

He stepped into the room. "Do you want me to take him to the park?"

She didn't answer.

"Gabrielle?"

She didn't turn her head, didn't give any indication she'd heard him speak. For half a distorted second, he thought he might be invisible because Peter didn't look up either, or break the furious rhythm of the string of wooden train cars.

"Gabrielle! Do you want me to take Peter to the park before it gets hot?"

Without turning, she said, "We're fine."

He leaned against the doorframe. He should ask her what was wrong. He should sit on the floor with them. There were any number of things he should do. Every single day of the week, he faced some sort of dramatic event. He couldn't eat a meal, lead a worship service, leave the house to visit someone in the hospital, or even go to bed without a scene. "I'm going to the driving range. I'll be back around noon." He took a deep breath. "Should I bring home something for lunch? Or I can pull it together when I get here."

She didn't turn. A curtain of hair fell over the side of her face, hiding her expression. Not that he'd be able to interpret it. He was stunned that she could sit in one position without flickering an eyelash or seeming to take a breath. The only movement came from Peter, rotating his body to follow the path of the train around the track.

"How about it?" Mark said.

"I'm perfectly capable of fixing lunch. After all, that's the only thing I have to do. Clean your house, cook your meals, and take care of your son."

He spoke against his better judgement. "Do you want to talk about what's bothering you?"

"Nothing is bothering *me*."

A sob shoved its way up through his chest. He wanted to go into the bedroom, fall on the mattress, and sleep. Never wake up. Life was not supposed to be this much work. He went out to the garage and pulled his golf clubs off the shelf that ran along one side. They were coated with a thin film of dust that was held in place by greasy residue floating in the air of the garage. It didn't matter. He'd polish the few clubs he needed at the driving range. He might stick with his five iron the whole time. Or a driver. Why bother with the whole bag? Definitely a driver. Send the ball flying as far as possible. He couldn't remember how long it had been since he'd hit golf balls, much less played a game. Golf wasn't something that fit easily into their budget. And since Peter's birth, he hadn't had much freedom to play golf on his one, measly day off.

WHEN HE RETURNED from the driving range, he was calmer. A plate covered with plastic film sat on the kitchen table. Another warning that his company wasn't welcome until Gabrielle decided it was the right time for their next fight, which would most likely be the moment he reached over to switch off his bedside lamp. Peter was parked in front of an animated retelling of the story of Noah's ark. At the other end of the house, the vacuum cleaner roared. The sound confused him, but he couldn't think why.

He peeled the plastic off the plate. Slices of tomato, a serving of pasta salad, and an apricot. Although he didn't always care for her vegetable-centric meals, and her strange substitutes for meat, he was always impressed with Gabrielle's cooking. He missed the roasts and gravies his mother used to make on Sundays, but Gabrielle had a knack with food. He picked up a tomato slice and popped it into his mouth, too hungry to wait until he'd pulled the chair out from the table.

He sat down and took a forkful of pasta salad. It had water chestnuts and tiny slices of onion, a creamy dressing with a hint of garlic and lime, and chopped pistachios. The only flaw on the plate was the apricot. He didn't want to think about why she'd included it. She knew how he felt about apricots. He set the fruit on the table and gobbled up the salad and tomatoes. When he was finished, he rinsed the plate and fork, dropped the apricot into the garbage under the sink, and pulled up the sides of the white trash bag. He yanked the plastic straps tight and looped them into a knot.

Stepping into the backyard, he was assaulted by the stench of rotting apricots. Despite nausea generated by the odor, he knew he should spend the afternoon picking the decayed fruit out of the grass and sealing it up in a garbage bag. He realized why it had struck him that Gabrielle was running the vacuum cleaner — when he'd come into the house the night before, he'd been overwhelmed with the scent of disinfectant, telling him she'd spent the day scrubbing bathrooms. He'd seen the tracks left by the wheels of the vacuum cleaner on the living room carpet. The whole house sparkled. Why was she vacuuming again? A shiver ran down his arms. He was very afraid for some reason he couldn't form into a coherent thought. Right now might be the best time to get going on ridding the yard of the offensive smelling apricots.

He went around to the side yard, dropped the kitchen garbage into the trashcan, and went back into the house. He pulled two trash bags from the box under the sink. He put one into the garbage can and took the other out to the back yard. With a few violent shakes, the bag billowed open. After studying the shiny flesh of the rotten apricots, he went back into the house and pulled a plastic sandwich bag out of the drawer. He slid it over his hand like a mitten. The bag insulated him from the goop, but he was still queasy as he crouched under the first tree, scraping fruit off the blades of grass. The thin plastic did not protect his fingers from the slippery consistency. He cursed Gabrielle for not cleaning up the mess. She was the one that wanted to keep the trees. She loved picking the fruit, eating the fruit, and figuring out more unappetizing ways to serve it. Every summer, she preserved it and produced endless jars of jam. People at church seemed to enjoy receiving a jar at Christmas, so that was good. But in the meantime, he had to watch it drop all over the lawn and smell the decay. If he had his way, they'd uproot the trees and plant something fruitless.

When he finished, he peeled the slimy sandwich bag off his hand and dropped it into the garbage bag. He tied it closed and disposed of the entire mess, pushing away the prick of guilt as he walked past the yard waste bin where the fruit should have been deposited.

Between golf and bending over the apricots in the heat, the energy had drained from his body. A nap would be just the thing to get his strength up to listen to Gabrielle. If he had more than one day off a week, life wouldn't feel like such a treadmill. He'd have time to enjoy her company. She really could be fun. Their intermittent love-making had created some kind of sexual obsession in her. It was his own fault that things had deteriorated to this point.

The house was silent. After the bright sun, the kitchen appeared dark, and it took a moment for his eyes to adjust. He stepped into the hallway. The only sound was the hum of the kitchen clock that seemed to be audible from one end of the house to the other when no other noises were competing with it. He peered into Peter's room. Peter and Gabrielle were asleep on the floor. Peter's head was tucked up next to his mother's shoulder. They looked like two angels, fallen out of heaven. How could he think she was impossible? He underestimated the amount of energy Peter demanded. She made it all look so easy. He really did love her. She looked so sweet, lying on the floor with her eyes closed, all the fire in her body subsided. Having a wife was a good thing. A family. He'd always wanted a family, hadn't he? Didn't everyone?

HE WAS AWAKENED from his nap by water running full blast, pounding into the tub in the hall bathroom. The searing odor of bleach wafted into the bedroom. He struggled to the edge of the mattress and raised himself to a sitting position. His head ached. The thought of asking Gabrielle why she was cleaning, again, the promise of a stonily silent dinner, and the effort of projecting a cheerful tone for Peter, rushed at him in dark waves. Why was she so angry? She'd known what she was getting into when she married him — the job of being a minister's wife. It was like a full time, unpaid job, but she'd seemed eager to build a life around the church. Hadn't she?

When he wasn't overtired, he loved his work. He liked the stimulation of a schedule packed with people, the challenge of helping them find God's peace, planning events, and studying and teaching. He felt alive when he counseled a couple about financial problems or stumbling blocks in their marriage, and they took his advice. There was no greater feeling than receiving praise for providing new insights or shifting a mood from despair to hope.

He rarely found the right words for Gabrielle. Not that she asked his advice. She didn't respect his spiritual authority and knowledge. Her themes of taking second place to the church and not having enough sex never varied. Who defined *enough*? In all the marital counseling sessions he'd conducted, he'd never encountered a woman who wanted sex with such ferocity. It had been months since he'd been given an opportunity to slip away to the bathhouse where he could meet a man trapped in circumstances similar to his own, occasionally a man who was free from the agony of living two distinct lives.

In all fairness to Gabrielle, getting married hadn't been the best decision of his life. But at the time, he'd thought God might miraculously alter his desires. Or that God was at least on his side, that He understood and accepted the situation. The last thing he'd expected was a woman who put sex at the top of her priority list. No matter what his self deceits were, he knew that wasn't normal. Especially for a woman who was supposed to be glowing in the reflection of her new child.

His thoughts were broken by the sound of a large quantity of water slopping onto the floor. Pushing away the clogged feeling in his head, he hurried to the bathroom door. She'd poured half a bucket of water on the linoleum. It moved ominously toward the carpet. The bleach stung his nostrils. "What are you doing?"

She looked up. Her eyes were red and teary from the fumes. "What does it look like? Cleaning the bathroom."

"The bleach is going to get into the carpet. And what if Peter comes wandering in? Move over, and I'll help you mop it up."

"No! I have to do this myself."

"What?"

"I need to do it myself."

He didn't want to understand what she meant. "Mop it up! Now."

Water undulated closer to the metal strip separating the linoleum from the carpet. He grabbed the mop out of her hand and began pushing the water back toward the center of the room. Gabrielle wrenched the mop away from him. She wrung it into the tub and pushed the pool of water toward the side wall. The puddle was still thick. He opened the cabinet, grabbed three pale green towels, and threw them onto the floor.

"You're ruining our towels. Get out of here! I said I have

to do this myself. It's my role as the woman to keep our home pure, and I have to cleanse the impurities myself, or it won't mean anything."

"I have no idea what you're talking about."

"Just go away. Take Peter to the park. Dinner will be ready when you come home."

"Let me help clean up this mess."

"Leave me alone." Her voice was softer, almost a whisper.

He backed out of the doorway and went into Peter's bedroom. He didn't want to think about what was happening and what it might mean for his ministry. What it would mean for his son, so young and malleable, looking to his parents as if they were gods. This was his punishment for misinterpreting God's will. He was stuck with a woman who was gradually losing her mind. Half the things she said made no sense. And when he asked for an explanation, he got more senseless words or a terrifying barrage of anger.

It wasn't until he was pushing Peter in the swing that Mark thought about how he'd obediently trotted down the hall, scooped up his son, plopped him into the stroller, and hurried to the park. He'd darted away like a frightened squirrel. All that nonsense about purity probably came from those people at Gethsemane. She'd been teetering on the edge before, always wanting more, more, more. But she hadn't become completely incomprehensible until she hooked up with them. After she went to one of their prayer meetings, she would come home and sit in Allysan's car, sometimes for more than an hour, talking about God knew what.

He pushed Peter harder. Peter squealed.

He needed to put his foot down about the Gethsemane activities. Get her back with normal people, like Susan, and some of the other women with small children. Extremists were feeding her already unstable personality. He felt calmer. Was it really only a few hours since he'd been so satisfied with cleaning all the apricot goop out of his lawn? Only a few hours since he'd thought Gabrielle looked angelic?

When they returned from the park, the atmosphere inside the house was brittle with bleach and silence. The water was gone, and the bathroom floor glistened. He washed Peter's hands in the clean sink.

When he sat down at the table, a plate of flour tortillas was in the center, surrounded by bowls containing chopped tomatoes, slivers of red onion, shredded lettuce, pinto beans, grated cheddar cheese, and a creamy mountain of guacamole. Peter had a flour tortilla to gnaw on, little bits of tomato, and a cup of beans. Mark folded the beans and toppings into the tortilla and rolled it up. They ate in silence.

For the rest of the evening, Gabrielle behaved as if she were encased in thick plastic — playing with Peter, reading him stories, bathing him in the sparkling bathroom, and tucking him into bed with a flurry of kisses. Mark followed her around, useless. Trying to figure out where this dreamy, mechanical demeanor had come from and what it meant. Could a man have a nervous breakdown because his spouse turned into a different person every time he left the room? His nerves crackled like popcorn pinging off the sides of an aluminum pot, building into a mass of stiff, white stuff that left no room for air.

By nine-thirty, the kitchen was cleared, wiped, and mopped. Peter was sleeping peacefully. Mark sat on the futon, trying to decide whether he should go to sleep or watch some news. The pinging in his nerves had worn him out, but enough tension remained to convince him sleep would not come easily. At least Gabrielle had channeled her excess energy into something useful. The house looked great. He smiled. It might be pleasant if she had the same hyper mood tomorrow and drilled it into the weeds that had popped up along the back fence. He reached to the end table for the remote. He pressed the power button and felt a wave of sludge pass out of his veins. The images on the screen didn't require anything beyond idle curiosity. He could watch the parade of stories about fires and crimes and political shenanigans. These would be followed by stories of people whose problems were heaped higher than any human could seem to bear. The news put his frustrations into perspective. He didn't have insurmountable physical handicaps. He didn't have astronomical bills he couldn't hope to pay or trouble with a faceless bureaucracy that refused to listen to reason. His house hadn't burned to the ground.

Suddenly, Gabrielle was standing in front of the TV, her hair hanging in clumps around her slack arms. Her expression was blank. Her skin and lips were so pale, the only color on her face came from her greenish eyes. The glow of the screen shone through the space between her arms and waist, back-lighting the upper half of her body.

"Are you going to ignore me and the problems in our marriage forever?"

A pain shot through his neck. His eyes felt full of sand. She turned and flicked off the TV, twirling back to face him as if performing some kind of life-destroying dance. Anyone would agree that it would be perfectly reasonable if he pointed out that he was watching the news. A normal person also would have asked her to move the moment she stepped in front of the screen. For that matter, a normal person wouldn't have a wife who...he interrupted his own thoughts. What was the point? She'd decided now was the time to speak her mind, and there was nothing he could do about it. Thinking about normal behavior was counter-productive.

"Well?" she said. "You won't even answer my question? That's how unimportant I am?"

"What do you want? I tried to talk to you this afternoon. Twice. You told me to leave you alone. You ordered me out of the house."

"That shows how clueless you are if you think we can talk about these problems when our son is awake and listening. Look how he was during dinner. Not a sound. He knows something's wrong."

"Okay. Fine. Come sit down and tell me what you want to

talk about." He swallowed a yawn.

"Don't tell me to sit down."

"It's a little hard to talk with you standing across the room."

She didn't move. The desire to yawn became more pressing. He couldn't speak another word unless he allowed his body to release its weariness with a long, lung filling yawn. It was nearing ten o'clock. All day. She'd had all day, yet she'd waited until now to start a conversation that was sure to last for an hour or more. "Please," he said. "Please sit down." The whining in his voice filled him with disgust.

She looked like a child, with her thin body, her tangled hair. Yet here he was, a full-grown man, an educated man with the respect of a large community of intelligent, God-fearing people, trembling in front of this fragile girl. What an illusion — she was anything but fragile. Even her physical strength amazed him, but her psyche was so much more powerful than his own, he felt like he was in the presence of a force beyond the human realm.

"Maybe we should go into the bedroom." Her voice had a mocking quality. "That's where we have all our fights."

"We don't have to fight."

"You live your life as if I don't exist. You're trying to squash me into some paper doll minister's wife who doesn't require any attention or have any needs. You want to eat away at my spirit until I'm nothing. Of course you don't want to fight. You want me to shut up and meekly appear whenever it's convenient for you, carrying your adorable child. You want your devoted parishioners, your suburban house, your landscaped yard, your brilliant son, and cute wife. All you want are possessions to make you look good, and I'm just one more thing — at the bottom of the list. I'm not even a human being to you. I'm certainly not your wife in the way I'm supposed to be. You don't tell me your feelings. I know nothing about what you do all day. You keep secrets about your job, and I don't know who your friends are. You care nothing about what I'm thinking, and you don't need my body."

He laced his fingers together behind his neck, pulling his hands forward to relieve the pressure building at the base of his skull. His pipe would be nice right now, but getting up and going into the backyard was out of the question. Thinking about his pipe made him ache for it. In some ways, she was right. He even needed the pipe more than he needed her. Graceful, slow-moving smoke, escaping through his lips, the earthy scent, the feel of the stem between his teeth. He took his hands out from behind his neck and lifted his left leg, so it was crossed at an angle over his right knee. He cupped his hands around his kneecap. "I don't know what to say."

"That's obvious."

"Won't you please come sit down so we can have a calm conversation?"

"You mean, won't I come sit down so you can feel more in control? You don't like sitting over there like we all have to sit and listen to you? Every week I sit there quietly while you stand above me and tell me what God wants me to do. Well, I don't need you to tell me what He thinks anymore. I've started listening to God myself. And it's been quite a revelation."

"Why don't you tell me about it."

She tossed her head, sending her hair flying off her shoulders. Her limp arms remained at her sides like half-cooked spaghetti. Why couldn't she put her hands on her hips — a natural pose for an argument?

"You sound so superior when you talk like that. I hate it. Do you talk that way to people when they come to see you in your office? I guess not because they keep coming. Floods of them wanting their pastor. Making you a substitute for God."

He'd already forgotten what he'd said to prompt that comment, so he kept quiet.

"They're all screwed up. Asking another person to tell you what God wants doesn't work. I asked Susan. When I told her you never touched me, that I felt like I was living in the middle of the desert, needing sex or I would die, do you know what she said? As if it was *God's* idea? Implying it was God's will for me?"

It was pointless to say anything. She had some unknowable destination, and all he did by trying to make it a two-way conversation was prolong the trip to wherever she was headed. He shifted, stretching his arm across the back of the futon, trying to steady himself.

"Susan's brilliant insight into God's will for me was that He should meet my needs. She thought I should *hand it over*, that's what she said — *hand it over to God*. He would satisfy my desire!"

"Don't yell at *me*. She's the one who said it." It seemed so long since he'd tried that himself — handing it over. It was easy to choose a few random verses, tie them together into a neat package of guarantees. Then, *Voila!* God would either remove or fulfill the desire. It hadn't worked for him. He completely understood her frustration.

"You're my husband! You're supposed to want me. And instead, my best friend tells me I'm the one with a problem for wanting *you*, for wanting to feel your body, wanting to be touched. *I'm* the one who's supposed to yield to God? Like I'm supposed to have an affair with a Spirit? I need real hands, I need real skin touching mine!" Her voice rose with each sentence until she sounded like she was sobbing, but there were no tears.

If she would just cry, she might feel better. She let all this pressure build inside her, and she never cried. Always, her reaction was fury.

"I can't make God my lover! And the thing He revealed to me, in a dream I had, is…well, never mind about that. It's sickening to have to beg you to make love to me. I feel like I'm repulsive. You have no right to make me feel that way."

Her words sucked at his brain like leeches. There was no telling what wild ideas she would come up with if she believed her dreams were infallible revelations. He was very nervous. He felt the leeches sucking harder, pulling his brain out of shape, making it difficult to think, as if there were gouges where brain matter had been devoured. "A dream? What kind of dream? God doesn't speak to people in dreams."

"He did in the Bible."

"He doesn't do that in modern times."

She lunged toward the coffee table. He yanked his arm off the back of the futon and pulled into himself. She stopped a few feet away and grabbed her always present Bible off the table. A table that normally had tiny oily prints from Peter's hands along the edges. Today it glowed. It didn't even look as if there was a child living in the house. Looking around, he noticed the whole room had taken on that appearance. Cleaner than it had been before they had a child.

"How do you know He doesn't speak in dreams? You've put everything into a tiny box and made God a spectator."

She must be quoting Allysan or someone else from that church.

"God has revealed some very interesting things to me, and if you'll stop interrupting me and acting so superior, I'll tell you. One thing that's been revealed is that Grace is a church without any spirit. We go through the motions, we read prayers out of books, and we sing songs that march through the verses in the same order every time. There's no worship. It's just a ritual that makes everyone think they've done their duty. They're missing the whole point."

He wasn't going to debate church doctrine with her. It frightened him that she might start mentioning these heretical views to people at church. It was one thing to think his wife might be unbalanced, but another thing entirely if his parishioners recognized it. His flock, his taskmasters, ultimately and always, his employers.

Her nostrils were pinched, her face whiter than ever. Her eyes were large shadowy sockets, and he could hardly see the iris. "I'm getting off the subject."

He couldn't disagree with that.

"God doesn't expect me to make Him my lover. I was created with these desires. He made me appealing to men. He's shown me that something evil has come into our home. It's blinding you to my beauty and milking you of all desire so that you're turning into a shell of a man. He told me to clean the house, scrub it from top to bottom, and I did. Then He told me to clean it again."

"You're telling me that God directed you to clean the entire house every day? Do you hear how crazy you sound?"

"You can make fun of it all you want. I know it was God. I've been spending a lot of time in prayer. And I fasted. At that time, God didn't speak to me. After the fast was over, though, He showed me the need to clean. To wipe out the evil forces that are trying to take you away from me, the ugly, vicious demons that make you reject me. See, there's no spirit in the way you lead the church, and there's no spirit in our marriage. The spirit is our desire for each other. Our passion. I have it, but you don't. I fasted and prayed and asked for a vision."

Mark put his face in his hands. The tips of his fingers were hard and cold. The sucking sensation in his head continued to increase. He'd worried she suspected he was attracted to men, but his problem was much bigger. In one step, she had moved from the edge of religious fanaticism over the precipice where she was now dangling by her fingertips. He didn't want to think about what it would take to snap the threads holding her in place.

"Don't hide your face from me. You act like you have the burden of the entire world on your back. Sit up and look at me. Talk to me."

"How can I talk? Before I can get my thoughts together, you launch into another subject. Your thoughts are like heroin racing through a junkie's blood vessels." He was pleased with his illustration. He might want to make a note of it for use in a sermon or an article for the newsletter.

She slurped air into her lungs, inflating the entire cavity of her torso. Slowly she let the air escape between her teeth. Such small, perfect teeth, forming a sweet smile on the occasions when she decided to use it. He could hardly remember what her smile looked like. Unrestrained, bursting with energy and delight. Now, she looked ill. Her body was gaunt. Her large round breasts that had lingered for a short time after she'd weaned Peter were gone, withered into pods, barely visible under the baggy blue tee shirt with faded white lettering, announcing the tour of some country-western group she used to adore. Tan knit shorts sagged around her legs, brushing delicately against the long, thin muscles of her thighs. Her knees were gray from crawling around the floors.

"I don't even know what we're talking about. I'm assuming it's the same old thing."

"It is not the same old thing. We're talking about new revelations. We're talking about the emptiness in this marriage."

"To me, it is the same old thing. You pick the worst possible time — I'm tired, ready to crash, and suddenly we're going to talk about our relationship. And it's always about sex."

"That's because there's never a good time!" She leaned forward and grabbed the edges of the coffee table. She gave it a hard shake. "You tell me when it's a good time. Tell me when you're not tired. Never. You're always exhausted, always thinking about someone else. I'm single-handedly holding this family together. I'm caring for our child and our home, and as if I'm not doing enough, God has shown me I also have to rid our home of evil spirits. When the widow lost the coin, she swept the house from top to bottom, looking for it."

"That has absolutely nothing to do with this. The point of that story is…"

"Don't preach to me. You take all those stories at face value. There are hidden messages."

Was it his imagination that the glass door vibrated from the intensity of her voice? She no longer seemed concerned whether Peter heard them. He dug the heels of his hands into the edge of the futon and pushed himself forward. There had to be a way to get her calmed down. Movement would make something happen. Free him from this trapped feeling, weak in the face of her fury. "Okay. I'm sorry." He half stood up.

"Don't get up. You're not leaving this room."

He settled back. Although she was still too loud, her voice didn't have the frantic edge that infected it when she thought she was quoting God.

"You stay where you are. I'll show you what I'm talking about as if you didn't know. But if you want to pretend. If you want to act like you're so innocent, go right ahead. I'll show you in just a minute. But don't you move off that couch."

She whirled around. Her hair flew out in tangled cords, her t-shirt billowed like a parachute. She darted up the stairs. A puff of air came out of his lungs. He hadn't noticed he was holding in all that oxygen, waiting for something he couldn't predict. His heart fluttered like it couldn't quite regain its regular beat, forcing him to take another deep breath. This time he let it out carefully, and his heart slowed to a steady rhythm.

Gabrielle ran back down the hall, leaping past the steps into the living room, landing on the floor with a thud. She grabbed her Bible and flung it open. She flipped through the pages, from the center toward the beginning of the book. The onion skin paper rattled in her hands, and she shook the pages off as they stuck to her fingers. She stopped near the front so that the bulk of the Bible lay toward her right, and just a few pages floated on the left. He tipped his head to peer curiously at the page she had been looking for. It was the book of Exodus.

"The ten commandments, in case you're wondering. Although you ought to know what I was looking for. How stupid do you think I am? You're always preaching at me, always telling me how to interpret the Bible. Acting like you're so important because you have degrees, and I don't. I'm not as stupid as you think. Not when it comes to the important things, like knowing when I'm being lied to. Like knowing my husband should be craving my body, not trying to find ways to work longer hours. I know what's going on, Mark."

She opened her clenched fist and dropped three square packets onto the Bible. At first, in the dim light, he wasn't sure what they were. He leaned forward. He stared as if he might decode a hidden message in the way the packages had fallen. His brain felt as if it had been dropped into a bucket of dry ice. He had to say something. He wanted to make it clear. But he didn't have the courage to probe even the tip of a finger at the flaming aura around her.

Defending himself in his own mind had been easy, he'd done it for years. But thinking of how the words would sound spoken aloud for the first time was terrifying. The confidence that God accepted even allowed his feelings for men, seemed clear and well thought out. But how would that belief sound in the stillness of the living room? How would those ideas land on Gabrielle's ears? They would sound ridiculous. Without even trying them out, he knew that. Not because they didn't make sense, but because he could see her throw her head back. He could see her long white neck stretching out. See her mouth open wide, shouting, *Ha!* Then, she would follow with...something. He realized he didn't know what she'd say. Never, in all this time, had he seriously considered telling her of his attraction to men. And in his blind arrogance, he hadn't rehearsed the conversation, like he might rehearse a sermon, picturing her in front of him, imagining how she might respond. It never crossed his mind to plan for a day like this. In fact, that's why he'd been too casual with the condoms. What a fool he was for keeping them where she might find them. A fool for even bringing them into the house.

Was it possible to convince her they were there for a legitimate reason? The fact that he hadn't hidden them spoke in his favor. Any sensible person, trying to keep something hidden, wouldn't leave them in such an obvious place. Of course, she might stumble across them at some point. How could you not stumble across the hygienic belongings of the person with whom you shared a tiny, four-foot by six-foot bathroom seven days a week?

Birth control sometimes failed. He would tell her the condoms were for them. Extra protection. One method fails, and the backup method kicks in. He was so pleased with his solution, he almost smiled. She hadn't found a thing. His private life was still between him and God. He pressed his lips together, forcing the smile back into his throat.

"Obviously, you have nothing to say for yourself."

He raised his head and looked at her. The specter that had loomed over him, pushing against the walls and the sliding glass door, was gone. He was eager to see the shocked look on her face when he explained why he'd purchased them. For a moment, he was sad, a little ashamed, that he was so good at lying. It was sad that he had to lie to his wife. He'd started out wanting it to be different. Somehow. Although he'd never really thought that through either. There were too many things to keep in check.

"Tell me," she said, "Tell me your affair is not with one of the women from church. Not with someone I know. And at least...at least admit you understand what I'm saying about the invasion of something evil into our lives."

He jerked his head back. The fear that she'd discovered he was gay had so consumed him, it hadn't occurred to him she might draw another, more obvious conclusion. "Oh, no. How could you think that?" He stood and moved around the coffee table, reaching to take her in his arms. He had one hand on her waist before she moved back, flinging his arm away from her like it was a snake.

"I don't want you to hold me out of pity. Get away from me."

He risked a step closer.

She backed away.

"I'm not having an affair. You're the only woman I love."

"I don't believe you. God revealed it to me. The condoms prove it."

He stayed where he was. "I bought them for us." The lie dragged across his throat like thick mucous. What had seemed brilliant in his thoughts was leaden when he spoke. It sounded like a lie to him, and it was degrading to her. In spite of all her complaints that he thought she was stupid, he didn't. She was smart. She didn't deserve this, but he didn't have any other choice. "I'm afraid. When we have sex…"

"That's a joke. We don't even *have sex*, as you so romantically put it. We don't make love. And the diaphragm is perfectly safe. Don't make stupid excuses."

"But it can fail. I've been worried, so I decided to buy some. I don't want to take any chances." He finished meekly, as flaccid as he felt after their infrequent rounds in bed.

She backed slowly across the room. She kept her eyes on his. She didn't blink or brush the strand of hair off her face where it hung, playing across her lips when she talked. She stopped when she was standing near the steps that led up to the dining area. "Don't talk to me about birth control and making love. Don't you dare try to touch me or hug me. I know you're having an affair. And I better not find out you've humiliated me in front of the whole church. The truth will come into the light. I've cleansed the house, and I know my heart is pure."

"Gabrielle, listen to me. I'm not having an affair. There isn't any woman who could even come close to you." That was true in more ways than one. He wasn't so blind that he couldn't see how beautiful she was, or she had been before she started starving herself. Men looked at her all the time. Even in church, he'd seen men's eyes dart in her direction.

"You're lying!"

He was safe. In spite of her supposed revelations, the truth was still hidden. Somehow he'd work his way around this. Confidence swelled inside him. Without the immediate fear of his secret being discovered, he was filled with a strange peace. It was the trust in his own ability to draw her back over to rational thinking. "I hope I can find a way to show you it's all in your mind."

"God will punish you, Mark. Just wait and see. I know He will. You not only betrayed me, now you won't even give me the dignity of talking about it honestly. God will punish you."

Twelve

THE VIBRATING CELL PHONE woke Gabrielle. She'd turned off the sound but forgotten to lower the volume. It sounded like a bee the size of her fist, beating its wings and humming within inches of her ear. She vaguely remembered murmuring to Mark that he should take Peter with him to church because she needed to sleep. She grabbed the phone — a missed call from Susan. She stumbled out of bed, tripping as her foot caught the sheet and dragged it over the side. Her brain was fuzzy. After Mark had gone to bed, she sat in the rocking chair and drank two glasses of wine.

She staggered down the hall to the kitchen, resisting the urge to collapse on the living room floor, letting sleep once again take her safely away from the swollen feeling in her chest. The condoms were proof that Mark was having sex with someone else, and still, he'd refused to give her the courtesy of admitting the truth.

His arrogance was unbelievable. He'd brushed aside her

revelations like they were nonsense.

The phone vibrated with a message. She pressed the play button. Susan's voice was hoarse. "Hi." She paused. "Please don't be mad at me. Can't we patch things up? I'm not even sure what I did. I guess you think I was out of line to give advice on your..." She paused again. "Can I come over? The kids would love to see each other. Call me."

Gabrielle made a clucking sound with her tongue. She yanked the tea kettle off the back burner. She held a yellow plastic funnel in the mouth of the kettle, poured bottled water into it, and turned on the gas. She took hold of the counter edge in front of the sink and lowered herself into a plié. She held the flexed position for several seconds. She did seventy-five more pliés until the kettle began to hiss. She pulled a bag of cinnamon tea out of the tin and dropped it into a mug, managing eight more pliés before the kettle let out its piercing whistle. While the tea steeped, she touched her toes, stretched her arms over her head, and twisted to both sides. She felt her blood was starting to flow normally.

The awful night was behind her. It was time to ask God what He wanted her to do now. Before she could even think of calling Susan, she'd read a few Bible passages and spend some time praying, searching for the right course of action. She had a vague memory of promising to pick Peter up at noon, but what did it matter? Mark could wait. It was more important that she clear her head and make sure she was heading in the direction God had ordained.

She took her tea into the living room, sat on the floor, and crossed her legs at the ankles. Dragging her Bible onto her lap, she blew on the hot, cloudy surface of the tea and set the mug carefully on the carpet. She settled her back against the front edge of the futon, anxious and excited to see what message would be given to her this morning. When you knew, absolutely *knew,* and believed that God was going to give a personal message through those delicate pages, the whole book took on a new significance. She stroked the comforting leather. Even though some poor animal had given its life for this, she loved the texture. The heft of the thing thrilled her. She opened to the book of Philippians. The words at the top of the page drew her attention — *I urge Euodia, and I urge Syntyche to live in harmony…*She slammed the Bible closed. The instructions couldn't be more clear. She wasn't meant to read any further. It was right there in a single sentence — it was meant for her and Susan to become friends again. No matter how unspiritual Susan was. No matter how pig-headed and self-satisfied Susan was, God wanted Gabrielle to rebuild their friendship. Susan had been her first true friend, probably the only true friend in her adult life.

The sun, beating through the glass door, filled her with ecstasy. God was letting His presence fill her living room, with its tired carpet and mismatched furniture.

She needed to call Susan right this instant. It was somewhat disappointing that she hadn't received a message about Mark's cheating and lying, but it was too upsetting to think about him. If she followed the instructions she was given, it would open the door for God to perform a miracle with Mark. There couldn't be any roadblocks on her part, any unspiritual attitudes to create an open wound where evil spirits could further insert their hooks.

She took a long, slurping sip of tea. The cinnamon filled her mouth and sinuses with a calming fragrance that made her feel alive. She carried the mug into the kitchen, picked up her phone, and pressed *return call.*

Susan answered.

"Sure," Gabrielle said as if the conversation had continued unbroken.

Susan followed her lead, an easy rhythm developed through years of friendship. "What time would be good?"

"Peter's at church with Mark. I just got up."

"Wow. How nice."

"It would have been, but I was awake until three this morning."

"Is Peter sick?"

"No."

Susan didn't push. "I can drop by the church and pick him up for you."

"Would you? Thanks, that's a huge help." The warm, trusting feeling spread further. She should value Susan more. It was just hard not to be angry at someone who flaunted the very thing Gabrielle was deprived of. She shoved that thought aside. "I'll tell Mark you're stopping by. See ya'." She paused for a few seconds. "It'll be nice…to get together." She felt exposed. But the peaceful feeling swelled — her reward for humbling herself.

After they disconnected, she stood at the back door and drank the rest of her tea, looking across the patio at the thick, wet shade of the apricot trees. The grass was matted, badly in need of a mowing. Just like their marriage. Invasive weeds were out of control. Tomorrow. She would take care of it tomorrow. And clean the kitchen, maybe the garage too.

She took a shower, made the bed, and called Mark to let him know Susan was picking up Peter. After that, she wandered up and down the hall. Her mind was wiped clean. She was calm, but deep beneath the smooth surface, something gnawed at her. What was it? Maybe she should be making lunch. It was almost noon. She strolled into the kitchen. It seemed darker than usual. No direct sunlight was coming in at this hour, and all the lights were off. Everything looked unfamiliar. She glanced toward the family room area, her attention landing on Mark's desk, almost hidden by even darker shadows in that corner of the room. It was a mess. How had she missed his desk in her cleansing efforts? Maybe the areas she'd neglected were the cause of his refusal to admit to his affair.

Hadn't the message clearly told her she was to clean absolutely everything? No corner was to go untouched. The kitchen cabinets hadn't been cleaned out and washed, but his desk was the worst offense of all. There were stacks of credit card statements and bill stubs that needed filing and a pile of magazines in danger of sliding over the edge. Dust coated the screen of the computer he hardly used, preferring pen and paper for his sermon preparation. A dirty coffee cup sat next to the magazines, and pages of sketches and hand-written notes stuck out from the centers of five or six books stacked on top of each other.

She'd get to work the minute Susan left, while Peter was down for his nap. By next weekend, everything would be in order. Then she could relax and wait for the Spirit to compel Mark to do his part. No wonder things hadn't gone well last night. Her cleaning had been slipshod. She drifted to the sliding glass door and opened it. The scent of warming grass pushed against the screen. It would be better for the house to be closed up, keeping out the heat as long as possible. But she needed the burning heat to come inside, eating up whatever dank things lurked out of sight. She closed her eyes and breathed in the smells from the back yard. Bees hummed around the Pyracantha bushes that lined the back fence.

She opened her eyes. She needed to figure out what she could serve for lunch. Susan wouldn't be particular. What was it like, to not care so intensely? What was it like to let life wash over your shoulders? Susan stood there, not trying, and the heavens opened up, pouring money, children, and a lustful husband into her arms. She didn't have to grasp for anything.

Gabrielle opened the refrigerator and grabbed a bottle of water. She took a long drink. Unkind thoughts kept pushing their way into her mind. She didn't know how to be rid of them, and it seemed like a lot of work to keep fighting them. Why did it have to be so difficult? Why was everything so easy for Susan and so hard for her? She pulled open the vegetable drawer. There was a plastic bag full of mushrooms she'd forgotten about. They were a little dark and damp for a salad, but she could make mushroom risotto out of a box from the health food store. The moderately fresh mushrooms would make it tastier. A side of wheat bread would satisfy everyone.

When they sat down for lunch, Susan complimented the risotto. Peter fed himself, leaving a smear of creamy white dotted with bits of risotto across his cheeks. Cara removed all the mushrooms and lined them around the edge of the plate-like discarded buttons.

After Gabrielle washed Peter's face and rinsed the dishes, she and Susan settled on the back lawn under the apricot trees. Cara and Peter climbed into his sandbox. While Susan fed Sam, Gabrielle inched her way toward the vegetable garden, plucking out the weeds that were within easy reach. She could listen to Susan and work toward total cleansing at the same time. She dug her fingers into the dirt, gently probing for a secure grip on the roots of a weed. "So, I have a question," she said.

"Mmm?"

"What was all that about being invasive when we were giving the visitation reports the other night?"

Susan was silent.

"You know, when you freaked out about whatever Victoria Latimer said."

"I don't want to get into that."

"What's the big deal? Since when are you too pure to gossip?"

"It wasn't the gossip. It was just…"

"Come on. Tell me. No wonder we feel alienated from each other. We never talk, never say what's going on. If it bugged you, why can't you tell me about it?"

Susan lifted Sam to her shoulder and thumped his back. She sighed. "Victoria won't come to church because she got angry at my father and never got over it. Okay? I didn't want to say something negative about him in front of everyone."

Gabrielle sidled to the next row. She plucked out two weeds. "What was she mad about?"

"She was married to someone else before Charlie. Since he grew up there, Charlie really wanted to get married at Grace. My father wouldn't perform the wedding. He told her what the Bible says about divorce, that they would be committing adultery for the rest of their lives."

"How awful."

Susan slapped Sam's back too hard, and he spewed formula on her shoulder. She moved him onto her lap, ignoring the mess. "See. That's why I didn't want to talk about it. My father was firm in his beliefs, and most people can't handle that. I don't want to hear him criticized for not being afraid to speak the truth. And it's not awful. It's true. A lot of people want to ignore that. He was just standing up for his principles. For God's Word." She pulled the cloth off her shoulder and rolled it into a tube, hiding the spit up.

"But to tell someone they're committing adultery for the rest of their lives? Refuse to marry them? It sounds like something from the middle ages. It's creepy."

"It is not. That's what the Bible says. Divorce is a slap in God's face. People should stay together and work things out. They give up too easily. No marriage is perfect, you learn to care for the person and work around your problems."

"Maybe some problems are too big to work around."

"I don't believe that."

Gabrielle stood and brushed pebbles and dirt off her knees. She stomped her feet to get the blood flowing back through her calves and ankles. "Why don't we go inside and have a glass of water. Or I can make lemonade. It's getting too hot out here."

"That's because you're crawling around like a madwoman. Can't you let a few weeds grow for now? It's not like your plants are so small they'll get choked out."

"I hate weeds."

"Okay. Relax. It's just that it's so hot, I don't think you need to do it right this minute. Especially when we're trying to talk."

Gabrielle walked toward the patio. She stopped and looked back, waiting for Susan to follow.

Susan stood up, jostling the baby's head. He started to whimper. She rubbed his fuzzy head and kissed his nose.

"Come help me clean up Mark's desk."

Susan followed her to the back door. "Why would I want to clean Mark's desk? I'm not sure why you think I'd want to help you clean anything, but definitely not that. That's his space."

"It's a mess. And it's just a desk." Gabrielle flung open the screen door and stepped into the house. She walked over to the desk. She wadded her hair in her hands, twisted it into a coil, and stuffed the ends inside. "There, that feels better." She moved the coffee cup and flung the magazines onto the floor. She yanked open the drawer at the bottom, filled with cardboard folders hanging on a metal frame. She flicked her fingers over the folders, pushing them to the front until she found one labeled *bills to pay*. She scooped up the pile of unopened envelopes and stuffed them in the folder.

"I don't want to help you clean," Susan said. "And it looks awfully like snooping. A pastor's desk is sacred."

"It's a mess. You can see that." Gabrielle knelt in front of the open drawer and started tucking papers back into the folders where they'd inched their way out of place.

Susan stepped toward the back door and called through the screen, "Let's go, Cara. We need to get home." Peter started to scream.

"Peter still wants to play," Gabrielle said. "Don't yank her away like that. This thing is a mess. Mark used to be so neat, I don't know what's happened lately." She grabbed a fistful of folders and tossed them on the floor. "I can't stand this mess. It's all out of control."

"You're the one that's out of control," Susan said. "I don't know what's happening to you. I can't even talk to you anymore. When you're ready to act like a normal human being, call me." She strode to the front door, grabbed the baby's diaper bag, and slung it over her shoulder. Cara trotted after her, and they went out the door.

Peter howled as if he was in pain.

Gabrielle went outside. "Don't cry, honey. Susan's not feeling well. They'll come back another day." Peter cried louder, banging his bucket against the wood frame of the sandbox. "Stop that!" She lifted him onto her hip. He kicked his legs like he was trying to swim. She held him with a firm grip and carried him into the house. "I know what's wrong, my little man. You're late for your nap. It's off to bed with you."

His legs thrashed wildly against her right thigh as she took a bottle of water and poured a few inches into a cup. Still struggling to keep him from throwing himself off her hip, she snapped on the plastic sipper lid. She held the cup to his lips. He swung his head away from her. She put the cup into his hand. He flung it across the kitchen. It sailed through the doorway and into the hall.

"Well, that was a fine throw, but no water for you."

She strode down the hall, using all her strength to hold him firmly in place. She lifted him over the rail and laid him on his back. Peter stood up and grabbed the rail. He screamed louder, his face growing redder, tears billowing from his eyes.

"You'll just have to work it out. I know it's not your fault, honey boy. There's something wicked in this house. You take your nap, and I'll keep working to get rid of it. Don't you worry."

She pulled the blinds, twisting the wand to make the room semi-dark. She closed the door tightly and nearly ran back down the hall. She wiped up the spilled water and hurried to Mark's desk. She dumped the contents of the drawers on the floor and scooped the top clean. She wiped it carefully with a dust cloth, taking care to work around each knob. She dampened a paper towel, using it to clean out the grit in the drawers. She dragged the garbage can over and began tossing in pens that looked unattractive. Some were labeled with the names and addresses of funeral homes and hospitals — reminders of death and disease. She threw away paper clips and little scraps of paper with cryptic notes on them. She straightened the contents of the file folders and put them back into the drawer in alphabetical order.

It was interesting to read a few pages of his notes from counseling sessions. She couldn't tell who they were about. They must be old, surely he kept all his current things at the church. In fact, why was he keeping these? Pages of people's problems. Ugly things that shouldn't be inside their fortress. She shredded them into long strips, a few sheets at a time, and stuffed them into the garbage. The desk looked beautiful, the surface smooth and free of clutter. The drawers were tidy.

She should do the kitchen cupboards next, but the room had grown too hot. Her scalp and back were damp. The garage would be cooler. She tied the straps of the garbage bag into a knot. She put a fresh bag in the trash can and pulled a giant, black plastic trash bag out of the box under the sink. She hated contributing to landfills, but she couldn't think about that right now. There was no other way to entirely rid their home of every speck of dirt.

She went into the garage. Along the left side was a three-foot-high plywood shelf. Underneath was another row of shelving filled with neatly stacked boxes, all properly labeled. There was no need to get into that, but over the past year or so, everything they didn't want in the house had been piled, one item at a time, on the top shelf, until the stuff teetered dangerously. A jolt from the garage door slamming shut could send it all tumbling onto the gritty floor. She lifted down empty boxes and began to pull them apart, folding them flat, and stacking them behind her for storage on the rafters. Bags of Peter's baby clothes that she'd meant to sort stood shoulder to shoulder. She pushed them aside. Walking the length of the shelf, she tried to decide how best to organize it. Really, everything should come off so the top could be swept clean, but that was awfully ambitious for a hot afternoon, with dinnertime only a few hours away.

At the end of the shelf, near the garage door, Mark's bag

of golf clubs lay on its side. Next to the golf bag was a gas mask. She'd forgotten she had it. She held it to her face and breathed through the musty filter. When her father retired from the Navy, her mother had gone on a crusade to rid the house of everything that reminded her of the military — *I want every God-damned thing that makes me think of the US Navy out of this house! They stole my husband. They stole my life.* Gabrielle couldn't imagine what the gas mask was doing lying out on the shelf. Mark must have tossed it there when he was digging through one of the boxes on the lower shelves. She pushed it to the back.

The gas mask had been lying on top of Mark's golf shoes, which were encrusted with dried grass. That wasn't like him. Why wasn't he taking better care of them? His golf equipment used to be his pride and joy. She pulled the bag off the shelf and stood it upright on the floor next to her. Attached to the side was a small wire brush. She unhooked it and went to work brushing grass and dried clumps of dirt out from between the plastic spikes on the bottoms of his shoes. When they were clean, she stuffed them into the large side pocket of the golf bag. She flipped the face of one of the clubs. The bag wobbled ominously. Some of the clubs needed cleaning, but that would be going too far. Surely, evil spirits wouldn't infiltrate their house through the faces of golf clubs, would they? She didn't really know. The details of the cleansing were somewhat overwhelming. When she'd first received the message, she hadn't thought through all the implications of a house swept perfectly clean in every corner. She straightened the clubs. She was tempted to weed through those too. But that might be a mistake. There must be a reason he had so many.

A dirty white towel protruded from one of the pockets. She pulled it out. A handful of golf tees, a ball smudged with dirt, two crumpled napkins, and a book of matches fell onto the floor. She reached for the book of matches. Squinting at the label, although the printing was perfectly clear, she tried to picture Mark with his pipe. She couldn't recall the last time he'd smoked it. Did he smoke his pipe when he played golf? She wasn't sure. The matchbook was glossy red with black printing — *This 'n That Club*. Below the name was a phone number and a web address.

When did he go to a nightclub? They certainly didn't do that kind of thing together. Leaving the tees scattered on the floor, she went into the house and picked up her phone. She entered the number. Would a nightclub be open on a Tuesday afternoon? She didn't even know why she was calling. What would she say? It was crazy to ask if they'd seen her husband there with another woman. How would she describe him? And she had no idea what the woman looked like.

After four rings, a recorded message began. *Thank you for calling This 'n That! No one can take your call right now, but we'd love to have you join us for an evening or a late-night romp in a completely safe and healthy atmosphere at the South bay's premier gay bathhouse. We serve non-alcoholic beverages and...*

She ended the call and pressed the phone to her chest. She couldn't breathe. She put the phone on the counter and slid to the floor, her back against the cabinets. A knob pressed into her shoulder blade. Opening her hand, she saw that she'd crushed the matchbook. The pressure of her grip had left a red stain on her palm and the insides of her fingers.

Thirteen

THE ODOR OF FISH hit Mark like a mildewed blanket when he walked in the front door. It clung to the walls and draped itself over his face. The air seemed to contain the sweat of raw fish. After several days of ammonia and cleanser, it was a shocking change.

In the kitchen, Peter sat on the floor, banging a pot with a wooden spoon. His grin helped ease the aching deep inside Mark's ear from the clash of solid wood on stainless steel. "Gabrielle?"

The fish sizzled in the oven, and a covered pot sat on the stove. There were steamed green beans in a covered bowl, and the bottom of the sink was littered with the sliced off ends. He picked up several pieces with the long, grainy stems attached and dropped them into the trash. The room looked different, but he couldn't identify the change. He put his tablet case on the table, then thought better of it and carried it back out to the hall and set it by the front door. He turned the deadbolt. One less thing to think about later.

Where was she? He didn't like seeing Peter alone in the kitchen with the stove turned on. It didn't matter that the pot was tucked out of reach on the back burner. She couldn't know when Peter would take it into his head to start climbing. He went back into the kitchen and squatted next to Peter. "Hi, buddy. Give Daddy a hug." Peter hit the pot harder. He paused and wrapped one arm around Mark's neck, still clutching the wooden spoon. Mark held him for a long minute, squeezing more tightly than necessary. He wanted to collapse onto the floor and lie there, holding his child. It seemed as if a rush of forgotten plans flowed through Peter's small arms into the base of Mark's skull. What had happened to their vision for raising a well-nurtured child? Between the building program and the tension in their marriage, Peter was growing older every day under the semi-unconscious attention of his parents.

Peter struggled to end the hug. Mark kissed his cheek and let go. The banging resumed. Mark dug through the cabinet and pulled out a large plastic bowl. He set it in front of Peter. "Try this one." Peter hit the pot three times in quick succession.

Mark walked back into the entryway. Peter tried a single beat on the plastic bowl. The sound was almost soothing compared with the racket from the pot. Mark walked down the hall. "Gabrielle?" He stepped into Peter's room. "Gabrielle? Where are you?"

He turned and went past the open bathroom door. Their bedroom was also empty. The blue satin quilt lay precisely on the bed, six inches hanging over the foot and on each side. The pillows were lined up evenly along the headboard, plump and dignified. The floor was a fluffy sea of dark blue, recently vacuumed. The tops of their dressers were smooth, and most of the odds and ends that usually cluttered the surface were tucked out of sight. He walked back to the entryway. "Gabrielle?" Where the hell was she? He had a foolish urge to look inside the hall closet as if they were playing hide and seek.

He stepped down into the living room and walked to the screen door. A fly sat on the outside of the screen, waiting for him to open the door so it could slip into the house, unnoticed until they were eating dinner, or worse, lying in bed trying to sleep. Then it would start buzzing around, hiding when they switched on the light, taking off again the minute the room was dark. He pressed his face against the screen. Gabrielle was sitting under the apricot tree. She was staring at something in her hand, but the screen prevented him from seeing what it was. He raised his voice to carry across the yard. "What are you doing?"

She didn't answer. He sighed. Maybe she honestly hadn't heard him. He stepped up into the kitchen so he could outsmart the fly by letting himself out through the door from the dining area.

Now he noticed what had eluded him earlier when he'd felt

the room was different. The surface of his desk was empty. Magazines, bills, papers, even the cup that held pens, were gone. The wood gleamed. Sparks of irritation pricked at the back of his head. Normally he didn't let his desk get so messy, but things had been hectic. And on his day off, he'd been consumed with trying to steer a wide path around Gabrielle. He hadn't even thought about catching up on his reading or checking that he was on top of the bills. He rubbed his eyes. One thing at a time. He couldn't get distracted by the immaculate desk. He needed to know why his wife was sitting in the backyard as if she hadn't a thing in the world to do, while dinner cooked itself to death inside, and her son pounded his eardrums to a pulp with a wooden spoon. He opened the screen and stepped outside. "Gabrielle!"

She continued to stare at whatever was in her hand. He sharpened his tone. "Gabrielle! What are you doing?"

She looked up, moving her head slowly, making him feel as if he were watching her underwater. He wanted her to snap her head up, jump to her feet, suddenly realizing she'd left Peter alone in front of a hot stove, suddenly noticing she'd lost track of time. A tremor of fear ran through him. Gabrielle didn't care for seafood, and he couldn't imagine what had prompted her to choose it for dinner. There seemed to be a vast space from where he stood by the back door to the spot where she sat under the tree. She dropped what she was holding, and he saw that it was only a hard, green apricot that had fallen off ages ago. He pushed away anxious questions about why she was staring at a piece of fruit as if it held the secret of the universe. "What are you doing? Peter's alone in front of the stove."

Laboriously, she pushed herself up to her feet. She stretched her arms over her head and pointed her toes. He wanted to fly across the patio, grab her arm, and drag her into the house. He wanted to shake her and shout that she'd better get her act together, or they'd find a doctor to help her with whatever was making her crazy. Instead, he shoved his hands into his pockets. Just as forcefully, he pulled them out again, turned, and went into the house, convinced his authoritative move would shake her loose and compel her to follow him. Peter hadn't broken the rhythm of his drumming since Mark handed him the plastic bowl. He beat it with dull thuds, then switched his drumstick to the pot, grinning at the racket. Mark pulled the musical instruments out of Peter's hands and put them in the sink for washing.

"No!" Peter cried.

Mark picked him up and flung him halfway over his shoulder, so Peter was hanging upside down, facing his back. Peter giggled, and Mark dropped him a few inches lower. Then he pulled him back up into his arms.

The screen door scraped along the track. Gabrielle turned and closed the door carefully. He wanted to ask why they were eating fish on a scorching day when the heat had a way of making the smell more offensive. He wanted to know why she was sitting under the tree, wanted to know why she'd stripped his desk of everything he was working on. He clenched his jaw, forcing the questions down his throat. He put Peter on the floor. "Should I take him to wash his hands?"

"That would be helpful." Her words came out slowly, dreamily, and rose to linger in the steamy air hovering near the ceiling.

When he and Peter returned to the kitchen, the food was on the table. They ate, carefully putting food into their mouths, their eyes focused on their plates. The fish wasn't a type he recognized. He nibbled tiny bites. It was spicy, but the flesh had a slight jelly texture. He scooped large forkfuls of brown rice with each bite, and between the spices and the thick, chewy rice, managed to gag his way through it. He envied Peter, who got to eat cut up strawberries, steamed green beans, and a piece of bread. Never before had he longed for a vegetarian dinner like he did now. His haste at urging her into the house seemed misplaced. The fish might have fared better with a few more minutes in the oven.

"How do you like the catfish?" she said.

"It's not bad. I didn't know it was catfish. What kind of spices?" He wanted to keep talking, delay her response.

"Cajun. They did it at the market."

He was relieved and pleased with her pleasant, non-combative response. "I've never had catfish."

"It was the cheapest. It's garbage fish." She stood and

began clearing the table.

It was clear they were going to continue to argue about his supposed affair. Right now, he almost wanted to tell her the truth. All the tension and arguments were a result of his secret. Although she was off the mark with the details, the fact that she was suspicious of something she couldn't see, couldn't identify, was accurate. Telling her the truth might bring relief. But he couldn't. It wasn't possible. A man didn't tell his wife he'd married her, hoping God might change his desires. Or that God accepted the solution of his occasional, fleeting encounters with strangers.

Obviously, annoyed with his failure to take the bait from her comment about garbage fish, she turned on the faucet full force, sending water spraying across her arms, and splattering against the backsplash. A few drops hit the clean window and sat there like tiny jewels. "Damn," she said. "Now, I have to polish that window again." The water continued to gush out of the faucet. She began rinsing plates and standing them up in the dishwasher. She carried the fish pan to the sink. His stomach heaved as he watched soapy water fill the pan, causing the gray skin of the fish to float like something still living. She tipped the pan at a forty-five-degree angle and scraped at the glass with a metal spatula. The remains slithered into the sink.

Mark lifted Peter out of his high chair and took him to the bathroom to clean up his face and hands. Sand was crusted between Peter's toes. He called out to Gabrielle. "I'll give

Peter a bath."

After Peter's bath, Mark's gut felt somewhat more stable. A big cup of coffee might kill the rest of the unsettled feeling. The opposite end of the house was enveloped in silence. He peppered Peter with information, just to make noise while he carried him to the bedroom. "Clean pajamas will feel great," he said. He pulled cotton knit pants over Peter's legs. "When you're dressed, we'll build a block tower. Then I'll read you two stories."

For all his dreams of being more engaged and nurturing than his father had been, Gabrielle was the one who was always reading to Peter, playing with him, teaching him new words. She handled most of his physical needs. Mark felt as if he was intruding on her perfectly ordered world. It wasn't right that a father should feel excluded. But things would change. In another year or two, when Peter could talk and was more mobile, he would seek out his father.

After Peter was tucked into bed, Mark went into the living room. Gabrielle was seated on the futon. The lights were off. Her silent presence filled the room. A moth had managed to find its way inside. It beat its wings against the screen, trying to escape. They always wanted to come into the house, but it seemed it wasn't happy there after all.

"Peter wants to kiss you good night," he said.

She stood up and walked past him. Her hair brushed against the lower part of his arm. He shivered. Even though he knew it was her hair, it felt like the moth, tickling his dry skin with its fragile wings. After she passed, he stepped down into the living room. He turned on the light. The remote wasn't on the end table. He opened the drawer. She might have put it out of Peter's reach. The drawer was full of old church bulletins, coupons, and coasters. The remote was near the back. He pressed the power button, and a sitcom sprang to life. Before his finger could find the arrow to move to another channel, Gabrielle ran down the hall, into the living room, and over to where he stood.

"You're not watching TV. We need to talk."

As if he'd been caught sneaking a mid-day drink or indulging in some other vice, he fumbled for the power button. He placed the remote on the end table and settled onto the futon. She glided over, opened the drawer, picked up the remote, and dropped it inside. The irrational guilt returned. He felt as if she was dropping contraband into a garbage can. He expected her to brush her hands together and wipe them on her pants to remove the contamination. She moved across the room and sat in the rocking chair.

Now, the moth hugged the wall over the entrance to the kitchen. Moths sometimes sat for so long, it seemed as if they were dead. Then, without warning, they sprang to life and flew in your face. Brushing their silky wings across your skin, making you feel as if bugs were crawling all over your body, seeking a resting place on the back of your neck. He wanted the moth outside where it belonged. He wanted a normal life — watching TV with his wife by his side, his son falling into a peaceful sleep, without any thoughts of malevolent insects.

"I guess I was a fool," she said.

"Why's that?" The words would not have sounded any stiffer if she'd handed him a sheet of notes, saying, *Here's what you'll be saying in this evening's drama. For our entertainment tonight, we have Mark and Gabrielle. That's Gabrielle, not Gabby, Atwater. They'll be demonstrating their twisted wreck of a marriage. A minister and his wife sit in their living room for nightly arguments. Come, listen to them fight about sex, vegetarian food, and theology.*

"You know why."

"No, I don't."

"Don't lie to me."

"How can I lie when I don't know what the conversation is about?"

She rocked the chair. Back and forth, steady and rapid as his heartbeat. Her calf muscles tightened and stood out from the bone when she pushed back, her feet arched, her toes spread on the carpet. The chair came forward again, and her heels hit the floor, up and down in some weird dance. "You've made a fool of me. Or maybe you didn't have to. I'm so stupidly naïve, I never stopped to think about what it all meant. Now everything makes sense."

"Everything but you. I have no idea what you're talking about." As he said the words, something flicked at his forehead. He brushed at his face, but nothing was there. He ran his hand across the back of his neck. It came away with dead skin balled up in sweat.

"Quit fidgeting. That's how I know you're lying."

"Can you *please* tell me what you're talking about."

"I'm talking about this 'n that."

He said nothing. He refused to say another word until she got to the point. He was sick and tired of her games, her mysterious comments suggesting he was supposed to read her mind.

She stopped rocking. The refrigerator hummed. The moth still clung to its spot. More than anything, he wanted to get up and fix the screen. It would be terrible if more moths joined that one, covering the walls, waiting for their opportunity to fly at him, swarming across his face.

"This 'n That. Doesn't it mean anything to you."

He didn't answer.

She half rose out of the chair and screamed, "The South bay's premier gay bathhouse!"

His lips convulsed. He closed his eyes, but his eyelids twitched rapidly. He'd had advance notice. He should have seen it coming. *Why* hadn't he taken the time to think about what to say? And how did she know?

"How…"

"How did I find out, you lying shit?" She flopped back down in the chair and began rocking.

He tried to swallow. He deserved this. Everything had been a lie. Even if he hadn't formed untruthful words and told her stories that were blatantly false, he'd lied with all the things he'd left unsaid. He'd lied to the church. Worst of all, he'd lied to himself. Lied to God, even. When he drove to meet men, as he handed cash to the clerk at the front desk, and helped himself to free condoms, he'd lied because half his mind insisted he and God had an understanding. The other half said *I will change. Being married will change me. It just takes time*. He clenched his fists.

It was true, he'd made mistakes, terrible mistakes, but he couldn't collapse in a puddle of self-doubt in front of her. He needed to be firm and sure of himself. Bold. All those years ago, he and God had come to an agreement. It might have been a mistake to marry Gabrielle, but how could he say it was a mistake to have Peter? They were destined to be together, or Peter wouldn't exist. And what about her over-zealous need for sex? The situation wouldn't have reached this point if she was more normal. Instead, she wanted to consume him, she wanted to devour his body, own his mind, control every fiber of his being. She was ravenous — an insatiable termite, munching and chewing her way through him.

"You can just sit there like a lump. I suppose that's your natural inclination. Make me do all the work. Just like when we make love. Now I understand." Her voice heaved as she choked on a sob, but her eyes remained dry. "Of course I have to do the work because you don't even want to be there. You want me to be a man."

Her face blazed like a piece of coal.

"I know I've let you down. But can I explain?"

"Let me down? Our marriage is a farce. You lied about who you are and how you feel about me. Every time you touched me, it was a lie. I don't even know who you are."

"Can I tell you where I was coming from?"

"You make it sound like you're explaining why you bought a new car without asking me."

"Please." He willed his face to be smooth, easing the clenched muscles that ran through his jaw and cheeks.

She didn't answer.

Watching him squirm was her greatest pleasure. The moon would sink below the trees, the moth might die, and they would still be sitting here while Gabrielle delighted in his discomfort. She sat in that rocking chair like a queen, ordering her subject to confess his sins, while she decided what the punishment would be. And it was his stupidity that had forced him into this position. "How did you find out?"

"There was a matchbook in your golf bag, you moron. A shrink might say you wanted me to find out."

She was right. A psychiatrist would say some buried part of his psyche wanted her to know, while all his conscious strength, every shred of energy, every day, went to protecting his career and public image. He didn't remember putting the matchbook into the golf bag. It must have been ages ago. "Please don't be so harsh. Can you try to have an open mind?"

"I'll be however I damn well please."

"What do you want me to tell you? Do you want to hear

about my life?"

"You can start with why in the hell you married me."

He wished she wouldn't keep cursing. It made him nervous. He was afraid she would let those words slip out in front of his parishioners, but asking her to stop was out of the question. He studied the moth. If he kept staring at it, used it as a focal point, he would appear to be looking Gabrielle in the eye. Right now, seeing the moth leave its perch and fly at him was less terrifying than looking at those glassy green eyes. By looking at the moth, he would know the moment it did let go of the wall, so it couldn't take him by surprise, and cause him to jump out of his seat like a nervous old woman. "I married you because I loved you. Do love you."

"Bullshit."

That was the fourth curse word. She was doing it to make him angry. He wouldn't bite. He was calm, still confident, a little, of the conclusion God had led him to so many years ago. She had to understand what he'd suffered. Those were the things he needed to think about. "When I was a little kid, I realized that God made me different from the other guys I knew." He sounded hysterical, anxious. He tried to relax his shoulders.

"Don't you dare blame this on God."

"I'm not blaming anyone. But I didn't *decide* to be attracted to men." He rushed on, afraid she'd interrupt. "I begged God to change my feelings. Begged. But He didn't answer. I wanted to look at naked boys. I wanted to touch and cuddle with my friends. In high school, I tried going out with girls. I really tried, but it didn't work. In my freshman year of college, I met a guy. Andy. I finally had a relationship like other people did. I was so happy. I felt normal and wanted. Then, during the summer, he disappeared. When I went back in the fall, he'd withdrawn from school, and I never heard from him again. It was horrible."

"I'm sure." She rocked the chair faster.

Think about the moth. Keep your eyes on the moth. If you keep your eyes focused, your mind will be focused. As long as the moth remained still, it was soothing. Only the sudden moves, the erratic flying, startled him, made him tremble.

"I put all my energy into studying. School was easy for me, and it made me feel good about myself." From the outer edge of his vision, he sensed Gabrielle poking her tongue through her lips. She hated it when he *bragged about his brains*, as she called it. It couldn't be helped. If she wanted honesty, he needed to tell her exactly what his life had been like. Well, almost exactly. She didn't need to know everything. He owed her an explanation, and she had a right to be upset, hurt, even furious, but he had a right to some privacy. She didn't own him, and he refused to allow her to suck his brain out of his skull so she could possess every thought and feeling. If he let her, she would take every piece of his life, hold it in her hand, and examine it as if she were an entomologist.

"Without Andy, I had time to think. I got scared. How could I be a minister? I knew I wasn't what God wanted. I heard it in church, I read it in the Bible. The specifics were forced down my throat at summer camp. But I'd wanted to be a preacher since I was a little kid. Then, I started to notice that all the well-known leaders of God's people had sex lives that weren't traditional relationships. Abraham slept with his maid. Jacob married one woman, then married her sister. King David had a man killed in order to keep the guy's wife for himself. And I realized, if God chose them to be leaders, I could be certain he'd chosen me."

He took his gaze off the moth. Gabrielle's mouth was open. The edges of her lips were crusty, but she didn't lick them. She took short gasps of air. Her mouth was a great, gaping hole. Hopefully, the moth wouldn't fly inside.

Speaking his views out loud gave them a self-serving quality. But he couldn't let himself down now. "The only reason Kind David was punished was because he ordered his lover's husband killed — not for committing adultery. Judah picked up a prostitute who turned out to be his daughter-in-law. And he was the leader of one of the twelve tribes of Israel!"

Gabrielle's mouth snapped closed.

"I know it sounds a little crazy, but I felt peaceful after that. I knew I couldn't change myself. I'd spent hours on my knees, years of prayer, asking God to change me, and He hadn't. You would think if He didn't like what I was, He would have answered that prayer. It suddenly made sense that men who are called to be ministers are allowed to be imperfect. I mean, everyone is imperfect. But ministers are in a different category, I think."

"That is the most arrogant thing I've ever heard. You sound like a politician. You think because you're a minister that you're in some special class? You don't have to follow the same rules as the rest of us? Is that what gave you the right to lie to me too? What about love? And my feelings? You're absolutely amazing."

How could he make her understand? He hadn't explained clearly enough how tormented his life had been. She didn't realize how hard he'd tried to stir up a desire for females, how he'd tried to control his thoughts. But they came uninvited in his dreams.

She stood suddenly, the chair continued moving as she turned and went into the kitchen. The light came on, flooding down the steps onto the carpet at one entrance and out into the hallway on the opposite side. He heard her take a glass from the cabinet, snap open the cap on a bottle of water, and pour it into the glass with a soft, gulping sound. Did he dare ask her to bring him a glass of water? For several minutes, there was silence. He pictured her standing in front of the sink, looking out into the darkness, drinking the water. Not only wouldn't she pour him a glass, she wasn't even going to bring hers into the living room so he could ask for a sip. The rest of the water chugged out of the bottle, followed by another moment or two of silence. The glass clicked on the tile. The light went out, and the puddles of white at the edges of the room were gone.

She slipped back into the room and walked to the fireplace. "Is that all?"

"For the most part."

"Sounds pretty lame."

"I don't think you understand how impossible this has been for me. I've been in a battle since I was a little boy. My entire life."

"Oh, poor you. I'm supposed to feel sad for you because you lied to me? Our relationship, our entire marriage, is a big fat lie."

"Can you think about how I feel?"

"That's all I think about."

"It's been torture." He bent his head down. His shirt billowed forward, and cold drops of sweat trickled down his chest.

"Don't look so pathetic," she said.

"You don't know how bad I feel." His voice was soft, hesitant. "When I was a kid, my Dad acted like there was something wrong with me. He always liked my brother better, said he felt like he and Alan were *on the same wavelength*. He said being a minister was something regular men didn't think about. He called me a girl because I ducked when a volleyball came at me. He would be sick if he knew. I was constantly afraid they would find out. Afraid kids at school would bully me. I was afraid of everything. I lived my whole life in a state of terror. At first, I didn't even know what I was afraid of. I didn't have a word for it. I didn't think about sex, I was just a kid, but I knew I wasn't like them. When my friends started getting crushes on girls, I couldn't understand. I felt left out. It was so lonely. You can't imagine. I had to pretend I felt the same way. I said stuff I didn't mean, and I worried they would realize I was a fake. Mostly I just hoped they didn't notice me." He took a breath. His hands trembled, and he squeezed them together to stop the shaking.

Now that he'd begun, he couldn't stop. "When I was older, I really felt like a freak. I took out lots of girls, so I didn't have to get into a relationship with just one. They acted hurt when I didn't kiss them goodnight or try to do anything. But I didn't want to touch them. I couldn't. I hid in my room at night, looking at *Sports Illustrated* because it was the only time I could look at men without them knowing I was staring, and calling me a fag. I didn't have my own computer. We all shared the one in the family room." He coughed. "And I begged." His voice wavered. "You have no idea how I begged God to change me. I thought I'd never have what everyone else had. If He didn't change me, I couldn't be a minister. I couldn't get married, and I'd never have children. I'd be shut out from all the stuff that forms society. I wanted those things. I might as well die because who I was didn't fit anything in my experiences. I knew about the pride movement, but it wasn't for Christians. It had nothing to do with my family or my church or my friends. I yelled and screamed at God. I thought He hated me. I wondered if I'd been destined for hell before I was even born." He tried to take a deep breath. Mucous filled his sinuses, and thick tears washed across the surface of his eyes. His whole face was swelling up with water.

"I'm sure that was hard for you." Her words crunched as if she was biting them off the end of a carrot. "But why did you have to drag me into your miserable life? Now I'm stuck. God won't let me get a divorce, so I'm doomed to live without sex. It's not fair! I feel like an old woman. My life is over."

"I do love you."

"Ha."

"Love isn't just about sex. Doesn't God want you to love me? Doesn't he want us to try to figure this out so we can be there for Peter?"

"There wouldn't be anything to figure out if you hadn't lied to me every single day since I met you. You lied when you said you wanted to go out with me. You knew you were deceiving me. You lied when you asked me to marry you. Every night in bed, you *lied*! And now I'm supposed to feel sorry for you?" She whirled around from the fireplace. She grabbed her Bible off the coffee table and plucked the condoms out from between the pages where she'd left them. She hurled them at his face. They didn't go very far, tapping the floor like pats of butter. Closing the Bible, she grasped it by the spine and threw it at him.

He ducked. The Bible hit the back of the futon and fell to

the floor behind it.

"You're scum! I can't ever clean hard enough to cleanse our house of this evil thing. I've wasted hours, my whole life, praying for the wrong thing!"

He wanted to ask what she was going to do. His muscles fluttered uncontrollably. She could ruin his life. One word from her and his ministry would crumble. Without an income, without any other skills to earn a living, she could take Peter away from him. Did she know she held his life in her fingers?

Shadows of rage swept over her face. One after another, they flickered past, darkening her eyes, making the white shimmer of her skin fade to gray, and tightening her lips into hard edges. Just as quickly, the shadows slid away, and her eyes returned to their brilliant green. Her face and lips took on a pink hue, making her look vulnerable. He imagined that any second she would soften and kind words would come out of her mouth. He had no idea what those words would be, but somehow they would reassure him that she wouldn't destroy his life

It wouldn't take much for him to be on the street, keeping company with the homeless people he tried to help with food and sometimes a night or two in a cheap motel. What could a man with a bachelor's degree in history and a master's degree from the Lutheran church do to earn a living? He saw himself lying in the park, trying to stay warm. Hungry and filthy. People walking past with looks of disdain. Invisible to most of the population, because they didn't want to think about how easily they could land in the same spot. Silently drifting up and down El Camino Real, pushing a cart full of nameless junk. He forced his eyes to stay open, preventing the image from growing more vivid. "What are you going to do?"

"How should I know?" It sounded as if she'd been waiting for his question. "I keep seeing my life repeated like a re-run. Except this time, it looks completely different. This time it's a horror movie."

"I'm sorry. What else could I do?"

"Anything. You could have done anything. You could have stayed single. You could have accepted your natural state and not become a minister."

He felt bad for lying. It wasn't right, but when had there ever been a different choice? There was a slow, barely noticeable series of choices. He'd graduated from college, still confused. Part of him had been certain that God would make the same allowances for him that he'd made for the Old Testament leaders and kings. Those men that lived in ancient times were applauded today as righteous heroes. When he went to the seminary, a small part of him also clung to the thought that God might still change him. All he needed to do was avoid thinking about sex. Make himself into a man who had higher aspirations. It worked for a while. It wasn't as if he'd made a calculated decision to form a life that was false in every respect.

During those years, he'd sometimes gone for a few weeks without thinking about who and what he was. Then, without warning, in the midst of swinging a golf club or writing a research paper on some obscure aspect of church doctrine, his activity suddenly became pointless. He was overcome with the need to be touched. Desire immobilized him, making him barely able to climb out of bed in the morning and lift a spoonful of cereal to his mouth. Life meant nothing without love, and he wanted a man to touch his face, stroke his hair, hold him close. Love him. Just as quickly, those tender desires would pass, and all he wanted was sex. It was like needing to run or lift weights. A tension that couldn't be relieved without doing something. Occasionally he fought it, other times, he didn't. He couldn't. After, he felt peace. His body came under control again. His mind was able to think about other things. On one day, he would sense God walking right by his side, the next, he'd feel as if God was light-years away.

Why *had* he married Gabrielle? He wasn't sure he could answer that question, even to himself. She was beautiful. Anyone could see that. Her long, thick hair, her pale skin and rose-colored lips. She was slim. She walked confidently, shoulders back so that even though she was only five and a half feet tall, she gave the impression she could take on the world.

They'd met at a dinner at Susan's apartment. Susan and Jack were engaged, Susan eager to play matchmaker for her best friend and her young pastor. She wanted another couple to hang out with and had decided Mark and Gabrielle would be a good fit. Susan had set up a large round table in the center of her living room, the only place where it would fit in her one-bedroom apartment. Jack carried in a cookie sheet with hamburgers he'd barbecued on a portable grill. The burgers were already nestled inside buns that Susan had warmed in the oven. It was their first dinner party if you could call it that. Gabrielle had lifted the top bun on one of the burgers and said, "How can you eat a smashed up, broiled piece of dead cow?"

Mark had admired her bluntness. She didn't add any qualifying words about not meaning to insult them. At the same time, her voice didn't sound ugly and critical. There was a lightness to her tone that made the words half amusing, making him pause for a moment, realizing that all she was doing was speaking the truth. They pretended that what they were eating wasn't a dead, ground-up cow. She'd said it casually and proudly. And no one disliked her for it. He was awed by people who said exactly what they thought without fear of offending or hurting. Avoiding offensive words was a driving force in his life, so of course, he was attracted to the polar opposite. By that time, he'd spent several years taking great care to protect every aspect of his reputation, to do things that would keep him above criticism since he was trying with every fiber of his being to fit in.

Jack had taken a big bite of his burger before even smearing it with ketchup. He grinned and chewed with exaggerated movements. "It may be dead, but it sure tastes good."

They all laughed. Gabrielle didn't eat a hamburger that night. Neither did she go on and on about her preferences. He admired her conviction.

Five years later, he'd learned it was true what they said. You grew to hate the things you'd first loved in another person. He never knew it would happen so fast and that it would be so severe. Hatred seemed like a benign word when you read it in a book.

He'd loved watching her — always moving. He didn't watch with desire but simply admired her like he would a living piece of art. She was graceful, floating through the world like a ballerina. Her fluid movements soothed him.

Their relationship had taken on a life of its own. Like molten lead, Mark and Gabrielle conformed to the mold created by their church and their stage in life. In the eyes of Grace, a man and woman of marriageable age, attractive together, seemingly interested in each other, were prodded into becoming a couple. Why not get married? Why not take the ultimate step to fit in with society? He wanted a child. He wanted a home, and he wanted to be with other families at church, not the odd man out. During that awful sex talk, his father had assured him women lost interest in sex once they had children. The belief was confirmed in his brief experience as a minister. It was the men who came to the pastor to discuss a lack of sex in their marriages. Women never visited him with that complaint. He never foresaw it as a long term problem in his relationship with Gabrielle.

His thoughts of the past, racing through his mind in time to the tempo of Gabrielle's rocking, made him feel warm toward her again. He'd forgotten what she used to be like. Under the hard shell she'd developed, buried beneath all the religious jargon she'd been fed by Allysan, she was the same person. He'd forgotten the most important thing of all — she loved him. He stood and stepped around the end of the table. He walked to the rocking chair. He stopped with his knees inches from her. He took her hands. She didn't yank them away. She rested them limply in his. He tried to pull her out of the chair, but she resisted.

"Will you hold me?" he said.

She looked up at him. Her expression changed, but he couldn't read it. Slowly she rose out of the rocking chair.

All she wanted was physical affection. She focused her conversation on sex, but that wasn't what she wanted. In his fear of that, he'd hardly touched her. If he could let go of some of that fear, hold her more. Hug her, take her hand in his, and stay close to her in bed — everything would be okay.

She stood with her arms at her sides, but she didn't stiffen or pull away as he slipped his arms around her back. He held her narrow waist, wrapping his arms nearly all the way around her body. She felt so thin and light. Her hair brushed across his arms. He stiffened his back so he wouldn't shudder. He willed himself not to push her hair out of the way. Waves of fruit scent from her shampoo filled his nostrils. He buried his face against her neck. Shallow, weak breaths filled his ear. He held on, not relaxing his arms, not moving.

"I'm sorry I lied to you," he said.

After several minutes, she put her arms loosely around his shoulders.

"I didn't know what else to do. Things just sort of happened. I didn't think of it as lying. I suppose I just never knew how to tell you. And it didn't seem important."

She turned rigid in his arms. He'd said the wrong thing. "I don't mean it wasn't important. I guess I didn't know sex would be that important to you, and so it didn't seem to matter. When we got married, I thought I would have enough other things in my life that sex wouldn't matter so much to me either. I thought everything would work out."

His words sounded weak. But the weakness seemed to be pleasing Gabrielle. She didn't try to move away, and her arms tightened slightly around his shoulders. He felt calm. He could do this more. Nothing would come of it, and it felt kind of good. As long as she didn't want to start kissing and sucking on each other's lips, or didn't want to drag him into bed, force him into a command performance.

After a few minutes, she moved away.

"Maybe the cleansing was what we needed. You seem different. Not so arrogant. What are we going to do now?"

"What do you mean?" Why did they have to *do* something?

"Let's sit down." She went around one end of the coffee

table, and he walked around the other. She sat with her shoulder touching his. She kept her arms close to her sides, her hands resting on her lap. She leaned her head back, stretching her neck. Tendons pressed against her skin. He looked away.

"Now that the cleansing is almost complete, we have to pull close together so nothing can get inside our lives again. We have to be completely open and honest with each other in every single area. We have to talk about every single thing we're feeling. We can't have any secrets. We have to talk every day. And hold each other. And we need to pray together. This can work. I think God allowed you to have those crazy ideas about the Old Testament people getting away with whatever they wanted until you got close to me. Until you were ready to open up to someone."

He closed his eyes, trying to follow her train of thought. He wanted to go to sleep. It was all over now. Did they have to talk about this tonight? Was there really anything to talk about? He couldn't let his mind drift. He had to pay attention to what she was saying. If he said something that indicated he hadn't been listening, she would explode.

"We need to believe that God's power will now come forth unhindered. I think the reason He never answered your prayer for a change in your desires is He wanted to show you, in a mighty way, the power of joint prayer. Like at Gethsemane. This will be such a dramatic, incredible way for Him to show you, and me too, that what you can't achieve on your own, we can achieve together. We'll pray and believe together that He'll give you normal desires."

She leaped off the couch and spun around to face him. She looked drunk, her eyes unfocused. She flung her arms out. "This is so exciting. We're going to witness a miracle together. It will revolutionize our lives, our family, the entire church. Change won't come from the stupid building program, it will come from us."

She hugged herself and rocked from side to side. Any minute, he expected her to ask him what he thought. But she didn't. She was in another world, inside her own mind. She saw a vision of some life that included a man she had constructed in her imagination. His thoughts were superfluous to her ideas, to what she thought God was planting in her mind. It was good she didn't ask what he thought. He didn't know himself.

Fourteen

EVERYTHING HAD CHANGED. For three weeks, the outside circumstances of Gabrielle's life aligned perfectly with the new marriage that God had created. In the evenings, Mark stayed home. He canceled or asked others to run meetings. The two of them sprawled on the living room floor and built block towers or new train configurations with Peter. Some evenings, they buckled Peter into his stroller and walked to the park. Peter rode halfway, then twisted and thrashed under the straps until they set him free. He walked with his arms extended over his head to grasp the handles, pushing the stroller himself. This doubled the time it took to reach the park, but it didn't matter. They were together. Both boys were all hers. At night, they sat on the patio to escape the heat, or in the living room if the fog had come in to chill the evening air. They talked. Mostly, Mark talked.

HE TOLD HER, his earliest memory was sitting in the third

pew at St. Jude's Lutheran church. His father was on the aisle. Next to him was Alan, Mark's thirteen-year-old brother — taller than Mark, stronger than Mark — a boy who could throw and catch any ball devised by mankind. Mark sat between Alan and their mother.

Six-year-old Mark gazed up at the tableau before him. The wide steps led up to a marble altar that was eighteen feet long. Beyond that, a twenty-five-foot wooden cross, accented with gold, hung on the wall, reaching to the peak of the a-frame sanctuary. On the left side of the altar was a pulpit draped with red brocade. The sanctuary was filled with people sitting quietly, listening to the man dressed in white and black. A thick red stole hung around his neck, embroidered to match the brocade on the pulpit, and a larger piece draped across the length of the altar. His voice was deep and full of confidence. For twenty minutes, no one spoke. Every single person listened to that man's voice and considered what he had to say. Even Alan kept his mouth shut.

Mark didn't understand all that was said, but he understood how important it was to be that man. Other boys might want to be firefighters or football players, but he couldn't imagine a better life than standing in front of an audience, all eyes directed toward him, all ears listening. No matter whether they wanted to or not. When Mark announced at Sunday dinner that he wanted to be a preacher, Alan laughed — a single honk, like a goose. His mother told him he was a very special boy and his father said — *we'll see*. What did that mean? It wasn't as if his father got to decide what he'd become when he grew up. There was nothing to *see*. The decision was made.

He spent the next years carefully watching everything Reverend Johnson did and said. While Alan was safely out of the house, racing his skateboard up and down the street or shooting a basketball through the hoop in the backyard, Mark stood in front of the bedroom mirror. He held a Bible open in one hand and gestured with the other while he read the words in a slow, deep voice. He dragged a sheet out of the linen closet and draped it over his shoulders.

When he was eight, maybe seven, he couldn't remember, he began noticing the silken hair of his friends, their touchable lips that smiled so invitingly. He liked it when Brian slept over. Mark's father helped them set up the two-man tent in the backyard. Inside the tent, Mark and Brian waited until the lights in the house went out. They turned on their flashlights. They told stories of killers and monsters, relishing the shivers that ran down their spines. It was even better when they turned off the flashlights. Mark felt the warmth of Brian's body, their sleeping bags so close. He listened to the other boy's breath, moving slowly in and out as if it were moving into Mark's lungs. For hours, he was awake, thrilled to be alone in the protected space. When he slept, his sleep was more peaceful, dreamless, and he woke happier than he ever did in his own bed.

He began to realize that what he saw in the warm eyes and

desirable lips of other boys, Brian noticed in girls. Later, he came to understand that God was testing him, giving him unnatural desires. He knew they were unnatural because Alan laughed about *fags*, his father commented on *sickos*, and occasionally, Reverend Johnson preached about God's wrath toward *perversion*. Boys that wanted to touch other boys were queer. Creatures to be loathed.

But it was only a test of his faith and devotion. God making sure Mark was fit to serve Him. He wasn't a queer. Not at all. By then, he knew — he had a calling from God Himself. When he mentioned the desire to be a preacher, swallowing his words, Reverend Johnson's deep, strong voice assured him he would be tested, forces — flesh and blood and unseen — would try to divert him.

He'd only stumbled once in high school. Kyle Miller followed him home from school, asking if they could hang out at Mark's house. They sat close together on the couch and played video games for a few hours, then watched some lame TV shows. When Kyle got up to leave, he pushed Mark up against the hall closet door and pressed his warm lips on Mark's. His tongue slid inside of Mark's mouth. Mark thought he would die of pleasure and terror.

After that, he increased his daily devotional time from twenty to thirty minutes. He started lifting weights. He stopped writing his feelings in poorly constructed poems.

GABRIELLE COULDN'T ARGUE with anything Mark

told her. What was there to say? He brushed aside the questions she really wanted answered. How often did he visit *This 'n That?* She wanted to know what the routine was like, how the men behaved. How did he feel? Did he think about her? He turned her questions aside. *If we're putting all this behind us, why dwell on the past? Talking about it makes me think about it.*

Unasked questions and unwanted, voyeuristic curiosity haunted her.

Could a person feel shameful and self-righteous at the same moment in time? At two o'clock in the morning, her eyes would fly open as if she'd sensed another presence in their bedroom. She'd sit up, her body suggesting it was mid-day and she'd overslept, but it was dark. Some nights she'd twist in the sheets, turning from side to side, stretching her legs, then curling them close, rearranging her pillows. Other nights, she crept out of bed and walked down the dark hall to the living room, out into the kitchen. Imagined images of Mark making love, while she'd been sitting innocently, stupidly, at home, flashed through her mind. What did they talk about? Did he have favored partners or wind up with the guy that first captured his eye on any given evening? Did he whisper to a stranger the things she wanted to hear? She imagined him naked, his eyes hungrily stroking the bodies of men she'd never seen. There was a tight, sudden twist in her stomach as she thought of his smooth, familiar skin, warm against other skin, his lips devouring another mouth. She'd push the pictures aside like a series of out of focus photographs. After half a glass of wine and a few more turns through the kitchen, she'd return to their bedroom.

Lying on her side, staring at the blackness beyond the sliding glass door, split by the back porch light from the house next door, she tried to imagine when or how the miracle would take place.

They'd only made love once during that first week after they'd agreed to trust God for a miracle. They had agreed, hadn't they? She couldn't remember the details of what they'd said. In the days after they made love, Mark wanted to cuddle. *Turn on your side*, he'd say. Then he'd scoot up behind her, nestling his face in her hair and tucking his knees into the alcove formed by her bent legs. *I need to hold you. I love you.*

Hearing him say he needed her melted her heart into her stomach. Still, she tried to figure out how the miracle might happen. Would he suddenly want to make love every day? Every few days? How would she know? Would he be unable to keep his hands off her while they ate dinner, stare lustfully at her while he was singing hymns during the church service? She prayed for a sign. The very nature of a miracle is sudden, startling. A slowly growing desire for her wouldn't do at all.

Each night, before they fell asleep, she insisted they pray together. Informed by the prayers she heard at Gethsemane Temple, hers were long, laced with passionate language. Mark's prayers were brief. He spoke in halting phrases as if he couldn't quite settle on what he wanted to say. Gabrielle knew what she wanted, and she had no trouble expressing it.

NEAR THE END OF AUGUST, life began to dull around the edges. Their prayers began to sound the same every night. In spite of her new-found spiritual vocabulary, her words stiffened until they resembled decades-old prayers printed in the back of a hymnal. Where was the spontaneity? Her head ached from trying to invent new ways to ask for the same thing. She pleaded for a timeline. How long did it take for a miracle anyway? Moses and the people of Israel had wandered in the desert for forty years before they encountered the promised land. But the Israelites were given smaller, in-between miracles while they waited. They received manna sprinkled on the ground for bread every day, quail for food, and water that flowed miraculously from a rock. She wasn't about to wait forty *years*! She wanted a sign that something was happening now, soon.

During those weeks, they made love a few more times. But how was it any different from before she'd discovered his true desires? It was worse. Now, she worried he held a man in his imagination while he held her in his arms. She was frantic to know what ran through his mind but was forbidden to ask. Talking about it, asking questions, demonstrated a lack of faith. If she spoke about her worries, not only would Mark hear, but so would any evil spirits that lingered, sniffing around for a crack in their armor. She had to hold onto enough faith for both of them. She had to make herself believe the dark things she feared were not lingering inside of her husband.

A GASPING BREEZE came through the bedroom screen. Gabrielle and Mark lay on their backs, covered only by the sheet, the blanket and blue satin quilt bunched at the foot of the bed. Their hands rested on their rib cages, fingers laced. From above, they must have looked like two corpses. Their eyes were closed, their arched feet making a low tent of the sheet. Her breathing was shallow, keeping time with his. They always lay still for a few minutes when they finished with their respective prayers. After a moment, she would reach over and take his right hand, pulling it away from its mate. Their hands were tied together, as if the prayer continued, flowing through both of them, binding it into something permanent. Holding hands, they drifted to sleep. When she woke a few hours later, their hands had come apart, and Mark was on his left side, his back toward her.

Now that it was September, his evening meetings were becoming more frequent and unavoidable. Most weeks, he was gone three nights. Several times he came home after she was already asleep. Two Saturdays in a row, he had all day planning meetings. During the days, she didn't see another soul. She'd agreed to stop attending prayer meetings at Gethsemane. Mark rightly pointed out that they needed to be united in every way.

She began to feel as if she didn't have a voice, silent except when she spoke to Peter or the cashier at the health food store. She weeded the garden, cleaned the house from one end to the other. She moved through the day like a phantom, cooking, cleaning, harvesting vegetables, walking Peter to and from the park. When Peter slept, she napped. Waiting for a miracle was tedious work.

SUSAN CALLED. In a three-minute and twenty-three-second voicemail message, she choked out the words that their friendship had died tragically and without warning. She didn't know what she'd done wrong. She hadn't meant to offend, didn't mean to pry. She was sorry she'd flown off the handle, regretted getting so upset about the criticism of her father. She begged Gabrielle to tell her what was wrong and pleaded to meet up for lunch to spend the afternoon around the pool.

It was a hot day. One of those preludes to fall when everyone confidently dressed in jeans and warm shirts in the foggy morning, only to have the sun betray them in mid-afternoon, the heat dryer, and more harsh than August. The leaves were yellow, falling off branches, covering the sidewalks like pieces of cotton fabric instead of crunching underfoot. Gabrielle was sick of it. She wanted cold clear skies.

The following day she returned Susan's call. "Okay. We'll come over."

"You will? That would be so great." Susan's voice was giddy.

"I'll bring Peter's lunch," she said.

"I can make something healthy. What do you want?"

"Don't worry about it. It's easier if I bring something."

Susan's voice flattened with defeat. "What time?"

"Twelve-thirty."

Invited to eat lunch at Susan's. Looking ahead to an afternoon of swimming and staring at Susan's fresh toenail polish. Nothing was any different. She squeezed her eyes closed and conjured up an image of the miracle that was about to happen. Mark would come through the front door and kiss her for several long minutes until she could hardly breathe. He'd gobble down his dinner and help clean up the kitchen. He'd bathe Peter and read a story so they could hurry him into his crib the moment dusk descended. Any day now. It would be a day the same as every other, even a day like today. She would be standing at the kitchen counter chopping vegetables, getting a head start on dinner while Peter took a late nap. Mark would be early, overcome with a need for her that drove him out of his office.

Now, she feels him. Standing behind her, his entire body pressed against her, the intoxicating scent of fresh garlic fills their nostrils as he pulls her even closer and releases the knife from her hand. He draws her into himself. They drift to the living room and slide to the floor. He lays on top of her, kissing gently, then urgently with a hungry, famished mouth, deprived for so long. So gently, it feels like a breeze, he slips the straps of her tank top down her shoulders, exposing her breasts. She can feel him getting hard, digging into her. There's nothing but his weight on her body. His need for her overwhelms her so that she can hardly bear to touch him.

The vision is so close, but it slips away, and she can't bring it back.

Why wasn't it happening like that? Her devotion had faded in the stale August sunlight, but now it was time to reclaim it. She realized she shouldn't eat at Susan's. It was a day for fasting. She stood in the kitchen and drank two bottles of water without stopping. She packed two more bottles of water and a teabag into the backpack.

SITTING AT SUSAN'S kitchen table, the icy breath of the air conditioner blowing across her arms, Gabrielle sipped her water. Susan nibbled at half a sandwich and a handful of corn chips. She drank diet coke and looked morose. Finally, Susan abandoned the sandwich and stuffed the rest of the corn chips into her mouth. Gabrielle didn't care if Susan felt awkward eating alone, she was answering a calling that was higher than etiquette or the niceties of friendship.

They went outside and sat dangling their feet in the pool while Peter and Cara splashed around in a wading pool set up on the small patch of lawn.

"I've missed seeing you." Below the surface of the water, Susan's cherry toenails laughed at Gabrielle — a dancing, floating reminder that there was no miracle.

Gabrielle closed her eyes, "I've been lifted to a higher spiritual plane, my relationship with Mark is so intense, I honestly don't need social activities. Making small talk dilutes my connection to God." The contrast between the sun on her face and the cool water surrounding her feet and ankles felt glorious. Her heart beat furiously. The tips of her fingers and her jaw were slightly numb. The lack of food weakened the power of her body, preventing it from destroying her peaceful feelings with its pounding rage.

After a few minutes, Susan said, "You sound a little crazy."

"I don't expect you to understand. It's been an amazing summer. I've learned so many new things about living in God's presence. I can't begin to explain."

"Huh. So have all these new insights improved your sex life?"

Gabrielle yanked her feet out of the water. She scooted back from the edge of the pool and wrapped her arms around her knees. "My marriage is none of your business. And I don't know why you keep trying to stick your nose into it."

"You're the one who begged me to help you understand why your husband wasn't attracted to you. Ever since then, you've shut me out. I tried to give you some advice, and you turned on me like a shark."

"I never begged for anything in my life," Gabrielle said. "It was wrong to discuss it with you. Mark was exhausted from the burdens of Grace, and I over-reacted. End of story. Now that the initial pressure of the fund-raising campaign is over, he can't keep his hands off me. Like it's always been."

"I'm sorry," Susan said. "I won't mention it again. I just wanted to help."

Gabrielle stood up. She stomped her foot on the pebbled concrete. A sharp pain ran from her heel through her ankle bone and up to her hip. "We don't need your help. Our marriage is incredible. We've spent the whole summer talking about our relationship, expanding our connection. We're closer than we've ever been. Closer than we were when we first fell in love, and closer than we were even on our honeymoon." The lie was like a piece of glass in her throat. She strained to swallow. No, it was a statement of faith. She and Mark held each other every night, didn't they? Even if they didn't always make love, or didn't yet, they were on the precipice of a dramatic change.

"I'm worried about you. You might think your life is becoming more spiritual, but that's not what it looks like from where I'm sitting."

"And where are you sitting? How do you know what's going on inside me? Or inside my marriage?"

"It worries me that you didn't eat lunch. You've lost a lot of weight. Being spiritual isn't a contest. You can't be more spiritual than someone else. If you and Mark feel close, that's great." Covering her eyes with her left hand, and supporting herself with her right, she tipped her head back, straining to look up at Gabrielle's face.

Gabrielle took a step closer, positioning herself so that it was impossible for Susan to see her face from the angle where she sat. "I haven't lost that much weight. You're just sensitive about that issue."

Susan lowered her head and let her hand fall away from her brow. "I think you're lying about your marriage, and I feel sad that you don't have anyone to talk to."

"That's a terrible thing to say. I have no reason to lie. Mark and I are ecstatically happy."

"You sound hysterical. When someone is happy, they don't feel the need to explain it."

It was clear that Susan wanted to plant seeds of doubt. She wanted Gabrielle to suffer. She wasn't happy unless everyone around her was miserable — it made her feel needed and superior. Curiosity quivered on her pudgy face. At the same time, her mouth watered like someone who hadn't eaten in weeks, drooling for details of the savory secrets in Gabrielle's sex life. "I'm leaving. This is a pointless conversation." Gabrielle walked to the wading pool. She lifted Peter onto her hip, soaking the side of her skirt and leaving a dark stain on her shirt. She carried him to his towel. Strangely, he didn't protest. It must be God directing her, infusing Peter with compliance.

"Please don't leave. I didn't mean to upset you again. I'm just trying to be honest. I'm worried about you."

Furiously rubbing Peter's body with the towel, Gabrielle

ignored her. She pulled a shirt over Peter's head and hoisted him back to her hip.

"Please." Susan lifted her glossy toes out of the water and struggled to her feet.

"You're nothing but a bloodsucking ghoul."

"A what?"

"A ghoul. You want something to be wrong between Mark and me. I have something better than you, and you can't stand it." She walked into the house, picked up the backpack, and continued out the front door.

As she drove home, a lightheaded feeling wrapped around her brain. It felt strange, unfinished, walking out on someone. She'd never done it before. But Susan had done the same to her a few weeks ago. Gabrielle felt as if she'd had the final word.

When she walked into the house, her phone began vibrating against her hip. A part of her wanted to ignore it, but it might mean something. A sign. It was too much of a coincidence for the phone to ring the moment she crossed the threshold. Pushing Peter's leg to the side, she wriggled the phone out of her pocket.

"Hello?"

"Why so out of breath?" Mark said.

"Oh. Just a second." She let Peter slip slowly down her side. Once on the floor, he scurried off to his bedroom. She dropped the backpack off her opposite shoulder and sat down on the cool hardwood.

"We just got back from Susan's."

"Oh. Okay. I'm calling to ask what you think about inviting Joe for dinner tomorrow."

"Joe?"

"You know, my friend from college? He dropped off the check this afternoon. I think we need to thank him properly. And it would be great to catch up."

The check. Joe. The mysterious golf teammate. She'd forgotten all about him. She'd forgotten about the check. There was something not right about a guy who had never set foot in their church donating fifty thousand dollars. She couldn't imagine why he cared. Should she mention her suspicion, question the motivation again? They were supposed to be completely honest and open, sharing every thought. Complete transparency was necessary to make their marriage impenetrable. But she didn't want to start an argument. Not on the phone, and not when they'd come so far. It would be interesting to meet the generous, mysterious Joe. Maybe the check-giving would become clear once she met him. Maybe, somehow, it was the sign? "Sure!"

"Wow. I didn't expect so much enthusiasm. One favor, though. Please. Can you please serve meat?"

Worrying again what someone else would think. Not caring what she might want. With all the fervent prayer, had there been one, single, change in Mark? Why did the opinions of mere humans matter so much to him? His attitude certainly didn't point to an imminent miracle. She shoved the thought aside. Joe's visit would pave the way for the miracle. The ridiculously enormous amount of cash, the utter absence of a logical explanation, had all the marks of a miracle.

Fifteen

NOW SHE HAD A MISSION. Something to rescue her from the boredom of cleaning. The constant demands that she clean again and again had worn her down. The floors were spotless, and the windows glistened, yet she was compelled to clean them repeatedly. For a day or two, she could put that behind her.

It was shameful to admit, but having Joe to dinner also released her from the monotony of prayer. There was menu planning and shopping and cooking to occupy her mind. She would be performing prayers of action. A physical dance of food preparation that was a wordless prayer. The idea pleased her. She hadn't been judged for the fleeting thought that spending time on her knees was boring. A different door had opened, and she felt a renewed presence of the Spirit.

She pulled three cookbooks off the shelf. The largest one — *Vive La Veggie* — featured a photograph of a basket overflowing with broccoli, carrots, green beans, peppers, tomatoes, mushrooms, and onions. *Vive La Veggie* offered unusual recipes for preparing common vegetables. Mark had been clear that he didn't want a vegetarian meal. She'd have to figure out a way around that. Pleasing him was important, especially now, but what was he doing to please her? Not much.

She wanted most of the vegetables to come from her garden. A Caprese salad would be smooth and sweet, as well as filling. The bright red cherry tomatoes and creamy mozzarella would be visually appealing. She would make a loaf of her multi-grain bread, of course. What else? She opened *The Balanced Vegetarian*. Something comforting. She flipped back and forth through the book. Pages of broccoli baked, broccoli sautéed, and broccoli soufflé paraded past her. Her stomach rumbled as she considered the seductive photographs.

She rummaged in Mark's desk for a piece of paper and pen. She propped open the books and copied down ingredients, adding candles, and three bottles of Chardonnay. Why had she promised Mark she'd cook meat? Rice and sausage! She'd make white Basmati instead of brown, that would keep him from complaining. A soy-based sausage would look meaty, and if she drowned it in some kind of sauce, nestled it into heaping mounds of white rice, he wouldn't even notice the sausage didn't contain bits of animal flesh. She'd done it before, using chopped garden burgers hidden in tomato sauce over spaghetti, smiling with satisfaction as he thanked her for making something that *stuck to his ribs.*

THE NEXT DAY she was up before the sun. She threw the short denim skirt into the wicker clothes basket, telling herself to remember to do laundry as soon as she got back from the store. She loved that skirt and wanted to wear it that evening. Mark would see the firm, smooth skin of her thighs, and the way the skirt hugged her hips without grabbing too tightly or creeping and bunching around lumps of fat. Joe's presence would transform the evening into a normal social event. Without the scrutiny of parishioners, Mark would be more aware of her.

She spent an hour sweeping and mopping the kitchen floor. She scoured the rings around the burners of the stove. After her shower, she put on a loose white t-shirt and denim overall shorts and braided her hair. Mark was still burrowed under the blankets. She bent over him and kissed his neck. "I'm going to the store. I want to get an early start, and I want to concentrate on what I'm getting for dinner without Peter. He's starting to make noises, but he should be happy in the crib for another ten minutes. I'll be back in an hour. Can you just give him breakfast? No need to get him dressed."

Mark grunted. He rolled onto his stomach.

"Mark. Are you listening? I'm going to the grocery store."

"Hmmm. Yeah."

She took that as agreement. If he forgot or hadn't quite

heard what she'd said, Peter would make it clear to him.

At eight, the grocery store was nearly empty. The only people crowding the aisles were delivery men with racks of bread and carts of yogurt and milk. She stopped at the meat counter. The butcher was still putting out long metal trays of red meat, wrapped in thick white fat. Leaving the cart in front of the meat counter, she crossed the aisle and picked up a soft ball of fresh mozzarella and a brick of cheddar. She returned to the meat counter and ordered five large soy sausages just to be sure she didn't come up short. Pasta, a bag of rice, and sheets of dried fruit and oatmeal for Peter filled the bottom of her cart. She grabbed a carton of chocolate ice cream. In the produce section, she lingered over each pile of vegetables, some of them stacked higher than her head. She filled two plastic bags with broccoli, grabbed a bunch of green onions to supplement what was ready to harvest from her garden, a few pounds of mushrooms, cantaloupe, strawberries, cucumbers, basil, two potatoes, garlic, cilantro, baby carrots, and a head each of radicchio and butter lettuce.

The cart was brimming with food that she couldn't wait to put together. She could taste it already. There was nothing more satisfying than watching as individual foods, uninteresting on their own, were chopped and mixed and cooked together with partners and herbs and spices until they became dishes that not only satisfied your mouth and comforted your stomach, they nourished unseen organs and brain cells, improving the functioning of the body's ecosystem.

At the end of the produce aisle was a semi-circle shelf stacked with a variety of wines. She wasn't sure what made a wine worthy of the health food market. It must be that the grapes were raised without pesticides. Or maybe they weren't trying to be healthy at all. Whatever it was, she liked to experiment. After reading several labels, she settled on a coastal Chardonnay.

When she walked in the front door, Mark was sitting on the futon, his eyes glued to the door, his face hardened, reciting from memory, the story of *The Little Engine That Could*, while Peter turned the pages. Peter was naming all the characters stranded outside the big engine that was unable to make it over the hill into the town on the other side. The look on Mark's face and his black suit made him look like something carved out of stone. The suit and white shirt, the gray and blue striped tie announced that he had some kind of important meeting. He would never help drag fabric sacks full of pungent onions and garlic into the house.

As if he was opening a gate, he lifted the half of the book that was on his lap, stood up, and lowered it onto the futon next to Peter.

Peter shouted — "Da! Choo choo."

"We have to stop now. Daddy has to go to work. I'm late."

"I was out getting food for your friend," she said.

"It would have been nice if you'd told me. I wake up, and you're gone. Peter's standing up in bed yelling. Why couldn't you take him with you?"

She lowered the bags she was holding onto the floor. They sat on either side of her, like dogs waiting for her command. The unity of their marriage was eroding. Each day, some new thorn sprouted between them. When had Mark touched her willingly? The only change was that she had been more tender toward *him*. He was the same as always. Hiding his feelings, consumed with work, meeting the needs of everyone in the whole world except her.

"I wanted to make it nice. It's hard to concentrate on what I'm getting, hard to think about the menu now that Peter's talking. He chatters all the time, and I forget things." How dare he complain when he'd asked her to do this? Finally, they had something in their lives that wasn't a church function. Even this was ultimately tied to the church — money for the building program. She wished she'd never heard of the building program or Grant Miller and his plans for seed money and sacrificial giving. "Why are you so dressed up? Where are you going?"

"I'm meeting Bob and Grant for lunch this afternoon to talk about the next phase of the program."

"No one dresses up like that for work on a Friday."

"Bob does. He always wears a shirt and tie. And Grant probably will too."

"Oh." She didn't know what else to say. Nothing had changed. The thought rubbed beneath her skin like a piece of bark, scraping at her nerves. She didn't want a fight. Not when she'd looked forward to making this dinner. All of her ungodly feelings were resurfacing. Why was it so hard to stay peaceful, waiting for God to infect her life with something good? While she stood there, longing for passion, wanting Mark to wrap his arms around her and thank her for all the work she was doing to make his friend feel welcome, he walked into the kitchen. She heard him pick up his tablet case and keys. He came through the opposite door into the hallway, where she was still frozen between the grocery bags.

"I'll still make it to the office in time to get ready for the meeting. It's just irritating to wake up and not know what's going on. Hearing Peter shouting."

"Well, I do that every day."

"It's your job."

"I know that. But raising a child takes two people. And I told you I was going to the store."

"I'm sure the dinner will be great." His words were as starched as his shirt. He leaned over the bag of vegetables and brushed his lips across her forehead.

"I'll be home by four-thirty to keep Peter occupied while you finish up. I told Joe to come at six. Okay?"

"Sure."

She moved out from between her twin bags, so he could put his arms around her waist like he'd been doing each morning for the past few weeks. But he'd already stepped over the bag and had his hand on the doorknob.

"See you later. Maybe Peter can help you carry in some

groceries."

She laughed.

He stepped neatly out the front door, closing it softly behind him.

THE DAY HAD passed by like a DVD on fast-forward. At six-fifteen, Gabrielle was worried Joe wasn't going to show up. She fluttered to the backyard where Mark was throwing a blue and red ball to Peter, who heaved it up in his arms and threw it a few feet from his toes. She drifted back to the kitchen and lifted the lid on the rice and sausage casserole to check the temperature. She adjusted the position of the candles in the center of the table. She moved to the refrigerator. She opened the door to check that the wine bottles had a nice sheen, and the cut fruit wasn't looking dehydrated along the edges. She wandered down the hallway, glancing at the small window in the center of the door.

At 6:40, she was starting her tenth trip down the hall. The doorbell rang. She was grateful he couldn't see her — looking eager over a meal that had been her entire reason for living for the past twenty-four hours. She backed farther down the hallway, straightening her skirt so that the seams ran down the center of her hip on each side. She leaned forward, tossed her hair over her head, stood up, and flipped it over her shoulders, so it draped across most of her back. That movement required her to re-adjust her skirt. The doorbell rang again. She heard Mark open the screen door.

"Gabrielle?"

Rather than yelling and risk Joe hearing, she stepped quickly into the entryway and yanked open the door with too much force.

She nearly gasped. Joe was gorgeous. He was tall, a few inches over six feet. Even standing a few inches below her on the porch, he towered over her. His shoulders seemed to fill the entire doorframe. His hair was brown, clipped short on the sides and long enough on top that it fell across the bridge of his nose. He pushed it out of his face. Glasses with thin pewter frames shaped in small ovals highlighted his dark blue eyes and made him look intelligent and sophisticated. He had a charming grin filled with straight teeth. Resting across his right arm was a spray of gladiolas bursting with yellow blooms, and in the crook of his left elbow was a bottle of wine. He handed the spectacular flowers to her. Before she could say *thank you*, he thrust out his hand and took hers. "Hi, Gabrielle. I can't believe we've never met. I'm Joe Malik."

She moved back against the open door. "Come in."

With one stride, he stepped into the house and out of the range of the door. She closed it. "What amazing flowers. Thank you."

He wore a black t-shirt and faded blue jeans. His shoes were black leather and looked expensive. She couldn't help but like a man who cared about well-made shoes.

Walking in front of him as she led the way to the dining area, she felt small and delicate. Her overly large feet were dwarfed in comparison with his. She wanted to pirouette her way through the kitchen door. She put the flowers on the counter and dragged a chair over to the cupboard to look for a vase large enough to hold the gladiolas.

"Joe!" Mark came through the back door and stepped around the table to reach for Joe's hand.

"Hey!" Joe had to lean down slightly in order to dodge Mark's extended hand and give him a firm, back-slapping hug. "Nice house. You make the suburbs look appealing."

Mark laughed. Gabrielle stepped up on the chair and slid vases and half-burned candles around on the shelf, reaching to the back for her largest vase. She slid it toward the front of the cabinet and stepped to one side of the chair to get a better angle before lifting it down.

"Let me get that for you." Joe reached between her and the cabinet door. An image flashed through the center of her brain — *Joe...grabbing her waist with his free arm, lifting her off the chair at the same time he took the vase out of the cabinet and set it on the counter.* She closed her eyes, shocked by the wave of excitement that washed over her.

"Are you okay?" Mark said.

She took a deep breath, opened her eyes, and quickly closed the cabinet door. Joe set the vase on the counter. "I'm fine." She stepped off the chair, and Mark moved it back to its place at the table.

While she arranged the gladiolas in the vase, Mark poured three glasses of wine. He put them on a bamboo tray and went to the screen door. Before he could touch the handle, Joe was at his side. He slid the door open, and Mark carried the wine out to the patio. The vase of gladiolas was too tempting to put anywhere in the living room where Peter would make an immediate grab for it. She wandered through the entryway and back to the kitchen. It was too large for the center of the table, and it would look foolish sitting on Mark's desk. She made another loop through the living room, hoping to find a surface out of Peter's reach that she'd missed on her first pass. She couldn't walk around all evening carrying flowers. Finally, she settled the vase on the L-section of the kitchen counter. She placed crackers and thin slices of cheese and peppers and slivers of carrots on a large blue ceramic plate. She carried the plate outside, where Joe was nearly finished with his first glass of wine.

"Do you have anything stronger than this?" he grinned and swallowed what was left in the glass. "Or do you have California soaked into your blood, so the only acceptable beverage is wine? Or is it a Lutheran thing?"

Mark laughed. He didn't seem offended. His laugh was a deep, unfamiliar rumble that rose from his belly. Was his usual lack of laughter the result of marriage and parenthood? Did every part of you slowly decay and eventually die once those two milestones were achieved? Or was it the fate of ministers and their families? Always working, no boundaries between social life and work. Nothing was ever just for fun because the business of heaven never stopped.

Why was she thinking such things? She should be pleased. It was good to have Joe here. A little time with him, and maybe she and Mark would relax and return to their better selves.

"Wine is all we have," Mark said. "It'll have to do this time."

She felt a tremble of anticipation. *This time.* They'd be seeing more of Joe. Aside from his obvious good looks, and graceful charm, he'd turned everything in their house on its edge in the fifteen minutes since he'd walked in the door. Mark was laughing, Gabrielle was feeling like a normal woman for the first time since…she couldn't remember. She went into the house and brought the wine bottle out to the patio. She refilled Joe's glass and topped off Mark's. She'd barely had a sip of her own, feeling intoxicated with the thrill of a stranger in their house, the thrill of wondering what mysterious plan had brought him into their lives at this point in time

During dinner, Joe entertained them with anecdotes from his business travels all over the world. Between stories, he poured out compliments about her cooking. Gabrielle was starting her third glass of wine. She could feel her blood pumping closer to the surface of her skin. The tip of her nose was numb. Joe must have had at least a bottle and a half on his own. He didn't seem drunk. He smiled and talked as crisply and easily as when he'd first walked through the front door.

"I used to be a fanatical vegan, so I know a good soy sausage when I taste one," he said.

She avoided Mark's eyes, unsure whether it registered that Joe was referring to the soy sausage she had buried in the rice beneath a sweet and spicy pepper sauce.

"With all the late nights at the office, all the food that's brought in, it got too difficult to maintain. I sure felt better back then. And none of this." He patted a non-existent belly. "Incredible sauce."

He couldn't seem to stop — the bread was like nothing he'd ever tasted. The Caprese salad one of the best he'd ever had. He decreed her meal a work of art.

Her eyes filled with tears. "That's exactly how I feel." It seemed as if he'd looked inside her, seen how she felt about growing and preparing food, then put the perfect words to that experience.

While they talked, the room grew darker. The candles gave off a creamy glow, making their faces look warm and soft. Mark talked less and less, as he always did when he had more than one glass of wine. It put him on the edge of sleep. His eyelids looked thick. She wanted to pick him up and carry him to bed like she'd done with Peter. She was filled with tender feelings toward him. Things would improve. She'd been too impatient. Weren't they commanded to take a weekly day of rest? When did they ever sit like this, talking, not worrying whether everyone felt included in the group, not straining to socialize with so many differing personalities, making sure each person had equal attention from the pastor and his wife? Social events so often deteriorated into a dredging up of church problems, examined as if the Atwaters and their guests were turning empty wine glasses in their hands, looking at every possible angle, working to locate some small imperfection.

When the wine was gone, and Mark looked even sleepier, Joe pushed back his chair. "I should take off. It's been a long week, and I need to go into the office for a few hours tomorrow. I better get some sleep. I'm sure you two feel the same way." He winked at Gabrielle. "Can I help you put away the food? Wipe up some dishes?"

Mark leaped out of his chair. "We'll take care of it." He moved between Joe and the counter, took the plate out of Joe's hands, and put it down. "It was great to see you. With all the catching up, I forgot to say something. Part of the reason for the dinner was to let you know how much we appreciate the gift you gave to the building campaign. I can't tell you how much it means to the church and to me personally."

It was like a big plastic lid had been lowered onto a container, fitted onto the ridge, sealing them into an airless, stale-smelling bowl. She wondered if she'd imagined Mark's laughter, dreamt about the relaxing dinner and easy conversation, fantasized that her meal was called a work of art.

They walked in their silent vacuum to the front door. Joe hugged Mark. Then he turned to her, lifting her onto her toes in a sweeping hug. "Thanks for a great evening. The food was spectacular. Peter's a charmer. What a smart kid! I had a great time with you two. Take care." With the same long strides he'd used to take over their house for the evening, he stepped out the door and walked to the driveway. He got into a silver sports car, backed out of the driveway, and shot down the street, disappearing at the corner.

When they were settled in bed, she moved close to Mark and tucked her arm under the small of his back. His body felt as if he'd melted into the mattress. "That was fun. I like Joe," she said.

"He's a good guy."

She pulled him closer. He didn't resist, but he didn't turn toward her. Before she could say anything else, she heard the rumble of his breath coming from deep in his sinuses. She kept her arms around him and closed her eyes.

When Joe had first called, all those weeks ago, she'd resented him. But meeting him in person erased the feeling of being excluded. Energy raced from one end of her body to the other. This was definitely the first phase of the miracle. Her brain was muddled from all the wine. She couldn't quite explain to herself what Joe had to do with their marriage or the answer to her prayers. She just knew she felt happier than she had in a very long time. Relaxing and having fun made her more willing to wait for Mark's desires to change shape. If he could just see that he needed to stop working twelve or fourteen hours a day, six days a week, if he could relax, they could spend more time touching each other, having fun. That was it. They never did anything fun.

Her thoughts straddled that confusing space between consciousness and dreams. She liked Joe a lot and wanted him to spend more time at their house. She had expected to dislike him, and she hadn't. She should enjoy the warm, peaceful feeling, and try not to think about when the miracle would take place or how it would unfold. For now, she was content to hold her sleeping husband. Making love would come soon, she was sure of it. Maybe sooner than she imagined.

Sixteen

GABRIELLE HATED SEPTEMBER. How could it be in the high seventies one day and rain the next? The air smelled foul — like wet, dirty tar. She wanted Mark to close the minivan window, so she didn't have to breathe it in, but he insisted on keeping it open because the interior turned muggy when it was closed. She didn't even want to be in the minivan. She didn't want to be visiting the Olefsons. It was their final fundraising visit, postponed because the Olefsons had been on the East coast all summer, visiting Carrie Olefson's sister.

Gabrielle wanted the building program to go away. She was tired of church members, tired of making conversation with people twenty or thirty years older than her, some of whom she didn't particularly like. She was a young, healthy woman, but she spent half her life around middle-aged and elderly people. Why couldn't there be people like Joe in their church? People like the members of Gethsemane Temple? Young, exciting people. Instead, Grace was made up of couples plodding through conventional lives. Their biggest thrill was arguing about constructing a new sanctuary where they would continue to do everything exactly as they had for the past forty years.

She leaned against the door. She had a vaguely formed desire for the door to fly open, the movement of the minivan flinging her onto the damp pavement. At least it would be something interesting and exciting. Maybe if she went back to Gethsemane, things would be better. It was too much work trying to maintain an elevated spiritual state all by herself. It wasn't supposed to be a solitary effort. There should be a community of ecstatic supporters.

Everything was the same. Everything! She didn't even know with absolute certainty whether Mark's visits to *This 'n That* had stopped. She was condemned to a life of sameness. A life with no passion, without miracles. It was all too paralyzing to think about.

"Why are you sulking?" Mark said.

"I'm not sulking."

"You're sulking. I hope you aren't going to be in a mood at the Olefsons."

"I'm tired of visiting people. That's all."

"It's almost over." He actually sounded sympathetic, as if he was tired of the visits too.

"It will never be over," she said. "There's always something. We'll finish the visits, and it will be time for Advent services and the Christmas fair, and all the concerts and parties. Then it will be construction plans and meetings about what kind of wood we want for the pews. And committee meetings for carpets and windows. We'll never have time for our marriage. You don't even want to have time for me. You don't want to change."

"We can't have this fight right now."

"It's not a fight. It's our life."

"Please."

"Do you want me? Are your feelings changing? You're not even trying. We have to spend time alone."

"I can't talk about this right now. We're going to visit these people, and I can't talk about sex five minutes before we walk in the door. Please don't do this to me."

"Fine. Then when? When can we talk about it?"

"This weekend. I promise."

She pressed harder against the door, wondering if the latch would hold. Without the armrest poking her ribs and the cold glass against her temple, everything would fall apart. She didn't believe for one minute that they'd talk about it or spend time alone over the weekend. Something would come up. When had he ever had time for her on a Saturday?

They turned onto Mariposa Court. The Olefsons lived in a tiny two-bedroom, one-bathroom house built in the nineteen forties. In those eleven hundred square feet, they had raised two daughters who now had children of their own. It was a pointless visit. The Olefsons were excited about the new sanctuary. They were convinced that a snazzy new building would bring young people like their daughters and grandchildren flocking to the church. It was another one of Grant's stupid rules that the Olefsons still had to be visited, even though they'd already donated money. Every member — no exceptions. At least it was an easy visit. They could skip the prescribed agenda that made her feel like a salesman trying to achieve a quota, pushing for a close on the deal, begging for a check.

The Olefson's front yard was a small, lush plot of grass, vibrant despite the drought. Around the lawn was a two-foot border of rich-looking soil, planted every foot and a half with a rose bush. The precision irritated her. It disturbed an aesthetic sense that craved irregularity. The bushes were planted in a perfectly repeating pattern — white, red, pink, salmon, yellow, white, red... A waist-high iron fence ran around the edge. Some of the rose blossoms strained to escape their perfect world, shooting out through the iron bars. The house was yellow, and although it had never been remodeled, it looked almost new. There wasn't a speck of dirt on any of the windows. The concrete driveway was white and free of oil spots. The front porch was swept clean, a clay flower pot in each corner, purple pansies spilling over the sides.

Herb Olefson opened the front door before they pressed the bell.

"So good to see you, Pastor." He grabbed Mark's hand and shook it vigorously. "Come on in." With one hand, he opened the door wider, and with the other, he clung to Mark's hand, pulling him into the tiny entryway. He tugged Mark into the living room and nearly pushed him into a squatty green and pink floral armchair with an extraordinarily low back.

Carrie Olefson appeared and ushered Gabrielle to a matching chair near the one where Mark was seated. A round table with a tiny railing circling the edge sat between the two chairs. Crowded into the fenced circle were two silver coasters, three ceramic angels, a tiny lamp with a ceramic base painted with pink rosebuds, and a milky white candy dish. The candy dish had a lid with circular bumps all over it, making it look like a pile of petrified cotton balls.

Carrie lifted the lid. "Have a candy, Pastor."

The dish was filled with colored balls wrapped in plastic, perfect for choking to death. Mark took a piece of candy. Gabrielle shook her head.

Carrie scurried off to the kitchen and returned with a plate of lemon bars. She set them on the coffee table. "Have a lemon bar, dear. Herb loves them." She sidled up to Herb and patted his stomach. "It's a good source of vitamin C, all that lemon."

Imagine thinking you could get the benefits of vitamin C in a cookie saturated with sugar and a bit of lemon rind that had been cooked to death.

Gabrielle pressed her lips together. "No thanks."

From the corner of her eye, she saw Mark glaring at her. She smiled to soften the refusal. "I'll just enjoy a cup of tea first."

Mark appeared to relax. She could count on him to eat so many lemon bars that Carrie would think they'd both consumed them when she wasn't looking.

Carrie disappeared into the kitchen again. She returned with coffee for Herb and Mark. The cups containing tea hovered precariously at the other end of the tray as if she might mix up the coffee and tea if the cups were set too close to each other. When the tray was settled safely on the table between the lemon bars and a pile of National Geographic magazines, Gabrielle let out a long breath. In spite of her age, Carrie Olefson seemed to be completely in control of her lemon bars and the room. She moved easily in the tight quarters created by excessive amounts of furniture. There was a piano tucked in one corner and a couch flanked by two square tables that matched the coffee table. Besides the two chairs where Mark and Gabrielle were seated, there was a large, floral wing chair with its own end table. Carrie settled on the couch, sitting so close to Herb, her weight on the thick cushion forced him to lean toward her.

Gabrielle reached for her teacup and took a sip. The heat stabbed her tongue like the tip of a steak knife.

Carrie left her teacup sitting on the tray. She wasn't interested in her lemon bars or her tea. Herb was equally disinterested in his cup of coffee. They snuggled up to each other as if they were alone in the room. Carried wrapped her arm around Herb's round stomach, pulling him close to her. He grunted with satisfaction. Gabrielle looked away. She sipped more tea, angry that there was nothing else to do but sip tea, scorching the tender flesh inside her mouth. Mark was rambling on about something, but she couldn't focus on the words. Herb fiddled with the white plastic beads on Carrie's bracelet, then moved his hand to his wife's plump thigh, pressed up against his own. Gabrielle put her teacup down with a slight clatter, earning another sharp look from Mark, who was still talking incoherently about the new building. She didn't want any more tea. Since Mark wasn't eating any lemon bars, pressure to consume her fair share of sugar would begin at any moment.

Herb and Carrie seemed oblivious to what Mark was saying. They pawed each other, rubbing each other's legs. Carrie leaned her head against Herb's shoulder, sighing with pleasure. Gabrielle wanted to scream. She wanted to fling her thin teacup against the fireplace, shocking Mark out of his complacent monologue. Even old people — plump, sagging, bleary-eyed people who lived in a house with a stuffy, over-crowded living room had passion oozing out of them. It was an outrage that someone like Carrie Olefson had a man cuddling and stroking her powdery white skin, while Gabrielle had to sit and watch. She was doomed to go home and crawl into bed with a man who wanted other men. What would the Olefsons say if they knew that? Would they be so simpering with their *Pastor this* and *Pastor that?*

Gabrielle's teacup was empty.

"Can I get you more tea, dear?" Carrie said.

"Sure," Gabrielle said. She could feel Mark's eyes on her again. Why was it that the only time she felt his eyes on her was when he was upset, or trying to correct her behavior? As if piercing stares would cut into her, slice out the parts of her personality that annoyed him, and leave her sweet and agreeable.

Carrie was back with a pot of hot water in one hand and a small bowl for Gabrielle's used teabag in the other. She shoved the bowl between the ceramic angels and pulled a frowsy teabag out of a wide pocket that spanned her left thigh on the front of her dress. She placed the teabag in the cup like she was placing a dead bird into a grave. It lay there while she poured steaming water over it. The bag floated to the surface. Carrie took the kettle back to the kitchen and returned to urge lemon bars on them, holding the plate in front of Mark until he took two.

"You'll just love my lemon bars," Carrie said. "Everyone does. Try one. You don't know what you're missing."

Herb piped up. "I could eat Carrie's lemon bars for breakfast, lunch, and dinner. They're that good. Tart and sweet, just like a good woman." He winked.

Gabrielle gagged, but Mark didn't seem to notice. He laughed too loud and too fast. Gabrielle let her eyes creep up Carrie's face.

Carrie was blushing, pressing her lips together to stifle a giggle. "Oh, Herb," she said. She moved toward Gabrielle, holding the plate expectantly.

Mark stuffed a lemon bar into his mouth.

Gabrielle was making a monumental effort to stand by her husband, to wait patiently for a change in his inclination. Instead of answering her devoted prayers, God was mocking her! She couldn't go anywhere without having another couple's sex life shoved down her throat like the oxygen-sapping lemon bars. The combination of powdered sugar and lemon made it difficult to breathe, the fine powder and sour taste sucked the air right out of your throat. She'd eaten the deadly things before at countless church potlucks. Carrie Olefson wasn't the only woman at Grace who considered lemon bars her specialty. It hurt that God was so insensitive to her feelings. She was doing everything right, everything she'd been told to do. Others, who did nothing more than show up at a church service once a week had all their desires satisfied. Her lot was to suffer an ache in her bones that would *never* be eased.

Carrie wouldn't move. She remained a few inches from Gabrielle's knees, holding the plate close enough for Gabrielle to smell the sweetened lemon. Carrie's hands began to tremble. Gabrielle plucked at the smallest bar she could find. Her fingers sank into the narrow sides of the soft, lemony stuff. The bar clung to the plate like a barnacle. As the center slowly came loose, the ends collapsed, refusing to let go. She pressed her fingers more tightly, making big dents, powdered sugar creeping into her nails and cuticles. She applied even more pressure, finally scooping it free of the plate. It hung limply in her fingers. She had no choice but to shove the entire thing into her mouth at once or risk losing it onto her lap. She clenched her shoulders to restrain a pressing compulsion to tap the bottom of the plate and upend the whole thing into a sticky mound of broken ceramic and lemon custard on the dark brown carpet, lemon ooze adhering to the strands of the shag, and the powdered sugar floating gracefully across the rug, settling like snow on Carrie's shoes.

Carrie stepped toward Mark. "Just one more?"

Mark grabbed one. He was as deprived of sugar as she was of sex. Maybe it was the same thing.

"Sweet and tart," mumbled Herb, inexplicably. "I'll have another one, honey."

Carrie trotted over to the couch, managing to slip her round body between the coffee table and Herb's legs. He took two bars, shoved one into his mouth, and held the other in the palm of his left hand, gazing at it with a partial smile on his lips. With his right hand, he patted his wife's hip, rubbing it slightly. Carrie turned and set the plate on the table.

Gabrielle hated herself for succumbing to the pressure to eat something that made her stomach clutch itself in terror. But when someone stood over you, her knees almost pressing into your own, breathing sweet, warm breath onto your face, and your husband wanted nothing from you but politeness, you choked down the sugar.

Carrie was almost purring under Herb's thick, wide hands. Gabrielle couldn't comprehend why a man would be drawn to Carrie. Her hair was dyed honey blonde. The top part of her body was small, almost delicate, with narrow shoulders. Her neck was thin, and her head, under the cloud of single-hue hair, was small and round. Her hips ballooned out, pushing at the fabric of her dress, drawing attention away from her elegant shoulders. They were huge hips that had never deflated after giving birth, accompanied by a full belly and thick thighs that rubbed against each other. Her breasts were old and nondescript, dwarfed by those hips. Yet it was increasingly clear that Herb wanted the Pastor and his wife to leave so he could be alone with the woman he craved. He couldn't keep his eyes off her body, or his hands off her lemon bars. As soon as she sat down, he shoved the lemon bar into his mouth and stroked her leg, ignoring his sugar-tipped fingers.

Gabrielle thrust her teacup forward. "May I have some more tea? It's delicious."

This earned her another harsh look from Mark. She grimaced at him. The little worm. That's what her husband looked like, sitting without a sturdy chair to support his spine. He looked limp and nervous. The stunning blue eyes and muscular shoulders were lies. The entire core of his being was a lie. He married her, knowing he would never be attracted to her. She'd been foolish and naïve. It all came from marrying him on the rebound after Paul abandoned her, just like her mother had warned. Gabrielle had only seen what she wanted to — Mark's good looks, his charming public persona. If only she'd waited, but she was so hell-bent on proving her mother wrong, on proving to herself that she was a desirable woman. If she'd had any sense at all, she would have seen what he was.

Her lengthy prayers and devotional cleaning weren't fooling anyone but herself. Mark was gay, hiding behind her and Peter. She'd been faithful. She'd stood by him and helped him appeal to God for a change in his desires. Of course nothing had happened. He wasn't even trying. All he cared about was what people saw on the outside. If he wanted to change, if he really wanted to listen to God, it was all on him now. It wasn't fair that she had to do everything.

The room swam in front of her eyes. The crowded furniture pressed at her muscles until they twitched and shuddered with desire for some space in which to get up and move around. She sipped the burning water that Carrie had poured into her cup. It hadn't steeped through the teabag.

Carrie was back on the couch, snuggling with Herb. Old, lumpy, dyed Carrie had a man who adored her. After more than forty years of marriage, he wanted her so much he couldn't stop fondling her.

It wasn't fair that she did everything God asked, and He stuck her with a man who didn't want her. Maybe it wasn't fair to blame God. Mark was the liar. God must have something better in store for her. She just hadn't seen it yet.

Seventeen

NEARLY ALL THE MONEY required to start construction on the new sanctuary and office buildings had been raised. Or more accurately, had been promised. Over one million dollars pledged by the members of Grace. Mark was ecstatic. Gabrielle was shocked. Susan was defeated, but she hid it well. The three of them stood near the patio entrance to the parish hall and watched people line up at the buffet table to fill their plates with food for the pledge dinner. All of the women had provided a casserole and either a salad or a dessert. They'd whipped up hamburger with canned soup, chicken and noodle casseroles, and plates of fried chicken, huge bowls of lettuce and tomatoes, Jell-O molds, and plates of cookies.

Gabrielle was sickened by Grant Miller's gloating, *I-told-you-so,* attitude that he wore like an expensive coat as he strolled around congratulating people on their incredible faith. He should be congratulating them on living frugal lives. Praising them for having the luck to purchase houses in Silicon Valley years before average, three-bedroom tract homes appreciated to six or seven or ten times their original value before interest rates dropped, and homeowners refinanced their way to greater disposable incomes.

She caught Allysan's eye across the room and knew her thoughts in an instant — disgust with the group of lemmings who patted themselves on the back for raising so much cash. As if God cared what kind of building they had, especially their office building. Allysan glided over to Gabrielle's side. "They think stained glass and stone floors and carved pews will bring them closer to God. It's so sad."

Gabrielle wasn't feeling particularly close to God herself, but she nodded. It seemed the only thing to do. "I want to go to a prayer meeting at Gethsemane with you again."

"Any time."

Hearing the word *Gethsemane* flow out of her lips released a flood of hope, easing the knot of fear that she was doomed to a dry, bleak life.

"In ancient cultures, there were women who were designated mourners," Allysan said.

Gabrielle didn't know what to make of this comment. Men and women trudged past the tables of food, filling their plates and arteries with fat that made some of their bodies hideous, reflecting what was happening inside.

"I feel like I'm the designated mourner for these people," Allysan said.

"Why are you mourning?" She didn't really care what Allysan's answer might be. She wanted someone to mourn for her sex life. God had let her down. Why couldn't she have married someone like Joe? He'd swept into the room a few minutes ago, pacifying Mark by agreeing to come to the potluck. Even though he'd sharply pointed out, "Why would I go to a dinner to be applauded for my gift? I make considerably more than most of the people in your church. What I'm able to give is disproportionate."

He'd winked at Gabrielle when he said it, and a little shiver ran through her arms. No man had ever winked at her. It was clear she'd gotten married when she was too young. Married the wrong man. Now she was trapped. The law of God glued her to Mark for eternity.

Allysan's voice slammed against her thoughts. "I look at all these people, and I want to mourn because they're like the dry bones in the book of Ezekiel — bones without flesh. They stand at the tables, heaping their plates, filling their bodies, talking nonsense. They have no connection with anything beyond the physical. They don't want anything more than food in their stomachs and a sense of stability, so they don't have to think about the vastness of God and be afraid. They want to be small, it makes them feel secure."

Gabrielle was having a hard time following Allysan's train of thought. Each comment sent her brain reeling off in another direction. The food looked horrid, and the smells created a rotten feeling in her stomach.

Mark moved through the crowd like a politician, asking questions, shaking hands, patting old folks on the arm, helping those with canes transport sagging plates to one of the round, cloth-covered tables. In a few minutes, everyone would be seated. Gabrielle would be placed next to Mark like a potted plant at the head table. She and Mark and the Schneiders and Grant Miller would line one side of a rectangular table, set apart from the others. It was impossible to talk, difficult to keep Peter in place. She envied the others, choosing their dinner companions, not parked at a separate table like a miscast bridal party.

"Should we line up for our food?" she said. "I have to sit at the head table, so I can't talk any more."

"Why is there a head table?" Allysan said.

"That's just the way we do it. I guess everyone feels nervous if they can't see their Pastor set in one spot."

"Then, don't sit there. You're not the pastor."

"Mark wants me there."

"Do you do everything Mark wants?"

It wasn't as if Mark made her do anything. It seemed like that was her job. Why *did* she go along? She let out a harsh, bitter laugh.

Allysan turned to look at her. "Hit a nerve, did I?" She smiled and glided toward the thick paper plates stacked at the end of one table. She pried one loose and picked up a napkin rolled around plastic utensils, tied with a bright blue ribbon.

Gabrielle followed. She moved past three Jell-O molds,

pretending not to hear the woman on the other side of the table — *You have to try the lime. It's absolutely the most refreshing thing you'll ever taste.* When they reached the end of the line, Joe was standing there, his plate piled so high with food, the edges bent out precariously. Gabrielle hoped he'd put it on a table before the whole thing collapsed on his feet.

"Where are you sitting?" he said.

"You're talking to a VIP," Allysan said. "She sits at the head table." She winked at Joe. "Hi, I'm Allysan Krohl."

"Hi Allysan, I'm Joe." He grinned. "This is all completely unfamiliar territory to me. Maybe you can help me navigate the subtleties of a potluck dinner. Start by telling me why it's called a potluck." They turned and started walking toward the side of the hall, where a few tables were still half empty. Joe glanced back and lifted his chin toward Gabrielle. "See ya'."

Gabrielle didn't know whether she was furious with Mark for expecting her to sit at a table isolated from everyone else, or angry at Joe for being equally charming to Allysan, or disgusted with Allysan for so quickly shedding her spirituality. What happened to the mysterious, barefooted Allysan who was too ethereal to talk to anyone else at the church, much less a man she'd never met? A man who cared nothing for spiritual things, as far as Gabrielle knew. She stared at Joe's back, his wide shoulders, watched his loping stride. Allysan floated next to him, not seeming to have any difficulty keeping up with his pace. They walked easily together as if they'd known and absorbed each other's rhythms for years. A white heat flared inside of her. She wanted it to consume her. She wanted to drop the plate of toxic food on the floor and run after them. She wanted Allysan to go back to being a feathery, nymph-like creature, an angel hovering at Gabrielle's side.

Mark signaled her to join him. She glanced toward the side of the room where Allysan and Joe were eating. Allysan monopolized his attention, drawing him into herself with those wide, dark eyes. Joe gazed back at her, listening as if she were revealing the secrets of the universe to him. Mark's hand signals grew more intense, indicating she was to get to his side immediately. She sighed and carried her softening paper plate to the front of the room. She sat next to Mark. He leaned toward her. "You need to do a better job keeping your eye on Peter. I caught him standing on a folding chair."

She settled Peter onto her lap and scooped several forkfuls of noodles onto a separate plate for him.

While they ate, several people, including Larry Brackner, spoke about the success of the fundraising program. While the speakers carried on, people drifted quietly from their tables, dropping soggy plates into the plastic-lined garbage cans, and lining up for fresh paper plates on which they could pile cookies, slices of pie, and wedges of chocolate cake. Gabrielle had finished dinner quickly. She stood at the back of the room. Peter sat near her feet, racing his miniature cars around the floor, excited that the slick surface made them move faster than they did on the linoleum at home.

Her body jerked as Carrie Olefson suddenly materialized at her side.

"I'm sorry, did I startle you?" She patted Gabrielle's arm. "Go get some dessert, dear. I'll watch Peter for a minute or two."

"I'm fine," Gabrielle said.

Carrie looked as if she was winking her wrinkled eyelid at Gabrielle. "You know, they say when you startle easily, it's the sign of a guilty conscience."

"There's nothing wrong with my conscience."

"I was teasing, dear. Come have some dessert."

"I don't care for any."

Carrie rested her hand on Gabrielle's arm. Gabrielle shook it off. Tears sprang into Carrie's eyes. Gabrielle didn't care. She wanted to be left alone. She didn't have a guilty conscience. Dessert was never on her list of things to do, and she wondered when these people would get it through their thick skulls that she didn't eat sweets. Some of them sucked up an endless quantity of sugars and fats, filling their plump cells, plugging arteries, huffing and puffing around, exhausted from trying to lug all that weight around with inadequate blood circulation. Mark wouldn't be away from home so much of the time, making hospital visits, if they weren't so busy killing themselves with their own cooking.

Mark seemed to appear out of nowhere. He leaned close. "Have some dessert."

On one side, Carrie's eyes glittered with tears, on the other,

Mark's were hard and commanding. Gabrielle looked away. Across the room, Allysan and Joe had their heads together, alone in the sea of people. They looked like lovers, soul mates who would talk until the hall was empty and the lights were turned off. They were oblivious to their surroundings. Peter tugged on Gabrielle's skirt, whining for a cookie. She didn't even know how he'd learned that word. He couldn't say *bread*, but he knew how to ask for a cookie. He certainly hadn't learned that from her.

Mark took her arm. His fingers were sharp on her elbow, steering her toward the desserts. She stumbled. He leaned his head close to hers, filling her ear with warm breath. Blood pounded through her chest, and she felt soft with desire until he spoke. "Peter wants a cookie," he said quietly. "You need to get a grip. Have a piece of dessert to please an old lady. You hurt these people when you reject their food."

"Let go of me." She yanked her arm away with a wide upward swing, banging her wrist against his chin, forcing his fingers to lose their hold on the bones of her elbow. "No one is going to force me to eat something I don't want. You don't own my body. You can't grab me, and you can't force me to eat food that disgusts me. You lost that right. And if you want to give Peter a cookie, go ahead. But don't expect me to do it."

His eyes seemed to lose focus. Waves of shame washed across his face, letting her know that his fear of attracting unfavorable attention had overcome his fear that she was hurting Carrie's feelings. He stepped back and took Peter's hand. Susan stood off to one side, watching. Her face was slack, her eyes filled with false pity. On the other side of the room, Allysan and Joe had managed to free themselves from their private universe. Allysan had a soulful look that filled her eyes and poured down across her face, forming her lips into a generous, concerned frown. Joe looked amused, as he always did in the short time she'd known him. It must feel good to always be an observer of life, to be entertained, not caring what the outcome was because every possibility was interesting. Carrie was staring at her, joined by a few others.

Gabrielle hated them all. She wanted to smack her hand across all of their faces, one after the other, screaming at them to stop trying to control what she ate, to stop pitying her because her body was unwanted. The circle of glaring eyes grew larger.

Mark moved in again. She leaped back as if he meant to hit her. His eyes were filled with angry tears, and his lips were bloodless. At last, something she'd done had stirred some emotion in him. *Now* he was passionate. Maybe not the wild desire she wanted, but at least it was something.

"Don't make a scene," he said. "I'm getting a cookie for Peter, and I would really appreciate it if you would calm down and act like a lady by taking a small piece of dessert. You've crushed Carrie's feelings, and she deserves an apology. You aren't standing up for your faith here, it's just a dessert."

She took a step away from him and bumped into Carrie.

The soft cushion of flesh bounced against her back. She had no idea how Carrie had managed to maneuver behind her. They crowded closer. It was as if they'd been directed where to stand, so they contracted like a sea anemone closing in on itself as it was prodded and poked. Fanned out a few feet in front of her to her left were Mark and Peter. Susan faced her head-on. Joe and Allysan now stood to her right. Beyond this inner circle was another row of parishioners, trying not to stare. Allysan's eyes were closed as if she was deep in prayer. Gabrielle turned away. She didn't require divine intervention. God was already on her side.

Susan stepped up close, her breath hot, her voice carrying beyond the small group of onlookers. "You're embarrassing Mark and you're making a fool of yourself." She reached for Gabrielle's wrist. "Let's go sit down, and you can cool off."

Gabrielle narrowed her eyes. She lowered her voice to a fierce whisper. "I don't need to cool off, and I don't need you butting in where you don't belong. Don't tell me what to do and don't hand me your superior attitude. Just stay out of my life."

"Hey." Joe moved quickly to her side and draped his arm loosely across her shoulders. A wave of blood pulsed through her veins. "Give the woman some breathing room. What's the big deal here? Mark, get the kid a cookie." He turned to face her, keeping his arm resting across her shoulders. "How about a ride home? I know I've had just about enough pot *luck* for one evening."

The rage shrank to a small flame, deep inside. She laughed. "I think I've had enough pot luck for an entire year."

Joe laughed. Mark's eyes were bitter, but he led Peter to the table and pointed to a plate of cookies. Peter selected his cookie more quickly than he'd ever made a decision in his short life. He clutched it in his hand while Mark scooped him up, handed him to Gabrielle, turned, and stalked to the front of the hall. Instead of turning and asking people to settle down with their desserts, he kept going, disappearing through the door that lead to the area behind the stage.

Gabrielle couldn't stop smiling. Joe had rescued her from an angry mob that was about to pick up stones and hurl them at her until she bled to death. If Mark hadn't tricked her into marrying him, none of this would be happening. Since Old Testament times, it was always the woman who was blamed when things went wrong. She was certain that none of these people thought she deserved adoration, even though Susan and Carrie and hordes of other women, attractive or not, had all the sex they wanted. All her life she'd been shoved aside. It was so completely unfair she could hardly find the strength to carry Peter out to Joe's silver BMW. She didn't deserve the life that had been shoved into her hands.

Eighteen

JOE PULLED HIS car into the driveway and turned off the engine. The pewter frames of his glasses glinted under the streetlight coming through the passenger side window. He glanced at her and smiled. The remaining tension drained out of her shoulders. How easy life would be with someone who smiled as often as he spoke.

"Do you want a glass of wine?" she said.

"Sure." Before the words were out of his mouth, he opened the door, easily extracting his long legs. Before she could unbuckle her belt, he was standing on the passenger side of the car. He opened her door.

She got out and lifted a drowsy Peter out of his car seat. She stepped to the side, cradling him against her shoulder. "Can you get the car seat? Just leave it on the front porch, I'll put it away later."

She went inside. Without turning on any lights, she walked down the hall to Peter's bedroom. His diaper felt dry, so she slipped him off her arm into the crib, holding his head securely, so he didn't wake. Leaning over the rail, she unbuckled his sandals and slipped them off his hot little feet. She leaned further into the crib. The rail dug into her ribs as she kissed the top of each foot. She smoothed his hair back from his forehead and placed the quilt over his legs. She closed the blinds and tiptoed out of the room, closing the door with a soft click.

The car seat was in the front hall, propped in the corner. The front door was closed, and Joe had already opened the sliding glass door letting moist air laced with the scent of ripe tomatoes into the room. He'd turned on the lamp at one end of the couch and was standing in front of the iPod dock, scrolling through their music. "Not much for music variety other than the occasional country rock, are you?"

"Not really. I love country rock, but God uses music to fill our thoughts with the ideas He wants us to think about, so we usually listen to praise songs."

Joe straightened and looked at her until she had to shift her gaze away from his face. "Do you really believe that?"

She felt as if he'd slapped her. "I think so," she said softly. Right now, she didn't know what she believed. About anything. And she didn't want to try to figure it out.

He moved closer. He touched her forearm. "I didn't mean to offend you. Just making conversation. Don't take it seriously. Curiosity killed the cat, huh?"

"You didn't offend me. How about that glass of wine?"

She turned quickly and went up the steps, around the corner, and into the kitchen. She flicked on the light switch and opened the refrigerator. Of course, there was nothing cold. It wasn't as if she and Mark drank wine every day, or even once a week. What had she been thinking when she'd invited him to have a glass of wine? They served it often enough when church members came to dinner, but they only drank white, and rarely kept a bottle waiting in the refrigerator. She closed the door and looked out the window, trying to think. The clock hummed. Minutes glided past like water slipping down the drain. She didn't want to spoil the evening by saying she didn't have any wine. Didn't want to break the silence that filled the house with peace while she stared at the window and felt Joe's presence in the other room, waiting for her.

"Need help opening it?" His voice was so strong it sounded like he was right beside her.

She went to the doorway of the living room. She stepped down meekly and walked toward him, afraid her words would send him out the door. "I don't actually have any wine. I thought we did."

"No worries. I have a bottle in my trunk." He shoved his fingers into his right pocket and pulled out a small ring with a remote and two keys. So different from Mark's wad of keys, fitting all the locks at church, their house, the minivan, his motorcycle…so simple, so straightforward. Easy.

She laughed. "You carry wine in your trunk?"

"Not on a regular basis. But when I was at the market

today, I saw something I'd read about, and I grabbed it. I was only in the store for a candy bar on my way to work. Never had a chance to put the wine away. It was fortuitous."

"Must have been." Her smile felt weak as she watched him stride to the other side of the room, step up into the entryway, and open the front door.

"I hope you like Merlot," he said.

She'd never had Merlot. Would he realize how inexperienced she was? The evening felt like a first date.

He returned with a bottle wrapped in a thin paper bag. She followed him into the kitchen.

"Where's the opener?"

She moved to the drawer near the oven and pulled out a corkscrew. Joe peeled off the thick foil around the neck of the bottle. He inserted the corkscrew perfectly straight, twisting it firmly into the cork, and pulled it out with a soft, pleasing pop. Without asking where they were kept, he reached into the cabinet above the sink and pulled out two wine glasses. He filled them a third of the way, handed one to her, and led the way back to the living room.

He turned to face her, although facing her was more of a general idea than an actual fact. Her forehead barely reached his collarbone, white and smooth, dark hairs lapping over the curve of the bone. She put the glass to her lips, but before she could take a sip, he said, "Wait. First, a toast."

"What would we drink to? The building program?"

He laughed. "No." He brought his glass close to hers

without touching it. "To a new wine and new friends." He gently touched the side of his glass to hers. The glasses chimed. He took a small, careful sip.

Her father would have called him glib — *He's too smooth for his own good.* But Gabrielle liked it. The low, even sound of his voice vibrated through her bones. She wanted the evening to go on forever, even though only the past half hour had been pleasurable. She pushed away the image of Mark and the others crowding around her, threatening with their solemn faces, standing shoulder to shoulder. She wondered how long Mark would linger at church. If it was anything like usual, it could be hours. The wine was smooth. She took another sip.

"We're lucky the evening cooled off so fast, or this would have been too warm to drink. I was an idiot to let it sit in the trunk all day. Not a very good wine storage technique."

Gabrielle said nothing.

He stepped around the coffee table and settled onto the futon. He pushed the table away from the couch to make more room for his legs. Gabrielle sat at the other end, taking two more sips of wine. She couldn't shake the first date sensation.

"All we talked about the other night was my job and golf. Tell me about you. What's it like being married to a man of God?"

She laughed. Thankfully her mouth was empty of wine, so she didn't look ridiculous spitting it out on her lap.

"Why is that funny?"

"I don't know. I guess it's the last thing I'd expect you to say, calling him a man of God."

"Why?"

"Because you aren't religious. But you say it respectfully. A lot of people would be snarky." She sipped her wine. It was almost gone, and she wanted more. It was his wine. Should she serve it herself? Ask for more?

"So tell me what it's like. How is it, having all those people in your social life? The way Mark talks, it sounds like there's no line where the church ends, and your lives begin." He stood and went into the kitchen. He returned with the bottle of Merlot. He poured a half glass for himself, then paused in front of her. His jeans brushed her kneecaps. A warm shiver ran up the insides of her thighs.

"More?" He lifted the bottle.

She held out her glass, and he filled it to the same level as his. He put the bottle on the table and returned to his spot at the other end of the futon. Gabrielle took two quick sips. She shouldn't drink it so fast. She couldn't think straight, unsettled by the warm, buttery sensation that flooded her every time he came close. It was so wrong to have feelings for another man. Yet there was no guilt to accompany the attraction. He was so good looking, so easy to be with. He laughed a lot, and he made her laugh. It wasn't just Mark who never laughed. Peter's voice was the only happy sound in their house.

Joe looked at her, sipping his wine, waiting for her to speak.

"Most of my time is taken up with Peter. I do a lot of stuff at church. And you're right, it feels like even when Mark has a day off, the church is still part of our lives. We share most of our weekends and evenings with them. But I guess it's who we are. All of our friends belong to Grace. Like you said, our whole social life is with Grace. Until you turned up." She sipped her wine.

"Turning things upside down, that's me." He set his glass on the table and stretched out his legs.

She didn't want to talk. She didn't want to think about her life, much less describe it. It sounded so dull. Nothing mattered right now except sipping this divine Merlot and looking at Joe every chance she got. She really ought to be able to uncover some thread of guilt for feeling drawn to a man who wasn't her husband. But it wasn't as if she went looking for him. He fell into her life like he'd dropped down from heaven. Aside from the lamp at Joe's right, the room was dark. A circle of light surrounded the lamp, blurred at the edges. When they'd come in, it had still been dusk, so she hadn't turned on the hall light, and when Joe went into the kitchen for the wine, he'd turned off the light on his way out. The effect was that of sitting on a stage that was carefully lit from a single spot to enhance a particular subject. And what subject was that?

He sat up straighter and reached for his glass. He finished the rest of the wine in one swallow and poured more. In the short time since he'd come for dinner, she'd forgotten how quickly he swallowed his way through a bottle of wine. Yet it didn't affect him. His eyes were lively, his words were clear.

She put the glass to her mouth and swallowed some more. It was so good. "Why did you give all that money for the new buildings? It's way over the top."

He looked thoughtful, struggling to give a truthful answer. He set his glass on the table and stood, shoving his hands into his pockets. He walked to the screen door. "I've known Mark since we were teenagers. We became adults together. All he ever wanted, since the day I met him was to be a minister. I never really got it, so I couldn't do anything to support him. I don't know what a minister even does. I'm not interested in religion, except when it makes people do stupid things. But other than that..."

She set down her glass. The weakness that had taken possession of her legs and belly had traveled to her arms and throat. He was so strong and in control, but also kind. For someone who didn't believe God commanded him to be considerate, he was more thoughtful than many of the religious men she knew. She rubbed her palms along her thighs.

"Anyway, this was the first thing I saw that I could do for him. We'd lost touch for so long. After all this time, the day I decide to call, he's wrapped up in this extravagant construction scheme. He wasn't sure it would get funded. Maybe there is a God because it's strange that something made me choose this time. Not last year, not next year. The minute he told me about it, I knew it was something I could do for him." He turned away from the door.

She couldn't read his expression. She wasn't sure why she thought she should be able to decipher it, this was only the second time she'd met him. But somehow, he felt like a much bigger part of her life than simply Mark's old college friend. She stood, rubbing her hip joints, wanting the jelly in her bones to solidify. There was nothing inside her but great pools of liquid, filling the spaces that should have been occupied by bone and muscle. She searched casually through her mind, wondering if she would find any guilt, or hear a voice telling her this was the wrong way to go. After all these weeks of clamoring, needling voices, commanding her to do first one thing, then another, her mind was eerily quiet. No sound. No impulse. It was an unruffled pool of water.

There wasn't a man anywhere on the planet who would think he was required to live without sex. If a man had been deprived of sex for years, he wouldn't have waited as long as she had. Claiming it as his right, just as most people would overlook a starving child's theft of a sandwich, a man would find someone to satisfy his need. It wasn't as if Mark had spent all these years depriving himself. He did what he wanted and justified it by twisting the Bible inside out. Why hadn't she considered that before? She was so filled with her own longing, trying so hard to spark his desire, burning all her energy into prayer, she hadn't thought of it. Mark got sex. Mark got whatever he wanted, and she got nothing.

Joe was standing there for the taking. She stepped closer

and slid her arms around his waist. He bent slightly, put his arms around her, and pulled her close. She kissed his cheek, smooth and clean smelling. She kissed his jaw. Terrified that he would pull away and remind her of his friendship with Mark, she moved her lips close to his. Her blood pulsed harder. She brushed his lips. His tongue moved softly inside her mouth. The jelly in her limbs dissolved. If he weren't holding her so firmly, her knees would buckle. She clung to him, feeling so much pleasure from his lips and tongue that she didn't think she needed anything more. The press of his hands on her back and the feeling of his mouth told her he desired her as much as she did him. Someone wanted her. Needed her. And not just anyone. A man that looked and acted like a god. This was what every other married woman had whenever she wanted. This was what she'd been deprived of by her selfish, lying husband.

After a while, the kiss faded, and they simply held each other. She sighed. He drew her even closer. She was so used to being pushed away after a few seconds in Mark's arms. She could stand here all night, feeling his body against hers, solid and warm.

Mark's kisses were limp pecks on her lips. Before they were married, she'd let it go. She'd thought he was trying to be chaste. After they were married, she'd pleaded with him to kiss her properly, but he simply pecked harder. She was too ashamed to ask for more. Who had to explain how to kiss? Didn't it sort of come naturally? She didn't want to be thinking of Mark. All she wanted to think of was this moment. Except it might end abruptly. How long had they been standing here? How many kisses had there been, or was it one long kiss that went on forever? Shocked that she was able to let go, she moved away.

"I suppose I should head out," he said.

She didn't need to mention that Mark could walk in the door any minute. They didn't need to say anything. Their minds were linked. They knew each other's thoughts.

"Goodnight." He brushed his lips across her earlobe. She trembled.

"Bye," she said softly. She followed him to the entryway. The front door closed with a whisper. She leaned against it, listening to his car door open and close. The engine started with a purr, not unlike the feeling inside her chest. She was glad he hadn't kissed her again at the door. They might not have been able to separate. There was no disguising the urgency he felt for her.

She went into the bedroom, stepped out of her sandals, and felt the carpet, thick and comforting beneath the soles of her feet. She took off her skirt and t-shirt and let them fall on the floor. She slipped out of her underwear and left it puddled nearby. She got into bed. The sheets stroked her skin. She pulled the top sheet up to her neck, closed her eyes, and recalled the sensation of Joe's mouth on hers.

Nineteen

THE BEDROOM WAS MURKY when Mark woke. He couldn't see the clock, and he wasn't sure if it was darkness or blurred eyes that prevented him from seeing. He threw off the covers and sat up. Monday. He flopped back down. It seemed like eons since he'd had a break. He pulled the clotted mass of sheet and blanket back over himself. He turned on his side and bent his knees, longing for a return to sleep.

In a rush, the humiliating scene of the night before came back to him. He flipped to his right side, his back to the window. He squeezed his eyes closed until they ached, but it didn't shut out the memory of standing in front of the dessert table watching Gabrielle hover on the brink of a tantrum. He opened his eyes. Where was she? The house was silent, meaning she was either feverishly praying in the living room, or she'd done another one of her disappearing acts. She hadn't spent as much time praying during the past week or so. Their nightly prayers, when she'd wrapped herself around him, groping around inside his brain with words in the same way she twisted her legs around him, had stopped. Strange that he hadn't noticed until this moment. He shivered and pulled the blankets tighter.

Had she deliberately tried to humiliate him? Planned to threaten his career? A warning of her power over him? Or was it just her nature, nothing intentional, an insatiable desire to be the center of attention? She wasn't the sole person in his life, and it was eating her alive. Which explained her marathon prayer sessions and constant hounding for sex. It wasn't that she really wanted *him*, it was another manifestation of her craving for attention. He threw off the covers, got up, and plodded out of the bedroom and down the hall to the kitchen. He paused at the living room, his eyes locking on the empty bottle of wine and two glasses. He hadn't noticed them the night before.

The coffee pot was cold, dark with the sludge of yesterday's coffee. He rinsed it out and filled the machine with fresh grounds and eight cups of water. He paced, stopping to look at the damp lawn in the back yard. The grass needed cutting. He turned and wandered back in the other direction, listening to the agonizingly slow drip of coffee. It was tempting to yank the pot off the hot plate and stick his cup in its place, fill it with coffee, then replace the pot to finish the job. But that would create a mess of burned coffee. He walked down the hall to check on Peter. The door was closed tight. He didn't dare open it, for fear of waking him too early, shattering the peace and quiet he needed in order to enjoy his coffee.

Where was Gabrielle? He walked back to the kitchen. Nine-thirty. Later than he'd realized. She must have gone to the grocery store. Finally, the coffee maker grunted, signaling that it was spewing out its last few tablespoons of caffeine. He poured a full mug, feeling his blood begin to percolate as the aroma drifted into his nostrils. The first sip was heavenly. He felt alive again. By the end of two cups, he'd be ready for Peter's energy, maybe even prepared to face whatever Gabrielle wanted to fling in his direction.

He was reading an article about the housing market when the doorbell rang. At the same time, Peter yelled from behind his closed door, "Ma-ma!"

He couldn't imagine who would show up unannounced on a Monday morning. Peter could handle five minutes before panic set in. He probably hadn't even reached the standing up, clinging to the rails of the crib stage yet. Mark looked for a coaster. The wine bottle sat coaster-less, forming a sticky red ring on the glass. He sighed and stood up, carrying his mug to the door. With his free hand, he pulled his robe more tightly across his chest so that only his neck showed, in case it was a parishioner. Through the small window, he saw Susan, her face distorted by the frosted glass. Had she and Gabrielle made plans? It didn't seem likely after last night. Although Susan was bull-headed enough to keep an appointment even if Gabrielle had slapped her across the face. He took a sip of coffee as he opened the door.

"Hi," she said. "How's it going?"

"Come on in." He said it out of habit, regretting it before he was done speaking. He stepped back, clutching his mug like a life preserver. He was in no mood to deal with a surprise visitor before he'd eaten or showered, with a missing wife and a son who would be screaming for help any minute. He backed away from her, not wanting her to notice an odor, either from his skin, or his breath. He felt stale and exposed.

"I'm concerned about Gabrielle," Susan said. "And I think you should be too."

He stared, unsure what to say. He took a long sip of coffee and squeezed his hand more tightly around the thick handle. "How so?"

"I don't think she's eating. Don't you see how skinny she is?" She continued, somewhat pompously. "I can't betray her confidence, but she's told me some stuff that makes me think she's headed in the wrong direction."

"What did she tell you?" His heart pounded. His awareness of his skin, sticky and unclean, increased. He wanted to pull the robe even tighter, but one hand was occupied with the heavy mug. He longed for socks, or to be sitting on the couch with a blanket wrapped around him. Better yet, he wished he hadn't answered the door, hadn't gotten out of bed. He waited, refusing to fill the silence with any words that would expose his fear.

Susan waved her hand like she was swatting away a fly. "It

was a while ago. Just stuff."

He let out his breath slowly.

"The point is, something's wrong with her. She doesn't eat, you must see how skinny she is."

"She's always been thin."

"She looks anorexic."

"No she doesn't." It was amazing how he could be so angry at Gabrielle, tired of her, yet hearing her attacked made him feel protective. "She eats a lot of vegetables. So she stays lean." What a word. Why did he say *lean*? He made her sound like a hunk of meat. He shrugged his shoulders, trying to brush off the inappropriate word as well as Susan's deliberate stare that bored into him, waiting for him to agree and confess Gabrielle's faults.

"Don't just brush it off. There's something wrong with her. She was acting strangely all summer. And you saw her last night. She looked like she was going to have a fit. I expected her to start foaming at the mouth."

"Oh, you did not. Don't be dramatic."

Peter was rattling the crib rail. Any minute he would start yelling. Mark moved to the other side of Susan, forcing her to back up toward the door. "Where are your kids?"

"Jack's working from home this morning. I felt like I needed to come over."

Why was she really here? He didn't want to know. All he wanted was to get her out the door and on her way, minding her own business.

"Gabrielle isn't even home, is she," Susan said.

Peter was bouncing and shaking the crib. She knew if Gabrielle had been home, she'd be in Peter's room in a heartbeat. Mark didn't want to discuss Gabrielle's weight, or where she might be, or her potential for throwing a fit. Couldn't Susan see this was a bad time?

She touched his arm. "I'm here as a friend, not as a member of the church. I want to help."

He didn't need or want her help. And no one, he realized for the hundredth time, could be *just* a friend. Ultimately, they were all members of his church. He didn't serve God, but the two-hundred-seventy-five members of Grace Lutheran Church. Each one with their own squirming bundle of needs and opinions. But that didn't mean he had to let Susan stand in his hallway on his day off when he hadn't showered, his wife was missing, his stomach was growling, and his son was rattling his crib like a caged animal.

He pulled his arm out from under Susan's concerned fingers. He turned and stepped down into the living room. He set his mug on the table, foregoing the coaster after all. Straightening his shoulders, pulling firmly on the belt of his robe, so it cinched his waist beyond comfort, he stepped back up to the entryway. "Thanks for your concern. Gabrielle is fine. She's under a lot of pressure from the building program." He moved closer, but she didn't back toward the door as he'd expected.

"Don't dismiss me. What I saw last night was more than

pressure over the building program. Besides, what has she done for the building program? Why would she feel pressured? I think it's more than that. And I also think it looked strange having some guy that no one knows taking her home."

Had Susan noticed the bottle of wine and the two glasses? He moved further to the left to block her view of the coffee table. He put his hand on her elbow, guiding her to the door. "Speaking of fits," he tried to laugh, but it came out like he was gargling, "Peter is going to have one if I don't get him up right now. Thanks for stopping by."

"Don't shove me out the door. Where's Gabrielle?"

"She's not here."

"Where is she?"

"Susan, you need to leave." He gulped in air, mustering all his strength. "This isn't a good time. I'm just waking up, and I need to get Peter. I'm sorry," he said, hoping to soften the coldness in his voice. He leaned past her and pushed open the screen door. "Call me later if you want."

Unable to move anywhere but back, Susan stepped outside. "You're making a mistake. I've known her longer than you. I'm her friend, and I know what I saw. She needs help. Professional counseling maybe. You're too close to see, but something isn't right."

He could see all right, but he wasn't about to admit it to Susan. "Okay, thanks. Bye." He closed the door and leaned against it, breathing hard.

AT ELEVEN-THIRTY, he was sitting on the living room floor reading a story to Peter, worn out from the balancing act of dressing and feeding both of them. The front door was open, letting the warm fall air filter through the screen. He enjoyed the quiet of not listening to Gabrielle. Even her sulking sounded like noise.

He heard the minivan pull into the driveway. The door slammed. Then the side door slid open and slammed shut. A rattling sound approached the screen door with Gabrielle. The screen flew open, and she breezed through, dragging three oversized shopping bags. The bag facing his direction had a Nordstrom logo. He stared as she pivoted and turned down the hall toward their bedroom. Since when did Gabrielle shop at Nordstrom?

Peter pounded his arm. "'eed."

"Just a minute." Mark handed the book to Peter, praying he'd be entertained by the pictures for a few minutes. Peter knew the story by heart, and this was the third time they'd been through it in the past hour. Mark stood and followed Gabrielle down the hall.

She'd thrown the shopping bags on the bed. Clothes spilled out, a silky beige thing he couldn't identify, and a short skirt, also very silky. The contents of the second bag stayed hidden, and the third bulged with the hard edges of shoeboxes. One thing she didn't need was more shoes. He closed his eyes. He wouldn't comment on the shoes. It was best not to acknowledge any of the bags. He swallowed the question of where she'd been since the answer was scattered across the unmade bed.

She relieved him of trying to search for innocuous words to break the silence. "What do you want?"

"What do you mean, *what do I want?* I came in to see what you were doing." This was not the tone he'd hoped for and was just as unimportant as asking where she'd been all morning. "Susan came by."

"Don't care."

"She's worried about you."

"Imagine that."

"She thinks you're too thin." His voice sounded as feeble as an old woman's. There was something dismissive and terrifying about Gabrielle's mood, more than any of her tantrums or fanciful religious ideas. She was cold and much too calm.

"Well, she's too fat."

This was not headed toward a positive outcome. He longed for everything to return to how it had been, but he couldn't think what point in time he desired. Before the fundraising effort? Right after Peter was born? Not then, with her hysterical comments about God letting her down by giving her a son when He knew she'd wanted a daughter. After she'd recovered from that, things had been peaceful and pleasant, hadn't they? He couldn't remember. The room felt as if it were growing colder from the icy vapor that seemed to rise from her skin. "Where have you been?"

"What does it look like?"

"I thought we'd spend the day together. Take Peter somewhere…"

"Since when do we spend the day together? I have plans."

"What plans?"

"None of your business." She pulled the shoeboxes out of the bag and stacked them on the rumpled blanket. She folded the shopping bag into a rectangle. Without opening the lids to show him what was inside like she usually did, she carried the boxes to the closet, slid open the door, and added them to the double column of boxed shoes. She tucked the bag into another large shopping bag on the floor of the closet where she collected them. "You need to take care of Peter."

He said nothing. It was clear that she no longer cared what he said. Even if he couldn't go back to some vaguely easier, pleasant time in their marriage, he wanted to unwind the past few weeks. When had they stopped praying and holding each other? That had been working out all right. She'd seemed content. For a while, he'd managed to avoid the craving to find an anonymous lover. He shoved that thought out of his mind. Now was not the time for desire to suddenly show its face and further complicate his life.

"Why all the new clothes?"

She kept her back toward him. "I needed some new things, and I needed to get out of here. I needed a break."

I need. He pressed his lips together and waited.

"I couldn't sleep, and I was starving. I went to *Eggstravaganza* and had a big, fat omelet and two sides of bacon. Then I went shopping. Now I'm going to take a shower and put on something besides denim for the first time in two years. Is that enough information for you?" As if to punctuate her plans, she unzipped her skirt and stepped out of it.

He instinctively turned away from the long expanse of skin, barely covered by her thin cotton underpants.

Gabrielle snorted. "Maybe you better leave. You wouldn't want to see anything more." She laughed for several seconds, ending with a giggle.

As he stepped into the hallway, she began laughing again. She pulled off her t-shirt and unhooked her bra, flinging it against the wall. The hooks of the bra made a tapping sound. She kicked the door shut.

He closed his eyes and pressed his fingers into the corners. Peter was singing to himself in the living room. Gabrielle was still laughing like a madwoman behind the door. He stood motionless, his mind empty until he heard the squeak of the shower faucet. He walked down the hall. He was hungry but couldn't think of what he wanted for lunch. He wasn't used to planning food that Peter could eat. Maybe he would introduce Peter to fast food. French fries. If Gabrielle had suddenly decided to eat omelets and bacon, there was no telling what could happen. She might not care if Peter had a little fat and cholesterol for once in his life. An omelet and bacon. It was a terrifying image. For Gabrielle, eating bacon was like selling her soul.

Twenty

AS MARK WALKED AWAY from the bedroom door, anticipation swam inside her, bursting out in a dancing sound of laughter she'd forgotten existed. Was it possible she'd never laughed like this? Deeply, with abandon, almost unable to stop? Joe had done this. Being wanted by a man. Flesh and blood, not a Spirit she couldn't see or feel, a Being she couldn't taste or touch anywhere but inside the shadowy corners of her mind. She walked to the sliding glass door and yanked the cord, opening the blinds to let sunlight into the room. She lifted her new clothes off the rumpled bed and set them on the chair in the corner. If he wanted, Mark could look directly into the bedroom through the slider in the eating area, but he never wanted to watch her dress. He was immune to her body. It didn't matter anymore.

She turned back to the bed and pulled the sheet, tugging it toward the top edge of the mattress. She smoothed her hands across it, making her way to Mark's side to be sure it was evenly placed, then pulled the blanket up, and tucked both between the mattress and box spring. She pulled the quilt gently across the surface as if she were placing a shroud over a loved one's body. She scooped the pillows off the floor and arranged them along the headboard. The new clothes spread out on the blue satin looked even more inviting.

She'd thought Mark would ask what she'd spent on the obviously expensive clothes, but he hadn't, proving he was afraid of her newfound power. She hadn't recognized that until last night. Watching him stand there helplessly, trying to argue her into calming down, she'd seen that he was terrified of what she might do to embarrass him. And it was so easy. Absolutely everything embarrassed him. He fretted that her thrift store clothes would tarnish his reputation. People would interpret it as some kind of message that the congregation wasn't paying him enough. He fretted her skirts would generate gossip because they were too short. When she talked too much, he worried she sounded selfish and silly. When she held her tongue, he said she came across like a snob. It seemed that her very existence embarrassed her husband.

Joe, on the other hand, was comfortable in his own skin. With Joe, she could have taken all that disgusting potluck food and flung it on the floor. He would have smiled with detached amusement. There wasn't a single flaw in the man. He towered over her with all that thick, beautiful hair and those confident, defiant eyes. He laughed so easily. He was charming. And although she'd always said she didn't care about money, he had plenty. How lovely to not worry what things cost. She ran her hand across the raw silk skirt. The sleeveless top would fall loosely from her shoulders, showing the shape of her breasts without hugging them too tightly. With her new dark chocolate leather Ferragamo pumps, she could compete with any woman at Joe's office. No one would guess she was the mother of a toddler, the wife of a minister. Joe would be flattered and excited.

She opened the closet and pulled out one of the shoeboxes. Mark must be dying to know what was in the boxes and what they'd cost, but of course, he was too afraid to ask. Sooner or later, he would. He'd complain about the excessive number of shoes she owned, all much too expensive for someone with their income. Her mother had always said — *Wear whatever you want, but never scrimp on shoes. Painful feet make you look ugly. You scrunch up your face and hunch your shoulders and lose all the grace in your walk. Buy nice shoes, spend a little extra, and you can't go wrong.* Gabrielle intended to follow that advice religiously from here on out.

She slipped off her underpants and scooped up her bra where it had fallen by the door. She carried them into the bathroom and dropped them into the clothes basket. She turned on the hot water and left it running. She bent over and dragged the brush through her hair, letting the bristles dig deep into her scalp. As she straightened, she flipped her hair up and over, then brushed it from the top.

The bathroom was filling with steam. The only image

visible in the mirror was a drape of golden-brown hair and the foggiest outline of her face and shoulders. She added cold water to the mix, sticking her hand into the spray to feel the temperature. It was a little too hot, but she wanted her skin to tingle and burn. She stepped into the stall. She soaped and shaved her legs and under her arms, making double laps up her legs to be sure every nub of hair was sliced away. She poured a puddle of shampoo into her palm and massaged it into her scalp. A second puddle went into the damp length of hair that hung between her shoulder blades. It lathered up into a cloud of froth. She rinsed it for several minutes and ran conditioner through the ends. While it soaked in, she held the rail on the inside of the shower door and did thirty demi-pliés. The conditioner slid off in a river down her back, making it feel as if the strands of hair had melted into one long, piece of silk. She turned off the water and grabbed the clean towel she'd left folded on the lip of the sink. She dried herself and dropped the towel on the floor. Let Mark pick up a wet towel for once. She squirted a deep pool of vanilla lotion into her palm and spread it across her breasts and arms and down her legs. She stood on one leg, then the other, rubbing the lotion into her feet. She dried her hair on a low setting, then went into the bedroom and opened the third shopping bag.

Inside was a thong the color of tea. She stepped into it, looking down to admire the way it made her thighs look longer, emphasized the sleekness of her hips. Tears sprang into her eyes, and her throat tightened. She'd never owned expensive lingerie. The second drawer of her dresser was full of cotton underpants in a variety of colors. Dull and worn, next to her two, slightly bedraggled, silky teddies and matching underwear from Target. She pulled a sheer, matching bra out of the bag, and bit the plastic string that held a cluster of tags. She tucked her breasts inside and hooked the front, pausing to admire herself in the mirror. Even the Bible said a woman was a work of beauty. A young man was commanded to drink in his wife's satin skin and soft hair. The *Song of Songs* made it clear that her husband was supposed to adore her — worship her. He'd failed miserably. It didn't even matter why. All she knew was that now she would finally get what she'd longed for, what she deserved. Joe admired her. He would touch her with awe. He craved her with a gnawing hunger that matched her own.

She stuffed the tags into the plastic bag, rolled it into a ball, and put it into the wastebasket in the bathroom. She gazed at herself again. There wasn't a flaw anywhere on her, as long as she didn't look in a full-length mirror that reflected her feet, always creepy with their protruding bones and oversized toes. But in her Ferragamo shoes, those flaws would be hidden behind creamy, firm leather. She slid into the skirt. The fabric caressed her legs like water. The tea color was two shades darker than the lingerie, perfect with the ecru top and chocolate brown shoes. She felt like a different woman. Turning slowly in front of the mirror, she saw her hair, hanging invitingly down her back, the clothes rippling and clinging at just the right spots. The high heels made her legs look extraordinarily long, even before the thong came into play.

Without warning, a heaviness made its way through her limbs, a heaviness she'd come to recognize as the presence of God. What kind of woman was she, parading in front of her mirror, admiring her body, calculating how she might invite a man to seduce her? She sat in the chair by the glass door and leaned forward. What was she thinking? Although she looked undeniably spectacular, it wasn't for the husband God had given her. Had she ever dressed like this for Mark? Before she was married, these kinds of clothes weren't part of her life, and since their marriage, she couldn't afford things like this. She clutched her head and tried to define which thoughts were true and which were not. Wicked thoughts. From the devil. She rubbed her temples and clenched the skin of her face.

That was the wrong thing to do. Relaxation was the answer. She lifted her elbows off her thighs and leaned back carefully. She allowed her eyelids to soften, feeling them resting gently on her eyeballs. The light penetrating her eyelids glowed orange, easing the glittering shards of red caused by squeezing them too tightly. She felt better, but still uncertain about whether God was speaking to her, warning her against the half-formed plan. A few hours earlier, it had been more definite than a plan — a compulsion. Still feeling the touch of Joe's hands and lips, she'd climbed out of bed the moment she woke. Without thinking, she dressed and drove toward the omelet and bacon. Desperate for heavy, thick food, she ate, savoring the weight in her mouth and the fullness in her stomach. In the same trance-like condition, she'd driven to the mall and bought the clothes—first the lingerie, then the shoes, then the skirt and blouse.

She took a deep breath, and laced her fingers together, hoping for guidance. She would pay attention to the first calm thought. God would speak in a whisper, not this clamor of voices assaulting her now. One screamed, *You deserve it!* Another said sharply, *You're a mother!* A third hissed, *You harlot.* She took another breath and tried to empty her mind.

Mark is gay.

Yes! That one. *That* was the voice of God. Calm and reasonable. Truthful. She was married to a gay man. How long was she going to deny that fact? It was impossible for anything or anyone to intervene and rescue their marriage. She would not live a life without sex. God did not expect that of her, and that's why He'd brought Joe into her life. She inhaled slowly, filling her lungs until they ached, holding her breath as long as she could until she had to let it go. Her husband was gay. She'd married a man who wanted other men, not his beautiful wife. It had taken all summer to realize this, her entire married life to see the truth. How had she ended up in this situation? Why hadn't she seen it? At twenty-six years old, she had been tossed aside. It wasn't fair. It was completely, and totally, astronomically unfair. She married him, believing the things he'd said. Believing who he was. And he'd lied. Every single thing he'd done was a lie.

She stood up and returned to her spot in front of the mirror. She refused to be put out to pasture when she wasn't even thirty. She deserved more, and God knew she deserved more. He knew how hard she'd tried. How she tenderly touched her husband, how she'd waited for him night after night. He saw how she tried to arouse Mark's interest. He saw how she took care of herself, how she made supreme efforts to be a good and loving wife. He could see that she'd received nothing in return. She ran her palms slowly along the sides of her body, feeling the slight extension of her breasts, her rib cage, her soft waist, and her hips, craving the feel of the silky fabric like she craved a man's hands on her skin. It was so very clear that God had brought Joe into her life. The timing was too perfect.

She went into the bathroom, and without thinking about Mark or Joe or God or Grace or her son, she turned all of her thoughts to putting dark brown shadow and liner on her eyes. She smoothed a thin coat of gloss over her lips. Her lips looked soft and edible, and with the darkened lids, her eyes deep and inviting. She shut off the light, picked up her purse, and walked out to the entryway.

There was no sign of Mark. That was the final message. He didn't care what she was doing in the bedroom. She realized she'd been hoping he was watching, that his interest would be aroused. Only because it would feel nice to know that he noticed what he could no longer have. She wanted him to see that he'd lost her. But he didn't care.

He was sitting in a beach chair watching Peter in the sandbox, his back to the patio, unable to see the glass door leading to their bedroom. They'd be content. Neither one of them needed to know where she was going. Still…she walked to the living room door, past the wine bottle and the glasses with bloody-looking circles dried on the surface of the table. She slid open the door. "I'm going out."

Mark looked up. "So I'm supposed to spend the whole day by myself? With Peter?"

There was no suggestion that her appearance affected him. "Isn't that how it usually is for me?" She slid the door closed. She could see his mouth moving, hear his voice, but couldn't make out the words. He was most likely asking what they would have for dinner and at what time.

She looked again at the wine bottle, ready for whatever came next. She walked across the living room and felt that her movement past the front door was momentous. As if she were leaving the house, a virgin for the last time. She smiled to herself. In a way, she was.

Twenty-one

GABRIELLE DROVE PAST the main gates of Joe's office complex. The entrance was wide with faux marble pillars on either side, one bearing the company logo formed from some type of silvery metal that shimmered in the sunlight. The drive curved to the left, where it offered plenty of visitor parking. She parked and slid out of the minivan. The walkway leading to the lobby was covered by an iron archway thickly woven with jasmine. She walked slowly, breathing the scent, feeling that she was simultaneously in her own backyard, and entering another realm. Her heels echoed in the scented enclosure.

She hesitated for a moment inside the double glass doors. Several people were seated in the lobby. All but one turned to look at her. She straightened her back, tossed her hair behind her shoulders, and walked to the reception desk. The woman at the desk wore a white polo shirt with a blue logo that read *McBane Security*. Her dark hair was slicked back into a very tight ponytail, and she wore sienna lipstick. She was thin, managing to look exotic and harsh at the same time. Her long, sienna fingernails tapped and flicked at a pen lying on the desk. She looked at Gabrielle without a change in expression.

"I'm here to see Joe Malik," Gabrielle said.

The receptionist said, "And who's calling, please?"

"A personal friend."

"Your name?"

"Just say a friend is here and ask him to come down."

"You won't be allowed into the building without giving me your name and the company you represent."

"I said I was a personal friend. I don't represent anyone."

"And your name is?"

"Look," Gabrielle lowered her voice, leaning forward as if sharing a confidence, "I want to surprise him. Can you help me out?"

The receptionist leaned forward, suggesting she was ready to receive the secret that was being offered. "No. I can't. It's company policy that you give me your name and the company you represent before I call any employee on your behalf."

This wasn't how she'd planned it. She'd imagined catching him by surprise, observing the look of unexpected pleasure when he came around the corner, or better yet, down the sweeping staircase that curved behind the reception desk to the open hallway on the second floor. Perhaps if the lobby was inundated with visitors, she could slip unnoticed past the desk and up those lovely stairs. But she wouldn't know where to go, and it was unlikely that anyone in this security-obsessed organization would be willing to point her to Joe's office. If they even knew him. Beyond the floor to ceiling glass on the opposite side of the lobby, there were five or six multi-story buildings.

The receptionist stared, her gaze unwavering. If there was a way around this roadblock, Gabrielle couldn't see it. With a deep sigh, she said, "Gabrielle Atwater. Thanks for your help in spoiling the surprise."

"And your company Ms. Atwater?"

"I don't have a company. I told you already, I'm a personal friend."

"Don't know of any other kind." The receptionist tapped her keyboard, her nails clicking in the spaces between the keys. Gabrielle waited for one of the nails to trip her up, but they worked in perfect unison, oblivious to the treacherous spaces. The receptionist picked up the handset and punched in a few numbers too quickly for Gabrielle to note what they were. She stared past Gabrielle as she waited for an answer. After a few seconds, she pressed a key on her phone and said, "This is the receptionist in building one. Gabrielle Atwater is here to see you." She glared at Gabrielle. "She won't provide a company name." She replaced the handset. "Please have a seat. He'll either be over to meet you or call me back."

"How long will I have to wait?"

"How should I know? Since he wasn't expecting you, it

could be several hours if he's in a meeting."

The receptionist was trying to upset her. There was no way Joe could be busy for hours. Gabrielle walked to one of the benches facing the desk, then turned away. If she had to wait more than a few minutes, she wanted to be comfortable, not sit on a backless bench where she had to perch like an anxious bird, her hips and thighs clutching the cushion to prevent her from toppling over. She chose a small couch. She settled herself in the center and picked up a magazine off the black cube that served as a table. She flipped through the pages of articles and elaborate charts, photographs and diagrams. It had been fifteen minutes, according to the giant clock on the wall behind the reception desk.

Suddenly he was standing in front of the sofa. "This is a surprise. To what do I owe this pleasure?" He didn't look pleased. He wore the same smile and casual posture, but his eyes were harder than she remembered. They didn't match the grin on his face. He wore a black shirt and black slacks.

"You look good," Gabrielle said.

He didn't return the compliment. She tossed the magazine on the table and stood up. He reached out his hand. After making such a point of being a close friend, he was thrusting out his hand like she was an unwanted salesperson. She left her arms hanging at her sides. She refused to go along with his game, whatever it might be. She felt the receptionist watching. Maybe Joe didn't want the receptionist to know his personal business. He probably knew the woman was a bitch.

He wasn't dismissing Gabrielle, he was simply protecting their privacy. She raised her hand and took his. But she was too late. His hand was retreating, the skin around his mouth tight with irritation. Their wrists bumped awkwardly. Finally, their fingers found each other, and they managed a half-hearted handshake.

"Should we walk to the coffee bar and grab a cup?" he said.

"I thought we could go out for a late lunch." She smiled, widening her eyes so he could see their dark invitation. "Or a glass of wine."

"I ate an hour ago. I have meetings."

She scowled. Why was he being so difficult? "I suppose we can go to your office to talk."

"Do we need to talk about something?"

She arranged her hair behind her shoulders and wriggled her hips slightly, so her skirt hung straighter. "Let's get coffee. Then go to your office."

"You caught me off guard. I only have about twenty minutes before I have to run to my next meeting. Should we make an appointment for lunch later this week?"

"No." She blurted it out too loudly, then smiled. "I'm here now, let's go get coffee."

She walked beside him, half-listening as he pointed to the various buildings, describing the kind of work that went on in each one. Nothing was going the way she'd wanted. He behaved as if last night hadn't even happened. Still, he was at work. Apparently, he wasn't quite as carefree as he appeared outside of the office. Mark wasn't the only man who obsessed over the opinions of people he worked with. She trotted stiffly to keep up with him. They entered another glass-walled building, and he led her to a counter that looked like a commercial coffee shop. While she danced from one foot to the other, wishing she had the freedom to do a few pliés, Joe ordered two cups of coffee.

"Decaf!" she blurted out. He hadn't asked if she wanted coffee. Didn't he know she preferred healthy beverages? He must think she didn't care. And maybe she didn't. All she wanted was to be with him. But not here, not with all these people walking by, some of them nodding at Joe, several men casting sideways glances at her sleek legs and short skirt. She wanted to be in his office, with the door closed.

She walked beside him along the ridiculously narrow hallways, moving to the side every few steps to let someone pass, trying to keep steady the steaming cup of coffee. The office doors all had glass panels set in wood frames. How would they find privacy? She couldn't survive for another hour without feeling his hands on her body. Without the softness of his lips and the eager pressure of his tongue, the scent of his skin, she would die. Each time his sleeve brushed her arm, she felt flushed and wobbly.

They exited one building and entered the next. This building seemed newer, with different carpets and bright blue accent walls. From the outside, it had looked exactly the same as the others, but the hallways were wider with occasional alcoves containing easy chairs and potted plants. The office doors were different — the glass panels were frosted, turning the occupants into shadows. Her hand trembled, and coffee bubbled out of the hole in the plastic lid.

After several hallways and two flights of stairs, they reached his office. In less than ten minutes, they'd have to take the long walk back to the lobby so he could go off to his meeting. Surely he could fabricate some excuse for missing one meeting. She set her coffee on a bookshelf next to the chair he offered her. The adjacent wall was glass, looking down on the courtyard. Joe settled into the wheeled armchair tucked into the curve of his kidney-shaped desk. Behind him was a computer monitor where the company logo spun and danced, making her dizzy.

"What brought you all this way?" He leaned back slightly. His tone was demanding, as if he was interviewing, even interrogating her.

"I needed to see you. After last night." She didn't like the chair, confining her to a small spot, too far from him. The door was only half-closed. Every few minutes, someone walked by. She glanced out the window. There was a constant flow of people in both directions. Where were they all going? Didn't they sit in their offices and work? Did they all walk up and down the cobblestone path from the main building to whatever was at the back of the campus all day long? She shifted her gaze to his face. "Aren't you going to say anything?" She wanted to keep her voice light, but it came out shrill.

"I'm not sure why you're here."

"I told you — I couldn't..." The conversation was going nowhere. A bold move was called for. He must be feeling uncertain about the next step, about her willingness. She stood and closed the door. Maybe he'd misinterpreted everything. He thought she felt guilty about betraying Mark. She turned toward him, and in two quick steps, was at his side. She settled herself onto his lap and draped her arm around his neck. Did she imagine that he pulled away? Last night he couldn't keep his lips off her. His office was having a negative effect. Coming here might have been a mistake. But she didn't know where he lived, and she couldn't very well ask Mark for his phone number.

Shutting off the patter of negative thoughts, knowing she was doing the right thing, even if the circumstances were less than ideal, she kissed him lightly. She pressed her lips against his again, putting her other hand on his back. She pulled herself closer. Her skirt slid up her thigh, exposing the entire length of her leg. Joe arched his shoulders and head away from her. He lifted her arms off his neck and pushed her gently toward his knees. She teetered precariously.

"Please get up," he said.

"Why?"

"Are you out of your mind? Do you realize what could happen if someone stopped by my office?" He pushed her again, more firmly this time.

She had no choice but to stand up. "Last night, you wanted me!"

"This is my office. You don't invade it dressed like a…I don't know what, and assault me. I can't imagine what you're thinking. And since you brought it up, last night was an anomaly. It didn't mean anything. You're my best friend's wife, for God's sake."

She started to tremble. This couldn't be happening. God meant them to be together. This was a man who needed her. This was the man sent to fulfill her desire in an unconventional but spectacular manner. She shook more violently, unable to control her limbs.

"I didn't mean to upset you." He stood up.

She tried to think whether she should insist they leave his office and continue their conversation in a private place, or if she should kiss him again, forcing his body to rule his mind.

He stepped around her and opened the door. "I'll walk you back to the lobby. We'll pretend this didn't happen. I won't say anything to Mark."

"But last night! I know you wanted me. You still do."

"I was fooling around. You looked like you wanted to be kissed, so I kissed you. No big deal. Don't read something into it." He stepped into the hallway.

She didn't think she could bear the humiliation of walking all that way with him. Seeing the receptionist's mocking face, returning her visitor's badge to those hands with the dagger nails. But she couldn't possibly find her way alone. She ached for him, longing to melt into him, making him say it was a mistake. He wanted her, he couldn't sleep for thinking about her. At the same time, her fingers twitched, eager to rip out his eyes. She needed those long, fierce sienna nails, capable of great damage. She wanted to destroy him. How dare God mislead her like this. She didn't deserve this punishment — to be tossed aside by every man she loved.

Twenty-two

ON TUESDAY MORNING, Mark woke with a headache that felt like a section of his brain had been sliced out. Gabrielle had come home at ten past eleven the night before, heels clicking on the hardwood floor in the hallway. As much as he'd wanted to demand to know where she'd been, to chastise her for leaving him alone all day, he couldn't seem to find the courage. Was she thinking of leaving him? He could hear her, lecturing the church elders with the same tone she used to reprimand everyone's dietary choices, the same frantic flipping through her Bible he'd seen a few weeks earlier.

Being married to Mark is poisoning me. I need sex, and he's not interested in me. God gave me a message, and He understands my predicament.

He shuddered. He couldn't seem to bring up an image of his parishioners' faces.

Once I found out he was spending time at a gay club, having sex with all kinds of strangers, I knew I had to do something. God will show you

I'm right.

He couldn't put words around what the church leaders might say. It would never really happen. She wouldn't. He needed to stop panicking. She'd be fine. How would she support herself if she left him? And no matter how upset she was, she'd never take Peter away from him. She wasn't cold enough to destroy his entire life, was she? His hands shook.

Tears oozed into his right eye. The pain sliced across the side of his brow, behind his eye socket, like a spear embedded in his skull. It had been months, maybe a year, since he'd had a migraine. He needed to get up and take his medication, put an ice pack on the side of his head. But even raising himself partially off the pillow allowed the pain to make another virtual cut through his brain, forcing him back down. He groaned turned over, generating another flash of pain.

It was seven o'clock. Gabrielle was still asleep next to him. Aside from a crease in the skin on the left edge of her lips, forming a slight frown even in her sleep, her face was slack. The flashy new clothes were tossed on the chair in the corner. The unexpected shopping trip that would gouge their budget worried him, as did her neglect of Peter. Since the day she'd announced she was pregnant, ignoring her brief lapse, she'd had a single-hearted devotion to motherhood. She pursued healthy eating as if her unborn child's life depended on it. She couldn't be pried away from Peter. She nursed him whenever he pleased. She never complained when he woke her two, even three times a night. Her existence had centered around their child. Now, she acted as if she hardly noticed him. Was this because Mark had suggested it was time to stop breastfeeding? Had he broken the mother-child connection too soon?

He turned on his back. The pain of swollen capillaries pressed viciously against his skull. He had to get that ice. He needed to swallow the white prescription tablet.

Susan's concern over Gabrielle's bizarre behavior hit close to the bone. Implying to her that he wasn't concerned had been a flat out lie. How long would it be until others noticed? There was no career — aside from politics, maybe — where a wife's actions directly affected a job. The parallels between the political limelight and the role of a minister were stronger than he'd realized — judged for trying to maintain a private life, watched every hour of the day, always working even when you weren't performing official duties. His mistakes marched through his thoughts with each throb of his head. He'd made a fateful decision when he'd decided to hide his true self. Although, it wasn't as if that choice had occurred at a single moment in time. It was a series of choices — his inexplicable childhood desire to be a preacher in a conservative church now looked blind and utterly foolish. But he was good at preaching. His parishioners had said so week after week for the entire length of his short career. Still, why had he favored one aspect of his nature over the other? The Bible clearly said a man couldn't serve two masters. He should have chosen a long time ago — either embraced his desire and found a satisfying relationship with a man or adhered to the strict Biblical beliefs he'd been nurtured by since the day he was born.

He could have become a minister in a more liberal church or remained single and celibate and true to the views of his denomination. The former had seemed a betrayal of his soul.

Now, he straddled two worlds in never-ending torment. His head throbbed more violently. Forcing himself onto his left side, he thrust his legs out from under the blankets. He slowly raised himself and put his feet on the floor. The pain was unbearable. He couldn't open his right eye. He pressed his fingers against his temple and used his left hand to push himself up to a standing position. Bent forward, his head throbbing with every movement, he shuffled across the floor to the bathroom. He opened the drawer on his side of the counter and pulled out a packet of tablets. He tore one individually wrapped pill off the sheet. He trudged out of the bedroom and down the hall to the kitchen.

Once the tablet was successfully dissolving in his stomach, the ice pack wrapped in a thin towel and pressed against the side of his head, he lay on the living room floor. After twenty minutes, the throbbing was less intense, and he knew that in an hour, the medication would perform its miracle on the dilated capillaries in his brain.

There had to be a way to correct the slow disintegration of his life. He drifted to sleep.

When he woke, the springs in Peter's crib were squeaking.

No sound came from the master bedroom. The pain was gone. His head felt incredibly light. He stood and took the melted ice pack back to the freezer.

PETER WAS CHANGED, dressed, and fed, but Gabrielle was still asleep. Mark's drug-induced nap on the living room floor, three cups of coffee, and Peter's constant requests for *Mama* had given him the solution to his problem. It was his duty to force Gabrielle to take responsibility. He'd been too indulgent. She had a child to care for. They'd vowed to keep their marriage together for better or worse. He would help her see that they both needed to find a way to do what was right. They owed it to God, and they owed it to Grace. Most of all, they owed it to Peter. He went into the bedroom and shook her gently. Her eyes remained resolutely closed. He shook her more vigorously. The thin bone of her shoulder moved in his hand as if it were disconnected from the rest of her body. "Gabrielle!"

Surely she felt the grip of his hand, heard his voice. It was after nine. He shook harder, feeling a prick of guilt that he was too aggressive. Not a muscle twitched. No sign in her face that she was coming into consciousness. He spoke her name more loudly. She didn't respond. He could grab her shoulders and pull her out from under the blankets, forcing her to sit up, or he could take Peter to the church office with him. In spite of his momentary resolve to force her to stop acting like a child and take responsibility for her life, he didn't have the energy for a fight, especially a physical fight, which her limp body suggested. Already he felt the press of the voicemails that greeted him on Tuesday mornings. It was easier to let Peter tag along. Hadn't he wanted to spend more time with his son? Perhaps he hadn't fully taken his own share of responsibility.

Peter was thrilled to be buckled into his car seat. Finally, he stopped his mantra for *Mama* and started in with *car* and *Dada*. The sound of Peter's delighted voice washed away Mark's frustration. It would be great to spend another day with his son. He couldn't recall that he'd ever spent two days in a row caring for his child. They drove the few short blocks to church. There was a lot to do. He hadn't given a single thought to next week's sermon yet. Usually, the burst of creative adrenaline he needed to preach two sermons on a Sunday morning filled his mind with ideas for the following week, but this week his mind was dulled by fear.

As he pulled into the parking lot, he saw white Ford Taurus in the spot where he usually parked. The Olefson's car. He couldn't imagine what they were doing inside the church on a weekday morning. He unloaded Peter and the canvas bag full of toys. He let Peter make his confident march to the sidewalk alone. Mark glanced around the garden and the buildings, trying to figure out where the Olefson's might have gone. Rather than entering the main office, he walked to the side door of the parish hall. Peter toddled after him. The door was unlocked. He walked into the building, pausing while his eyes adjusted to the dim light. The voices of Carrie and Herb filtered out from the kitchen. He walked the length of the hall, calling out, *Good morning,* to ensure he didn't frighten them.

Herb stood near the center island, holding a can of insect spray. Carrie was at the sink, squeezing water out of a large pink sponge.

"Good morning, Pastor," Herb said. "We've had some ant problems the past few weeks, so we decided to stop by and make sure none had congregated since the potluck."

"Sometimes people don't clean up as well as they should," Carrie said. "It's an open invitation to the ants."

As if they were a single voice, her husband continued without a pause, "Sure enough, there was an enormous stream of ants across that wall." He jerked his head toward the stove. "No obvious signs of food left out, but just the same, Carrie's wiping down the sink and the counters. I already sprayed."

"Great," Mark said. "Glad you thought of it. I'll be in my office."

Outside the kitchen doorway, Peter screeched, excited by the echoing sound of his voice in the long, empty building. He squealed again, laughing at the sound.

"Oh," Carrie said. She followed him into the main hall. "You have Peter with you. Where's Gabby?"

Mark cringed on Gabrielle's behalf. She'd reminded him so many times how much she hated that bastardized version of her name, it was almost as if he hated it himself. What was it about marriage? Without even realizing it, you gradually adopted parts of another person and integrated them into your own personality. If he and Gabrielle were so intimately united that he could feel what she felt about the proper use of her name, he was absolutely certain they could patch up the other cracks in their marriage. "She prefers to be called Gabrielle," he said.

Carrie's eyeballs jittered, as if she wanted to roll them but resisted the temptation. Her expression said Gabrielle was pompous, and that he was silly for allowing her to be that way. He realized he'd spoken too sharply and offended her. A tremor of fear raced through him, wiping out the pleasure he'd felt just a moment before. He was supposed to feel love for these people, was supposed to be passionate about caring for their souls. Instead, he felt like they sat in perpetual judgement of him, waiting for him to screw up. They were an enormous writhing organism of demands, looking to him as God's representative to satisfy their whims. One person insisted she couldn't worship without lively music, her counterpart wanted the awe of traditional hymns. Another wanted an always-available ear to reassure her she was obeying the Bible in every minor decision. Still, another wished Mark was more gentle, presenting a kinder view of God, while others were equally adamant that the Pastor be strong in his convictions, unyielding in his proclamation of unvarnished truth. Every year his own thoughts and opinions were buried deeper under the clamor of his congregation until he feared he wouldn't know who he was in another decade.

"Gabrielle's taking a day off." He spoke as cheerfully as he could manage. He didn't like defending her laziness. Neither was he going to let Carrie see that he couldn't manage his family. "I'm gone so much," he said, "she doesn't get a lot of time to herself."

The sound that came out of Carrie resembled an old man's *harrumph*. "I never had time to myself. The idea didn't exist when I was raising my daughters. Why does a mother need time off? And Gabrielle only has one child, just wait until there are two or three running around."

He didn't know what to say without criticizing either Gabrielle or Carrie. There must be some non-committal phrase he could come up with, but his mind was empty.

Carrie stared at him, her gaze narrow and sharp. She wasn't going to let him off the hook.

"I suppose," he said.

"You suppose what? Speak your mind, don't be pussy-footing around."

"I don't know. I guess times have changed. Peter requires a lot of energy. We all need a change of pace, a Sabbath day once in a while, right?" He didn't understand why Carrie was being so combative. She must be upset about that little scene at the potluck dinner.

"The only thing that's changed is young women are lazy.

They expect their husbands to work hard all day, take care of the heavy tasks around the house, and then look after the children on top of that." Her face softened. "I think you work awfully hard, Pastor. I don't like seeing you forced into doing your wife's job as well. Is she sick? Is that it? She's looked rather thin lately. I noticed when you came to visit us. She looked very thin, and she doesn't eat anything. Motherhood requires stamina, and you don't get it by starving yourself to look like a model."

Now, her eyes were round, waiting expectantly for his answer, eager to find out something was wrong with Gabrielle. He wished Herb would hurry up with the can of insecticide he'd taken outside to coat the foundation around the kitchen area.

"She's not starving herself. And she's not ill. I thought I'd take Peter today, let him run around the church and explore the buildings. She doesn't expect me to do her job, I wanted her to have some time for herself."

Carrie looked like she couldn't think of any more prying questions. Her upper lip twitched, longing to make more pointed remarks about the laziness of women today. She didn't dare accuse him of lying about his own intentions. The conversation sickened him. He was furious at Gabrielle for abandoning her responsibility and forcing him to defend her indefensible actions. In one sense, Carrie looked soft and understanding, like a substitute grandmother. Part of him wanted to rest his head on her shoulder and sob that his wife was losing her sanity. He wanted to tell her he didn't know where Gabrielle spent her time, that she wouldn't support him in his life's work, and now she'd given up taking care of their son. But he couldn't. Gabrielle's reputation was his reputation.

Still looking dissatisfied, Carrie drifted back to the kitchen. Water pounded into the stainless steel sink. She was probably convinced that since she could smell the fumes of the bug spray, it still tainted the counters she'd already wiped. That was one trait he admired in older people — they were devoted to cleanliness. Gabrielle's housecleaning frenzy had been the most cleaning she'd done in the entire time they were married. Usually, she was satisfied with a quick sweep of the vacuum cleaner, and a swish of the mop. She never moved furniture or did any kind of serious spring cleaning. The one time she'd decided to do some old-fashioned cleaning, it became a bizarre compulsion to rid the house of evil.

He lifted Peter onto his shoulders, carrying him and the bag of toys to his office. The thin autumn light made the room dingy and flat. Even though he didn't need it, he turned on the light to brighten things up, hoping it would lighten his mood as well. He settled Peter on the floor with a pile of interlocking blocks. He shuffled through the pink slips of paper — messages taken by one of the office volunteers the day before. The entire congregation knew Monday was his day off, yet the number of phone calls on Mondays varied little from the rest of the week. It seemed they thought they would grab his attention first, get a jump on the others if they called on a Monday and left a message. None of these were emergencies, no deaths or hospitalizations. When serious incidents took place, the office volunteer called his cell phone. If no one answered the church line, the voicemail system gave callers his home landline, instructing them to call for immediate assistance. Sometimes he felt like he was as busy as God Himself. As if the pile of messages regarding comments on the sermon, requests for prayer, and general complaints wasn't enough, the phone rang.

"Grace Lutheran Church, Pastor Atwater speaking."

"It's Gabrielle."

"Hi, I hope I didn't scare you. I couldn't get you to wake up before I left. I assume you saw my note."

"Uh-huh. I'm going to a twenty-four-hour prayer meeting at Gethsemane tonight. There's plenty of food in the fridge. See you tomorrow."

"Wait! I can't keep Peter here all day and all evening. I have a council meeting tonight. You know that. And you were gone all day yesterday."

"Ask Susan to help. Involving herself in our family seems to interest her. If you can call it a family. If I weren't here, you'd think of something."

His hand trembled. He ignored the dig at Susan. "What do you mean?" The minute he asked, he wished he hadn't. She couldn't be threatening to kill herself. She was playing games, trying to manipulate him.

"You figure it out. I just know I need some serious prayer because I don't know what's going on, and I don't know what God wants from me."

"God wants you to take care of your son and be my wife."

"Well, you don't seem to need a wife." She ended the call.

He clutched the phone to his ear. His fingers pressed harder on the handset as if the intensity of his grip would bring her voice back on the line. After a few minutes, he replaced the handset. He propped his elbows on his desk and rested his head in his hands. Everything was wrong. He ached to be held. He wanted to pour out his heart to someone. Who was supposed to listen to the pastor's complaints? He wanted to lay his head on a man's shoulder, he wanted to be held and loved. Just once, he wanted someone to care about him. It had been a very long time. He pulled out his cell phone and scrolled through for the coded number in his contact list.

Twenty-three

GETHSEMANE TEMPLE DIDN'T maintain membership lists like traditional churches did. Dispensing with a list of who belonged was a source of pride. They liked to tell visitors that members' names were recorded in the heavenly roster. Their free-flowing worship had no fixed ending time, overflowing with spontaneous testimonials of answers to prayer, healings, and other miracles. It had been explained to Gabrielle that fixed times for services and short, pre-packaged prayers were rituals that shoved God into a box. The eternal could not be confined. Members of traditional churches, according to Allysan, had turned their backs on the supernatural. At Gethsemane, people were delivered from addictions, marriages were saved from the brink of divorce, and the occasional man rescued from the clutches of a *homosexual lifestyle*.

The building glittered like a beacon, as Gabrielle slowed to turn into the parking lot. She locked the minivan and walked toward the entrance. A sensation of hope took root inside of her. She started to run. Her chest swelled with the knowledge that she'd made a terrible mistake, trying to discern God's will on her own, trying to find strength by herself. This was the place to stay on course. The sting of Joe's rejection still burned, but here, she would find peace and a salve for the wound. As soon as she confessed publicly that she'd been wrong to desire a man who wasn't her husband, the shame of rejection would pass. The fierce longing she still felt for Joe's lips and arms would dissolve, replaced by a renewed love for her husband. After tonight, she would once more be able to obey God, to wait obediently for Mark's transformation. She tripped on the edge of the sidewalk. The foyer was empty. Voices rumbled behind the double doors that opened into the worship hall.

Inside the hall, forty or fifty people huddled in groups of three or four. Some had their heads bent forward, elbows resting on their knees. Others raised their hands to shoulder level, palms facing forward as if they were held at gunpoint, their faces tilted up toward the rafters. Murmuring filled the room, a sound loud enough to come from a group of a hundred or more. Voices rose and fell like waves splashing across the room, swelling, cresting, and curling gently as they fell to the shore. In some ways, the sound frightened her. At the same time, it was soothing, the voices flowing toward her, washing over her fear that she'd missed God's true message, wiping clean her anger.

Pastor Colin Glass and another man sat apart from the other groups. Heads bent over, their lips barely moving, praying silently, something Gabrielle rarely saw at this church where prayer was raised to the level of a sacrament. Prayer was everything at Gethsemane — the path to salvation, the key to unlocking the secrets in the Bible, the solution to every problem, the purpose of people on earth. Gabrielle moved further into the room, closing her eyes to absorb the voices.

After a moment, she opened her eyes and looked around the room. Allysan was seated near the front, her long tangled hair covering her head like a mantilla. The resentment Gabrielle had felt when Allysan swept Joe out from under her nose was gone. The incident seemed like it had taken place in another life, even though it had been only forty-eight hours. She was disoriented, unsure whether she'd been standing there all evening or only a few minutes. She didn't want to disrupt one of the little groups of praying people. What she really wanted was to talk to a human being, not pray, but she had to keep focused on her purpose in coming here. It would be a long night. She'd never prayed all night, never prayed for more than an hour at the most. Hopefully, they broke up the praying with other activities. As spiritual as it felt to declare she would pray all night, she didn't think she was up to sitting with a bowed head, thinking of Godly words to describe what filled her mind, hour after hour, while others listened. She chided herself. Without a doubt, God would provide the words. Wasn't that the point? To get caught up into another realm where you didn't self-consciously listen to your own voice, letting heavenly beings consume your thoughts.

Just when she thought she couldn't bear to stand there another minute, drowning in the voices, Pastor Colin stood and picked up his guitar. He strummed a chord. Slowly, the praying voices subsided, as if the volume control was gradually turned down. As the voices faded, the guitar grew louder. After a few minutes, the chords turned into a recognizable tune. The Pastor began to sing, and the others joined with the words of a familiar song about joy. Gabrielle added her voice, swaying in time with the music. Using her voice had the effect of connecting her to the group. As if Allysan felt that same growing connection, she turned and looked directly at Gabrielle.

Allysan rose from her chair and made her way to the back of the room. She wrapped her fingers around Gabrielle's upper arm, squeezed gently, and guided her to the circle where she'd been sitting. There was an empty chair at the edge of a nearby circle, and Allysan pulled it over next to her own. Gabrielle sat down, continuing to sing. She pushed her purse under her chair, wishing something as earthly as a purse didn't have to disrupt her mood. Allysan lifted her arms toward the ceiling, her fingers stretched out. Her face was covered with a look of rapture that implied she didn't see the ceiling at all. Instead, tiles and heating vents, insulation and roofing material had all been peeled back, allowing her to peer directly into heaven. She seemed to float in her chair, her hips lifting off the seat a few fractions of an inch, her skirt falling over the sides, so the legs were hidden, adding to the floating effect.

Gabrielle tried not to feel jealous. She was supposed to be enjoying her own rapturous experience. Forcing herself to close her eyes, she lifted her hands off her lap, raising her voice with the movement of her hands. Hadn't Allysan told her that if she didn't feel caught up with the Spirit, the best thing was to act as if she was? In response to faith, the ecstatic feeling would appear. Sometimes it did. Sometimes it didn't. She closed her eyes, and her thoughts drifted to Joe. Shame warmed her skin as she remembered how he'd pushed her off his lap. She wanted that horrible memory removed. She wanted the shouting voices to stop telling her she wasn't wanted. Every single man she'd ever loved had humiliated her. No one cared for her. Maybe God didn't care for her either!

When she was a child, no girl wanted to be her best friend — she was too bossy. When she was older, girlfriends were difficult to come by because the other girls envied her near-perfect appearance. Her father had preferred spending half of her life floating on the ocean. Her mother worshipped her at first, then shoved her aside. It was beginning to appear as if no one on the face of the earth adored her. Was it possible that God felt the same way? But He was supposed to love and cherish her. He'd *promised*. Over and over — those who were faithful would receive everything they wanted, every desire would be satisfied. *Every* desire.

She continued mouthing the words to the songs. They were simple words, phrases that repeated frequently. Her thoughts floated above the music. She had to work hard to keep from peeking at the others. She lifted her hands higher, forcing her mind to turn off the stream of bitter thoughts, to think about the meaning of the words. Before long, she was rewarded by a slowing of the music, followed by silence. After a few seconds of quiet, she lowered her hands and opened her eyes, relieved to see that those around her were doing the same. She turned her attention to Pastor Colin's commanding voice.

He gestured toward the man at his left. "Let me introduce Brad Jelinek. Brad has been led to share his testimony of seduction into a world of drugs. He went looking for the good feelings we all crave as part of our human makeup. Those feelings," his voice rose, "are meant to come from God. So many are misled, using drugs and alcohol to capture those pleasurable experiences. Brad followed that path, but then, a miracle of prayer set him on the road to glory. He's here to tell the stunning story of that miracle."

It wasn't fair that Brad whoever-he-was had a miracle. He couldn't be more than twenty years old. He got his prayer answered. Why was it that everyone else received miracles and answers to their prayers except Gabrielle Atwater? The unfairness roiled inside her stomach.

Brad stood and began to speak.

They listened as though every word and each pause came

from the mouth of God Himself. Brad told the brief story of his life. His parents had been absorbed in their careers, community activities, extensive travel, too busy to pay much attention to him. He drifted into smoking pot during high school. From there, the story followed a predictable pattern — a teenager without goals, heading off to college with the desire to party topping his agenda. Drugs were easy to come by, and he tried them all, settling on cocaine. Brad went on and on about how he couldn't stop chasing the feeling of power. *I felt utter rapture with the smallest details of the world. When I wasn't coked up, I felt nothing but emptiness.* Eventually, he couldn't live without it.

Gabrielle wanted him to be finished. She wanted the Pastor to ask for their prayer requests. When did she get to talk about what she needed? How was she supposed to relate to some single guy who was addicted to drugs? His supposed miracle was easy. He just had to stop taking drugs. And he had lots of people, Pastor Colin included, it turned out, helping him. Gabrielle had no one. She was alone in some sort of sexless jail cell, watching all the world being loved and touched, while she faced an endless ache for a man's hands on her body. She had no miracle. No love. No satisfying nights with her husband. She squeezed her eyes shut and silently commanded Brad to finish his boring, self-absorbed story, so they could get on to the real needs.

Finally, he was finished. Pastor Colin informed the group that in order to capture the full power of Brad's story, they would pray specifically for people who had addiction issues.

She hadn't known there were rules for prayer topics. She wanted the group to pray for her husband! Her marriage! This was completely unfair. Unless…maybe, she could call sex with men an addiction.

She turned to look at Allysan, forgetting for a moment that Allysan knew nothing about Mark's problems. She couldn't tell all these people that her body was unwanted. It was humiliating. Allysan's features were relaxed, her jaw loose. Gabrielle realized her own jaw was clenched so tightly her entire face hurt. She tried relaxing her facial muscles, but they refused to cooperate. Nothing in her life behaved as it should. She needed their prayers, immediately. It didn't matter that they wanted her to think of people with addictions. She didn't know anyone like that. The evening had been set up for prayer. It was only right that she should receive what she needed. If her miracle wasn't revived tonight, she wasn't sure she could go on living.

Several people had moved to the front of the room. One after another, they told sad, frightening stories of family members addicted to drugs, alcohol, pornography, even exercise. One person spoke about a daughter that was *addicted* to vomiting her meals. It was amazing the array of problems shoved into the category of addiction. Almost anything they didn't like in another person's life — sports, watching television, surfing the internet.

Surely she qualified. She shot out of her chair and marched

to the front of the room. When it was her turn, she moved closer to Pastor Colin as the others had done. He was taller than she'd realized. A light scent of soap emanated from his skin. She longed to move closer, to take a slow, deep breath and identify the aroma. His voice was smooth and creamy, like a satellite radio host for a deep track channel she'd heard several times in Susan's car. She closed her eyes, letting the gentle rhythm of his voice penetrate her skin. Standing next to him, aware of his height, made her feel small and delicate, just as she had when she stood beside Joe.

She shook her head, scattering thoughts of Joe like spilled rice. Every time his name crossed her mind, a feather floating across a stagnant pond, the shame returned, spreading from her neck, across her face, creeping up to her hairline, and over her scalp. If she never saw his cruel, mocking grin again, she'd be pleased. Perhaps even when he'd kissed her, holding her close to him, pressing his body against hers, he'd been playing a game with her. He'd wanted to see how far she'd go, how much she would betray her husband, or how easily she could be captured by his charm. She hated him. He had no right to deceive her, to make her feel wanted, then push her away and ridicule her.

The room was silent. She opened her eyes and saw Allysan's puzzled gaze. Pastor Colin must have asked a question. If she stood patiently, maybe he would ask again, so she didn't have to admit she'd been daydreaming. If he asked again, if she didn't have to make herself look foolish in front of all these people, it would be a sign that God was paying attention to her. Allysan's expression grew more puzzled. Gabrielle forced her own face to retreat in the opposite direction, into a relaxed, beatific pose. After a few moments of silence, she felt the weight of Colin's arm around her shoulders.

She knew all about pastors. They might be focused on God, they might have the eyes of hundreds of people on them at all times, but underneath it all, they were human beings. Flesh and blood, snoring and sneezing, needy, flawed human beings. She knew that better than anyone. The rest of the church ignored it, but the wives knew. Gabrielle had never seen Pastor Colin's wife. Was she good looking?

Under the weight of his arm, she knew he was enjoying holding a woman as gorgeous as herself. Her hair was bunched up over the place where his arm pressed against her back. He didn't let up on the pressure, unashamed to hold her in front of a crowd of people. Could it be he needed affection as much as she did? She wanted to move closer. But all those eyes on her waited expectantly. Let them wait. Let them gaze at the attractive couple standing in front of them.

This was the pastor she should be married to! This church was younger, more lively, more to her liking. This man knew how to hold a woman, and she could feel the vitality at every point where his body pressed against hers.

"I'm sensing you don't want to be specific about the addiction that's troubling you," he said.

His incredible sensitivity to her shame proved that God was going above and beyond to show concern for her! The atmosphere in the room transformed before her eyes. A pink glow throbbed at the edges. Love pulsated off the walls and flooded out of the pastor's muscular arm, assuring her that God cared for her. The fluorescent lights on the ceiling softened and gave off gentle rays of love that rested on the top of her head. The faces staring back at her shone with tenderness and anticipation. Allysan looked as if she was in awe of her new-found friend, eager to observe the miracle that would take place.

Of course, none of them would actually see the miracle because they didn't know what was wrong. But somehow, they would know anyway. They would know Gabrielle Atwater was special. She looked into Colin's face, waiting to hear his next words. Her heart pounded and fluttered against her ribs. Her fingers shook. She was so filled with heavenly energy, she could barely stand still under the protection of his embrace. She shifted her position, so she was nestled closer to him. Standing there waiting for him to offer his powerful prayers, waiting for him to anoint her head with magical, demon-defying oil, she still wanted to revel in the sense of his skin. It comforted her to know that in spite of his holiness, he wanted her, as a man wants a desirable woman.

"This young woman is hurting, and we're going to pray, but also ask the Spirit to reveal to each of our hearts the specific needs that she's unable to express."

She was disappointed he hadn't used her name. Surely he knew what it was. He knew everything about her. But that small disappointment wouldn't mar her excitement. Snuggling closer, she waited for the command to kneel before him.

Pastor Colin released her from his arm and stepped to one side. His voice deepened. "Please kneel before the throne of heaven."

Gabrielle lowered herself onto the soft pad on the floor in front of a small table that held a candle and a single fern in a narrow vase. She closed her eyes and let her head drop forward, feeling her hair wash across the sides of her face, knowing she looked angelic with her hair falling around her thin shoulders and straight back, her jeans pulling up slightly at the knee so that her slim, elegant ankles were exposed. Hopefully, he wouldn't notice the length of her feet, flatted out behind her. She let her arms hang as loosely as her hair. Remaining still felt spiritual, as well as challenging to her body. Pastor Colin touched the top of her head. He prayed for her peace of mind. Then he removed his hand. She knew he was slipping the small bottle of oil out of his pocket. She felt him touch the oily pad of his finger to each of her earlobes, passing over the wires of her earrings. He ran his warm finger across her forehead, smearing a thin layer of oil above her eyebrows. She could sense him closing the bottle and returning it to his pocket. Then his hand was resting heavily on top of her head. She took a deep breath and let herself fall into the rhythm of his words.

"Oh, God. This woman kneeling humbly before You is at the edge of a precipice. She's done all she can to be an obedient servant, and yet she hasn't received the desires of her grateful...yearning...anxious...faithful heart. You know what those desires are. For You put them there with Your own loving hand. Listen to her. Listen to all of us. Hear our prayers and answer. You command us to pray, promising answers to all our prayers when we ask...and seek...and knock. She has asked. Now, this woman seeks a miraculous change in her life. Pour out the things she desires, the heavenly things, the things that will make her know You more. Fill her with the joy of Your Spirit. Be the Heavenly Bridegroom to this yearning, hungry bride. Quench her thirst and satisfy her every desire."

He went on like this for quite some time. Gabrielle's knees grew stiff. Surely God had heard. If she were sitting in a chair, if she were able to form the words herself, she would be less anxious for it to end. At the same time, the warmth and affection she felt from Colin's steady hand made her want to remain forever. She wanted to kneel all night, feeling the press of his hand on her hair, the warmth penetrating her scalp, feeling the response in her blood vessels, and the muscles of her thighs and belly.

When he was finished, Colin reached down, took her hand in his, and helped her to her feet. He put an arm around her waist as if he knew she would be weak from the extended time on her knees. Her calves and feet tingled, and she leaned against him while she waited for the blood to return to her lower legs.

Speaking to the entire group, yet turning slightly to direct his gaze at her upturned face, Colin said, "Your miracle has been accomplished. Go home now and see what the Spirit will do for you. Seek the Lord in prayer and in His Word. Our vigil continues all night and tomorrow." He ended with a triumphant shout — "Come back and tell us what has occurred in your life."

Although the blood was now flowing normally through her legs, she felt weak. She couldn't walk. No words would come into her throat. She was filled with excitement and the absolute knowledge that her life was about to undergo an incredible, spectacular change.

Twenty-four

THE INTERIOR OF the minivan pulsated with the same love she'd felt inside the worship hall. It was almost ten o'clock. She flew past the traffic lights, hitting all of them green. She smiled and settled back in the seat, enjoying the steady speed. Angels were opening the way before her, like the water of the Red Sea parted for Moses. The hours of singing and prayer had removed all blockage between her and the heavenly realm. Until this night, her life had been filled with resistance, but going forward, it would flow smoothly. If only she'd seen that before. On the freeway, the world opened up before her as clearly as the road stretched empty into the darkness, inviting her to press harder on the accelerator, going seventy, seventy-five. She soared above the rough surface of the earth. She'd fought God at every turn. She'd been impatient. At long last, Mark would desire her. Pastor Colin had assured her it was so. The warmth of his hands and the slick oil continued to penetrate her skin.

The exit to Fremont Avenue appeared suddenly, and she veered off, gasping a bit when the minivan fishtailed as she turned a bit too hard to make the off-ramp in time. She braked gently, clenching the steering wheel to bring the vehicle back under control. She drove the rest of the way more slowly, keeping to the speed limit, allowing the lights to turn red if that was what they wished. As she made the turn onto her street, she took a long, deep breath, trying to ease the thumping of her heart.

A car was parked in front of her house, but she couldn't make it out from the end of the street. She squinted through the filmy windshield. Then she saw — Joe's silver BMW. She pulled in front of the house next door, momentarily diverted from the smooth path into Mark's arms. She eased the minivan close to the curb and turned off the engine. For a few minutes, she sat in the dark, feeling as if time had stopped. She wasn't sure how to interpret the presence of Joe's car. Her mind froze, unable to identify a possible explanation. She closed her eyes. Joe must have dropped by to remind her of his life-long friendship with Mark, to demonstrate that the three of them would be friends. He wanted to be certain Gabrielle knew she'd misinterpreted his actions. Thinking of his kisses blotted out the peace she'd been feeling since she knelt in front of Pastor Colin. The shame from the day before filled her afresh with a heat that transformed the skin of her face into a hot, ugly mask. He had no right to kiss her, to arouse uncontrolled passion, making her feel desirable, only to say it meant nothing. She pulled the key out of the ignition. The humiliation should be behind her now. Prayer had given birth to a miracle. Mark was no longer the aloof and arrogant man he'd been, confused by phony desires. He'd been set free. She was sure of it. She could see him in the center of her mind, sitting in his favorite spot on the futon. Closing his eyes and dreaming of his wife. Disappointed that he was condemned to spend the night without her. Longing for her return. The thoughts of Joe dissolved.

She opened the door, climbed out, and closed it softly. She moved stealthily toward the darkened house. A thin mist floated around the streetlight. The porch light was turned off, making the path to the front door difficult to see. Was this how Mark felt, creeping home when she was asleep? But Mark wasn't sleeping. Joe was there.

She changed course. Instead of walking up the path, past the birds of paradise, their leaves like grasping hands, she turned toward the side gate. She pushed it open and walked along the side of the garage. The door into the garage was never locked, but the door into the kitchen was. She opened it with the same key that opened the front door. The only light was the small spotlight over the kitchen sink. It glimmered across the clean counter. No soaking pots littered the surface like they did when she was alone for the evening. Not even a stray spoon or coffee cup marred the expanse of tile. She closed the garage door softly and leaned against it. Her heart continued to race in spite of the slow breaths she forced into her lungs.

Her hands shaking, she moved cautiously into the hallway. Her mind blazed with a white heat that prevented any thoughts from forming. All she knew was an apprehension she'd never felt in her life. An unformed thought told her what waited at the end of the hall. Slipping off her sandals in the alcove near the front door, she continued past the living room. Peter's door was open. Mark must have taken her suggestion to enlist Susan's help. She rounded the corner, drifting as if her body had no substance. Near the opening of the master bedroom door, she stopped.

The bedside lamp shone on smooth gleaming skin. Naked bodies moved slowly, limbs wrapped around one another as if they formed a single organism. She closed her eyes. Soft groans assaulted her ears, eating into the center of her brain. She turned away. Bile surged into her throat. She wanted to watch. She wanted to race down the hall and out the door, letting the retching have control, relieving her of the things swimming in her stomach, flooding her mind, gnawing at her heart. She turned back to see hands stroking hips and thighs. The nauseous feeling remained, but it was met by a sickening sense of longing. She wanted to join them. It had been an eternity since someone touched her. Their hands were so gentle, lingering on one another's skin. No rushing. And no begging. All her life, she'd been forced to beg for affection. Instead of desiring *her*, Mark and Joe lusted for each other. A tiny gasp burst out of her throat. She backed down the hall a few steps and flattened herself against the wall, pressing her hand over her mouth to keep a sob from escaping. It was quiet except for the soft breeze of the voices coming from the bedroom.

This wasn't something new. Joe had come from the Northwest looking to reconnect with Mark. And still, he'd seduced her. Through every sip of wine, every interesting question, and each brush of his lips and press of his hand on her back, he'd wanted Mark, not her. He must think she was unbearably naïve. With all the college degrees between the two of them, they thought they were so smart. Silly Gabrielle, would never see what was going on right under her stupid little nose. She was a mother, an innocent pastor's wife. What did she know?

Well, she wasn't stupid anymore. Now she knew everything. In one flash, the prayers of Gethsemane Temple had been answered. Something new had been revealed, as it was promised. She could see the truth. Mark and Joe had been lovers in college. Something had gone wrong, and they split up. Manipulative, lying, cheating Mark Atwater sought her out, took her on dates, told her he loved her and married her. What an effort it must have been for him to make love to her often enough to keep her suspicions subdued.

How surprised he must have been when their intermittent love-making created a child. No wonder he was so moody when she got pregnant. He didn't fear the responsibilities of fatherhood, he was unnerved that a gay man had fathered a child. And it was no surprise that he'd come around to be happy about her pregnancy. It was another confirmation in the eyes of the unsuspecting world that he was a good minister and devoted family man. He could lead the congregation and live his life as he pleased. Every Sunday morning, there was his pretty wife and his adorable son, proving to the world that he was a Godly and virile man. She was right in thinking she was nothing but a prop. A part of his twisted fantasy that God gave special permission for ministers to satisfy their desires any way they pleased. He thought he could keep her happy and quiet, raising his child and showing up at his church functions. A figurehead. In their arrogance, Mark and Joe would think she didn't know the meaning of the word figurehead. But she wasn't nearly as stupid as they thought. Not any more. How they must have laughed at her. Even tonight, they giggled together over her pathetic visit to Joe's office. They commiserated about her constant pleading for sex. She wanted to vomit right on the hall floor. But she forced her hand to stay clamped to her lips, relying on the clean scent of her skin to keep her stomach under control.

She tilted her head to the side so she could see into the room once more. Mark sat up and reached into the drawer of his bedside table. He pulled out a tiny bottle that looked exactly like the anointing oil Pastor Colin had used. He held the bottle in his right hand and unscrewed the tiny cap. He offered the bottle to Joe, who put it under his nostril and inhaled deeply. Joe handed the bottle back to Mark who took an audible breath through each nostril before screwing on the cap. They fell back on the bed. With elaborately slow movements, they continued where they'd left off.

Even now, she longed for one of them to notice her and touch her as lovingly as they touched each other. A horrid, shameful part of her still wanted to join them. She could lie between them, they'd gaze at her naked body, stroke her skin with the same slow, admiring caresses.

She moved away from the doorway. Her stomach twisted into knots. She tiptoed down the hall, pausing every few steps. At the front door, she picked up her sandals and carried them with her to the kitchen. She slipped out the garage door, turning the knob to gently replace the latch in its slot. She didn't bother to lock it. She stumbled through the garage and nearly fell out the door into the side yard. She ran past the fence, not stopping to close the gate. She threw her sandals on the seat of the van, inserted the key, started the engine, yanked the gear shift into drive, and shot into the street. A fleeting thought suggested she plow into Joe's car, but she resisted. She sped down the street, enjoying how the rapid motion forced her limp body forward, then back and over to one side as she veered around the corner. A few blocks away, she pulled to the curb. Falling forward onto the steering wheel, she began to scream. She pounded her fists against the window, throwing every thought, every piece of shame into her shoulders, sobbing and shaking until the minivan seemed to weep with her.

After a while, there were no more tears. Her nose ran profusely. She didn't know where her purse was, so she wiped her arm on the sleeve of her shirt, disgusted with herself. She hated him. Hated them both. They'd used her. Laughed at her. Destroyed her life. Every dream she'd ever had was a farce. She couldn't find words to think how much she hated Joe for his cruel game. She hated his grin, his charming laugh that sounded as if he loved everyone when, in reality, he hated her. Without even knowing her, he hated her enough to lead her into some sick charade, luring out her desires, then squashing them in her face. She hated Mark for his lies. She hated him for accusing her of wanting too much. For ignoring her, and keeping secrets. She hated his phoniness, acting as if he loved her. Praying night after night for changed desires. He knew he would never change. He didn't even *want* to change. More than anything, she hated him for making her cry. All her internal organs felt as if they had been ripped out of her throat, and her insides and skin felt bone dry.

She started the engine and drove aimlessly through the housing development surrounding Grace. Hatred boiled toward everyone at Grace, toward Susan. How they would pity her. She wanted the earth to open up and swallow her. She swiped her hand across her face again, but no tears remained. Her skin felt papery. She made an illegal U-turn on Fremont and headed toward the freeway. There was only one thing to do. Return to the prayer meeting and find out what she was supposed to do now. She wouldn't allow them to humiliate her. Reject her. Deprive her of love. They were mocking God, and they would be punished.

She couldn't figure this out on her own. Spending the rest of the night in prayer would give her the final answer. She heard a soft, deep voice speaking to her. Telling her to clean up this ugly, disgusting mess that was called her marriage.

Twenty-five

HER FACE WAS swollen from crying when Gabrielle arrived back at Gethsemane Temple. She was liable to break down completely at any minute. She slipped back into the same circle where the chair she'd occupied earlier was still slightly askew. When she sat down, she felt light, almost transparent. She had the ability to drift in and out of places without leaving any evidence of having been there. She'd walked into her house, seen what she'd seen without either of them becoming aware of her presence, and returned here, also unnoticed. Without warning, and for no apparent reason, Allysan, her eyes still closed, reached over and patted Gabrielle's leg, as if Gabrielle had been sitting beside her the entire time.

Prayer continued for another hour or so, then they broke out of their circles for a snack of sandwiches and homemade chocolate chip cookies. Gabrielle selected a roast beef sandwich from the tray. As she chewed, strength seeped into her blood from the meat. She devoured three cookies, hardly pausing to sip her coffee. The meat and sugar dulled the memory of what she'd seen in her bedroom. The food sank into her stomach and made her feel that she was regaining her substance. The unfamiliar, dangerous food felt like another creature entering her body, giving her power.

Brad, the freed drug addict, sat on the edge of the stage where the music leaders performed on Sunday mornings. He swung his legs like a child. He'd finished his sandwich and was diligently picking out unwanted walnuts from a cookie and placing them on a napkin.

Gabrielle hurried toward him. She stood close to him, almost touching his knees. He stopped swinging his legs.

"Can I ask you a question?" she said.

Up close, his face appeared much older than when he'd told his story. Looking at the dry, discolored skin made her regret eating all that poisonous food. Every rough spot and premature wrinkle demonstrated what unhealthy living did to you. And that was only what was visible, she couldn't imagine how damaged he was on the inside.

"Sure. Ask away."

"I'm guessing you know a lot about drugs."

"I suppose. Do you know someone with addiction issues?"

"Not exactly. I know someone who I think uses something illegal, but I don't know what it is."

"What kind of behavior does he, or she, exhibit? Depressed? Psychotic? Euphoric?"

"I haven't noticed any of that, I just saw him sniffing something. It was a little glass bottle, and he held it under his nose. It seemed like it relaxed him, or slowed him down, maybe. It was…" She didn't want Brad to think she was some kind of pervert who watched other people making love. "I don't know how to…" She had to know, but couldn't think of a simple way to describe the situation.

"Was it during sex?" Brad said.

"Yes." She nearly spit the word at him.

"Could be poppers. Amyl nitrate. It's somewhat unusual for a straight guy. But I guess some do if they've been around. It relaxes your muscles. Makes you more sensitive, enhances sensations. I've heard it makes you feel as if time is slowing down. Other than that, I don't know much about it. I've never tried it. No idea whether it's addictive."

"Uh-huh." She had what she needed. The conversation was over. She changed the subject back to the story of his life. She stood there for another few minutes, pretending to follow the thread of Brad's anecdotes, thinking about amyl nitrate.

TWENTY-FIVE STERILIZED half-pint jam jars were lined up on the kitchen counter. The other supplies she'd purchased online were in the garage, close at hand when she was ready for them.

The past two weeks seemed like the longest of her life. Returning to the prayer meeting that horrible night had been one of the hardest things she'd ever done. But it was worth it. She'd received her guidance.

Turning to the bags of apricots on the opposite counter, she squeezed a few to see if they were completely defrosted. Back in June, when they needed picking, it was easier to toss them all in the freezer, planning to wait until late summer to make jam. Here it was, already October. She shouldn't put it off any longer if she wanted to give jam as Christmas gifts. Of course, jam was not her primary purpose. She bent down and pulled a plastic-coated tablecloth out of the bottom drawer. Spreading it on the kitchen table, smoothing out the stiff wrinkles, she could feel power pulsing through her arms and hands. Every movement was deliberate and satisfying. She was empty of desire. She wanted nothing from Mark. If he wasn't home, it didn't affect her any more than if he was sitting in the living room, or trying to talk to her during dinner. That morning she'd told him very simply she was making jam.

"Please take Peter to work with you." The surprising thing was, he hadn't argued. He'd quietly packed up Peter's diaper bag and toys. There were no complaints about how busy he was.

The house was silent, enhancing her sense of power. She was complete. She didn't need anything. Not music, not the sound of human activity, not another voice. The atmosphere throbbed with the weight of the Spirit's presence, filling her task with divine purpose. She carried the plastic bags of thawed apricots to the table. She dumped them into her twelve-quart pot and set them on the stove to boil. When the skins were loose, she spooned them into several large glass bowls and put them on the table. Next to them, she placed the blender and a wooden spoon. She sat down and picked up the first apricot. After the skin was removed, she sliced it in half, removed the pit, and dumped the halves into the blender. She placed the pit into an empty bowl. She moved mechanically, pausing occasionally to stand up and attach the blender to its base, puree the fruit into pulp, and pour it into the other large pot sitting on the stovetop. She added lemon juice and honey. The only sounds were the ticking of the stove as the burner worked to maintain its temperature, the hum of the pewter clock, the blurp of the jam when it drew close to boiling, and her own breath.

By eleven-thirty, the twenty-five jars were filled with glistening, orange jam. The surface of the jam was coated with a thin layer of white wax that she'd melted in an empty coffee can. She'd gotten that can from her mother's kitchen the first time she made jam when she was fifteen years old. Every year when she heated the bars of wax, the new layering over the old, she thought about the layers of her life, wondering if the original wax still coated the insides, or if it evaporated to nothing, replaced by a year she couldn't identify.

She washed the pots, blender, and spoon and put everything in its proper place. She studied the bowl of pits.

They were slimy, bits of apricot clinging to the seam where the two halves of the pit were sealed. There were a lot of pits. She hadn't counted as she went, and now she wished she had. Easily a hundred. She didn't think she'd need that many, but there was no sense throwing them out. More was better. Safer. She carried the bowl to the sink. Balancing it on her hip, she turned the faucet on, pushing the handle to the left, then holding the faucet to feel the increasing heat. Before the water got too hot to touch, she eased back on the pressure and put the bowl under the faucet. She filled it halfway. Carefully lifting the bowl to the other side of the sink, opposite the rows of jam jars, she turned off the water and wiped her hands. She ran the sponge over the tablecloth. She rummaged in the drawer for the nutcracker, laying it next to the bowl of soaking pits.

In the garage, a bag of eye droppers and a small scale she'd bought a few days earlier lay on the metal shelf. There was also a bottle of chlorine from the pool supply store, a package of new rubber gloves, and a fresh silver oxide filter she'd ordered online for the gas mask. Next to her packages was a stone mortar and pestle that she'd purchased at Williams Sonoma. Hidden under a pile of rags was her father's gas mask. A useless piece of equipment, unless you needed it. What force had kept her from tossing it in the trash when she'd cleaned the garage? She carried her supplies into the kitchen and put them on the table.

She went down the hall to the bedroom. The bed was still

unmade, but she ignored it. There was no longer any need to make a pleasant environment for love. She went to the nightstand on Mark's side of the bed. She yanked open the top drawer and started flinging the contents onto the bed. Index cards for sermon notes, pens, one with *Carter Mortuary* printed on the side. How appropriate. She tucked the pen into the pocket of her jeans. There were some old cough drops, a packet of tissues, and a daily devotional pamphlet. The second drawer had a few pairs of gym socks folded into fat balls. She moved them around, feeling for the little bottle she'd seen Mark hand to Joe. It had to be here, but nothing felt like a possible container for the bottle. She shoved the drawer closed. Before she opened the third drawer, she ran her hands to the back corners of the shelf below the drawers. It was empty, full of dust and grit. She hadn't done much cleaning since her failed attempt to spiritually cleanse the house during the summer. No need for that anymore, either. The final cleansing was about to take place. As soon as she found that bottle. The third drawer contained gym shorts, a pair of weightlifting gloves, and more white balls of socks. How odd that he kept socks in the nightstand. The rest of his folded clothes, including his dark socks for suits, were all in his dresser. She opened the second drawer again and probed the folds of the socks. Tucked inside one pair, almost invisible because of the thick seams at the toes, she found not one, but two small tinted bottles with black caps. She laughed triumphantly. She replaced the contents of the drawer she'd emptied and ran back to the kitchen.

She poured the bowl of water and pits into a colander and scrubbed each pit to remove the remnants of pulp. She sat down with the nutcracker and began to snap open the pits. Some popped easily in half. Some refused to budge, so she tossed them into the garbage can sitting at her side. From the pits that opened willingly, she plucked out the tiny seeds nestled inside and placed them on top of the scale.

A little time spent on Google, aside from telling her she needed a fresh silver oxide filter to make the gas mask effective, and explaining the need for chlorine, had told her she needed five to seven grams of seeds to obtain a lethal quantity of cyanide — the powerful poison locked safely inside peach and apricot pits.

When she had a pile of nine grams, she put them into the mortar and began grinding them into powder. When all the chunks were pulverized, she brushed the powder into a jar. She dumped the powdered seeds into the pressure cooker. She added just enough water to allow the powder to dissolve, twisted the lid until the rubber ring held it snugly in place, and turned the stove to the highest setting.

She added the silver oxide filter to the cartridge. She sat at the table and watched until the valve on the top of the pressure cooker began to tremble.

When the pot was hissing furiously, she lifted it from the burner and turned off the heat. Using one of the eyedroppers, she patiently sucked liquid into the eyedropper and inserted it into one of the rinsed out bottles from Mark's drawer. She poured the rest of the contents, seeds, and water into a jar, closed it tightly, sealed it in a plastic freezer bag, and carried it to the garage. Just in case she needed more.

She strapped the gas mask to her face and pulled on the rubber gloves. She drew chlorine into the eyedropper, inserted the dropper tip into the bottle, squeezed, and quickly sealed it. She shook it and followed the same procedure with the second bottle.

She scrubbed clean the pressure cooker, the colander and bowl, the nutcracker and mortar and pestle, and the eyedroppers. She wiped off the table cloth again and left it to dry. When everything was clean, she removed the gas mask and took it back to the garage. She stuffed it into a box half full of Christmas decorations, covering it with tissue paper, and shoving the box back under the shelf.

The little bottles with their new, deadly contents fit snugly into the toe of a pair of socks. She lined up all the socks the way she'd found them, likes eggs in a carton.

With everything in place, she sat down at the kitchen table and stared at her jars of jam. It had all gone so smoothly, she wasn't sure what to do. She would have to draw on all her supernatural patience. They'd used her bed before, and they would use it again. All she had to do was figure out the right time to engineer her own and Peter's absence from the house. If she sat there long enough, the perfect occasion, a workable plan, would come to mind. She had faith.

Twenty-six

MARK PICKED UP the thirty-pound dumbbell, readying for his bicep curls. The rhythm of lifting weights was the only thing keeping his mind steady. The repetition slowed his thoughts in their mad race from one frightening scenario to another. In less than a year, less than six months, his life had collapsed. Pentecost Sunday — the start of the building program — was the last time he remembered being fully in control. And how he'd taken it for granted. Before his wife found out he was gay, before she lost her grip on reality, and before Joe came back into his life. No matter which direction he turned, all he could see was potential ruin. He put his elbow on his knee and began pressing his fist up toward his shoulder, feeling the pull and burn in his muscle, forcing his mind to think about breathing out, breathing in, counting the reps. He kept his eyes glued to the mirror, studying his form, not wanting to look at the other gym patrons. He wished they would all disappear, leaving him alone with the effort of lifting weights, and the greater challenge of controlling his thoughts.

It was one-thirty on a weekday afternoon, so the room was relatively empty. But several people using the weight machines and the older women on two of the five treadmills were enough to make him feel he was on display. His whole life was open to public view. Going into the ministry had, in some small part, been fueled by the desire to be noticed. He'd never considered the flip side of all that recognition — the unwanted attention, every day, all day. His marriage, his parenting, and his money management were acted out in front of hundreds. He couldn't even go to the hardware store unshaven and unwashed on a Monday morning without the fear, and often the reality, of running into someone from the congregation. At times, they seemed to be everywhere. And recently, he was aware that they were also in his bedroom. They might as well be standing in a semi-circle around the foot of his bed, for all the freedom he lacked. He grunted as he completed the last of twelve reps for the left arm. He switched the dumbbell to his right hand and began curling his fist toward his shoulder.

Because he'd wanted to project a perfect image, he was married to a woman dancing along the edge of a personality disorder, if not genuine madness. Because of his career choice, he was denied the affection of the man he loved. Life had been bearable when sex was fitted into a small, tight package at the fringe of his existence. He'd managed to keep

Gabrielle pacified, even enjoyed her company much of the time, hadn't he? He'd loved the challenge and the stimulation of his work. Communicating stories and feeling the thrill of people responding with contributions or volunteering for church and community projects. It was an addiction. He craved the response. He got high on the rush of knowing his persuasive power compelled another person to react. That had all been fine, interspersed with the occasional anonymous encounter, until Joe reappeared. He couldn't even remember anymore why he chose the ministry over Joe. Fear. Twenty years old. Still not ready to admit what he really wanted. A lifetime of believing the ministry was his calling. Half ashamed of his true self. Hating that he was different, raised with the belief he was cursed by God.

He'd forgotten how exciting Joe was. And he'd definitely forgotten what it was like to be completely loved. To adore another person, to be lost in his senses. Having Joe around again made him realize his life was an empty act. His marriage wrapped around him like locked chains. Fatherhood, in a household of warring adults, was horrific. He didn't know how to talk to his small son, didn't know what to do with him. He felt useless, except for the few minutes each day when Peter reached out his chubby little arms and cheered — *Da!* That part felt good, the rest was a blur, uselessly going through motions that didn't have any clear value, simply because those were the things a father was supposed to do. Did any of it really matter? What had his father done for him? Told him his career choice was a mistake. Assured him, women weren't interested in sex and made him feel guilty for even thinking about sex, half suggesting it was a teenage fascination that pretty much disappeared in adulthood. He'd seen that wasn't true, but somehow his father's voice drowned out reality. His father made him feel like a loser for not being able to play sports. Ridiculed him for his interest in cooking. Cooking was for women. Everything got defined by the gender assigned at conception. Not that he got to indulge his interest in gourmet cooking these days, Gabrielle had that all locked up with her healthy, hippy, vegetable obsessions. Another indication of her instability. Normal people didn't think ingesting meat was an act of murder.

He wanted Joe more than ever. The fragments of his life were nothing but obstacles to Joe. When he closed his eyes, he saw Joe's face. When he tried to organize his thoughts around a sermon topic, he thought about Joe's response and their conversation and debate over the truth of it. Recently, every person who called him or walked into his office made him feel as if a swarm of bees was trapped inside his clothing. And Gabrielle...living with her was like being confined to an insane asylum. She stared at the walls as if she could see through them. She glided through the house, looking at him as if he was an intruder. No matter where he settled, he was in the way. Peter treated him like a piece of furniture, pounding him with his fists, sitting on his belly if he stretched out on the floor to watch television, or like an amusement park ride, swinging on his extended foot when he crossed his legs to read the news or a book.

He dropped the dumbbell onto the rack and moved to the bench press. Seeing his profile in the mirror, he had to admit one thing was going right — the extra workouts were evident. He looked younger and more fit than any man his age. Gabrielle's healthy cooking had some benefit, as long as he supplemented it with protein. He set the weights at one hundred and fifty pounds and reclined on the bench. He raised and lowered the bar twenty times without stopping.

After he'd completed the remainder of his circuit, he took a shower and headed out to the parking lot. The sun was so intense it felt more like August than the end of October. Wearing shorts and t-shirts the day before Halloween was ridiculous. He let his mind drift into a fantasy of living in a seasonal climate. With all Joe's money, maybe he should leave the ministry, and they could move to the East coast. Then, as vivid as the mirage across the parking lot, the faces of the board of elders at Grace, his parents, Peter, rose before him, forcing the fantasy to sputter and die before he could mentally design the floor plan of the home he and Joe would create together. It would never happen. He was trapped. Death seemed like the only alternative to the iron-clad cage he'd created for himself over the years, one small choice after another. Most of them choices of silence.

He strapped his backpack over his shoulders and climbed onto his bike. In spite of the lack of cooling temperatures, the leaves on the liquid amber trees were managing to turn red. Everything else looked brittle and half dead, ready for a magnificent bonfire. But when he closed his eyes for a half-second at the traffic light, it felt like summer. The sensation confused him enormously.

He pulled into the driveway, irritated by the brown lawn. For someone who was home all day taking care of one child, Gabrielle might find time to water the grass. Sure, there was a drought, but that didn't mean it couldn't be watered occasionally. She kept the back soaked, looking like a tropical garden, but neglected the front, never seeming to care what their guests, or the neighbors, might think. The only live things were those blasted birds of paradise, which grew no matter how little they were watered. They blocked his path to the door, pointing their long stiff leaves like accusing fingers. For a moment, death truly did seem like a pleasant alternative to the shape of his life. He would be free from a son whose needs he couldn't meet, a wife who he couldn't even categorize, and a horde of parishioners who'd clung to him like leeches. It would feel so good to be free of the daily performance, crucifying his inner self again and again. The only thing he'd lose with death would be Joe. What would eternity be like without him? Or was God a complete mystery that none of them could begin to understand, in spite of their persistent, zealous efforts to define Him? If God was love, maybe any true love was the only thing that remained for eternity. Maybe it wasn't so black and white as they all wanted it to be — the thousands of religious organizations, in thousands of cities, in hundreds of countries, each with their own slender thread of truth. If he was contemplating death, why not leave the shocked and angry and disapproving faces to be with Joe?

Inside, Gabrielle was sitting on the living room floor. Peter stood facing her, a rapturous look on his face. Next to her was a pile of fabric. As Mark watched, Peter lifted his arms, and Gabrielle pulled his shirt up over his head and dropped it on the floor beside her. Out of the pile of fabric, she pulled a white blouse with sleeves twice as long as Peter's arms. She helped him poke his arms into the sleeves, then buttoned the front. She pushed the overly long sleeve of one arm up to his wrist and tied it in place with a piece of red ribbon. "There, see?" Peter studied her with a solemn expression. "You have a pirate shirt. Like the bad guys in Peter Pan."

Mark waited for her to acknowledge his presence. This was the kind of behavior that made him feel some sort of supernatural power was emanating from her. Her ability to make him feel invisible was uncanny. The atmosphere around her was the fruit of a mind that had slipped off its resting place in the center of the skull, skewed to one side like the pirate shirt that was bloused on one arm, and dangled off the other, swallowing Peter's hand. Mark half expected her to add a hook to the other sleeve. She knew he was standing there. If she hadn't heard his bike rumble into the driveway, she had definitely heard him open the screen door. As if he were held in some spell she'd cast, Peter also seemed oblivious to Mark's presence.

"Hi," Mark said. He could stand there all night. She could resist civility, not caring how stiff and silent the house was. Gone were her previous concerns about their son and the effects that sharp words or painful silences would have on his well being. She chattered about pirates as if Peter understood.

Peter's power of resistance wasn't completely in lock-step with hers. He turned. "Da! Da-da!" He ran to the living room step, and without being able to move fast enough to stop it, Mark saw what was going to happen. Peter, partially immobilized by the long shirt tails that reached to his feet, tripped on the dangling sleeve that Gabrielle hadn't yet tied into a balloon at his wrist. He crashed face down. His chin hit the edge of the step with a crack. His face contorted, and he screamed, tears cascading down his cheeks. He tore at the shirt, becoming more entangled. Gabrielle remained seated. Mark fell to his knees and fumbled with the shirt, furiously unbuttoning it while Peter screamed. He fumbled to untie the ribbon. When he tried to force open Peter's mouth to check for blood, Peter screamed louder. Gabrielle remained motionless, looking past Mark, staring at nothing.

There was no blood. Mark carried Peter to the kitchen. Holding Peter in one arm, he rummaged in the refrigerator for a handful of ice cubes. He sat Peter on the counter and wrapped the ice in a towel. The crying subsided. Peter whimpered when the cold pack was pressed against his jaw, but he looked at Mark gratefully. Mark smoothed the hair out of Peter's eyes. After a few minutes, he moved the ice pack from one side of the jaw to the other. He moved it under Peter's chin, unsure which spot absorbed the greatest impact. After a few minutes, he shook the towel over the sink until the cubes came unstuck from the fabric. He carried Peter back to the living room and sat on the couch, settling Peter on his lap. Peter leaned his head back against Mark's chest, snuggling into the circle of his father's arm. Yielding to the surreal atmosphere of the past few weeks, Mark ignored everything that had just happened.

"Why are you making him a pirate uniform?"

"It's not a uniform, it's a costume. A harvest festival costume."

"I thought that church was opposed to Halloween celebrations. Inviting in the evil spirits, and all that?" He was unable to stop the mocking tone from snaking around the words.

Speaking in a dull voice, Gabrielle intoned, "It's not a Halloween costume. Gethsemane Temple is holding a harvest festival on All Saints' Eve. There will be games and music, and entertainment for children. They can dress like imaginary characters, as long as there are no evil representations."

"Is that right? And are you now a member of Gethsemane Temple instead of Grace?"

"They don't have boring membership lists. It's a gathering of believers. Anyone is welcome. Peter and I are going."

"No, you're not."

Gabrielle leaped to her feet. "You can't tell me what to do."

"You're my wife. Peter is my son, and I don't want my son raised in that kind of cultish belief system." He couldn't believe he was invoking his rights as a father when just an hour before he didn't want anything to do with family life. But the fact remained that he *was* a father. He was also a minister with responsibilities and vows to keep. And part of that was to demonstrate through his family his qualification to guide other families. "What do you think it looks like when my wife and son are running off to some other church? What do you think it looks like to Grace when you prefer to listen to another preacher over your husband?"

"You talk about Grace as if it was another woman!"

She scooped up the pile of clothes. Clutching them in her arms, she cooed, "Come on, Peter. Let's go in your room and finish up your costume. You'll look just like the pirates in Peter Pan. You can play with your sword while I sew up the sleeves."

At the mention of the sword, Peter scrambled off Mark's lap.

"Don't walk out on me in the middle of a discussion," Mark said.

"It's not a discussion. All you care about is how things look. How it looks to have me going to another church is a dust mite compared with what's going on here. Don't tell me you care what it looks like. Attending a harvest festival at another church is nothing. Do you hear me? Nothing! And you know it."

He fell back against the futon. Gabrielle marched up the steps and down the hall. Peter tumbled at her heels like a puppy.

He didn't even know why he was throwing his weight around, why he was arguing. This was a gift from God. Tomorrow night was Halloween — *All Saints' Eve*, as she so pompously called it. If she and Peter would be gone for a defined amount of time, Joe could come over. They'd turn out the lights to ward off trick-or-treaters.

A warm, soft feeling like hot syrup rushed through him. Gone was the tension of the fight and his momentary joy that his son needed him. He couldn't visit Joe at his condo, where all of his neighbors knew Joe as a happy, confident, gay man. Trapped by the fear of running into someone he knew, he was forced to sit home and wait for scattered opportunities to arise. He was an idiot to argue with Gabrielle. He should help create the costume, usher them out the front door, and tell them to have a splendid time. He stood and went down the hall to Peter's bedroom. He'd help them get the costume ready. It would be an exciting evening for all of them. *All Saints' Eve.*

Twenty-seven

MARK HAD BEEN SO idiotically happy to help her get ready, Gabrielle knew he was planning to spend the evening with Joe. He couldn't wait to scuttle her out the door. He'd followed her around for nearly an hour, repeatedly saying — *Won't you be late? Make sure you have everything* — pressing her and Peter in the direction of the front door. His impatience glowed on his skin like oil.

Once Susan and her kids were loaded in the minivan, the drive to Gethsemane Temple was eerily quiet. Occasionally Susan barked out a question, trying to stir up conversation, but Gabrielle couldn't waste energy on trivia. No amount of pressure to be socially correct was going to divert her from the carefully constructed plan. She needed to keep her mind on each step, hyper-alert to every passing moment.

The early evening air was obnoxiously warm. It almost called for turning on the air conditioner, but she resisted, keeping both front windows partially open. It annoyed her that the weather, supposedly in God's control, wasn't cooperating with the atmosphere of the season. How could they get excited about the harvest when it was hot enough to swim? She rolled up to the stop sign and pressed the brake before turning left onto Hamilton Way. Dry leaves rattled in the gutters, crackling like slivers of glass. She stepped on the accelerator, then increased the pressure. Minutes were slipping past, but she couldn't just drop them off outside the church. She needed to make a show of participating in the event, spend a few minutes walking around the booths with Peter.

In the parking lot, Susan fumbled, pulling the seatbelt out of Sam's car seat. She put her face close to his and made cooing sounds before lifting the carrier out of the minivan. She attached the carrier to the stroller skeleton and hung the diaper bag over the handles.

They started toward the main doors. "I'm so glad you invited us," Susan said. "I'm curious about this church, and the festival should be fun for the kids. But mostly I'm so relieved that we're still friends. For a while, I thought you didn't want to be my friend anymore." She patted Gabrielle's arm, giving it a little squeeze. Her eyes watered. "I've missed you."

Inside the building, piles of dried cornstalks leaned against the walls. Huge, misshapen pumpkins rested cheerfully on bales of hay that propped up the cornstalks. Instead of the carved faces of jack-o-lanterns, the pumpkins' features were drawn with permanent markers —blue and brown eyes with long, dark lashes, and red, smiling mouths. They looked like the decapitated heads of circus clowns. The room was already full of people. Children were everywhere. The racket prompted Sam to add his excited shrieks to the mix. There were food booths with candied apples and popcorn. The odor of hot dogs wafted over everything. Around the perimeter of the room were makeshift booths, the roofs covered in straw. Nearly everything was painted orange and yellow, trying much too hard to remind everyone that this was a harvest festival, not a Halloween party. There wasn't a stroke of black paint in the entire hall, except for the exotic eyelashes on the pumpkins.

"Where should we start?" Gabrielle said. She had only moments to get Susan caught up in the activities. Then, Gabrielle would put on her show, designed to arrange a quick, uncontested escape. She was counting on Peter's devotion to Cara to solidify the plan. At least her son appeared to be attracted to females, unlike his father.

At their left was a large circle formed by numbered sheets of paper taped to the floor. Music played, and children walked around the circle. When the music stopped, a number was called, and the child standing in that spot got to choose a pumpkin from the pile in the corner.

"What should we do first?" Gabrielle said. "There's so much."

"Let's just walk around and see what they have."

Gabrielle raised her voice. "That's not a good idea. Peter will get bored. Can't you see how he's pulling on my hand? He wants to do something, not just walk and look."

"Don't get so excited," Susan said. "It was just a suggestion. Why are you so wound up?"

Gabrielle considered the words. Why wait? It wasn't as if there was a prescribed amount of activity that had to take place before she could beg her way out. Susan had given her a perfect opening, she needed to take it. She lowered her voice. "I need to get out of here."

Susan looked at her. "What's wrong?"

"You need to watch Peter for me." Gabrielle took a deep breath and forced a sob into her voice. "I have to go home! I never should have left Mark. We had a terrible fight because he didn't want me to come to the harvest festival." That part was true. It made it easier to continue accelerating her panic. "He hates it when I come to Gethsemane. I can't bear to be away from him when he's angry with me. I can't get rid of this horrible feeling. It was in my heart all the way to your house, and all the way here, and it won't go away. I thought it would, but it won't. It's getting worse. I feel like something terrible is going to happen if I don't go home right now. Please, please take care of Peter for me."

Susan's face was fluid with sympathy. Her eyes fluttered, and the edges of her lips seemed to be melting into her mouth. She patted Gabrielle's arm. "I know things haven't been good. But you also have an obligation to Peter. Look how excited he is. I'll keep him overnight for you, but you don't have to go right this minute. You and Mark need some space. We'll be finished early, then you can go home. Besides, we need a ride."

The problem was, Susan put no stock in premonitions or supernatural guidance. She wasn't buying Gabrielle's foreknowledge of the terrible thing about to happen. But her knowledge wasn't supernatural. Something terrible *was* going to happen. It might already be taking place. There was no more time. She was going to have to crank it up a notch. She stopped walking. She swayed as if she was about to pass out. She rolled her eyes back in their sockets, showing the maximum amount of white. She bit her lip, forcing her teeth in harder, barely feeling the pain, rewarded by the taste of blood.

Susan shifted the baby on her hip and tried to force the unruly wheels of the stroller toward the side of the hall so they could move away from the doorway where newcomers were crowding in behind them. Cara tugged on one handle of the stroller, making it even more difficult to maneuver. "Mom, can I do the pumpkin walk? Please? Mom? Mom!"

"Hush," Gabrielle said.

Susan whirled around, giving the stroller a final yank, pulling it away from the clot of people behind them. "Don't talk to her like that." She squinted. "Your lip is bleeding."

"Something terrible is going to happen to Mark and me. I can feel it." Gabrielle covered her face with her hand.

Susan and Cara stared at her with a mixture of disgust and fear.

"Mom, can I please do the pumpkin walk?"

Susan turned back to her daughter. "Sure. But you can't start right now. After this song finishes."

Cara nodded, inching closer to the circle of marching children so that she was almost in their path. They swerved around her, not missing a beat.

"Do you think Peter will march with her? Do you think if they win that both of them will get pumpkins?" Susan said.

Gabrielle wanted to wrap her hands around Susan's throat and shake her until her teeth came loose and scattered across the floor. All Susan could think about was the mundane and irrelevant. She was the most spiritually obtuse person imaginable. What could Gabrielle do to break through that thick skull, to frighten her enough to earn an escape from the talking, eating, laughing, pressing bodies? Voices swelled around them like clouds of sound, ignorant of the angels standing above, their swords ready to deliver justice.

At that very moment, less than six miles away, Joe was arriving at her front door. Did they drink wine first? Talk about their respective days for a while? Or were they unable to keep their hands off each other? She imagined them sharing a glass or two of wine like she and Joe had done. Then they would kiss and wander toward the bedroom. How long after they got into bed, did they indulge in the bottle of chemicals that they needed to make their sex life more enjoyable? That was proof they didn't really love each other. If they truly cared for each other, they wouldn't need an artificial assistant. Was Mark always so unselfish? Did he sometimes sniff the popper first, or did he always offer it to Joe…or to some other partner…how many partners over the years of their marriage? She shivered.

"What's the matter with you?"

"I told you." Gabrielle rolled her eyes back, biting down on her lip again.

"Don't do that! Your lip is bleeding. Did you do that to yourself?"

Gabrielle bit harder, tasting a fresh infusion of blood.

"Stop it!" Susan grabbed her arm and shook her. "People are staring."

"I'm just so scared. I don't like being separated from Mark when we've had a fight. It makes everything worse. I need to be with him."

"Then why did you come here? Why did you invite us? I can't watch all three kids, and I don't have a ride back. If you leave, I'm stuck."

Gabrielle looked frantically around the room, searching for Allysan's wild mass of hair. Allysan had said she would be helping in one of the game booths. Gabrielle drifted toward the row of booths, skirting the cluster of parents watching their children march relentlessly toward disappointment — only one would get a pumpkin. She licked her bottom lip, tasting blood. All Susan needed was a ride home, and she would gladly be rid of Gabrielle. She smiled. Susan had been quite disturbed by the lip biting.

Like a tropical flower in the overheated room, Allysan was swathed head to ankle in orange and yellow, her dark hair floating and shimmering under the florescent lights. She swayed lazily to some unheard music. Gabrielle darted across the center of the room. Her heart raced, envisioning Joe and Mark already sitting close to each other on the couch, starting a second glass of wine. She couldn't let the hammer of God fall without being there to witness it. She had to see who was chosen to die. If Mark plucked the bottle out of his socks and sniffed first, he would fall down in agony while Joe... what would he do? Get dressed? Call 9-1-1? If it was Joe, would Mark cry? Would he call for help? Or would he be too afraid of what the paramedics might think? If it was Mark, would Joe even recognize that God was the one delivering punishment?

She reached Allysan's side. She grabbed the orange-wrapped arm. The loose, soft fabric inflated itself on either side of her fingers, and her hand felt like it was sinking through foam onto the surprisingly muscular flesh of Allysan's upper arm. Allysan turned.

"You look upset," Allysan said.

"Please help me. You have to help me. I left Mark, we were in a terrible fight, and I have to go home."

Allysan's dark eyebrows rose gracefully. "You left Mark?"

"I don't mean I left him, I mean I walked out in the middle

of a fight. He didn't want me to come here. It's too complicated to explain. But my friend Susan is here with her kids. I really have to go home. But she's all freaked out that she won't have a ride and that she can't handle her kids and watch Peter for me."

"You look like the one who's freaked out."

Gabrielle leaned close. "I must go home. It's been revealed to me that something terrible is going to happen if I'm not there. I'm overcome with the Spirit's presence. You know how it is. I need you to stay with Susan, help her with the kids, and drive her home. You have to help me. Please."

"Calm down. You know…usually, when the Spirit is giving you guidance, it's a peaceful feeling. You're hysterical."

Gabrielle waved her hand, still clutching Allysan's arm with the other. "This is different. I said we had a fight. It was vicious." She wasn't lying. They had been having a terrible fight for months, years, ever since their wedding day. She forced her eyes to remain open, knowing the strain would cause them to fill with tears. After a moment or two, tears dutifully rose to the surface. "Please help me. I'm begging you. Something is holding my throat, squeezing the breath out of me." She let go of Allysan's arm and lowered herself to her knees. She grabbed Allysan's skirt. "Please."

"For heaven's sake," Allysan said. "Get up."

"You have to see how desperately I need your help. You have to know how the Spirit is compelling me."

"Is Susan okay with this? I don't even know her."

"Yes." Gabrielle's breath came in short bursts. She stood and tugged Allysan toward the other side of the room where Cara was marching in the pumpkin circle, holding tightly to Peter's hand.

Gabrielle introduced Susan and Allysan. Before either one could say anything more, she kissed Peter's head and slipped away in the crowd.

At last, she was out of the steamy, noisy building, walking into the darkness. It felt good to be away from the clamor. The noise made her crazy. She could hardly think. Never had she imagined it would be so difficult to get Susan, who was always begging to help, to cooperate and actually do something useful. She started running. She drove home as fast as she could, confident God was once again transporting her through the traffic lights that glowed green for blocks ahead of her. She didn't see any trick-or-treaters until she turned off the freeway and headed into their neighborhood. Joe's car was parked primly at the curb. It seemed like days, but she'd been gone for less than two hours.

God would choose which one should die. On the one hand, Joe deserved it more, for tempting Mark when he was trying to change. It came to her that Joe had given money to the church in order to lure Mark back to him. To make him feel indebted. And then there was the way he completely misled and humiliated her. But Mark wasn't blameless. Pretending to love her. Marrying her. Knowing the entire time what he was. He used her to make himself acceptable to

Grace. Both of them deserved punishment. It was really hard to make up her mind who deserved it more. Mark had wounded her the most — so deeply, so pervasively, she would carry the scar forever. But Joe had teased out her vulnerability and then maliciously lacerated her heart. That's why it must be God's decision which one would inhale the cyanide fumes. Whoever breathed first would die. She really had nothing to do with it.

All Saints' Day

GABRIELLE SHIVERED. AFTER the brittle, oppressive heat of the day, followed by the muggy atmosphere inside the hall at Gethsemane, she was finally cool. Now she longed for a sweatshirt to cover her bare shoulders.

Across the kitchen table, Mark's blue eyes stared at her, around her, past her. They stared into another dimension that only he could see. They were blank and unfocused. His eyes were uncomprehending, unwilling to grasp God's decisive punishment. He refused to understand that it hadn't been her doing. She was only an instrument. His sin had brought about this judgement. The Bible instructed him to rejoice in the wife of his youth, to be satisfied with her breasts at all times. It said that — at *all* times — and he'd discarded her. He chose someone else over her. He was an adulterer, and he knew it. He chose to use illicit drugs. Everything was his own doing.

"We can't sit here all night," she said. "You have to help me move Joe's body. To his condo, I think. Don't you agree? There isn't a lot of time left."

His stare remained fixed.

"Stop looking so shocked. You have to see that God finally took action. You knew you couldn't manipulate Him forever."

"God hasn't done anything."

"There's a corpse in our bedroom. We can't sit here all night." She pushed out her chair, shivering as the wood legs squeaked on the linoleum.

"Sit down. I have to think."

"We've been sitting here for hours. It's one o'clock." She turned her head to the clock behind her to confirm her guess. "Almost one-thirty. There's nothing left to think about."

She'd worked out a plan. Once they got the body to Joe's condo, a friend would eventually find it. There was no connection to Mark. She would dispose of the amyl nitrate bottle in their own trash. The police would be at a dead-end, questioning Joe's neighbors and friends, but they'd get nowhere because none of them knew Mark even existed. Since God had chosen Mark's life over Joe's, it was meant for Mark and her to continue as before. Joe's attempt to mess up their lives was a test. They'd return to fervent prayer. Maybe they'd attend Gethsemane together. The whole experience with Joe had been nothing but an infatuation with a very charismatic guy, a first love that Mark had never let go of. Now, Mark would see that he wasn't gay at all, he'd simply clung to distorted, romanticized memories. She'd read somewhere that many teenaged boys experimented with other guys. They outgrew it.

"If you think about it, we're exactly alike," she said. "We were both infatuated with Joe." She giggled. A bubbling sensation swelled inside her throat. She giggled more. She threw back her head, feeling the weight of her hair pull it down toward her shoulder blades, stretching her neck as she laughed. Her laughter turned to shrieks. "We're exactly alike! We both need sex, we both want to be desired. You were obsessed with Joe, and so was I."

Mark jumped to his feet. The chair crashed to the floor behind him. "Stop that. Stop laughing. We're nothing alike."

"It's funny. Can't you see it? We both wanted sex, and we weren't getting it. We need the same thing." Her laugh subsided, but the giggles wouldn't stop. It was really, very funny. She liked the pattern of it all. It made her feel calm. It made her confident they would be reunited now. Their desires would turn toward each other where they belonged — between husband and wife.

"We're nothing alike!" Mark was shouting, his face blanched, his eyes watery and faded. "I'm not a murderer."

She wrapped her hand around his forearm. He thrashed, shaking her off. He backed up to the wall. "Don't touch me."

"I'm not a murderer, Mark. God chose the person who would die. Yes, I put some cyanide in that little bottle. But what were you doing using illegal drugs? Where did you even get something like that? They don't sell it at the mall."

"Stop talking. I told you I have to think."

"There's nothing to think about. I didn't murder anyone. God…"

"Don't talk to me about God. All my life, I tried to do what God wanted. But He wouldn't listen. He ignored my prayers and refused to change me. He made me so I don't fit into this kind of church. I thought it was okay, but I was wrong. I'm tired of lying. I can't pretend anymore."

"Well, it's about time."

"I don't mean that. I'm sorry I wasn't honest with you. I haven't been honest with the whole world. With myself. With God. I want to live as the person I really am, not hiding. I loved Joe." The words sounded as if they were torn out of his throat, but no tears followed. He gasped, leaning over and clutching his stomach. "I'm calling the police."

"I didn't do anything wrong."

"Why did you kill him? I loved him!"

"He made a fool of me. He made me think he wanted me. I'm glad God chose him because now we can start over."

"You made a fool of *yourself*. I lied to you, and I'm sorry about that. But you killed him." He stepped around the table. "I'm calling the police."

"You can't. Everything will come out. How will you explain a dead, naked man in your bed?"

"I don't care. I said I'm tired of hiding. This isn't a life. I feel like I don't even exist. No one knows who I really am. Except Joe."

"I know who you are."

"Not really."

"You'll lose your job. What about me?"

"Whatever happens, happens."

"You can't do this to me."

"All you care about is yourself. What about Peter? What about me? What about Joe?"

She had to convince him. Where was the sense of God's presence? She really needed His assurance right now. She needed Him to make Mark understand that everything was okay. He wasn't giving God a chance to finish acting.

"You killed the man I loved. I'm sorry that I hurt you so badly. So very sorry. But I'm not going to let you get away with killing someone."

"He deserved to die. You both did. But God preserved your life over Joe's. Can't you see that? It's a chance for us."

"God didn't do anything. You did."

"I wanted to be loved the way I deserve!"

"Well, murder wasn't the appropriate solution. Didn't you ever hear of divorce?"

She waited for God to change Mark's heart. Any minute it would happen. He was breathing heavily. She could hear his heart thudding. The clock hummed. Why wouldn't it shut up? Time was slipping away. She wanted Mark to wrap her in his arms, tell her they would work it out together. He had to tell her he'd been completely mistaken. That he longed for her. "God hates divorce," she said.

"But not murder?"

"It wasn't murder," she whispered. "It's God's judgement. A man should leave his father and mother and cleave to his wife. A man's desire should be for the wife of his youth." She wanted a man. She would die without one. She wanted this man. But it was no good trying to force him to love her. It spoiled everything. She would have to yield herself into the hands of God and wait to see what He would do next. "You'll come to love me. All of that other stuff will fade. God will take it away if we pray together."

He turned his head, so he wasn't facing her. "I've spent my entire life watching and listening to people, even people who didn't know me, say the core of who I am, excludes me from so many things that they're allowed to take for granted. I've watched and listened as I was told that I could not be loved; could not be happy; could not experience a complete life on this earth. I absorbed those lessons as a child and believed them. No more."

She relaxed all her muscles. Letting herself go limp. She slid down along the side of the counter. She fell on her side, wrapping her hands around her shoulders, trying to keep warm, pleased by the tender sensation of her fingers against her skin. God would satisfy *every* desire. He'd promised.

MARK WATCHED GABRIELLE WILT onto the floor. He slumped against the wall, savoring the quiet. Tears rolled down his face as he thought of Joe's empty body lying on his bed. Dear, sweet Joe. He could see now that pride in his career, his relationship to his child, everything was empty until Joe swept back into his life, laughing, drinking a little too much, generous beyond reason. If only he'd made a different choice, but he couldn't remember which fork in the road had been the wrong one. Hiding his pre-teen yearnings? Dating girls, thinking he might change? Believing too much in some mysterious call of God into the ministry at a church where every line of the Bible was taken literally and out of context for its time and its writers? Thinking he had divine permission to live outside the prescribed rules? Thinking marriage to a woman would change him? Not putting his love for Joe above everything? He'd treated Gabrielle despicably, but it was too late to change that. There was no point in analyzing which mistaken path led so inevitably to this point.

He needed to pick up the phone, call the police, reveal the truth, but he wasn't ready. He wasn't ready to see Joe carried out of his life for the last time. He wasn't ready to be left alone with a small child and no job — no public esteem, tossed out of the church. He would lose his home. What would they say? Images of his parishioners raced across his mind. He saw their faces — their disappointment, their disapproval, their disgust.

He stepped around Gabrielle. Her arm flopped out as if she wanted to grab his ankle, but either she lacked strength or didn't intend that after all. He left the kitchen and walked slowly down the hall. He paused outside of Peter's open bedroom door. The drapes with Winnie the Pooh and the dresser, neatly arranged with figurines and a small lamp, looked forlorn as he tried to think what his son's future would be. At least Gabrielle hadn't dragged him into this. Peter must be with Susan, safely tucked in bed for the night. Protected, for now. He pulled the door closed and turned the corner.

There were so many questions. He didn't know how she'd gotten her hands on cyanide, and he didn't know how she'd discovered the popper bottle or known the contents would be inhaled. Had her cleaning frenzy led her to re-wash all his clothes? Was she looking for more evidence of his hidden life and stumbled across the bottles? He'd been stupid to leave so many things in the house, so easily found. Maybe he had wanted her to discover everything. Maybe his deeper self, his true self, was crying out for an escape route and had worked overtime to provide one. But when had she decided that murder was the path she should take? Did she really believe God had orchestrated her activities? He closed his eyes. His head throbbed. He didn't care. The only important question was, what would he do now?

He stepped into the bedroom. Fortunately, he couldn't immediately see Joe's face. Although, he had to look eventually. He had to say good-bye without Gabrielle panting and screaming in his ear. She'd actually stood in the doorway and watched a man die, her heart colder than he ever could have imagined.

It all happened so fast, he hadn't even had a moment to call for help before he knew Joe was gone. His face had looked hideous, his eyes sliding up beneath the lids, so all that was visible was the soul-less whites. The guttural sounds and the spasms of his body, completely out of control. Spilling vomit across his face, choking. Joe would have hated that. And then he was gone, not breathing, no pulse.

If Mark was honest, his own reactions had been violent and conflicting. First fear for Joe, for his life, but that fear over what looked like imminent death was immediately poisoned by thoughts of being found out. That was the worst part of all, knowing his love hadn't been pure enough to focus solely on Joe. Saving his own skin immobilized him. Then, he'd seen Gabrielle in the doorway. Smiling. *Smiling!* Rage had further prevented him from thinking clearly.

Now, Joe was sprawled on his face, the sheet twisted around his legs and his left arm as if he'd been put in a straitjacket. He laughed miserably. Gabrielle was the one who belonged in a straitjacket. He walked to the bed and sat on the corner. Joe's face was still blocked by the pillows. He had to prepare himself for removing the obstacles. For a moment, he was content to sit there. He closed his eyes to see whether he could sense Joe's presence, his outsized spirit. The room felt empty. Moving his hand across the mattress, plucking at the folds of the sheet, he found Joe's ankle and took hold of it. His skin wasn't cold, but the temperature was reduced enough to tell him there was no life. As if he needed that reminder. He gripped hard, feeling the bone, stretching his fingers up to touch muscle, and the thin scattering of silken hairs.

After several minutes, he let go of the ankle and opened his eyes. He moved closer to Joe's hips and nudged the pillows out of the way. He'd hoped for a peaceful expression. Or, knowing Joe, a look of triumph. All he saw was agony. The eyes partially opened, revealing the whites, milky as an uncooked egg. The unnatural color of his skin — gray or with a yellow tinge, or too pale. He couldn't define it. The mouth was partially opened, the tongue close to the teeth, and the lips stretched in a grimace.

He took the loose part of the sheet and placed it over Joe's face. When they came to take him away, they might not like that — disturbing the evidence, but no one should look at that ruined face.

He took his phone off the nightstand and went to the sliding glass door. It was dark, but not for long. Gabrielle was insane — wanting to cover this up and go on as they had, whatever that meant. He was done making deals with God, done with the effort of creating a separate self. Being someone else was soul-sucking work.

The tears continued in a smooth flow down his face, weeping for Joe, and himself, as he thought about his desolate future. But it would be free. He would be free. He would be a better father, a better man. And although the Church hierarchy wouldn't be happy with that, God might be.

The loneliness couldn't possibly be any worse than it had

been most of his life, locked inside a sarcophagus, a stranger's face carved on the outside. Now, he could expose his true face, his flesh and blood face, to the world.

About the Author

CATHRYN GRANT IS the author of Suburban Noir novels, ghost stories, and short fiction. Her writing has been described as "making the mundane menacing".

Cathryn's fiction has appeared in *Alfred Hitchcock* and *Ellery Queen Mystery Magazines*, *The Shroud Quarterly Journal*, and *The Best of Every Day Fiction*. Her short story, "I Was Young Once" received an honorable mention in the 2007 *Zoetrope All-story* Short Fiction contest.

When she's not writing, Cathryn reads fiction, eavesdrops whenever she can, and plays very high handicap golf. She lives on the central California coast with her husband and two cats. Visit her website at SuburbanNoir.com or email her at CathrynGrant.com